WHO IS DAVIS SPANX?

TRUTH

HONOUR

RESPECT

By L J GRANDI

another little gem from
PINK DIAMOND PRESS

First published in 2013 by Pink Diamond Press

An imprint of Pink Diamond Publishing Pty Ltd

www.pinkdiamondpress.com

A CIP catalogue record of this book is available from the National Library of Australia

ISBN 9780987439635

Fonts used with permission from Microsoft

For anyone who's ever dared to dream…

Glossary of Aussie Slang

I thought I'd include an Aussie slang glossary for all of my international friends - which will help solve the riddle of what the heck us Aussies are talking about. Soon dear reader, you'll be understanding, and speaking, the bonzer Aussie language in all of its colorful glory.

Arvo - Afternoon.

Barbie - Usually means a BBQ, chargrilling the flesh of animals over a hot outdoor flame - rather than referring to a doll, although the doll is loved by Aussie kids too.

Beaut - Great, fantastic. We're such a happy bunch in our glorious country that it's important to have lots of different words to express how good something is.

Beamer - BMW car.

Bikkie - Biscuit, e.g. a chockie bikkie is a chocolate biscuit.

Bloke - Man.

Bogan - A very unfashionable & rough individual, which can be either male or female - may be referred to in the USA as trailer trash.

Bonzer - Great, fantastic, another word for beaut.

Bugger - An expletive used in the same fashion as damn, darn, or drat.

Buggered - A bit trickier as it has more contexts, e.g. "Buggered if I know" translates to "I have no idea", "I'll be buggered" translates to "You're kidding!" or "I don't believe it", while "I'm buggered" could mean "I'm exhausted" or "I'm screwed!" Then you've got "It's buggered" which means it's stuffed, i.e. worn out, broken or of no further use. A bit bloody tricky eh?

Chinwag – A prolonged conversation.

Chockie - Chocolate.

Cop - Yes we call policemen cops, but we also use the word cop to mean have or take, e.g. "Cop a look" means have a look. "Cop a feel" is to feel someone up. "Cop that" means take that.

Daks - Long legged pants, trousers.

Dag - A person behaving like an idiot or a clown. Everyone's a dag sometimes, and we often call each other a dag in an affectionate way.

Decked out – Usually referring to the clothes someone is wearing, but can refer to how something is equipped or decorated, e.g. "The house was decked out for Christmas" or "His car is decked out with an awesome sound system, fluffy dice, and sheepskin seat covers."

Divvy van - Police van for transporting criminals.

Dolled up - Again the clothes someone is wearing, but this time they've pulled out all the stops and have really dressed up. Women often slather on the makeup when they get 'dolled up'.

Dunny or **Loo** - Toilet.

Egg someone on, or **being egged on** - Strangely this has nothing to do with eggs. It's a term used when you coax, taunt or talk someone else into doing something. Or you get talked into doing something yourself.

Family jewels - Male genitalia.

Flanno shirt - A warm shirt made of checkered flannelette fabric. Bogans often wear them.

Footy - Australian rules football. The term footy can refer to the actual game, or the ball used to play it, e.g. "I'm going to the footy this weekend", or "Let's kick the footy around."

Gobsmacked - Shocked.

Grog - Alcohol.

Howzat - How's that.

Jocks - To us jocks are men's underpants, not football players.

Kerfuffle - A fuss, scuffle or commotion about something.

Lob - Go somewhere, usually to another person's house, e.g. "I'm gonna lob at your place soon."

Lobbed up - Arrived at desired destination.

Mobile - Mobile phone, cell phone.

Nibblies - Snacks, munchies.

Onya - Short for "Good on you", i.e. "Good job, well done."

Pash - A passionate kiss involving tongues.

Perv - To look lustfully at the opposite sex.

Pics - Pictures.

Pissed - Our American friends use this term when they're angry. For us it refers to someone being drunk.

Pissed off – really upset or angry - **to piss someone off** would mean to *make* them upset or angry.

Pisshead - Someone who drinks too much grog.

Piss off - To leave, go away, e.g. "I'm gonna piss off home in a minute", or "I wish you would just piss off".

Reckon - What you think about something, e.g. "I reckon I love you," means "I think I love you."

Rib - Not only is this a body part, to us the term rib also means to tease someone. We often give someone "a good ribbing".

Ripper - Great, fantastic, e.g. "that's a ripper of an idea" means "that's a great idea."

Sangas - Sandwiches.

Servo - service station, gas station, a place to fill your car up with petrol/gas.

Skull - Down a drink in one go, to gulp it down. You often hear the chant of "skull, skull, skull" at a pub or party, where someone eggs on their fellow drinker.

Schmicko – Very special.

Snags - Sausages.

Spew - Throw up, be sick.

Spewing/spewin' - Very upset or angry. Also vomiting.

Stoked - Happy, rapt, ecstatic.

Sunnies - Sunglasses.

Suss - A suspicious person or situation, as in "That's a bit suss."

Sussed out - Looked into, found out info on person or situation. You can suss anything out, e.g. "I sussed out this book called 'Who Is Davis Spanx?' - it looks like a ripper."

Trackie daks - Tracksuit pants, sweatpants.

Tradie - Tradesperson - a plumber, carpenter etc.

Undies - Is another word we use for underpants, for both chicks and blokes.

Ute - It's like a pick-up truck, it's got an open tray on the back. Tradies often drive them, putting their tools and materials in the back. Ute's are a big deal here in Australia – where they were invented. We even have our own Ute musters where blokes with pimped up Utes congregate to show off their pride and joy.

Uni - Short for University.

Wanker - Idiot, dickhead.

Wanky - Stupid, silly.

Whaddaya - What do you, e.g. "Whaddaya reckon?" translates to "What do you think?"

How to pronounce the names of some of our cities like an Aussie, not a tourist.

If you want to immediately sound like a local here's a few tips.

Melbourne: Drop the "bourne" and say it like this – Melbn. I was going to suggest Melbin, but the "i" is kind of silent. It's also referred to as Melbs.

Brisbane: More commonly referred to as "Brizzy". Drop the "bane" and say it like this – Brisbn. Again it's similar to Brisbin, but the "i" is silent. It's also known as Bris Vegas, God knows why, there's only one casino and it's nothing like Las Vegas.

The Gold Coast: We affectionately call it The Goldie.

Canberra: It's just Canbra to us.

Chapter 1

They said it couldn't be done, they said there was no way that I could achieve it. In fact most people laughed until they cried when I told them about my plan. But I proved them all wrong, and here I stand next to my man-idol Mr Hugh Jackman, on the red carpet, at the premier of his latest movie in L.A. Just like I told them I would. In fact it gets even better. Hugh just told me that he wants to make my story into a movie, he's got the perfect guy to play me, and he can't wait to work with me.

Are you freakin' kidding me? I mean I knew I'd be on the red carpet with him, that was one of my goals, but now he wants to work with me. Me, a twenty nine year old, non-talented factory worker from Melbourne. My mission to become a celebrity, delivering a good message, has surpassed all of my expectations. So much has happened in the last month it blows my mind. The cars, the girls, the travel, and of course having my own number one hit. Oh and did I mention the money? Yeah the money, wow. What a life changer that is. I even have my own weekly segment on morning TV, and plans are in place for me to do an hour long show each Saturday night. Everyone wants a piece of Davis Spanx, and I'm only too happy to oblige. Of course it wasn't always this way.

One month earlier

"For fuck's sake Davis, can't you go any faster?" Unfortunately that's not my girlfriend Claire yelling at me but my bloody boss Beaker. All the boys here at Fantastic Plastics call him Beaker due to his extraordinary similarity to the Muppet character with said name. He's got the same bulgy eyes, red hair and no chin. Of course we don't call him Beaker to his face, although Jonno our production manager once did and it nearly got him fired.

"Don't get your knickers in a knot. I've got it all under control," I mutter. Like hell I do. We're understaffed, have got too many job orders to fill, and the warehouse is a shambles. I'm watching what should be a nice neat roll of plastic come off the extruder line in a messy, bundled heap. It flies off the winder station and lands at Beaker's feet. Shit. He rolls his eyes at me and shakes his head in disgust.

"Don't worry Mr Brooks," I yell above the machinery noise, "this is just an issue of quality control. The resin was inferior that's all. This glitch will be right in no time. Don't stress, we'll have the order filled within the hour." I give him a winning smile as I scoop up the offending bundle of plastic at his feet.

Silently I wish that he'd just piss off back to Sydney and leave us all alone. He flies down once a month to keep an eye on everything, he's really got no idea about the plastics industry - which is great because if he did, he'd know that that little stuff up had nothing to do with the resin and everything to do with me and my daydreaming. But I seem to have placated him, I'm a pretty good bullshitter when I want to be.

Beaker nods angrily at me and yells, "Well just make sure you keep the orders on time. Time is money Davis," and he stomps off towards the office. I feel for the poor girls in there and what they're probably about to cop.

The morning tea bell rings, you beauty, I need a little pick me up after that. I give Benji a high five as he takes my place on the production floor, and I hurry off.

Mitch and Scott are already at the urn when I get into the tea room, the aroma of instant coffee permeates the air. Jonno, our production manager, is sitting at the table engrossed in the latest copy of *Zoot* magazine, grinning from ear to ear. Mitch and Scott are heatedly debating whether Richmond or Essendon will win this week's footy. Grabbing my carton of Sexy Juice out of the fridge, I take a seat at the table opposite Jonno. The guys always rib me for drinking my juice, but hey, it's organic, it tastes good, and the name cracks me up. Jonno doesn't acknowledge me or even look up, it must be a pretty good set of tits he's perving at. The other two head out for a smoke so I'm left with pervy Jonno. Great.

Taking a swig of juice I scan the cover of Jonno's mag. He's now holding it up right in front of his face, and a collage of semi naked chicks with pert titties faces me. The headline reads 'Celebrity status:

You can be famous *now*!' Jonno notices that I'm looking at his mag and cocks an inquiring eyebrow.

"Bit of talent in there eh?" I ask.

"Fuck yeah, check this out."

He turns the mag around so I can see. A very busty blonde is sitting astride a BMX, and there's several other pictures of her in various poses with the bike.

"Nice use of a bike," I quip. "That's a new take on an old formula."

Jonno looks at me with a blank expression. I obviously need to explain what I mean.

"Yeah, a new take on the old. They always used to use motorbikes for that sort of shot, so it's ah, nice to see them using something different for a change. Don't ya reckon?"

Jonno is still looking at me like I'm an idiot. "Well I guess it shows she's an outdoorsy kind of girl, I like outdoorsy kinds of girls," he mutters.

"Mate you like any sort of girl," I retort.

Jonno's a married man but he's still the biggest perve out there. I feel a bit sorry for his wife Rita.

He narrows his eyes at me and says, "Yeah well at least I'm not pussy whipped like you are. Claire's got you by the short and curlies Davis, you'd better watch out."

"Watch out for what?" I demand.

Jonno holds his mag up again and says, "That she'll finally say yes to one of your lousy proposals ya goose, then you'll be stuffed." He starts cackling like a madman and continues his perving.

Mitch and Scott come back in. I reckon it only took them five drags to finish their smokes. I used to be out there with them until a few months ago when my Dad had a minor heart attack. He's fine now but it scared the bejeezus out of the whole family. I've got an older brother and two sisters, and we all smoked - Mum included – until Dad's heart attack. Then we all gave up together to support him, none of us wanted to be the excuse for him to start again. So health-kick-city here I am.

Mitch and Scott have a perv over Jonno's shoulder.

"Niiice," they say in unison.

Scott's an alright bloke, he's pretty quiet though, never says much. Mitch on the other hand gives me the shits. He's always whinging and bitching about someone or something. Nothing's ever good enough for him. He's one of those blokes that are a real downer to be around, so I try and avoid him as much as possible.

I'm eyeing off the headline again. 'Celebrity Status,' now that *would* be good. I'm itching to read what the article is about. It says '*You* can be famous *now*!' I really want to know how, but I also realize that there's no way Jonno's going to let me take that mag off him, even if it's only for a second. We've got a hierarchy going on here and Jonno is the top dog, we all know better than to mess with his prized magazines, especially if it's a new one.

A brilliant idea forms as I sip my juice and ponder on how to get my hands on that mag. I'll sneak it into the loo with me later, read it in there while Jonno's busy, then put it straight back. He'll never even know I pinched it. Slurping the last of my juice I stand up, toss the waxed cardboard carton on the floor and stamp my foot heavily on it, causing it to pop loudly. Jonno jumps with surprise and throws a few curses my way. Giving him a cheeky grin, I pick it up, give him a wink and slam dunk it into the rubbish bin just as the tea bell rings, announcing that our break is over. Jonno grumbles, reluctantly places his mag on the table, and we all head back out to the production floor.

$$\$\$\$\$\$\$\$\$\$$

It turns out that my brilliant plan isn't quite so brilliant after all. No probs getting the mag into the loo, but big dramas when I exit with it. Beaker and Shelly, our office manager, are standing right outside the dunny door having a pow-wow. I wasn't aware of this until I opened the door - holding the titty mag in my hot little hand. They both look at me, then both sets of eyes travel down and take in the semi naked chicks on the cover. Shelly's eyes widen in horror. I peek down at the mag too. Shit. I quickly try to hide it behind my back, which is a big mistake because it probably gives off a waft of guilt. Shelly looks completely disgusted with me. Beaker's eyes are the bulgiest I've ever seen them, he's turned a shade of purpley red and looks as though he's about to explode. All this happens in seconds, yet it seems as though time has slowed down, like it's all happening in slow motion.

"No," I say while shaking my head at them. "No this isn't what you think, I just wanted to read an article. I didn't do anything else."

U-huh, yeah right, as if they're going to believe that. A guy exiting a toilet with a titty mag normally only means one thing and it sure isn't reading the articles!

"Do something!" Shelly implores Beaker.

Pointing his finger at me he growls, "My office, right now."

Jeezus, this is bullshit, how am I going to get out of this? I follow him up into his office, which is on the second story overlooking the production floor. As I walk in, I look out the window and see Shelly talking with Jonno. They're both looking up at the office and Jonno's laughing his head off. Bugger. If Jonno knows, then everyone knows. This is not good.

"Hand it over Davis," Beaker commands, holding out his hand to me.

I hand him the offending mag, flick my eyes over to the window again and inwardly groan. All the guys are now huddled in a group looking up at the office and most of them are laughing. The bastards! Shelly has gone, but a couple of the office girls are there and they look just as shocked as Shelly had.

Beaker settles himself behind his desk and spreads the mag out in front him. He's shaking his head at me. Man I'd better do some damage control quick smart, tell him what really happened. Taking a deep breath I go for it.

"I really didn't do any wanking Mr Brooks." Did I just say that out loud? Shit!

"I mean I really did only read the article, I know that's hard to believe but it's the truth, honestly Mr Brooks, I'm not that sort of guy. I mean sure, I have a wank every now and then, who doesn't. But not at work, I'd never do it on company time, I…." I'm babbling, panic has set in and I've turned into a wank orating idiot. I mean who uses the word wank with their big boss? I'm a bloody idiot.

Beaker holds up a hand to stop my verbal diarrhoea and I'm glad he has.

15

"Listen Davis, this is a very serious matter." He's now flipping through the pages of the mag, stopping every now and then to have a quick perv. Suddenly he slams the magazine shut and eyeballs me.

"If it had only been me who saw you, well I might have been a bit more lenient, but as it is, with Shelly present, I'm going to have to make an example of you." I've got a sickening feeling in my gut, this is not going well. Beaker looks at me intently. "So which article is it that you wanted to read so desperately?"

"Uh the one that's on the cover. Celebrity Status, you can be famous now! "

"Well, was it a good article, Davis?" he sneers at me. "Was it worth having to smuggle it into the toilets to read? It must have been very entertaining." He raises his eyebrows at me, a look of expectation is on his face.

For a second I forget the gravity of the situation, my brain must be in total meltdown because I say rather cockily while nodding my head, "Actually it wasn't too bad, not what I was expecting, but I got something out of it."

This obviously isn't the answer he's expecting. Slamming his palm down on the desk he bellows, "You got something out of it did you? I bet you did! Do you want to be a celebrity Davis?"

"Yeah well who wouldn't want to be one?" I blurt before I can censor myself. God I've got to get a grip. Taking a couple of quick breaths my brain kicks into gear again. I realise that I need to try and explain why I had to smuggle the mag into the loo in the first place, I need to get my defence speech happening here.

Clearing my throat I start to say, "The reason why I had to take the mag into the dunny with me is because of Jonno…," but Beaker holds his hand up again, signalling for me to stop talking. Bugger I've left it too late, I'm probably well and truly stuffed now.

"Stop Davis, stop right there, don't try to blame your foreman, don't try and make any more excuses. I'm glad you liked the article. In fact I'm really glad that you want to be a celebrity and that you've discovered how." He pauses for a moment, steeples his fingers, then continues. "I'm also very glad that all of you boys were put onto casual rates recently, because it means that I can now do this. As of now Davis Spanx, your employment here is terminated. You have fifteen minutes to get your things and get out."

Throwing the mag into the bin he grins at me evilly and snaps, "Now you'll have the perfect opportunity to claim the celebrity status that you so fervently desire."

"But...," I stammer.

I can't believe this is happening, I'm in shock. He hasn't even listened to me. I might be in shock but I'm getting very pissed off very quickly. This is totally unfair, I haven't done anything wrong. Sure it may have looked like I did, but I've been falsely accused. Beaker hasn't even listened to me, he hasn't given me the respect I deserve.

"No buts Davis, get your things and get out now," he bellows at me while pointing to the door.

Two different scenarios are running through my head simultaneously. Plan A: Call him a fucking arsehole, smash up the office and storm out of here. Or plan B: Thank him for employing me for the past four years, tell him I disagree with his verdict - but since he's the boss it's ok for him to treat me like shit, and leave quietly. Suddenly plan C rears its head, it's a nice mix of the two. This is the one I go with.

Putting my hands on my hips and widening my stance I tell him, "Now you listen to me Beaker, you have no proof that I was wanking, unless you have cameras in the loo, and that would be way too weird. You haven't even listened to my side of things properly, you've just jumped to conclusions." Placing my hands on his desk, I lean forward slightly and eyeball him. "Respect, that's all I want. I've worked for you for four years, been a great employee, and you show me no respect at all. You should be ashamed of yourself." Making a snap decision, I narrow my eyes at him and declare, "I *am* going to become a celebrity, because that's what lost me this bloody job. I'm gonna use what I learnt in the crapper and make me a star - a star who teaches others about respect!"

At this point I stand up straight, do a nice kind of rapper hand move, and while pointing to myself say confidently, "Watch this space!" Then I swagger out the office door.

Beaker is laughing his head off as I walk out, but I don't care.

"You'll never be famous Davis, you're a nobody," he shouts out after me.

Respect man, that's what it's all about. Whatever happened to respect? He might be laughing at me now but I feel bloody good about standing up for myself, and somehow I know I'll have the last laugh.

$$$$$$$$$$

As soon as I reach the production floor everyone crowds around me demanding to know what happened.

"Wanker," calls out Mitch.

"Yeah, nice one wanker," puts in Scott. Trust him to follow Mitch's lead.

"Shut up, the lot of you," Jonno orders. "What happened in there?" he asks.

Looking each of them in the eye I say, "I just want to get one thing straight here. I did not have a wank in the bloody toilet. I've been wrongly accused."

"Wanker," quips Mitch again.

"Shut up," barks Jonno. He puts his arm around my shoulders in a manly display of support and says, "Now listen, all this'll blow over before you know it, everything'll be fine. You've had a shock, but you'll get over it."

He gives my shoulder a squeeze as he let's go. I've always liked Jonno. He may be the biggest perv out there, and he's rough as guts, but he's always looked out for us all.

Running a hand through my hair I reply, "Actually, no, it's not going to be fine, and it won't blow over, because Beaker's just fired me. I've got fifteen minutes to get my stuff and get out of here."

Jonno shakes his head violently. "He can't do that, that's not right."

"Well he wants to make an example of me. Because Shelly was there I'm fucked. And he can fire me because we're all just casuals now, so he can get away with it."

I can see that Jonno's getting angry.

"That's unfair dismissal, you can put in a claim," he fumes.

I sigh and start walking towards the tea room. The girls head back to the office but the guys crowd around me as I go.

"Well I don't bloody want to put in a claim. He's shown his real colours. He doesn't respect me or any of you lot. All he cares about is making money. There's nothing wrong with making money as long as you treat people right. I don't want to work for someone like him, I deserve better. I deserve some bloody respect!"

There's a general murmur of agreement among the boys.

"What did ya take the mag into the loo for anyway then, if ya didn't have a wank?" Mitch asks.

I'm now rummaging around in my locker getting my gear together, and turn round to face them all again. "I just wanted to read the article on celebrity status. It's Jonno's new mag, everyone knows they've got no chance of getting hold of it until he's got the next week's issue in his hands." Again there's a general murmur of agreement. "I didn't want to wait till next week, I wanted to read the article now," I explain.

"Was it worth it?" Jonno asks.

"Beaker asked me that too. It wasn't what I thought it'd be, it's just about getting your chick's photo in the mag so you can both claim celebrity status for the week. But I did get something out of it. It's given me a great idea."

"What's that?" Mitch wants to know.

Grinning cheekily at everyone I announce, "I'm gonna make me a star! I'll become a bloody celebrity, a celebrity that spreads the message of respect. It's what society needs right now, there's not enough of it around these days."

"Yeah right," sneers Mitch. "How ya gonna do that?"

I shake my head at him. "Mate, where's your bloody respect? You're as bad a Beaker! I have no idea how I'm gonna do it. All I know is that I'm now on a mission, a mission to bring back the respect."

Jonno claps me on the back. "Well good onya Davis, I'd just like to say that's it's been a pleasure workin' with ya, you're a top bloke, and I hope you get what ya want. You spread that respect shit!"

I can't help but laugh and we shake hands. I shake hands with the other guys and they wish me well. As I start to head for the door I turn around and tell the boys, "Oh yeah, I got to call him Beaker to his face! And I told him that I did wank, but not on company time!"

Everyone cracks up at this. Jonno walks me to the door and we shake hands again.

"I'll keep ya posted on my celebrity success eh Jonno?"

"You do that Davis, you do that."

Next thing I'm out the door heading for my new life, wondering how the hell I'm going to tell my girlfriend Claire, my family, and my mates about how I lost my job. They'll hit the roof, if they don't kill themselves laughing first!

Chapter 2

On the drive home reality sets in, who the hell do I think I am? It was easy talking the talk about becoming a celebrity back at work when I was all fired up, but now I'm having serious doubts. I'm 29 and I'm unemployed. Great. At least I don't have a mortgage.

Claire and I were going to buy a house in Melton, which is about forty k's out of Melbourne. Well I wanted to buy a house in Melton but Claire wasn't so sure, so she talked me into renting there first to see if we liked it. I'm bloody happy I listened to her, 'cos I think it's a fucking shithole. There's a few plusses for living out there though. Number one, it's cheap. Number two, it's easy to get to work in Port Melbourne, it's a nice straight run down the freeway. And number three, which was the clincher for me, is that there's a bowling alley and pistol club there. I've loved bowling since I was a kid, and luckily I've converted Claire into it. Friday night is always disco bowling night. As for shooting, I've been doing that since I was a kid as well. My two grans taught me when I was eleven. They were both crack shots back then, but now only Grandma Drummond can still shoot at the range. Grandma Spanx had to give it away a couple of years ago due to her osteoporosis, but she still whips my arse on PlayStation.

Thank God we're not locked into living in Melton forever though. Before we moved there, Claire and I had been renting in inner Melbourne for two years, but with property prices so high there was no way we could afford to buy there. So Melton looked like a great option. Before that, I'd been living at home with the folks in Carlton. There are certain perks to being the youngest of four kids. Mum was trying to keep her last baby in the nest for that little bit longer, even though I'd left home a few years earlier to do the backpacking thing around Europe.

That's where I met Claire, on a Contiki camping tour. We sat next to each other on the bus that first day. By the third day I'd convinced the chick who was sharing Claire's tent to swap with me, and a beautiful romance was born. We drank and shagged our way all around Europe. I know it's corny, but for me it was love at first sight. Well maybe lust. She's one hot looking babe, I still think so even after all these years. We've been together for five years now, and I'd marry her tomorrow if she'd let me. I've already asked her twice and been turned down both times. Doesn't worry me though, one day she'll say yes. Last time, she said that I needed to be more successful. The time before that she said I needed to grow up. Who would think it eh? A chick that isn't panting to get a ring on her finger. She's a rare one is my Claire, in more ways than one. My mates are dead jealous, they're always asking me where they can find themselves a Claire, instead of a clinger.

$$\$\$\$\$\$\$\$\$\$\$$$

I'm listening to Triple M as I'm driving, and they're talking about Kim Kardashian. Yeah she's not a bad looking sort, I think to myself. They start talking about how much money she's made, and I nearly swerve into the next lane and have an accident when they say she's worth forty million dollars. According to last year's Forbes Rich List she made eighteen million! Fuck me, that's a shit load of money. What does she do anyway?

Maccas is coming up so I decide to turn off the freeway and grab an early lunch, the drive-thru is beckoning. The radio's still on but it's all just blah blah blah to me now. All I can think about is how much money Kim's made, and she's not even a proper celebrity. Our society is so bizarre, she's famous for being famous and not much else. I place my order and suddenly refocus on what the radio hosts are saying. Apparently Kim gets paid forty thousand dollars per episode of her reality TV show, and she can charge up to ten thousand dollars for each tweet she does for her sponsors. Nice one Kim!

The drive-thru chick gives me a half-arsed smile. I take my bag of food from her and say an automatic thanks, but then I really look at her properly. She's fat, and she probably really hates her job, so I decide it's my duty to put a genuine smile on her face.

I look at her name badge. "Hey Ajala, I want you to know that you're doing a really great job. You've got a great smile, and you know what? I bet that smile is really going to take you places. Thanks for the great service, you've made my day."

She looks shocked at first, but then beams her full wattage smile at me.

Bobbling her head from side to side she gushes, "Oh that's really nice. Thanks, *you've* made *my* day."

I'm bopping along to the radio as I pass a huge billboard with 'Billboard Mania - get you're ad seen by thousands' on it. I smile as I think of my mate Eric who runs Billboard Mania. We went to uni together, for about five minutes. Well technically the first semester, then I dropped out. But we've been good mates ever since. How different our lives have become, he now runs a very successful advertising business, he's a multi-millionaire, and I'm jobless and close to broke. Maybe if I'd stayed at uni and got into the advertising industry I'd have my own business too. But after dropping out I worked as a builder's labourer for around five years before heading off overseas. So I'm now a bit of a jack of all trades, master of none. I've never really known what I wanted to do work wise, and when I got back from overseas I kind of fell into a rut with a warehouse position at the plastics factory, which led to becoming an extrusion operator. I can't believe that I've been stuck in that shithole for the past four years. Maybe getting fired today is the best thing that could have happened to me, at least now something has changed. At least now something different can happen.

As I'm eating and driving, the radio hosts talk more about Kim and how she had a multimillion dollar trust fund that got her started, as well as access to A-listers. I need to hear this stuff about Kim Kardashian, I'm getting pumped again. Man if she can do it, so can I. I mean how hard can it be? I've got nothing else to do now that I'm jobless, so I may as well devote all of my efforts to this experiment of becoming a celebrity.

I turn off the radio. I need to think this out, how the hell am I going to become a celebrity? What can I do to get the ball rolling? I need an advertising campaign and I need to brand myself. I also need a catch phrase. Then a thought hits me. I don't have a multimillion dollar trust fund like Kim, or access to A-listers, but I do have a mate who has a billboard. What if I put a picture of myself on that billboard? That could be the start of my campaign, the campaign to brand myself as a celebrity!

It's a good thing that it's a long drive out to Melton, because by the time I get home I have a basic action plan in place. Sure it's very basic, but at least I've got something cooking, which makes me feel better. As I pull into my driveway, Bruce from next door switches off his mower and ambles over. He probably mows his lawns at least twice a week, even in winter. I personally think he's nuts, but he reckons it keeps his little lady happy, so he's happy. 'Happy wife, happy life' is one of his favourite sayings. We're best mates, and he and his wife Tracy always come disco bowling with us on a Friday night. He's going to love how I got fired. Shit, that reminds me, I still haven't called Claire, I've been too busy thinking.

"Maaaate!" Bruce says, as I climb out of the ute.

"Maaate, how's it hangin'?" I enquire in return.

Cupping his dick with his left hand he gives a few lusty thrusts, while screwing up his face in mock ecstasy. He tells me he's great, then asks, "How come your home so early?"

"Finish your lawn, then come over for a beer, I got something to tell ya. It'll knock your socks off."

He gives me a quizzical look and says, "No worries, won't be long. Didn't get fired did ya?"

Trying to keep a straight face I say, "I'll fill you in when you come over," and with that we head our separate ways.

I give Claire a quick call on her mobile and it goes straight to voicemail, so I leave a short message telling her that I love her and that I'll talk to her later. No point in telling her anything now, I'll do it later when I see her. I could have called the café's phone, but at this hour the place will be jam packed. She'll be flat chat with the lunchtime rush, so she won't be able to talk anyway. Feeling that my duty is done, that I at least made an effort to talk to her, I change out of my overalls and crack open a beer, just as Bruce lets himself in through the sliding door in the lounge.

I grab another can and hand it to him. "Here get this into ya."

"Ta, now spill, what's happened?" he demands.

So I tell him everything. Everything that happened at work that is, I still haven't filled him in on my basic celebrity plan yet. Which is just as well, because my getting fired story has already prompted fits of laughter. In fact he's turned into a heaving, shaking mess. I had to take his beer off him at one point, because he was laughing so hysterically he wasn't capable of holding it.

I'm getting used to this reaction, the reaction of people laughing at my misfortune. I guess I've made it into the mystical 'Wanking Hall Of Fame'. It'd be nice if someone would let me finish the story without laughing so hard though. And it would be really nice if someone actually believed I was innocent. At least it takes the edge off the bad news of being unemployed. I'm hoping this will make it easier for me to tell Claire and my Mum.

Bruce finally calms down and asks, "So what are you gonna do? You were tellin' me just last week how tight things were, how you couldn't afford that new iPhone."

"Yeah, well I've got a plan. That bloody 'become a celebrity' article in Jonno's mag got me fired. So, I've decided that for my new career," I do a drum roll on the edge of the coffee table to build the drama, "I'll become a celebrity and spread the message of respect. Mate, I want to bring back the respect!"

Bruce scoffs, but I continue on.

"Can't be that hard. Kim-bloody-Kardashian's worth forty mill and she does jack-shit."

Between snorts of laughter Bruce asks, "Let me get this straight, you're gonna become a celebrity, is that correct? Is that your plan?"

"Yep," I nod as I take a swig of beer.

"Ok," says Bruce "let's go through this systematically then, let's work out which of your many talents will make you a celebrity. Can you sing?"

I shake my head. "Nup."

"Can you dance? Dunno why I'm asking you this, I know bloody well that you can't sing *or* dance, you're a disgrace at disco bowling. Ok let's try to pinpoint some of your other talents."

We stare blankly at each other for a few moments, neither of us are able to come up with anything. It seems like ages that we just sit there in total silence, deep in thought.

Then I pipe up, "Acting, I'm a good actor, I've bullshitted my way out of heaps of stuff!"

He shakes his head at me. "Yeah, but that's not real acting is it, that's just, oh I dunno… fake acting."

"What the fuck do you think acting is?" I demand. "Of course it's bloody fake, that's what an actor's job is – they're paid to be fake."

"Nuh," Bruce breathes, "they've got to be real, or else no one's gonna believe them. But I do give you credit for being a good bullshitter. The way you persuaded Mrs McLure to lend us her beach house last year was just pure genius to watch. So ok you're a good bullshitter, what else have we got?"

"Yeah," I agree. "I did a pretty good sales pitch on her. The clincher was that we'd mow the lawn for her - which is something you can do in your bloody sleep!"

We both crack up and I get Bruce another beer, but don't get one for myself. I still relate having a beer with having a smoke, and a craving for one is trying to kick in right now. I figure I'd better nip it in the bud and stay clear of the grog, so I grab a coke instead. All this thinking and talking is thirsty work. We lounge around trying to figure out what other celebrity talents I might possess, but we can't come up with anything. It appears that I'm talentless. Bugger!

"You're fucked Davis," Bruce declares. "You can't sing, dance, or act, and you've got no famous mates or anything. I reckon you're dreaming. I don't want to rain on your parade or anything, but maaate, you'll be pushing shit up hill to become a celebrity. You definitely need a new plan."

Running a hand through my hair I eyeball him. "Nup, I'm gonna do it," I say determinedly. "My experiment will work, I'm on a bloody mission Bruce. What talents does Kim Kardashian have eh?"

"A nice set of tits, a big fat arse," Bruce jokes.

I snigger and say, "Yeah well a boob job might have gotten her forty mill, but I draw the line at doing that! What I'm saying is that she doesn't have any talent either. She's not famous for singing, dancing or acting. She's famous for nothing, just for being famous. If she can do it, so can I."

Bruce starts nodding his head. "Yeah I guess you're right. She does have her own TV show though."

"I'll get my own reality TV show too, although that'll be a bit further down the line. Do ya wanna be in it Bruce? Do ya wanna be in my show?" I grin at him, egging him on.

Now he nods his head exaggeratedly and says very sarcastically, "Ooh yeah, I'll be a star too. I'd better bloody be in it ya dick, I'm your best mate aren't I? Although I do have one condition."

"What's that?"

"If I'm gonna be on your show then I'll be wanting to drive a Mercedes Benz SLS AMG alright? And it's gotta be red, with the red and black interior." His eyes are starting to glaze over. It's no secret, anyone who knows Bruce knows that he's been lusting after this car for ages. It's his ultimate dream machine.

"Consider it done!" I say cockily. "Maaaate, I'll be driving my new Porsche Cayman S Black Edition. There's only five hundred of those babies, and I'm gonna get me one!"

Bruce shakes his head at me as a look of pity spreads across his face. He probably thinks I'm nuts, but I don't care. I'm already picturing the look of awe on his face as I rock up in my Porsche and hand him the keys to his new Mercedes. It's gonna be freakin' awesome!

We crap on for a bit longer. I decide not tell him at this point about my basic plan, it can wait for another time. I had him going for a while there, but totally lost him with the reality TV stuff. I figure it's best to cut my losses and just shut up about it for now. He polishes off another beer and eventually heads back to his place

I've decided that I'd better make Claire a nice dinner to soften the blow of my job loss. Actually that could be a good sales pitch for my stay at home status. I'll become a house husband and do all the cooking and cleaning. She'd love that! And tonight I'll start by preparing her favourite dinner.

Shit, what is her favourite? Claire loves food, so I've got to get my thinking cap on as there's a lot to choose from. Pasta? Nah. Steak? She loves a good steak. Nah, not special enough. Suddenly I've got it - Mexican! I whip up a pretty mean taco, but I'm thinking 'Brownie Points' here - are tacos up to the challenge? I don't reckon they'll cut it, but a brilliant plan comes to mind. I'll take her out for dinner at the local Mexican restaurant, she'll love that. But that's not all. Because I don't have to waste time cooking, it means I can whip around the house tidying up. I might even make an effort to clean the bathroom, it always looks like a tip in there. I'm on a winner here because this way I get kudos for cleaning the house, she feels special because I'm taking her out to dinner; and once she's had a few margaritas and feeling no pain, I'll break the news about getting fired. Perfect. God I'm a legend.

Now, I'd better not do too good a job on cleaning the house or she'll get suspicious!

$$$$$$$$$

The restaurant is packed and it's only Thursday night. I was thinking it'd be quiet, but this is great. There's plenty of distractions, they've even got a mariachi band playing, and there's a very good vibe going on here. Claire was exceptionally appreciative of my tidying the house, so appreciative that we had a quickie before dinner. Result!

She almost inhaled her first margarita, it was gone that quick. She's had a very shitty day at work, which is perfect for me because she's now onto her second drink, and hasn't stopped whinging about her crappy co-workers. That suits me fine, I get to do the supportive man thing by nodding a lot and saying "I hear you" without actually having to contribute much. I'm feeling really nervous about telling her my news, I mean I'm meant to be the breadwinner and here I am job-less. She's blabbing away and I must confess to zoning out for a minute, but what a minute it is!

I was watching the mariachi band serenade a lady at another table and it's given me a fantastic idea. Man everything's going great tonight, and I've just figured out the ultimate way to break the news to her.

"Can you get me another margarita hon? I just need to go to the loo," she coos.

"Sure love, no probs," I reply enthusiastically.

And she's off, perfect timing. The band has finished serenading that lady and now they're just ambling around the restaurant playing at random. I quickly wave them over to our table.

"Guys, can you sing a song to my lady with some very specific words in it?" I ask.

"Sure, we can do anything," says one of the band members as he rubs his fingers together, giving the international money sign.

"Great," I say, rubbing my hands together with glee. "Ok here's what I'd like you to sing, 'I lost my job today, but everything's going to be alright because I'm going to be a celebrity,' do you think you can get those particular words in a song?"

All four sombreros bob up and down together, they all have huge grins on their faces.

"This is no problem for us," says the ringleader.

"How much will it cost me?"

"Seeing as you have just lost your job, we will give you a very special price tonight." He looks at all the other band members and they nod together in agreement.

"It will only cost you fifty dollars. This is a very good price for a personalised song," he states.

All the sombreros bobble in agreement once more. I could probably haggle with them, but I figure fifty bucks is a small price to pay for helping me get out of the shit.

"Sold!" I agree excitedly. "Can you wait till a bit later to sing it? I want my girl to have a couple more drinks first."

The head honcho smiles at me knowingly. "This is no problem," he assures me with a wink, "just wave to us when you are ready. You will enjoy the song."

I hand over the cash and they mosey on off. I'm feeling good about this, but I have to time it right because I don't want Claire asking me how my day was. I can't lie to her, we never bullshit each other, and I'm not going to start now.

We get halfway through the main course and then she finally asks me the dreaded question. Damn, I was hoping to wait until dessert. But at least I got a few shots of tequila into her, as well as the margaritas. I can tell the grog is kicking in because her chest has gone all red and blotchy. This only happens when she's getting pissy.

I quickly give the band a wave and they hurry on over. The band leader says to Claire, "Tonight we have a very special song for you from your man here, it is especially written just for you."

Now Claire's gone completely bright red, but she's looking stoked, and I suddenly wonder if she's thinking that I'm about to propose to her. Again.

The band starts up. I like their style, the first minute of the song is just "I love you, I love you, you mean so much to me" over and over again. Then they get to the punch line which they repeat quite a few times as well, "I lost my job today, but everything's going to be alright

29

because I'm going to be a celebrity". And then they finish with "I love you, I love you, you mean so much to me" a few more times.

The whole restaurant is watching us, and Claire's jaw is nearly on the ground. She looks from the band to me and back again, her head swivelling to and fro repeatedly. I'm just sitting there nodding my head in time with the music, with a sort of grimaced smile on my face. Oh fuck, maybe this wasn't the best idea after all.

When they finish, the whole restaurant claps and I thank the band profusely, they really did an awesome job. Once they move off I notice that Claire has gone as white as a sheet, all the blotchiness and redness on her chest and neck has now disappeared. This is not a good sign.

"I'm going to be sick," she blurts, and rushes off towards the toilets with her hand over her mouth.

I sit there feeling like an idiot, heaps of people are looking at me. I sigh, shake my head, and say to no one in particular, "Must be those tequila shots, it does it to her every time," which is total crap because Claire can hold her grog really well.

Sitting there all alone has given me time to review the situation. I'm freaking out about what's going to happen when she gets back to the table. Suddenly one of the mariachi dudes comes over to our table again.

He holds a DVD out to me and says, "We videoed it, special present for you, special memories. No extra charge eh."

"Uh, thanks, that's very nice of you." I say, taking the DVD.

As he walks away he laughs and says, "See you on YouTube Mr Celebrity!"

Fuck me, did I hear that right? At first I'm horrified, but then massive excitement kicks in. Oh my God, this is the start of my celebrity life and it only cost me fifty bucks! This is gonna be a hit on YouTube, I can't wait to see it!

Today has certainly been an extreme emotional rollercoaster. I put my serious face back on when Claire gets back to the table, I don't want her to see me too happy.

"How are you feeling sweetie, are you ok? Did you have a spew?"

She's got her stern face on, this isn't a good sign. "You spin me out Davis. I can't believe you would tell me like that. It's just…"

She seems lost for words. This isn't the reaction I was expecting, I was expecting full blown fury. Then she does something I'm totally unprepared for. She starts laughing. She's shaking her head and laughing at me. Man, I seem to have the ability to make everyone laugh at me today.

"I have to give it to you, you get ten out of ten for originality babe." She giggles, then continues, "At first I thought you were going to propose again, but when I heard about your job and the celebrity thing, well it just wouldn't compute. I was hearing it but I couldn't understand it. Let me get this straight. You have lost your job haven't you?"

"Yep."

"And you reckon you're going to be a celebrity, have I got that right?"

"Yep." I'm going for less is more here.

"Riiight," she drawls.

I can't stop myself blurting, "Hey the celebrity thing's already started, the guys had someone filming their performance. It's going on YouTube, it'll be a sensation. And they gave me a copy of it. This is just the start babe," I say excitedly, "wait till you hear what else I've got planned!"

I quickly reign myself in, now's not the time to get carried away.

"Do you want to eat anything else or do you want to go home? I don't mind if you want to go home, I've put you through a pretty full on dinner."

Licking her lips she admits, "I didn't spew. Can we have dessert first, and then go home? I've been traumatised. I definitely need a chilli chocolate parfait to help me cope."

"Sure babe, you can have whatever you want. But is it ok if I wait until we get home to tell you how I got fired?"

She looks kind of puzzled but agrees. I'm stoked, everything's panned out really well, better than expected really.

At the end of the evening I go to pay the bill, but the waiter insists that our meal is on the house. It's such a nice gesture, and I'm really blown away by their generosity. I insist on paying our bar tab though. Respect!

As we are leaving, the mariachi band starts playing my song again. I take Claire's hand and we exit to the tune of "I love you I love you, you mean so much to me."

Chapter 3

Man that was a good sleep. Prying an eye open, I take a look at the bedside clock. Holy shit it's lunchtime already, no wonder I feel so good. I heard Claire leave earlier, but no way was I going to get up at six thirty - not on my first day of freedom from the factory. I've got a piss hard-on, better go take care of it. Stumbling to the ensuite I notice my mobile sitting on the chest of drawers, it's flashing so there must be a message, but it'll have to wait. I'm betting it's from Claire, she probably figured I'd sleep in to some ungodly hour and tried to wake me up with a phone call. I grin to myself, man she should know me better than that, I can sleep through anything.

The home phone rings as I'm sitting at the kitchen table having some brunch. It seems a pity to put down my nice hot vegemite and honey toast to answer it. Mmmm, vegemite and honey together, my favourite. So I stuff in a big mouthful as I pick up the phone. It's my Mum. The first words she utters are, "Is it true Davis?"

"Is what true?" I ask, spraying toast crumbs all over the table.

"That you've lost your job," she says in exasperation. Before I can reply she cuts in, saying, "Although I guess you wouldn't be home answering the phone if you still had a job to go to now would you? I did try you on your mobile but it went straight to voicemail."

Jeeze news travels fast, how the heck did my Mum find out so quickly? I was planning on calling her later today and setting up a family meeting. We usually all go over to Mum and Dad's every second Sunday for lunch, but today's Friday and the next scheduled lunch is for the weekend after this one. I can't wait that long. We're a pretty close family, and I figure it'd be easier to tell everyone all at once, rather than going through the same old story again and again.

Quickly swallowing my mouthful of toast I ask, "How did you find out? Who told you I got the sack?"

Letting out a dramatic sigh mum says, "Douglas called me a couple of hours ago. He said it's all over the internet. I haven't seen it myself yet, your Dad's used up all our download allowance again, so we're back on dial up speed for the rest of the month and it just won't load. But Douglas said something about a Mexican band singing to Claire? Singing that you'd lost your job but you loved her?"

Mum's voice has gone all high pitched towards the end of her sentences, a sure sign she's freaking out. Doug's my elder brother. He's a good sort but he's got a big mouth, which has always been a problem. He's six years older than me, and still thinks it's his job to look after me. Look after me my arse, more like dob me in any chance he can get. It's unbelievable that at thirty five he's still at it, he could have rung me first, instead of immediately blabbing to Mum. Taking a deep breath I cross my fingers and pray that she won't ask too many questions.

"Yes Mum, Doug's right. I did get fired, and some Mexicans did sing it in a song to Claire. It's hard to explain. I was going to ring you today and see if you can organise a family meeting for this weekend, that way I can tell everyone together. What do you think?"

I know I've hit the jackpot here. This will be a major distraction for her, Mum'll use anything as an excuse to get us all together.

"Ooh, it would be nice to see everyone this weekend," she says excitedly. "Yes, I can organise that. But darling I think we should make it for tonight, the sooner the better eh? Given the gravity of the situation."

Bingo! I knew she'd go for it. But I'm finding her enthusiasm a little off putting. Tonight's Friday night, and that means disco bowling night. I don't want to miss out on it. Putting on my best whingey voice I say "But I can't tonight Mum, it's disco bowling night." I realise how lame it sounds as soon as I've said it.

"Well this is much more important than bowling Davis. Darling this is your future. Besides, if this thing's gone viral then we definitely need a family meeting tonight. I think that would be best, don't you?"

I can see her point, but I try one last tactic. "But this is awfully late notice for you Mum. I don't want to put any pressure on you having to cook for us all tonight. How about we make it for lunch tomorrow?"

By the tone of her voice I can tell she's smiling. "You are such a sweetie Davis, trust you to think of me. But I know that Danielle and Mark are heading off to the snow tomorrow, and they're not coming back until Sunday night. So lunch tomorrow won't work, it'll have to be dinner tonight ok?"

Bugger, never mind. Better to get it all sorted out now I guess. "Ok Mum. Say seven o'clock for dinner? I'll bring my laptop so we can watch it on YouTube together. Love you, bye."

"Not so fast Mister," she snaps at me. "Davis, how *did* you lose your job?"

Damn, I thought I'd gotten away with not telling her anything. I really don't want to go through it all now, so I decide to try and brush her off. "I'll tell you tonight Mum, we'll see you at seven ok? Love you, bye." I hang up, feeling a bit guilty for my quick exit, but there's no way I'm going into details with her now.

Now I'm momentarily torn as to what to do next. Three different things are jostling for my attention. One, get on YouTube as soon as possible and check out my clip. Two, check my mobile messages. And three, go over to Bruce's and fill him in on what happened at the restaurant last night. I figure I'd better check my messages first, the other two things can wait a bit.

Bloody hell there's fifteen messages! Four of them are from Claire, and three of them are from Doug. So he did try and get in touch before he blabbed to Mum! A few are from my sisters Danielle and Holly. Even Jonno from work has left me one, as well as Eric and another mate Paul. Wow, I'm a popular guy!

Grabbing my laptop I rush over to Bruce's place. It's great that he works from home. When he opens the door he gives me a good once over from head to toe. Shit, in all the excitement I forgot that I haven't gotten dressed yet. I'm still in my pyjamas which consist of a very manky pair of trackie daks and a holey old Hoodoo Gurus t-shirt. Claire's banned me from wearing the t-shirt in public but I still get away with wearing it to bed, it's an old favourite that I can't bring myself to throw out. I've got a pair of red socks on, but no slippers or shoes. As if I'd wear slippers anyway.

"Jeeze you're a worry," Bruce shakes his head at me. "You'd better come in. Or do you want to go and slip into something a little bit more appropriate?" he leers at me.

"Oh fuck it, this'll do. Wait till you see this." I wave my laptop above my head like a lunatic. Bruce just opens the door wider to let me in.

We settle on stools in the kitchen, laptop opened before us on the bench. Bruce asks, "So how did last night go? Did she take the news well?"

Smiling at him I say mysteriously, "See for yourself."

I get onto YouTube and then realise I don't know what to search for it under. Bruce sees my hesitation and asks "You're not looking for a certain mariachi band serenading your girlfriend are you?"

Snapping my eyes up from the laptop to look at him, I cuff him on the head and exclaim, "You bastard, you already know!"

Grinning at me he says, "Maaate, it'd be a bit hard not to. It's going insane. When I saw it this morning it'd already had nearly a million hits!"

"Whaat?" I shout in astonishment. "I told you I was going to be a celebrity!! Come on, I haven't seen it yet, show it to me NOW!"

So Bruce gets it sorted. Fuck me, it's now been seen by one and a half million people! This is unreal. I watch it and crack up. It's hilarious. The quality of the film is great, they've captured it all perfectly. Claire's head swivelling back and forth and me doing the head nod thing is a pisser, not to mention the actual song. Those guys rocked it! They even filmed the bit when Claire got up to be sick.

"Oh man, it's fantastic," I say excitedly, "and it only cost me fifty bucks to get 'em to do the song, and they threw in the DVD for free, how good is that?"

We both cackle over it for a while, then Bruce looks at me and says, "Maaate, I thought you were shittin' me yesterday when you told me you were going to make yourself a celebrity. But Jeezus, you're actually doing it!"

"I know, and I haven't even told you about my plan yet." I can't sit still, I'm too excited, so I jump up from the stool and start pacing around the kitchen.

Bruce shuts the laptop and turns round to face me. "Yeah, well hang on a minute. I reckon your next move should be to put another YouTube video up. One about how you got fired. Imagine the hits that would get! Put 'em together and man you will be a star!"

I suddenly stop pacing, a huge grin lights up my face, and I clap him on the back. "Maaate, that's perfect! That's exactly what I should do. Then I'm gonna get Eric to put me on a billboard. I need a website too."

Bruce is nodding his head, now we're both grinning stupidly. "C'mon," he says. "I've got a webcam on my computer in the office. We can make your getting fired vid right now!"

Bruce is out of the kitchen and heading towards his office before I can stop him. When I catch up he's already busy in front of his computer getting things organised. It's great having a mate who's into all this computer shit. Personally I wouldn't have a clue, it's not my thing at all. Luckily Claire's right into it as well, so I can easily get away with just knowing the basic stuff. I know us guys are all meant to be tech savvy, but I'd rather go bowling or shooting for fun instead of piss-farting around on a computer.

"Come and sit here," commands Bruce.

It then dawns on me that I'm still wearing my grotty pyjama t-shirt. "I can't wear this to do it in," I whine at him.

"Ooh the celebrity's already a diva, demanding things already eh?" Bruce jokes.

"Maaate, I can't wear this! I need to make a good impression."

"So what is your look going to be, have you thought about that yet?"

Shaking my head I admit, "Nup, it hasn't even cross my mind."

Bruce runs a hand through his short wavy brown hair, gives me the once over and says, "Well you should think about it. You need a haircut. Maybe we should give you a makeover before we do the YouTube thing. Whaddaya reckon?"

I can see his point but, "If I change my look, get a new haircut, then nobody's gonna recognise me from the mariachi video. You're right though, I could do with a bit of sprucing up. Maybe I should go and visit Silvio."

Bruce rolls his eyes at me. "That's bullshit Davis. Forget bloody Silvio, he always gives you the same haircut. Every time. I know he's been your family barber since you were a kid, but you need a new look now. You're not a factory worker any more mate, you're a bloody ce-lebrity!"

We both snigger at Bruce's comment, but he's right, I do need a new look. However family honour demands that I get Silvio to cut my hair. Maybe if I beg him hard enough he'll give me a new style, although I don't like my chances.

Then I have a great idea. "Why don't you be my manager eh Bruce? I'm gonna need one."

He shakes his head at me. "No way, never mix business with friendship, so they say. Nup, I wouldn't have a clue, and I want us to stay mates."

Moving over to his bookshelf I look at one of his certificates. He's a bigwig in the network marketing industry, he's even got his own online training shop called Ultimate MLM Mastery dot com. I tell him "Yeah, but I don't have a clue about being a celebrity. We could do it together. How hard can it be?"

Eyeballing me Bruce states, "Nup, I'm not doing it. End of story. You should get that guy Max Marsden from *I'm A Celebrity Apprentice* to be your manager. He knows his stuff."

"Yeah, maybe you're right, I'll have to look into it. But I'd rather give money to you instead of him."

Leaning back in his chair he grins and says, "Hey I'm getting my red SLS AMG don't forget, that's payment enough. Nah, you need a professional, someone who's switched on about all this celebrity shit."

Moving over to the door I quip "Jeeze, at the rate I'm going, I probably won't even need a manager, everyone's gonna know who Davis Spanx is. I've made an executive decision though, I'm gonna go home and spruce myself up a bit before we do the YouTube thing."

Bruce looks up from the computer and says "Yeah ok, but don't take too long, we gotta get on this ASAP."

$$\$\$\$\$\$\$\$\$\$$

While I'm having a shave I have a great idea. It'd be cool to do a public launch of the video I'm about to make, we could call it my getting fired clip. I could launch it at Paul's pub in the city tonight, after dinner with the family. Paul's a mate who I met when I was backpacking overseas. We both worked at a pub in London, and he's gone on to build a franchise of Aussie pubs around the world. They're all called *The Watering Hole*. It's Aussie kitsch at its very best, but the tourists love it, and they've made him a fortune.

The more I think about it, the better this idea seems. It'll generate even more free publicity for me, which I can then film for another YouTube video. I'll probably need to tweet this to get the word out that it's happening tonight. Being a Friday night I figure that people are more likely to want to stay out late and, fingers crossed, hopefully come to my launch. It'll also enable me to invite everyone I know so they can all find out what's happened at the same time. The worst case scenario is that we just have a beer and a catch up, but I'd better return Paul's call from earlier and run it by him first before I get carried away with my ideas.

Awesome! Paul is totally up for the challenge. You little ripper! We've agreed that eleven would be a good time, as the band that he's booked finishes at ten thirty, so hopefully plenty of punters will hang around for the launch. Paul's got big screen TVs throughout the pub and says he'll post a blurb about my appearance tonight, and run it on loop along the bottom of the screens. He reckons I should try and get the mariachi band to come along as well, which is an awesome idea.

I give them a quick call, luckily their number is on the DVD they gave me. Turns out that they're booked for a party tonight, bummer, but they know where the pub is and if they can possibly make it they will. Louis the bandleader was stoked for me, and he's also rapt about the publicity it's given them. He said that they're now fully booked out for the next three months.

Now I need to ring Eric and see about that billboard. Surprisingly he doesn't want to talk about anything over the phone, and asks me when I can come into the office and see him. I tell him it would be a bit tricky today because Bruce and I are gonna do my YouTube video this arvo, and I have no idea how long it will take.

"Bring Bruce and get both your arses into my office ASAP. We can do your YouTube stuff in here. I gotta see you Davis. We gotta get this sorted. And don't do any tweeting or anything until I've seen you. Ok?" he orders.

"Yes sir! Fuck me Eric, you're making me feel like I'm at school with all this get into your office shit."

"Just do it," he laughs. "I'll have everything ready for you when you get here. Oh yeah. Make sure you wear something half decent will ya?" and he hangs up. That's Eric for you, a man of action. Bit like myself really, it's probably why we're such good mates.

$$\$\$\$\$\$\$\$\$\$\$$$

I finish shaving and showering and finally decide what to wear. God it must be murder being a chick and having to worry about what you look like every day, I have a new found respect for the effort Claire makes in looking so good all the time.

I'm checking myself out in the floor length mirror. Mmmm, not bad at all. People say I'm the spitting image of Andy Lee, of *Hamish and Andy* fame. I can see their point. I'm tall and dark, and kind of handsome in an offbeat way. My dark good looks are a throwback to my Greek heritage. Somewhere along the line Spanx has mutated from the name Spanakarkis, Dad reckons one of the rellos probably couldn't spell or write properly, and putting an x at the end was the easy option. I'm seventh generation Greek-Australian – from one of the oldest lines in Australia. We're actually descended from the very first Greek immigrants to come to Australia in 1829. Immigrants my arse, more like convicts! It gets even better. Great Great Great Great Grandaddy Spanakarkis was convicted of being a pirate!! There were eight of them captured and transported out here together, but only three of them stayed in Australia after they were pardoned. Leonidas Spanakarkis was one of them. Being related to a pirate is pretty damn cool, it was my claim to fame as a kid.

None of my brothers and sisters are swarthy and dark haired like me, even Dad doesn't look Greek. I'm the only one who you could pick for having a bit of Greek heritage. Mum's background is Irish, although she's second generation Aussie, so that's helped dilute an already extremely weak Greek gene pool.

Taking one last look in the mirror, ruffling my dark, unruly hair into place, I grab my mobile and head over to Bruce's. He seems impressed with my outfit and gives me the thumbs up. I've gone for a nice black leather jacket, black retro shirt with black jeans and black boots.

I tell Bruce about my conversation with Eric and he insists that he drive us there, which is fine by me. His four wheel drive is much nicer than my crappy old Ute. Eric's office is in North Melbourne which is nice and handy. On the way in I show Bruce the billboard that I hope to be on soon. This time he doesn't laugh but says, "Yeah that'll be excellent exposure for you."

I give him a bemused look, boy what a difference twenty four hours makes. This time yesterday when I told him I was going to be a celebrity, he nearly pissed himself laughing. Now here he is agreeing about excellent exposure for me. I tell ya life is certainly some incredible ride, you just don't know what's going to happen to you next.

On the way I phone Claire and fill her in on tonight's plans. She's excited to be going out for dinner again, she also can't believe the response my clip has had on YouTube. She watched it at work and reckons she cringed at the bit where she dashes for the loo. I ask her to tell any and every one to come to Paul's pub tonight for my launch, we blow a few kisses to each other and hang up. So far she's the only one who's let me finish the story of how Beaker sacked me without killing herself laughing. When I finally got round to telling her last night, she was outraged that Beaker would fire me like that without hearing my side of things.

Eric's office is in an old warehouse and it's pretty groovy. Marissa the receptionist shows us into the boardroom and asks if we'd like anything to drink. I decline, but Bruce opts for a coffee. She tells us that Eric won't be too long and rushes off to answer a ringing phone. To fill in time Bruce and I both stroll around the boardroom admiring the artwork. The walls are covered in all the big billboard ads that Eric's done over the years. A lot of them are just so familiar, they've been seen by tons of people, and some of them have become iconic. A shiver of excitement runs through me when I think that mine will hopefully become just as familiar to multitudes of people.

I'm dragged away from my daydreams as Eric comes into the room. He's all business, shaking hands with both of us. Eric's a big guy, big in every way. He's tall and put bluntly, built like a brick shithouse. His bald head only adds to his sense of stature. He kind of looks like Bert Newton, kind of. He's got the moon face thing going on but not the dodgy hairpiece, Eric's bald as an egg. But for some strange reason the chicks absolutely love him, they always have. Maybe it's because he oozes self-confidence, and has a deep smooth voice. We used to joke that he should have been a news reader, he'd be perfect for it.

Because he's a chick magnet the lucky bastard's been able to enjoy a sex life I can only dream about. Some of the stories he's told me are incredible, but so far none of his conquests have managed to tie him down. He reckons he'll be a bachelor for at least another ten years, then he *might* consider settling down.

Today he's wearing a dark blue suit, which is unusual as he's normally a casual kind of guy. Once our greetings are exchanged he slams the door shut and shouts with excitement.

"Have you got any idea what you've started Davis? This is nuts, I just checked you out on YouTube again, you've now had two point two million hits. That's freakin' insane!"

I nod my head like this stuff happens to me every day. "Pretty cool eh? Although this is just part of my plan. Nice suit by the way!"

Patting himself down he replies "Yeah I had a meeting with some important dudes this morning. I'm thinking of expanding my business, branching out into mobile billboards as well. There's an existing setup I'm thinking of buying, it'd save me the headfuck of figuring it all out myself."

"Hey that's a great idea, you can put me on those too," I joke.

He narrows his eyes at me as we all sit down around the boardroom table. "So tell me what your plan is."

I fill him in on how the launch is happening tonight at Paul's pub, and that I want to have the whole night filmed so it can be used in another YouTube clip. I explain how branding myself is definitely the way to go, how the mariachi band might be there but might not be, how I want to have my picture on a billboard and, now he's mentioned it, those mobile ones sound good too. Taking a deep breath I continue on, stating that I need a website, and that Bruce and I are going to do a video on how I lost my job and premiere it at the launch tonight.

When I finish spewing all of this out, I can see that he's trying to process it all and put it all together, but the pieces just aren't fitting for him. Then it dawns on me that he really needs to know about how I lost my job, and he needs to know *right now*. That way he can get the full picture and understand everything properly. So next I launch into the whole story to get him up to speed. When I finish telling him, I'm almost out of breath. I've been talking so fast that I haven't had time to breathe properly, but I get a chance to fill my lungs now - while Eric pisses himself laughing. He's laughing so hard that he's slid off his chair and is now collapsed on the floor. Like Bruce, he's a shaking heaving mass of hysterical laughter, tears are streaming down his face and snot is coming out of his nose.

Finally he splutters, "Jeezus Davis you're a marketer's dream! You sure make this easy don't you! Fuck, I've never heard anything so funny. You crack me up you bloody wanker."

Clawing himself back onto his chair like he's climbing Everest, he blows his nose loudly and wipes his eyes, regaining a certain air of respectability. I notice that his suit is now well and truly crumpled, but he's still grinning, and utters a snort every now and then. Marissa comes in with a plate of biscuits and coffee for Bruce and Eric. Popping them on the table she looks at all of us and asks if everything's ok. We all just nod as she quickly backs out of the room, a worried look upon her face. Her reaction sets Eric off again, he can't stop laughing.

"Was I that bad when you told me?" Bruce asks.

"Yep, I had to hold your beer for you remember?"

"Yeah, that's right" he breathes.

After a while Eric calms down again, reaches for a biscuit and says. "Davis, anyone who's got a pulse is going to crack up at hearing that, it's bloody hilarious. But Beaker's a bastard for firing you like that mate. I think it's good you want to push the respect message though, I reckon you'll get a lot of support with that. It's a strong, powerful message."

Nodding in agreement I say "Yeah and I've come up with a catch phrase too. It goes like this: 'Respect yourself and respect other people.' What do you think?"

"I like it," says Bruce.

"So do I," says Eric. "It's gonna be easy to brand you Davis. Something must have sunk in all those years ago at uni, even though you were only there for one semester." He looks at me seriously and asks. "So you're completely sure you want to be a celebrity? With all this going on it should be doable, but are you really sure you want this?

It'll change everything you know. Have you and Claire talked about it?"

Looking from Eric to Bruce and back again I reply, "Hey I only decided yesterday that I was gonna to do this celebrity caper, and hell yeah, bring it on! Claire, schmare. She'll be right. It'll be a laugh."

"What about chicks?" Bruce asks.

"What do you mean, what about chicks?" I retort. I'm puzzled by his question.

"Well, if you're a celebrity, then the chicks are all gonna want you. How ya gonna handle that? Or more's to the point, how's Claire going to handle that?" Bruce leans back in his chair raising his eyebrows at me in query.

Bugger. I haven't thought that far ahead, so I do some quick thinking. Actually, I just say the first thing that comes into my head, and fortunately it makes sense.

"I'll get my sister Danielle to make up some contracts for me. Appearance contracts, so that if I have a chick on my arm, Claire will know it's only for show, nothing more. I'd never cheat on Claire. Respect guys. Now that could work couldn't it?" I ask hopefully.

Eric pipes up. "Actually that's not a bad idea Davis, that way you can get A-listers or up and coming stars to appear with you. It'd be of mutual benefit to both parties involved. More publicity all round, a win-win for everyone."

"Lucky you've got a sister that's a lawyer. Imagine having to explain that set-up to someone else," laughs Bruce.

"Yeah and the expense, it'd probably cost me a bloody fortune" I add.

We move on to the advertising action plan. Eric has three empty billboards at the moment and he reckons he wants me on all of them. Sweet. There's one on the Westgate Freeway, which is the one I saw yesterday and pointed out to Bruce on the way in this arvo. There's also one in Richmond on Swan St, and another on St Kilda Rd. All prime sites. I tell them both what I envision the billboards to look like.

"It's pretty basic really, nothing too flash. I just want it to drive the punters to my social media sites. In big letters I'd have 'Who is Davis Spanx?' I reckon a lime green background would work well. I'd also have a cool looking photo of me on it, with my website and the Twitter and Facebook logos. Simple as that. What do ya reckon?"

Bruce and Eric look at each other, then turn to face me. "Bloody brilliant" says Bruce.

"Fan-bloody-tastic," agrees Eric, "you should wear a t-shirt with respect on it. Or hang on a min ..." He's getting really excited now, he's bobbing up and down in his chair then he screams "It should have your slogan on it. Respect yourself and respect other people. Man that would be awesome!"

We all jump up out of our chairs and do a weird bobbing dance thing together. Don't know where that came from, but we're all so massively pumped up and excited. Eric looks at his watch. "It's only three o'clock, I'll give my mate Tai a ring and see if he can rustle up a t-shirt for us."

He gets his mobile out and starts dialling, but I grab his arm and shout, "Wait, what if we got more than one t-shirt made. What if we got say, fifty made for tonight's launch. We could probably flog them off there, and make a few bucks."

Bruce's eyes have gone wide. I can see dollar signs in them. "We should get two hundred made" he says excitedly.

"Fuck that shit," shouts Eric. "With the amount of hits you've had we should get five hundred made up. If we sell them as a limited edition we could get fifty bucks each."

It takes a minute to compute, then we all shout simultaneously, "That's twenty five thousand dollars!!"

The weird bobbing dance starts up again, then we're giving each other chest slams and high-tens. Fuck this is fun!

Eric calls his mate Tai, he can have them ready and delivered to Eric's office by six o'clock. Perfect! Of course Eric got a great deal on them. We've decided to all go thirds in the cost and share the profit, if there is any. The t-shirts will be black, with my respect slogan printed in red on both the front and back. Cool. We also agree to keep ten each for family and friends.

"We gotta get some tweets out, get the word out about the launch tonight," I say.

Eric nods at me. "Already onto it. Check this out, I reckon it'll get the crowds in."

Eric reads from a scribbled bit of paper he's holding. "Davis Spanx how I got fired launch. 11pm The Watering Hole, Bourke St Mall. Be part of my next YouTube clip. See u all there.'

"Nice one Eric, that's better than I could have come up with," I affirm.

Taking a sip of coffee he tells me, "That's why I didn't want you to tweet anything before we got together. How many followers do you have on Twitter at the moment?"

Looking off into space for a second I reply, "Oh, probably about 30." I might be exaggerating a bit there. Eric and Bruce both scoff, they know I'm bullshitting a bit. I am so not into Twitter and I don't even have a Facebook page. Who gives a shit about what someone's doing every second of the day?

"Well, get ready to watch your following explode," Eric says. "It's really important that you start posting tweets regularly. I know you're not into this shit, but you've got to work it Davis, keep the public plugged into you ok? Now let's get this out there, we'll do it now mate."

With the tweet sent we move onto what I will say in the YouTube clip. We all agree that I should be wearing a respect t-shirt for the video, and that I should do some rehearsals before the t-shirts arrive. I start off by introducing myself, then I run through the story, ending with my catchphrase. Eric wants me to censor the bit about calling Beaker a fucking arsehole in my head when I'm going through the options of how to react when he fires me.

"Look mate, you just can't say fucking arsehole on a YouTube vid, it's not family friendly and you want to pull in the crowds, so tame it down a bit and just say effing a. The adults'll know what it means, and hey, you're showing respect by toning it down a bit ok."

We all snigger, but I agree. "Yeah good idea, don't want to offend anyone. Eh."

Eric then takes us into the media room where a wall is already set up with a filming area. He tells me to go through the story again and says he'll film this one to see how I look, and to get the lighting and sound right.

Well as soon as I know I'm being filmed I kind of seize up, I get all self-conscious and can't talk properly. We do a few more takes.

Eric's got the lighting and sound perfect now, but I'm still shit. I'm getting really really frustrated. We do take after take, but I keep on getting it all wrong. Before we know it the t-shirts have arrived. Oh God it's six o'clock already, I've got to be at Mum and Dad's in an hour. I call Claire and tell her to meet me there.

The t-shirts look great, I immediately put one on. Eric's talking to the guy who's delivered them, then Eric leaves the room and comes back in with a few people in tow. He arranges some chairs in front of me and they all sit down.

"Right," he says, "here's what's going to happen. Davis, I want you to tell these guys what happened to you. Treat them like old friends. The camera won't be rolling so don't worry," he assures me.

I know he's bullshitting me, I can see the camera's red light is on, it only comes on when he's filming. But for some reason talking to the other people instead of the camera works, and of course they're all in hysterics as I'm telling it. Eric must have told them not to laugh too loud though, and this time I get it done successfully in the first take.

We playback the recording and it's great, having people laughing really adds to it. I give the guys a t-shirt each, thank them for their help, and ask them to come to the pub tonight with as many of their friends as possible. Bruce, Eric and I give each other a high five as everyone else leaves the room.

Then Eric wants to take some photos for the billboard, so I strike some poses. It's much easier than doing the video. He uploads the photos onto the computer and we dick around with the design for a while. Well Eric does, Bruce and I just give him some input. It's amazing how quickly this stuff can get done if you know what you're doing. He has it finished by the time I have to leave and it's freakin' awesome! I can't wait until it's up there on the billboards. We all agree that getting a webpage done is a top priority, and Eric puts his hand up for the job. So tomorrow's gonna be website design day, unreal.

We say our goodbyes for now, we'll all meet at the pub again later tonight. Eric's more than happy to film the launch tonight, he's such a legend. Now it's time to get to the folks place and fill them in on everything. Oh boy this is gonna be good …

Chapter 4

My taxi pulls up outside Mum and Dad's just as Claire arrives, and after giving each other a quick hug we walk to the front door together. My parents live in a double storey old Victorian terrace in Carlton. It's beautiful, but definitely a labour of love. This is where I get to shine with being a jack of all trades, as Dad's always ringing me up asking for help with something. He wouldn't know how to hammer in a nail by himself, lucky he's got me. I ring the doorbell and, just as Claire and I are having a quick pash, Mum opens the door. She's used to our shenanigans, because I learnt from the best - her and Dad. "Sprung bad," she laughs, welcoming us inside.

She ushers us into the lounge where the whole crew is gathered, it's a full house alright. I'm lucky to have such a great family. Sure we give each other shit, and we have our dramas, but the truth is we'd do anything to help each other out.

Doug's the eldest son. He's 35, and has taken over Dad's real estate agency. He's bloody good at it too. He and Janelle are the same age, and got married when they were twenty one. No one thought it would last, but they've made it work. I can't believe their twins Jack and Jill are twelve already. We all had a fit when they named them that, but it's grown on us, it actually suits them.

Danielle's my oldest sister, she's 34 and a top notch lawyer. Her and Mark have been married for two years but don't have any kids, and they don't want any either.

Then there's Holly, she's the baby of the family even though I'm younger than her. She's always been spoilt and I guess she always will be. She's 32, and what you'd call a free spirit - if you were being nice. A cock loving whore is more like it! Now I say that with love but it's the truth, that girl has had more roots than hot dinners. She has no idea who the father of eight year old Kaci is, there's three blokes in the running for the title and it doesn't worry Holly at all. The funny thing is that two of the prospective fathers still give Holly whatever she wants. What Holly asks for she gets, she has that power over everyone in her life, and it doesn't matter if it's a guy or a chick. It's bizarre, but her chickie friends will do anything for her as well. Dunno how she does it but it certainly works for her. Her latest boyfriend Tobie seems like a good sort though. Holly works reception at the real estate agency that Doug now runs. Dad used to let her get away with two hour lunch breaks, but I know that her poor work ethics are really starting to piss Doug off. She'd better watch it or she'll have to get a real job. God knows what else she'd do, she's only ever worked in the family business.

The two grans are an absolute classic. They live in the same retirement village, *Sunny Days*, and have units next door to each other. They do everything together, as if they're joined at the hip. Both their husbands have passed away now. I never knew Grandpa Spanx, he died before I was born, and Grandpa Drummond died when I was eight. I remember a bit about him, but not heaps.

The two grans are feisty, and they know so much useless crap it's mind-boggling. I love taking them to the pistol club with me, it's a total crack up. Unfortunately Grandma Spanx isn't allowed to shoot anymore because of her osteoporosis, at seventy seven she's finally starting to feel her age. Grandma Drummond is still a crack shot though, and at seventy three she's still got it. She often gives me a run for my money at the range. Literally.

All conversation suddenly stops as we make our entrance, but the silence only lasts for a second. Then suddenly everyone's talking at once and we're being mobbed. They all crowd around me and Claire, jostling for a good position. Then Dad does the head of the family thing and takes control of the situation.

Clapping his hands a few times to get everyone's attention he loudly says, "Ok everyone, pipe down, and give Davis and Claire some room to move. They're not going anywhere, there's plenty of time to get all your questions answered."

He comes over, gives me a hug and ruffles my hair. "My son the celebrity eh, who would have guessed it?" he says proudly.

Then its hugs all round as we greet everybody. Mum appears holding a tray loaded with glasses with little umbrellas in them.

"Virgin piña coladas for everyone," she announces excitedly. "Come on, come and help yourselves!"

"You're a gem love," says Dad. He gives her bum a squeeze and saunters off, glass in hand.

"Daaavid!" she squeals with delight, nearly dropping the tray.

This is a perfect example of why Mum doesn't bat an eyelash if she catches me and Claire snogging or copping a quick feel of each other. Her and Dad are the champions of gratuitous kissing and cuddling, they're always at it and always have been. As a kid it was always an embarrassment, but now as an adult, I admire their style. They've been together forever and still can't get enough of each other. It's pretty cool really.

What also used to embarrass me as a kid was my name. Davis means son of David. Now we're not Jewish, which is where the name stems from, but Dad wouldn't give up on his crusade to have a son named after him. Doug got lucky, Dad had wanted to name him David Junior but Mum wouldn't have a bar of it, so he settled on naming him after his favourite scotch whiskey instead. So when I came along, he again did his best to get a son named after him, and Davis was finally agreed upon.

I used to cop plenty of shit at school about how stupid my name was. Davis wasn't the only part of my name to cop it either, Spanx was fair game as well. The other kids used to call me Manxie Spanxie, which soon got shortened to just Spanxie. I was picked on relentlessly, never a day went by where I didn't get teased. It used to drive me mental, until I finally reached the point where I just ignored it. It also helped that the two grans taught me how to shoot a pistol when I was eleven. When word got round that I was a crack shot, well nobody wanted to mess with someone who could blow their brains out. Not that I'd ever do that, but it was nice to have an aura of menace about me for a change. I still hate being called Spanxie though.

Doug raises his glass and declares that we should all have a toast to the new celebrity of the household. He craps on for a while, then ends the toast with "May you prosper and share your wealth, little brother!" to which everyone loudly agrees.

I'm thinking that now is the perfect time to show off my custom t-shirt, so I give Claire my glass to hold while I turn my back to everyone and whip my jacket open. Turning back around while pointing to my chest I say, "Check it out, I've already got my own respect t-shirt's. What do ya think?"

Grandma Spanx wants to know what it says, she hasn't got her glasses on. So I tell her my catchphrase. 'Respect yourself and respect other people.'

"Very nice, that's a good clear message dear," she nods approvingly.

"Interesting, it's not very snappy though," says Doug, raising his eyebrows. He doesn't look so convinced.

"Well I think it's perfect," Dad declares. "Society's stuffed, people have got no idea about respect these days. So good onya Davis for wanting to bring it back."

"Cheers Dad." I give him a grin, then ask everyone "Now who hasn't seen my YouTube vid? Everybody raise your hand if you *haven't* seen it yet."

Turns out that Mum and Dad are the only ones who haven't seen it. In my excitement and my rush to get to Eric's, I totally forgot to bring my laptop. Whoops. So I ask if anyone's got one in their car. They all shake their heads, but then Danielle pulls her iPad out of her bag and waves it around. She gets it sorted while we sit Mum and Dad on one of the couches, then we all try and crowd around behind them. It's a pretty tight squeeze, so I opt for crouching down next to them.

Bloody hell, I've now had three million hits! Mum ceremoniously presses play, and for the next few minutes I get to watch her and Dad pull a succession of funny faces. By the end of it everyone is cracking up laughing.

Mum turns around and reaches for Claire. "Oh you poor love, I thought he was going to propose to you at the very beginning."

"So did I," laughs Claire. "I was shocked, horrified, and rapt, all at the same time."

"Yes, you're face gives it all away," Mum agrees, then adds, "but then, to find out Davis has been sacked like that, really! No wonder you went to throw up, you poor thing."

Mum turns back around to look at me. She's pursing her lips, looking exasperated. Dad's still laughing. "Why ever did you decide to tell poor Claire like that Davis? What got into you?" she accuses.

"Mum, it just seemed like a good idea at the time ok?"

Dad wants to watch it again, so we do. A few more times actually. No one can get enough.

I decide that this is probably the best time to tell them all about how I got fired. I'd better plug the launch at the pub first - to give myself some kudos. I stand up in front of them all and start, "Ok first things first. If anyone wants to come tonight, and I'd love to see you all there, I'm having a launch party for my new YouTube video at Paul's pub in the city. It starts at eleven o'clock, hopefully we're going to sell five hundred of my t-shirts."

"For how much each?" Dad immediately asks.

"Fifty bucks," I smirk, "they're limited edition, so we reckon they'll sell well."

There's a stunned silence. Then Danielle pipes up, "That's twenty five thousand dollars Davis!"

"I know!" I shout. "It's awesome eh! Eric, Bruce and I are splitting the profits. We all kept ten t-shirts each for family and friends though." I'm grinning and nodding my head. Everyone's just staring at me with their mouths open in shock.

"That's bloody brilliant!" Doug shouts, "*I'm* coming tonight."

Everyone nods and agrees that they are definitely coming tonight, even the Grandmas, they say they don't want to miss out on anything. Holly wants to know if I have any t-shirts with me, and can she wear one now? She's giving me her 'I want it now' look but it has no effect, because I don't have any with me. I left them all at Eric's, which was a dumb move, I could have kitted out some of the family in them.

I've just had a great thought, if I can delay telling them all how I got fired and wait until the launch, then I can get all of their reactions on video. It'll be even funnier and hey, it might even become part of family folklore, like Leonidas the Pirate! I'm not sure if they'll go for it, so I'll have to try and sweeten the deal. Here goes nothing.

"Ok, now I've just had a great idea on how I can share my fame with you guys. How would you all like to be on YouTube, and have bragging rights over all your friends?"

Everyone's looking at each other, then Grandma Spanx says, "Hell yeah, I want to shut that Maisie Smith up. She keeps crapping on about how wonderful her great-grandkids are, and it's making me sick. I'll be happy go on YouTube. That should keep her quiet for a bit."

Yes, I'm thinking, good one Grandma Spanx! She's got the ball rolling nicely, and soon everyone's agreeing. The twins and Kaci are doing a happy dance around the lounge room.

"Here's the deal guys," I say after everyone's settled down. "I've made another YouTube clip, one about how I got fired. We filmed it at Eric's office today, and it's gonna be launched at the pub tonight." Rubbing my hands together and looking at everyone I continue. "What I propose, is that I hang off telling you guys how I got fired *now*, and you wait until you see it at the launch. Eric's filming the whole thing tonight, and I'm gonna ask him to make sure he gets all of your reactions. So, you'll all become part of the next you tube video I put out there - the one taken at the launch. What do ya think?"

It's a mixed reaction. Some people get it, others don't.

"But why would you want to video our reactions?" Mum wants to know. I knew she'd be a hard sell.

"Let me put it this way Mum. I got fired for doing something that I didn't actually do, I got fired for something that's pretty shocking, something that doesn't normally happen at work."

I can tell that this has just confused her more, so I look pleadingly at Claire for help. "Claire, would you say it's a bizarre way to get fired?"

She comes to my rescue, bless her. "Davis is right. It's funny, but it's also something you'd never expect to hear. That's why getting all of your reactions filmed would be so good. It's a train wreck, you'll want to look away, but you won't be able to."

I like where she's going with this, she's so eloquent is my Claire.

She continues, "When Davis told me what happened I was in shock, but I know that Bruce laughed till he cried. In fact so far everyone else Davis has told has found it hilarious."

"So you think we should wait?" Dad asks.

Claire and I nod together.

"Ok then," Dad says, "I've made an executive family decision. We all wait and watch it at the pub tonight, no arguments," and he gives Mum a stern look.

This is going to be great. I'm turning into a marketing machine!

Mum decides it's dinner time, so we all head towards the kitchen. On the way Doug grabs my arm and pulls me into the bathroom.

"C'mon Davis, tell me what happened *now*. I don't want to wait till later. Spill for me bro," he begs.

"No way, you gotta wait, like the rest of the family," I chuckle at him.

"Ah c'mon," he whinges.

It's not often I've got one over Doug, so I plan on milking it for all its worth. "Actually, the kids really shouldn't be there tonight" I say. Leaning in close to his ear I loudly whisper "there's some adult language being used in the vid." I take a step back to watch his reaction.

He's just staring at me, in a rather hypnotising way. He's probably trying to use some mind power shit to make me spill. He's right into that personal development stuff, he's always spouting the latest tips he's read or listened to. I guess that's why he's such a good real estate agent. Dad's the same, they often go to leadership and motivational conferences together. They're stoked about an upcoming Anthony Robbins seminar, they've been raving on about it for ages. They've even talked Danielle into going with them too, Dad reckons she'll make partner in her law firm easy if she goes.

Crossing my arms I tell him "Don't look at me like that, I'm serious Doug, it's got adult content. The kids really should stay at home."

"Yeah and who's gonna look after them? We're all coming to see you."

"Good point," I counter. "Maybe we could ask Mrs Morgan next door to look after them."

Doug narrows his eyes at me. "What adult content could there possibly be Davis? What sort of words are you talking about here?"

I've got to do some quick thinking here, I don't want to give away too much. "Well, wanker comes up a lot. I called my boss that, as you do when you're getting fired" I bluff.

"The kids have heard that before, what else is in it?" he demands.

"Look just trust me, let's ask Mrs Morgan ok? Anyway, Kaci's too young to hear that shit."

Primping in front of the bathroom mirror he finally gives in. "Yeah I guess you're right. Bugger, you're really not going to tell me anything now are you?" He sounds so disappointed.

"Afraid not big bro, you're just going to have to wait and see."

We exit the bathroom together, and once in the kitchen Doug informs everyone that there's adult content in the video, using his fingers as quotation marks to emphasise *adult content* - he's such a dag. This causes a stir amongst the family. I suggest Mrs Morgan next door for babysitting, but Mum says they're away on holidays. Luckily Tobie puts his hand up, he reckons he's knackered and doesn't mind staying behind to look after the kids. Personally I think he's crazy, but it's up to him. Of course the kids go into total meltdown when they realise they can't come, and the nagging immediately starts. There's a chorus of 'it's not fair' etc. from them, but bad bloody luck. I tell them I'll give them a limited edition t-shirt to make it up to them. That settles them down a bit, but they're still not too happy about it.

Everyone's milling around in the kitchen, the smells are divine. Mum's an awesome cook, so is Dad. Whenever they have a dinner party Dad does all the cooking, but for family gatherings it's Mum's domain. I mosey on over to Danielle and ask her if I can have a word, and we head into the dining room together. I want to ask her if there is, or could be, such a thing as an appearance contract. Then I realise that I haven't told Claire about this, so I go and get her.

When I tell them what I'm thinking, they both look at me as if I'm crazy. I think they just got stuck on the fact that I'd have chicks, famous chicks, on my arm. They don't get it, so I need to dumb it down for them a bit. Taking a deep breath I start again.

"Ok, so what I'm suggesting here is this. Now that I'm a celebrity, I need to go and do celebrity things. And at these celebrity things, it would be good publicity to have another famous person, or up and coming famous person, with me for mutual exposure. Nothing else, just for us to get more publicity."

I think they're getting it this time round, so I continue. "So Danielle, what I was wondering is, can I possibly get a contract for the chicks to sign before we're seen in public together. A contract that states it's all just for show, you know, that they aren't entitled to any money or anything, and that it's only a business arrangement. There will definitely not be any hanky-panky. I want to make that clear. I want to protect our relationship Claire. Am I making any sense?"

I can see the lights go on, they've got it. They both look at each other, then back at me. They both start laughing, then Claire takes my face in her hands and kisses me.

"You're unbelievable. You've got this all figured out haven't you?" she asks.

"Well Eric thought it was a good idea."

Danielle's still giggling but manages to say, "Actually it's not a bad idea, and yes it can be done. Any sort of contract can be drawn up, so it shouldn't be a problem."

As Danielle is saying this, Dad and the others come in, carrying assorted casserole dishes. "What's not such a bad idea?" Dad wants to know.

So it becomes the general topic of dinner discussion. Holly wants to know what sort of celebrity things I'll be going to. "No idea," I reply. "But there's gotta be parties and stuff," which causes all the girls' ears prick up.

Eyeballing all the women around the table, I say, "Now, just because I'll be having celebrity chicks on my arm sometimes, doesn't mean that I won't be taking any of you lovely ladies with me at other times ok? It will just depend on the occasion."

"Oooh, you'll have to let us know well in advance when you're going to take *us* somewhere Davis. We'll need to get our hair done won't we?" quips Grandma Drummond, looking to Grandma Spanx, who is vigorously nodding her head in agreement.

I grin. I love the idea of taking those two out somewhere special with me. "No worries, I'll give you both plenty of notice, I promise."

Turning to Claire who's sitting next to me, I give her knee a squeeze under the table then, stand up to announce. "You all know that Hugh Jackman is my man-idol. So I'm stating here and now, that my goal is to stand next to him on the red carpet, at the premiere of his next movie. And there's only one special lady that I want on my arm at *that* event."

I hold Claire's hand up and give it a kiss. "Will you accompany me to that my love?"

"Yeah well, I'll have to check my diary, but I think I can fit you in," she says cheekily.

Everyone laughs, and the general consensus is that the appearance contract is a goer.

Dinner is superb, Mum's done it again. She's done a Spanish theme tonight and everything is absolutely delicious. Just as we are finishing off our desserts my mobile rings.

It's Paul, he wants to know if I can get to the pub early. He says the place is already packed, it's so full of people that they're spilling out into the mall, and he's had to hire extra security for the night. He also tells me that a TV crew is there as well. Cool!

He wants to know if he should hire a giant mobile TV screen to put out the front, so that the punters in the mall can watch the launch. I think it's a fantastic idea, so I give him the go ahead. He reckons it'll cost about five hundred bucks, but I'm cool with that. He's already sussed out the hire company, and they say they can get it all set up within half an hour. I quiz him on how they'll get the live feed to the TV outside, and he tells me not to worry, he's got it sorted. I look at my watch, it's nine thirty, so I tell him I'll be there soon. Just as I'm about to hang up he says to make sure I come in through the back entrance, through the kitchen, otherwise I'll probably get mobbed.

When everyone hears that I'm leaving early, that there's a TV crew at the pub, and that the crowd is pretty big, chaos erupts. The kids go mental and start nagging again, and all the adults start shouting, "I'm coming with you Davis."

There's a mad scramble for a second, but then Dad takes control of the situation once again and bellows, "Right-oh! Doug, you call for a couple of maxi-taxis. Everyone else, get your skates on, we've got a launch to go to!"

Chapter 5

On the way to the pub I send out a tweet of my imminent arrival. I'm doing what Eric asked me to do, gotta keep the fans happy. And fans I have! I've gone from having less than thirty Twitter friends, to suddenly having four hundred and fifty thousand! Oh my freakin' God! Claire does a double take when I show her, she can't believe it. Even the taxi driver knows who I am, and he wants my autograph. Fuck me!

The maxi-taxis drop us off in Little Collins Street and we walk up The Causeway to the back entrance of The Watering Hole. There's a goods delivery bell, I press the button and wait. We certainly are a funny looking bunch. The Grandmas have dolled themselves up with a nice coral lipstick, Dad's got his 'I love Elvis' cap on, and Mum's got her lucky ABBA handbag with her. Yep that's my family, full of fashion victims, but lovable.

While we're all huddled together waiting to be let in, I tell everyone how grateful I am for their support. "Thanks again, for coming tonight guys, it really means a lot to me."

Dad ruffles my hair and Mum gives my arm a squeeze. The others are just grinning at me.

Then Danielle pipes up, "Yeah well it's not every day your little brother nearly melts YouTube with so many hits."

"*I* can't wait to get my t-shirt, that's gonna be so cool," Holly gushes.

Suddenly the door opens and we're all blinded by the bright lights of a camera crew shining in our faces. We haven't even got in the door yet, but Kirk Stefanobik from *Good Morning Today* shoves a microphone in my face and asks how it feels to be a celebrity.

"Fuck me," I breathe. Then I realise this isn't the best thing to say on telly.

Kirk's laughing, he's got that funny head bobbing thing that he does going on.

"Ahem, what I mean is, aah, wow, good to see you Kirk, this is a really nice surprise."

Holding the mic up he says, "We heard that you were doing your launch here tonight at The Watering Hole in the Bourke Street Mall.

And seeing as you're a YouTube sensation, we thought it was an important story to cover. Are you nervous about tonight Davis?"

I take a deep breath. "Well I hadn't been until now Kirk! I was just excited, but I might be starting to freak out now, you know, just a little bit."

"I hear you brother, this *is* your first celebrity appearance, so it's only to be expected. Now, can we meet your lovely family here?"

So introductions are made. Grandma Spanx is beside herself with excitement, she's always had a big crush on Kirk. I hope she's got her Depend on, don't want her wetting herself. Eww, yuck, the thought totally grosses me out. Why do I think this weird shit?

Holly is now gushing at Kirk, but he must be able to sense an opportunist at a hundred paces, because he quickly cuts her off and focuses his attention on Mum.

"You must be very proud Mrs Spanx."

Nodding her head in agreement, Mum holds the microphone up to her mouth with one hand and blurts, "Oh Kirk, you can call me Jan." Batting her eyelashes at him she then says, "You're right, I am proud, we always knew Davis was special, it's just taken him a while to find his calling."

She's flailing her ABBA handbag around with her other hand as she's talking. I see Kirk take note of it and I inwardly groan. Not the ABBA story Mum, please don't tell him the ABBA story. But it's too late, Kirk has just remarked on what a lovely bag it is. Sadist! He can also probably sense an embarrassing story coming up. Well it'll be gold, Kirk, ABBA Gold! Mum holds her bag up for all to see.

"Oh this old thing! It's my lucky bag Kirk. I had it with me when I went to see ABBA at the Melbourne Town Hall. It was the fifth of March nineteen seventy seven, in the arvo, before their first concert that night. I was only nineteen, but I still remember it like it was yesterday," she says dreamily. "They all stood on the balcony like royalty and waved down to us. I got separated from my girlfriends, the crowd was unbelievable. There were over four thousand people there all screaming their heads off, everyone was pushing and shoving, it got pretty scary Kirk. I thought I was going to faint, but then suddenly a strong pair of hands stopped me from collapsing. That's when I met David, Davis's father. My knight in shining armour. I'm sure I would have gotten trampled if he hadn't saved me. That night we went to the ABBA concert together at the Sidney Myer Music Bowl, and a little bit of magic happened that night Kirk. I had my very first orgasm, and Doug was conceived. David still calls me his Dancing Queen, don't you David."

The look on Kirk's face is priceless, he wasn't expecting something as good as *that*. Dad's nodding his head, a dreamy smile is plastered on his face too. It always amazes me that Mum never thinks of herself as a dirty little stop-out for giving up her goods to Dad so quickly. Instead she tells it like it's the best love story in the world, which I guess it is, because it's her love story.

"Wow, that's amazing, what a fantastic story to pass down to your kids and grandkids," enthuses Kirk.

I can tell he's trying really hard to keep a straight face, and being the consummate professional he is, he somehow pulls it off. So now the whole of Australia knows when my Mum popped her cherry. Great. I look over at Doug. He's gone bright red, and is looking down at the ground, probably willing it to open up and swallow him alive. Kirk sees another great opportunity and quickly shoves his microphone into Doug's face.

"Wow Doug. That's a pretty special way to be brought in to the world. Are you musical?"

Doug avoids all eye contact with Kirk and just mumbles, "No". He seems to have lost the ability to speak, which is understandable.

Kirk gets it and moves things on. "Well we better let you all get inside and enjoy the evening. We're streaming live from here tonight, so we'll see you guys later on, ok?"

I realise that I've still got my jacket on and nobody's seen my respect t-shirt yet. So I take it off, ready to give myself a quick plug. "Hey Kirk, I'd just like to unveil the limited edition respect t-shirt. They'll be on sale here tonight, but you'd better be quick, there's not that many of them."

"Nice t-shirt Davis," Kirk affirms, then he looks right into the camera and says, "You heard it here first folks. Come down to the Watering Hole on the Bourke Street Mall, and get your limited edition respect t-shirts while you can. Stocks are limited, so don't miss out. They're one hundred dollars each, and it's strictly cash only."

While he's saying this I'm standing next to him, striking some poses and pointing to the message on the front of the t-shirt. What the? He just said a hundred bucks each! No one's gonna pay that for a lousy t-shirt. Oh well, he gave us a good plug. And speaking of plugs, Kirk's certainly giving The Watering Hole some nice airtime. I bet Paul put him up to it, the canny wee bastard. Good on him.

We finally get inside and I'm not sure what I was expecting, but it certainly isn't this. As we make our way through the kitchen, the staff line up and start clapping and whistling. I just smile, wave, and give a few high fives, acting like this happens all the time. Paul emerges from the bar and we give each other a man-hug.

"Hey, Kirk was giving the place a nice plug just now. How did you get him to do that?" I ask.

"Easy, I told him he could have an exclusive with you if he plugged the pub. Simple as that. Another TV crew are outside, but I told Kirk that if he keeps plugging the pub all night, he can stay inside and catch all the action. He's happy, I'm happy. Mate, this is out of control. You should see the mall, it's packed, and we can't fit any more inside here. Have a peek through the door."

I take a look through the glass porthole, it's standing room only out there, people are squashed together like sardines. It's crazy. The band is rocking on, they must be stoked to have such a huge crowd to play to.

The family are currently engaged with high-fiving the kitchen staff, but soon start scoffing the finger food that's thrust at them by the head chef. There's a bit of jostling between everyone when some prawn spring rolls are offered around. Paul and I shake our heads, grinning at each other. Show my family some free food and it's on for young and old. Elbowing and stamping one another's feet are standard tactics for gaining the advantage in such a situation. If we all go to a buffet, like we used to do at least once a month, well let me just say it's not a pretty sight.

It was a sad day for the Spanx family when the *Sizzle Saloon* all you can eat restaurants closed down in Victoria. I say sad, but I was kind of relieved too, because those buffets would send everyone into a feeding frenzy. It's kind of weird seeing your normally mild man-nered Mum pushing and shoving her way towards the dessert bar. Of course *I* always behaved myself – Ha! Like hell I did! I'd be there, happily elbowing anyone who was in my way. We took Paul with us once and he nearly died of embarrassment. He said we were like pigs at a trough. He was pretty spot on, and funnily enough, he never did come with us to the *Sizzle Saloon* ever again.

Narrowing my eyes at him I ask, "Did you set up this food on purpose?"

Paul laughs. "You bet! Nothing's bloody changed with you lot. I knew we'd need a bit of time to go over a few things, so I figured this'll keep the troops happy for a minute."

"Too right," I agree. "You know they'll be raving about this for ages."

"The Grandma Report," we say together knowingly.

If the Grandmas eat anything, anywhere, you're guaranteed a full report on what it was, what it tasted like, if they would have it again, blah blah blah. I tend to tune out after the first few minutes, they can go on for bloody ages. I once asked them why they're so focused on this shit, and they reckon it's because of growing up during the Second World War. They used to have limited supplies, and had to use coupons for food. So if they did eat anything good or yummy they'd discuss it at length, reliving the delicious experience. It's just become a habit I guess, one that's been passed down the family. Even Holly and Danielle tend to be pretty obsessed with food, and will always discuss the merits of any meal eaten out.

Paul clears his throat and announces "Now, what I was thinking was you guys need a VIP area, we especially want to keep the Grandmas safe. Trust them to come tonight, bet they didn't want to miss out eh?"

I nod. Paul's got a soft spot for my Grandmas. Sometimes we all go shooting together. That's another throwback to the war, both ladies were taught how to use a gun in case they needed to defend themselves.

"So I'm thinking," Paul continues, "that the stage will be perfect, you'll all be up there together, out of harm's way. The bouncers will have the stage fully covered, so the crowd shouldn't be a problem."

I look over to the stage area again and start nodding. Then something occurs to me. "But we won't be able to see the TV from there, we'll have a shit view of my video," I complain.

"Nah, I've got it sorted, you can watch it on this one. You can see everything from the stage ok." He points to a big screen above the bar, and I see his point, it'll work fine. Then he continues on, "Eric and I have already gone through everything, and it's actually better to have the family on stage. It'll be easier for Eric to film everyone."

"Good point. Yeah, I haven't told them anything yet, so they'll find out at the same time as everyone else," I grin cheekily. "I'm hoping for a good reaction here."

"So no one knows?" Paul asks in amazement.

"Only Claire."

"Jeeze Davis, you sure know how to build a bit of drama don'tcha! Come into the office and have a look at the security cameras. The view outside will blow you away."

I clap my hands to get the family's attention. Dad's got sweet chilli dipping sauce dribbling down his chin, and Doug has shoved so much food into his mouth he can barely chew. I inform them that we should all move into the office, and there's an audible groan. No one want's to be separated from the freebie finger food, so they all load up, carrying as many spring rolls and mini dim sims as possible. Finally everyone's ready to make a move. I notice Grandma Drummond put a couple of spring rolls into her purse for later - man she grosses me out sometimes.

We all file into the office after Paul. It's a bit of a tight squeeze, and a bit smelly due to the waft of the mini dim sims. Paul points to a security monitor, flicks a switch, and the outside camera starts to pan around. Oh my God, it's a sea of people out there. It looks like the whole mall is packed. We see Kirk and the crew interviewing some people. Everyone seems very excited.

Paul turns around and asks me, "Hey, do you want to say anything to them? They'll hear you on our speaker system. There's speakers out the front of the pub, we use them if it looks like trouble's brewing. Most people freak out when they hear someone talking to them and piss off. But you could use it to say hi to everyone, let them know you're here. Whaddaya reckon?"

I hesitate, but everyone's egging me on. Man, you've got to think on your feet when you're a celebrity. I have no idea what to say. Lucky I'm a good bullshitter though. I look at my watch and then go for it.

"Hey you're a good looking crowd. This isn't Big Brother, it's Davis Spanx, and I'd like to thank you all for coming along to see me tonight. We'll get the show on the road in about forty minutes, so don't go anywhere or you'll miss out on all the fun. Bye for now and don't forget, respect yourself and respect other people."

At first people's heads are swivelling around trying to pinpoint where the voice is coming from, but they figure it out pretty quickly, pointing to the speakers on the ceiling of the verandah. Then they spot the camera and start waving at it. Soon a massive Mexican wave has started up. All of this is for me? Man, it's so cool!

I ask Paul if he's seen Bruce or Eric. He reckons they're out in the main bar having a beer.

"Do you think I should go out there yet?" I ask.

Paul chews his bottom lip and says, "You can if you want, but I'd advise the rest of the family to stay here until we can get them all safely onto the stage."

"Yeah ok," I agree. "I want to touch base with the guys, we gotta sort out these t-shirts. Where do you think we should sell them from?"

Paul crinkles his nose in distaste, the smell in here is really gross now. "Mate, I'd just do it from the stage, that way you've got a bit of control of the situation. Do it as soon as your videos finish, that way the punters will be pumped and willing to part with the cash."

The family are happy to stay in the office and finish their finger food, while I go and find Eric and Bruce. On the way out I order a tray full of Virgin Marys to keep them all happy, they'll need something to wash down all that food.

Peeking through another door's porthole, I spot the guys immediately. Luckily they're right near the bar outside the door, it's easy for me to get to them. Their faces light up when they see me.

"Fuck me this is unbelievable!" I shout at them.

"Maaaate!" Bruce exclaims and claps me on the back.

"You're a legend already Davis, nice one," jokes Eric.

They clink glasses and I notice that some bouncers have moved around so that they're between us and the crowd, which is just as well, because it only takes a minute and the crowd cops onto me being there. At first I can hear people ask each other 'Is that him?' then it suddenly becomes a shout of 'There he is!' and they all start pushing forward.

The band happens to stop just at this moment, so I say in a loud voice, "Hey, let's give it up for the band, they've been great tonight."

The crowd goes ballistic, cheering and wolf whistling. When it dies down a bit I give a wave and say, "Great to see you all here tonight."

But before I can say anything else someone shouts out that they want a t-shirt. Then a chant starts up, 'We want a t-shirt, we want a t-shirt.' Bruce, Eric and I put our heads together and have a quick pow-wow. We decide to sell half now and half later. Eric wants to test the price of a hundred bucks each, and asks me to say something.

So I wave my arms around, to quieten down the crowd, then shout out, "Who's got their hundred bucks ready? Flash us your cash!"

A sea of hundred and fifty dollar bills is quickly held aloft. Holy shit! The guys and I grin at each other. We're going to make fifty grand, that's in-fucking-credible! Kirk must have sensed movement inside, because the crowd parts and in he comes, with the camera crew in tow. He's talking into his mike while the camera pans over the sea of fluttering money. Paul comes out of the door near us, shaking his head and laughing.

"We've been watching what's been happening on the office monitors. Jeezus, you guys are gonna pull in fifty grand tonight!" he says in amazement.

"I know," we all yell at him together. Our eyes are nearly popping out of our heads with excitement.

Paul puts his hand on my shoulder and says loudly over the noise, "I reckon we should sell them from the bar *opposite* the stage. I know I said to sell them from the stage before, but it'll actually be safer and easier to do it from behind the bar. You three can all get behind there and go for it. What do ya think?"

Nodding, I agree with him. "Sweet, sounds like a plan." I turn to the other two and they both agree.

Turning to the crowd I hold up my hands to quieten down the chant. It works, so I shout out that the bar opposite the stage will be selling t-shirts in ten minutes time.

Then I add, "Hey, it's all about respect guys, so once you've got your t-shirt please move aside so someone else can get theirs. Cheers."

The guys and I all file out of the bar, and the bouncers move to block the door from the crowd. Once we're out the back we all start screaming and high-fiving each other. We can't believe that people are almost throwing their money at us. As I give Paul a high-five I notice the TV crew is filming us through the porthole in the door, so I give them a wave. Man this celebrity shit is awesome! Fifty grand in the hand in one night. Woohoo, bring it on!

We poke our heads into the office to see how the family are going, and Dad quickly weasels his way into helping us sell the t-shirts.

Everyone wanted to help, but Paul said there was only room for one more behind the bar. So Dad pulled the head of the family card and won the spot. Mum's just wiped the sauce off his chin, thank God.

The guys, Dad and I are having a quick meeting before we face the crowd. Paul's given each of us a catering sized ice cream bucket with a lid to put the cash in. Very high tech I know, but there wasn't time for a crash course on how to work the bar tills. So, buckets in hand, we head for the bar. Paul's got some of his staff to carry and open the boxes of t-shirts for us.

When we come out the crowd goes wild, and a sea of money is fluttering before us. Kirk and the camera crew are now up on the stage, they've got a perfect view of us.

I put my hands up again to quieten the crowd, then shout "I'd like to introduce you all to my Dad, and my mates Eric and Bruce."

Dad, Eric and Bruce give the crowd a wave, and the crowd roars its approval.

"Who's ready to get their t-shirt?" I yell.

"I am!" screams the crowd back at me. Fuck me, I feel like a bloody rock star.

And with that, money is thrust into our faces. We can hardly keep up with it all. The punters are so happy to get their t-shirts, and we're so happy to get their cash! It's incredible. A couple of times I wave at someone to move along, so that others can get in. One chick even flashes her tits at us as she takes off her top and puts her new respect t-shirt on. Dad's loving it, his eyes are out on stalks!

67

They're a very well behaved crowd, with not too much pushing or shoving, which is kind of bizarre, but great. Our buckets are quickly crammed full of lovely cash, and it only takes about twenty minutes for us to sell out. When we run out I tell the crowd that we'll be selling more after the video launch, adding that the video will start in about ten minute's time. Now the crowd starts chanting 'Davis, Davis, Davis.' It's awesome.

The four of us head out the back and put our buckets down, then we all start doing that weird bobbing up and down dance thing again. Spookily enough, Dad knows just how it's done, it must be an ancient man ritual that's in all our male DNA. We're all screaming and shouting complete gibberish at this point, so we don't see Kirk and the crew filming us at first. They just seem to appear out of nowhere, how the hell do they do that? We acknowledge their presence by all turning to face the camera and doing our crazy dance for them. Kirk's cracking up, so Dad pulls him over and Kirk does the dance with us for a minute or so. We're all puffed and feeling a bit knackered. Paul takes the buckets and puts them in the strongroom for safe keeping. Kirk wants to ask me a few questions, but I don't really have time. I've got to get the family organised, we've only got five minutes until the launch is due to start.

Ok so we're running just a little bit late. Kirk has now moved himself and the camera crew off to the side, at the front of the stage, they have a perfect view of everything.

My family is taking to this celebrity status thing like ducks to water. When the two Grandmas hit the stage, do you think they would sit in their seats and behave, like two little old ladies should? No such luck. No, they decide that now would be the perfect time to embarrass me to the max!

Grandma Spanx goes up to the microphone and says, "You've seen Madonna and Britney do it, now you get to see us do it."

I'm not even on stage yet, I'm still standing to the side, and before I know what's happening Grandma Drummond has jumped out of her seat and is standing next to Grandma Spanx. Then they put their arms around each other and proceed to have a big granny pash. A what? That's right, a fucking granny pash. I do a double take, I can't believe what I'm seeing. I just can't believe it, it's so gross, yet I can't look away, it's like it's all happening in slow motion. This is like watching a car crash right in front of my eyes, how can they do this to me?

But then it gets worse. As they're pulling their mouths away from each other, Grandma Spanx's top set of false teeth fly out of her mouth and slide across the stage. Oh my fucking God, is this really happening? The crowd gasps as her teeth come to a sliding halt near the edge of the stage. Grandma Spanx starts cackling and orders Dad to go and pick them up.

I wince as she tells the audience, "Must have got us a nice bit of suction going on there kids!"

The crowd recovers from its shocked silence and claps in approval. Dad gingerly retrieves the teeth, and Grandma Spanx brushes them off on her dress and pops them back in her mouth. She's looking very pleased with herself.

I'm still in shock. Thank God there were no tongues involved, well none that I could see. They must have cooked this up in the office beforehand, bloody old tarts. I'm totally grossed out, but the crowd is absolutely loving it.

When the cheering dies down Grandma Spanx looks right into the TV camera, her coral lipstick smudged all over her face, and says "We're open for negotiations on doing a new TV show called *Grannies Behaving Badly*." Then she asks the crowd, "Would you all watch us in *Grannies Behaving Badly*?"

The crowd erupts, screaming yes it would. The two grans nod and wave to the crowd, then return to their seats. Grandma Spanx mouths at Kirk 'Call me' while holding her hand up to her ear like a phone.

Jeezus, here I am all about respect, and these two are all about behaving badly. It's a bit of an age role reversal isn't it? Ah well good on them, if it makes them happy go for it, although now I think about it, maybe there's been more to their relationship than I thought for years. I mean they *are* joined at the hip, I'll have to ask them later if they munch each other's carpets. But right now I've got my launch to do.

$$\$\$\$\$\$\$\$\$\$$

God, suddenly I'm nervous as hell. My heart's beating so fast it feels like I'm about to have a heart attack, and sweat is starting to trickle down my back, making my t-shirt all sticky. What if everyone hates my new video and they boo me off stage? What if they all just think I'm a wanker - literally? I take a deep breath. Oh man, why the fuck did I want to do this in the first place? This is seriously scary shit.

I take a look at my family. Danielle, Mark and Holly are standing up, high-fiving the grans. Mum looks like she's about to be sick, I'm not sure if it's because of the granny pash or too much finger food. Doug and Janelle are pissing themselves laughing, and Dad's just staring out at the crowd. He's got that silly dreamy look on his face, God knows what he's daydreaming about, although I've got a pretty good idea that it consists of chicks and pashing. Hopefully he didn't get off on seeing his mum pash his mother in law! Eww!

I seem to be the only one freaking out here, I need to get a grip. I look at Claire, she winks and gives me a double thumbs up, so I decide it's now or never and leap onto the stage to grab the microphone. It's wild to see so many people wearing my respect t-shirts.

"And that was my two lovely grans, they're a bloody riot aren't they?" I turn round and say to them, "Thanks for opening the show like that ladies, I'm not sure if I should be sick or throttle you."

The crowd laughs rowdily at this so I continue, "Ok that's enough about them, now it's all about me. You've all seen how I broke the news to my beautiful girlfriend Claire that I lost my job, so now I'd like to share with you *why* I lost my job. I'll let *you* be the judge on whether I was unfairly dismissed."

Now that I've made a start, my confidence is kicking in. There's a sea of faces riveted to what I'm saying, so I tell them, "I'm actually glad that this happened. If I hadn't been fired then I wouldn't be here with you all tonight, and I wouldn't be following my dream of becoming a celebrity and sharing my message of respect. So enjoy the video guys, and I'll see you after it. Don't forget to respect yourself and respect other people."

I move back a bit and stand side on, so that I can watch the reaction of my family and the audience simultaneously. Silence falls, the lights dim, and the clip starts playing. Kirk's film crew is panning around the audience, but Eric's got his camera trained directly on my family, ready to capture the reactions on their faces when they hear about what happened. As things get rolling I'm glad he's got it focused on them, because Mum looks like she's going to have another fit, while Dad's pissing himself laughing hysterically. The two grans have got their mouths open in shock, but after their public pashing fiasco they can hardly tell me off about anything! Danielle, Mark, Claire and Holly are all pissing themselves laughing, and so is the audience. As we get to the bit where I'm walking out the office door and Beaker yells after me, "You'll never be famous Davis, you're a nobody," the crowd boos.

When the video stops the place goes ballistic. I walk back over to the mike as people are laughing and cheering. There's a few cat calls of *wanker*, which is what I expected.

Shushing the crowd I tell them, "Ok, I'm going to answer five people's questions, who wants to ask me something?"

Hands immediately shoot up into the air everywhere.

I pick a guy near the front. "What would you like to know?"

"I wanna know if you really had a wank," he sneers.

I knew this would probably be the number one question on everyone's lips. I can feel everyone's eyes boring into me as my heart starts beating faster, but I answer the question honestly.

"No I didn't, I really only read the magazine article. That's the absolute, honest to God truth. That's why I was so pissed off that Beaker would fire me like that. It was totally unfair, I was a victim of circumstance, so I'll say it again, I did *not* wank at work that day. Now who else has a question?"

I pick a chick further back in the crowd and she demands, "Why are you guys allowed to read girly magazines at work?"

Shuffling uncomfortably, I clear my throat and answer, "I have no idea, we just are. It just happens, and as far as I know no one's ever complained. And we've got chicks that work in the office that use the tea room as well, but they don't seem to mind. It is what it is. Next question please."

I choose another bloke this time.

"How did you get so many hits on You Tube so quickly?"

Shrugging my shoulders I say, "Again, I have no idea, I guess you guys just liked it! It's blown me away. I only got fired yesterday, now here it is a day later, and I'm a bit of a celebrity. It's insane! I can't believe it's all happened so quickly. When I said to Beaker that I'd be a celebrity, I never dreamed it would happen this fast. So summing up the answer to that question, I have no idea why I'm so popular, but I'm grateful that I am. Next question please."

I point to a chick in the middle of the crowd.

"Will you sign my boobs for me?" she asks as she lifts up her t-shirt and flashes a nice set of tits.

The crowd cheers and I chuckle, "Well I'd better ask Claire if that's ok." Then I change my mind. "Actually, you know what? Honey, you need to respect yourself a little bit more. I *won't* sign your boobs, but I'll gladly sign the back of your t-shirt ok?"

She makes her way to the stage, and from somewhere a Texta appears and I sign the back of her white t-shirt. She's rapt.

"Ok last question now."

Hands shoot up everywhere, I pick an older guy.

"Do you want revenge on your old boss?" he calls out.

"Good question mate. Look, he didn't show me any respect, and in the video you heard how one of the scenarios going through my head was to call him an effing a… and smash up his office. But I didn't do that. I chose not to because that would have taken me down to his level. I heard somewhere that the best revenge is living a great life. So if you call that revenge then yeah, I plan on giving him plenty, because I plan on having a freakin' awesome life!!"

Another cheer erupts from the crowd.

Moving to the edge of the stage, I look out over everyone and say, "I'd like to thank you all again for showing your support and coming along tonight. We'll be selling more t-shirts in a minute, and soon I'll have my website up and running. You can also follow my progress on Twitter and Facebook. Thanks again, you're all awesome. And remember, respect yourself and respect other people. Oh yeah that reminds me, losing my job like this has really shown me how little respect is out there these days. So I want to bring it back. I want to bring back the respect, and I'm hoping that you can all help me with this. Do you guys want to help me bring back the respect?"

"Yes," the crowd chants, going wild.

I ask them again, "Do you want to help me bring back the respect? I can't do it without you!"

Once again the crowd roars its approval.

Punching the air I yell, "Respect!"

Then I turn around to Claire and motion her to over to me. She doesn't want to budge until Holly gives her a push off her chair. The crowd cheers as she walks up beside me. Taking her hand, I hold it up like she's a boxing champ. Then I pull her to me and kiss her thoroughly, which makes the crowd go absolutely crazy.

When we finish our kiss I say, "I'd just like to thank my beautiful lady for putting up with all of my crap, she's a gem." Turning to her and looking deeply into her eyes I say, "I love you so much Claire, thank you for being you."

All the chicks in the room let out a holler. Claire's got tears in her eyes, and when I look around I see a lot of people wiping their eyes. The crowd is cheering and clapping.

We exit the stage and then Eric, Bruce, Dad and I start selling the remaining t-shirts from behind the bar, while the rest of the family head out the back. The t-shirts sell out again in about twenty minutes, it's crazy.

When we make it back into the office I say, "Jeezus, fifty grand in forty minutes, that's over a grand a minute."

"Actually it's exactly $1250 a minute," says Dad. Trust him to know that, he's such a numbers man.

We all look at each other and go mental - you guessed it, the weird bobbing dance gets another go! We're all grinning like idiots. Fifty grand is a massive amount of money, it would normally take me a whole bloody year to earn that much!

Paul pokes his head in through the office door. "Drinks anyone?" He holds up a bottle of scotch.

Bruce and Eric scream out a yes. I look at Dad, he looks at me. Oh man, I so want to get shit faced with my mates, but I made a promise. I know damn well that if I have one, then Dad'll use it as an excuse to have one too, which will lead to both of us getting pissed and smoking our lungs out. Wow, I must be growing up in order to be thinking about the consequences of my actions.

It's like Dad can read my mind, in truth he's probably just following the strange sequence of faces I'm pulling as I'm thinking, but he gets it spot on. Patting me on the back he says, "Davis, you deserve to celebrate. Have a drink with your mates, I'll be fine."

It's spooky, almost like reverse psychology. Now he's told me to have a drink, I don't really want one, well I do, but I don't. Fuck, all this thinking is doing my head in!

"Nah, I'll give it a miss. I'll only want a smoke if I get pissed."

"Well, we could just have *one* drink together," he coaxes, "one drink'll be alright."

Here's the thing about my Dad, he's a master influencer. Sometimes you end up saying yes to the stupidest stuff, because he talks you into it in such a way that you've said yes before you even know the full story of what you're saying yes to. It's like he hypnotises you. *That's* why he had the top real estate agency in Australia for seven years in a row, his clients never knew what hit them, all they knew was that they *had* to pay full price for that house, and they had to pay it *right now*! So I have to keep my wits about me here, I know he's going to use his magic on me, I've just gotta stay strong.

"No way," I declare. "We're not drinking anything, you're still on medication. There's no way I'm letting you have any of that shit."

"Bugger," he says frowning at me, "thought I might get around ya. You're as bad as your Mum."

Hmmm, now that was too easy, what's he up to? Normally he doesn't give up half as easily. He strolls over to Eric and puts his arm around his shoulders, then murmurs something in his ear. The guys all know about Dad's heart attack and giving up the smokes, so I'm confident they won't let him have a drink. But I still want to be sure.

"No matter what he says to you Eric, and you too Bruce, and Paul, under no circumstances is Dad allowed to have any grog tonight. He's still on medication, so it's a no go alright?"

The guys all nod their agreement.

Dad looks amused by my little speech and says, "Aww Davis, it's nice to know you care son, come here," and he gives me a big hug.

Claire comes in as this is happening, "Nice to see some father son bonding going on here. I want a hug too."

So Dad spreads his arms wide, she walks into them, and we have a three way hug. I know it's not exactly what she was wanting, she was wanting a hug with me, her hero, but she goes along with it. Claire's such a good sport, so we all hug and have a laugh for minute.

Paul comes back in with a tray of glasses full of coke, I'm not sure if there's any scotch in them so I give Dad's a sniff before I pass it to him. Quality control check complete, Bruce raises a toast.

"To the best newest celebrity in the world!"

We all laugh and skull our drinks.

Paul quickly ducks out and returns with our money buckets in hand, swinging them around. "Who wants to see how rich you are? Do ya wanna count this pile of loot now or later?"

"Now," we all scream.

He hands us the buckets and a bag of rubber bands. As he's leaving he says to me "Kirk and the crew want one more interview with you, are you up for it?"

"Shit yeah, bring it on."

"Good, he's waiting out in the kitchen, the rest of your family are keeping him *entertained* out there."

I groan inwardly, God knows what they'll come out with this time, I'd better get out there as soon as possible to limit any damage. I ask Claire if she'll do the interview with me, she's not really keen but I talk her into doing it 'for me'. The guys are more than happy to count the money while we go off for our interview.

The scene that greets us in the kitchen is one of mayhem. Holly and Danielle are dancing on top of a kitchen bench. Mum and Mark, Danielle's husband, are cheering and egging them on. Doug and Janelle seem to be looking through cupboards, man they can't still be hungry can they? And the two grans are being interviewed by Kirk. Kirk's got a rather strained look on his face, God knows what those two have just told him. He spots us coming in, immediately wraps it up, and bustles over to us.

Shoving the microphone my way he asks, "Ah, and here we have the two lovebirds. How do you feel Davis?"

"Man I can't believe how incredible tonight's been. It's been amazing, better than I thought it could be. We even sold out of t-shirts, which is a total bonus."

Kirk nods. "Did you expect to get such a big response?"

Shaking my head I reply, "No way, I thought it'd be cool if a hundred people rocked up, but this has just been insane."

"Now Claire," Kirk says, "how does it feel to be Davis's girl? He clearly loves you a lot."

Claire immediately blushes at his comment. "Yeah, I was really scared of being on stage with him at first, but he's so sweet, he nearly made me cry up there. Next time I think I'll leave it to him though, I don't like being in the spotlight."

Kirk nods again, "There certainly was a lot of love in the room, I saw a lot of emotion here tonight." Then he starts laughing, "Davis I can't believe that's how you got fired. Does it bother you that you'll be called a wanker from now on?"

Jeezus, Kirk just said wanker on national TV, is he allowed to do that? I figure that if he can then I can too. Taking a deep breath I let out a sigh. "You know Kirk, everyone's a wanker sometimes, but in this case I'm not one. I swear to God I only read the article, and I never visited Mrs Palmer and her five daughters."

Kirk looks uncertain for a second, then the reference to Mrs Palmer, aka my wanking hand, computes in his brain, and he starts laughing again. "Well Davis, only *you* know what happened in there, but I must say that spreading the message of respect, of bringing back respect, is a pretty powerful thing."

"Yeah it is Kirk. And there's no way I could stand here and do any of this unless I was telling the truth, because if I was lying, I wouldn't be respecting myself, or anyone else for that matter. So I'm going to say it one more time." I look right into the camera. "I didn't do anything in the loo except read the article. Ok? I did *not* have a wank!"

Kirk thanks us for our time and wraps up the interview. When the camera stops rolling he asks me if I'll go on *Good Morning Today* on Monday morning.

"Hell yeah," I answer, so he tells me to be at the Channel Six studio at five thirty am sharp. I squeeze Claire's hand, this is so fucking cool. I'm going to be on telly, on a proper show. Now that's shit hot!

$$\$\$\$\$\$\$\$\$\$$

It turns out that we've made forty seven thousand dollars - in one bloody night - so we walk away with a bit over fifteen grand each. Un-bloody-believable! The family go home straight away, but Eric, Bruce, Claire and I decide to hang around for a bit. I'm too pumped to go home, and decide to have a couple of beers now that Dad's gone, but I stop at two - I'm getting good at this self-control shit. The crowd in the mall has dispersed but the pub is still packed. Paul comes into the office and gives me a high-five, he's grinning from ear to ear.

"What a night eh?" he enthuses. "Thanks to you the pub's had its biggest night ever. I just did a till reading and we've taken an insane amount of money. Thanks mate, this means I can get another Watering Hole opened up sooner than I expected!"

"Unreal mate, glad to help out man. Any time you need some publicity just ask old Davis here."

Paul laughs, "Yeah well I might just take you up on that buddy, watch out! Hey, I hear you're gonna be on Monday's *Good Morning Today*, is that right?"

"Yeah, Kirk's asked me to, it should be a good laugh. I can't bloody believe it though."

Bruce pipes up, "I still reckon you need an agent or manager to handle all this publicity shit."

"Nah," I say.

"Bruce's got a point though, how are ya gonna keep track of everything when you get really full-on busy?" Eric wants to know.

Suddenly I'm bone tired, the adrenaline must be wearing off because I feel shattered. I want to go home and just chill out, not think, just chill.

Claire must sense the change in me. "Hey it's only early days," she tells them, "he can work that out later, can't you Darl? But for now I'm absolutely knackered, is it ok if you take me home Babe?"

You little ripper! I'm so grateful I could kiss her, so I do. Now I won't look like a wuss in front of the guys for heading home, after all it's *Claire* who wants to leave, not me.

Eric wants to meet up tomorrow to get started on the website and stuff. My only criteria is that it's not too bloody early, and we finally agree that we should meet up at Eric's office again. Bruce offers us a lift home, but I know that he wants to keep on partying, so I insist on getting a taxi. Then it hits me, where's Tracy? She's normally attached to Bruce like a fly on shit, they do everything together. I'm curious as to why she didn't show up tonight, so I ask where she is.

A look of panicked shock spreads across Bruce's face. "Fuck me, oh man she's gonna kill me," he squeaks. Whipping out his phone he checks his messages. His face turns white while he's scrolling through them. Then he looks up at us, "She waited for two hours at disco bowling for us, then she got totally pissed off and went home. I fucking forgot to tell her to get her arse here. I can't believe I forgot to tell her. Oh God, I meant to call her from Eric's place earlier, but with all the excitement I just forgot."

He puts his head into his hands and starts rocking back and forth. I shake my head in pity for him. This is the man who mows his lawn twice a week to keep her happy, and now he's gone and totally pissed the little lady off. I'm glad I'm not in his shoes!

We all murmur some, "That's too bad" and "You poor thing" type of comments at him, Tracy is *not* someone you want to piss off. She turns into a screaming banshee, I've only witnessed it a few times, but that's enough. Patting him on the back I ask him if he wants to come home with us, but he vehemently refuses, saying that the longer he stays out the better. That way she'll be asleep when he gets home. Claire and I make a fast exit.

On the ride home I'm holding Claire's hand and pondering the evening's events. I mentally tally up what the whole of Australia has learnt about me tonight. One, my Mum popped her cherry at an ABBA concert and got pregnant with my older brother. Two, my two grans like to behave badly and enjoy pashing in public. And three, I'm an accused wanker! That's a pretty good trifecta. Suddenly the scene of Grandma Spanx asking Kirk to call her pops into my mind, Jeezus I hope he doesn't.

Chapter 6

I awaken the next morning to a very nice stroking of my cock.

"That's great babe," I murmur.

Me, I'm up for a shag any old time, but Claire's always horniest in the mornings. This usually poses a bit of a problem – during the week we don't have time as we're both rushing to get to work, and by the evening she's too bloody knackered. So we've turned into weekend shaggers, it's not ideal, but I'll take what I can get. It certainly makes me appreciate the attention my cock's getting right now!

I open my eyes and there she is, grinning at me cheekily, her green eyes are all sparkly with mischief. She's straddling my legs, her long curly golden locks are swinging forward. I gulp. Oh man, she's naked. Claire reminds me of a big cat, she's all slinky tight muscled sexiness. I reach up to tweak a nipple but she teases me and pulls back, so that she's just out of reach. The stroking of my cock increases. I really need a piss, so I squirm out from underneath her and head for the ensuite, giving her bum a slap on the way.

"Don't you dare move," I command.

None of that movie bullshit of having a pash as soon as you wake up, where do they get that crap from? There's a protocol to be adhered to, and it includes having a piss and brushing your teeth!

Suddenly there's very loud banging on the front door, followed by the high pitched sound of a female yelling. Jeezus, that sounds like Tracy, and she's on the warpath. Claire comes running into the ensuite, pulling on her dressing gown. Bugger.

"Can we pretend to hide?" she begs.

I wish we could, but say to her resignedly, "Nah, she knows we're home."

I'm pissed off. My Saturday morning root has disappeared right before my eyes. It would have made it two shags in two days, which would have been unreal. We've been a bit slack in the old shagging department lately, even on the weekends.

"Fuck this shit," I snap. "Why does she have to do this now? What's the time anyway?" I demand.

Claire goes and has a look at the bedside clock. "Well it *was* Cock o'clock," she says cheekily, "but now it's just plain old eight thirty."

I can't help but laugh. "Cock o'clock, nice one babe!" Then I get shitty again. "Eight thirty! Who the hell does she think she is, crapping on like this so early on a Saturday morning?"

I finish having my piss and decide not to bother brushing my teeth, Tracy can just bloody well put up with my morning breath, it'll serve her right. I'm looking a real treat in my grotty trackie daks and t-shirt, but I don't care.

"Ready?" I ask.

Claire nods and I give her the once over.

"Don't ya want to get a bit more dressed?" I can see her tits through the dressing gown.

"Nup, you didn't brush your teeth, so I'm not gonna get dressed. Maybe she'll get the message and go home."

I see her tactic and I like it, but I know that Tracy won't get it, she's too full of herself to worry about anyone else. It might sound as though I'm being a bit harsh on old Trace, but the woman's an ego-maniac. You can't have a conversation unless it's all about her, it really gives me the shits. I don't know how Bruce puts up with it. Well actually I can guess, we often hear them going for it. Trace's not just loud when she's angry, the whole bloody neighbourhood knows when those two are having a shag, especially when it's in their outdoor spa!

At least she's still a bit of a looker, for forty five she's not doing too badly - in a fake way. She's always dolled up to the nines is Trace, normally her tits are out on show. Bruce bought her a new set for her birthday last year, and she makes sure to flash them whenever she can. And she's always wearing skin tight pants, usually leopard print ones.

The banging and yelling at the door increases.

"I know you're in there Davis, open the bloody door!" Tracy screeches.

Claire and I look at each other. "Come on babe, let's get it over with," I sigh.

When I open the door Trace bustles inside, almost pushing Claire out of the way in her eagerness to get in, her high heels click clacking loudly on the tiled floor. Bruce follows her in, looking very sheepish, he doesn't want to look me in the eye.

"Sorry about this mate," he mutters, but his piss weak apology just doesn't cut it for me.

The girls are already in the kitchen, so I take advantage of the opportunity of having Bruce to myself for a second. I grab his arm and put my face right in his, so he has to look at me.

"Maaate, what the fucks going on? We were just about to have a root. What's Trace going on about?"

My comment seems to have snapped Bruce out of his pussy whipped state. It must have been the mention of me missing out on a root that did it, or maybe it was my morning breath. He suddenly snaps to attention.

"Fuck, shit, sorry mate," he says looking me in the eye, "I tried to stop her from coming over, but you know Trace. Once she gets something in her head, well, it's hard to stop her from doing whatever she wants."

Yeah, she's just like a spoiled brat, what Trace wants Trace gets. It's easy to see who wears the pants in their relationship, skin tight leopard skin pants! I'd love to say this to Bruce, but it goes against the man code to diss your best mate's wife, so I hold my tongue.

"But what started it? Is this all because she missed out on the launch last night?" I ask.

Bruce's about to answer but Tracy screeches from the kitchen, "Come on you two, get your butts in here. I need some answers Davis."

Bruce just looks at me, nods, and heads towards the kitchen.

Claire's busy getting some coffee sorted, bless her. Tracy starts her verbal assault as soon as I'm in the room. She's such a glamazon, even at this hour she's caked in makeup. She's got her trademark leopard skin pants on, and her silicon enhanced tits are straining against her top, threatening to pop out at any second.

Tossing her hair back, she looks at me coolly and says, "I'm just so disappointed with you Davis. *I* should have been up on that stage last night. But did anyone bother to tell me about it? No! Did anyone even think of poor Trace missing out on all the fun? No!"

She starts sniffing. Oh fuck, here we go, she's going to turn on the water works. "I just feel *so* left out Davis, can you understand that?"

And bingo, for maximum effect she starts crying. I knew it, I knew she'd go for the male pressure point of vulnerability. No guy likes to see a lady cry, you just feel fucking helpless, and you know that the only thing to do is fix the problem for them, make it all better so they stop with the stupid tears.

I look over at Claire who's standing behind Trace. She rolls her eyes at me, and I have to stifle a smile. If Claire was to start crying then I'd immediately go into hero mode, and do anything I could to make her feel better. But with Trace it's different, I know it's just her ego that needs a bit of a stroke. I've become immune to her shenanigans, she does this crying shit all the time just to pull a guilt trip to get what she wants, so I don't have the normal male reaction of wanting to help her. Maybe that's why we don't like each other. It's a silent, mutual dislike. I've never said anything to Bruce about how I feel, and I don't need to, it's none of his business.

Oh Jeeze, she's really pissing me off now, but I've got to pretend that I care - for Bruce's sake. I go over to her, put my arm around her shoulder, and lean in nice and close so that she gets a full hit of my morning breath. "I'm really sorry you feel that way Trace, we didn't mean to forget you, to leave you out. It was just such a crazy day, everything happened so quickly."

She visibly recoils away from me, but I've got my arm tight around her shoulders, so she can't get away. She squeezes out another tear, takes a dramatic breath and wails, "But I've missed out on all the fun! It's so unfair!"

She puts her head forward and launches into a full blown sobbing episode. It's Oscar worthy, but strangely there aren't enough tears to match the sobs. I shake my head in frustration, but I have a brilliant idea. I'll have to check something with Bruce first.

Patting her on the back I try to sooth her, saying, "Why don't you have a nice cup of coffee Trace, it'll make you feel better. Look, I'm really sorry about last night, but you've got to believe that we didn't do it on purpose. It was chaos. I'll make it up to you, I promise. Ok?"

She seems placated by this. Peeping up at me through her enormous false eyelashes she sniffs and asks in a little girl voice, "Promise?"

Giving her arm a squeeze I lean in nice and close again, "I promise Trace, just you wait and see."

This time she wiggles away from me and my morning breath, and takes the cup of coffee Claire is holding out to her. The girls start chatting, so I grab Bruce and pull him out into the lounge, which is really just an extension of the kitchen area. The kitchen and lounge are one big room, broken up by the breakfast bar. There's not much privacy for us, so I whisper to him, "Does Trace know how much we made on the t-shirts last night?"

"Nah, I haven't told her about that yet," he answers, his eyes nervously darting from me to the kitchen.

"Did she watch any of the launch on telly last night? Does she even know what really went on, how big it was?" I whisper urgently.

Concentrating on me for a moment he replies, "Nah, she came home and polished off a couple of bottles of wine while watching a movie. She was comatose when I got in, thank God. That's why she's so worked up about it, it's all fresh news to her."

Now I understand why she's being such a lunatic, not that it gives her an excuse or anything. It would have been so much better for Claire and I if she'd gotten all this off her chest with Bruce last night, then she probably wouldn't have barged in here this morning demanding answers. I think my brilliant idea will be just the ticket to get her out of my house, and off Bruce's back.

Grabbing Bruce's arm I pull him closer. "I reckon you should give Trace a couple of grand and send her on a shopping spree. She'd be rapt with that, and you'd be racking up the brownie points for sure."

Bruce's face lights up. "That's a bloody brilliant idea mate. Fuck yeah, that'll sort her out. Awesome!"

We do a small high-five and head back into the kitchen. "Bruce's just had a fantastic idea Trace, you're going to love it!" I announce.

Bruce looks at me and gives an imperceptible nod, acknowledging me for giving him the kudos for the idea. He's grinning from ear to ear.

Taking her hands in his he says excitedly, "That's right. How would you like to go on a shopping spree today Trace? As my way of saying sorry, I'm gonna give you two grand to spend any way your little heart desires. Would you like that Pumpkin?"

Jeezus I don't believe it, he's gone into pussy whipped mode again. He's sucking up to her like his life depends on it, which I suppose it does. Man she'd be a bloody idiot not to like it, what chick doesn't dream of their man giving them a wad of cash to go and blow?

She narrows her eyes at him and asks "Since when have you got two grand to spare, just floating around for me to spend? Have you been holding out on me Brucie? Have you?" she demands.

"No, no, it's not like that Trace," Bruce looks like a rabbit caught in headlights. "Davis, Eric and I sold some t-shirts at the launch last night that's all. We made a bit of money from them, that's all love."

Now I'm *really* hoping he won't spill the beans on exactly how much we made last night. She'll be wanting to get her taloned claws on the lot if she finds out.

"How much did you make Brucie?" she whines.

Oh no, do not tell her, please don't tell her mate, don't do it. I'm sending him a telepathic message; I hope to God he gets it.

Looking smugly at her he says, "We made just enough for me to send you on your shopping spree today Darl, isn't that great!" Stroking his chin, he asks her, "I wonder which shop you'll go to first, will it be Gucci or Chanel?"

I think to myself 'Yes! Nice deflection mate, you're a goddamn legend!' He must have sensed what I was thinking, because he turns to me and gives a cocky wink.

Trace looks satisfied, but then blurts, "I want Claire to come with me. She should have a shopping spree too, and we should go in a limo. A stretch limo."

Claire looks shocked, I'm not sure if it's because she gets to go and blow two grand or if it's because she has to spend the day with Tracy. Two hours of disco bowling is usually her limit of Tracy time, like me she's not her biggest fan. I'm not sure how she'll cope with having to spend the whole day with her, but I'd love her to have the experience of blowing that cash. And Tracy would be the ultimate shopper to go with, Claire's not really into high end fashion. Don't get me wrong, she always looks hot, but in an understated way. Maybe it's because she's never had loads to spend on clothes before. I decide I really want to give her that chance now.

For once Trace has said something that makes sense, so I pipe up "Hey that's a great idea Trace! Yeah you girls should *definitely* go in a stretch limo, get some champagne into ya while you shop till you drop. What do you think Claire?"

I can see she's still weighing up the pros and cons, so I decide to take some action. "I'll get the limo organised right now. Claire, you'd better go get dressed Babe. You two are gonna have a ball today." I walk off to get the phone book, I can feel Claire's dagger eyes on my back as I leave the room.

When I come back in Tracy's giving Claire an air kiss and telling her to come over to their place when she's dressed. With that she grabs Bruce's hand and heads for the front door. While holding it open she turns to me and says, "This shopping spree *nearly* makes up for me missing out on last night. Just as well you boys made some money out of those t-shirts Davis, so *I* can go shopping."

Typical Tracy, turning this into something about her. And then she's gone, leaving a trail of perfume behind her.

I can still feel Claire's eyes on me, and I'm a little bit scared of what she's going to say. After all, I did push her into this.

"I could kill you Davis!" she moans and swats my arm. "That was a really low thing to do to me. You know she gives me the shits. How am I gonna put up with her for the whole day?"

Taking her hands in mine, I look into her eyes, kiss her on the tip of her nose and say, "It's called champagne Darling."

Claire just glares at me and wipes her nose with her sleeve. Shit, I forgot about my morning breath. Wrapping my arms around her I try to make amends. "Sorry if I put you in it babe. But I really do want you to go blow some cash, and you've gotta admit that Trace knows her stuff when it comes to clothes."

Wriggling out of my grasp, she snaps, "Yeah, if you want to look like a bloody porn star. You know that's not my style."

"But she'll be able to take you to places you've never been before, you might like it," I coax.

Narrowing her eyes at me she asks, "Are we talking fashion or porn here Davis?"

Laughing at her, I take her hand again. "I'm just saying, how bad can it be to go to some top notch shops you wouldn't normally go to, and blow a wad of cash?"

Bingo! That got a smile on her face.

Giving me a hug she says, "I know what you're saying, and thanks for wanting to give me some money to spend. I'll have fun doing that, even if Trace does drive me nuts."

"See, I knew you'd like it. C'mon lets go brush our teeth, I need a kiss," and I drag her off to the bathroom.

$$\$\$\$\$\$\$\$\$\$$$

Unfortunately the kiss is just a kiss, we never do get time to have our morning shag. The magic moment has gone. Before I know it the stretch limo's arrived, and Claire's dressed and out the door. I hurry after her, I want a peek inside because I've never been in one before. Trace and Bruce come outside, and the chauffer opens a gull wing door. We all pile in and it's amazing, it's like a bloody spaceship inside. This isn't your normal stretch limo, but a stretch Hummer, and the interior is pimped to the max. It's like a freakin' disco!

Bruce and I look at each other, and I'm wondering if he's thinking what I'm thinking. I've gotta say something. "We should go pick up Eric and have our business meeting in here while the girls go shopping. How awesome would that be?"

"That's what I was thinking, give Eric a call see what he reckons."

I'm about to whip out my phone when I notice Tracy's face drop. Oh shit, here we go again.

She immediately goes into full pout mode again. "But that's not fair!" she wails, "The limo's just for *me*." Then she looks shifty and suddenly adds, "Well me and Claire. We don't want you *boys* coming along and wrecking our shopping trip." She looks over at Bruce and pouts even more. "Tell Davis you're not coming Brucie, tell him it's just for me and Claire."

Bruce looks at me like he's a broken man. God Tracy's really got him by the balls these days, I didn't realize it was this bad. I feel sorry for him, so I hold up my hand to quickly stop her from carrying on.

"Yeah you're right Trace, dunno what I was thinking. Of course this is just for you and Claire. We'll leave you girls to it eh?"

I lean over and give Claire a peck, tell her to have fun, then make a quick exit. Bruce is close behind me, and we give the girls a wave as the Hummer takes off.

I know that I shouldn't ask, but I can't help myself, I turn to Bruce and say, "Maaate, you know I wouldn't normally say anything, but what's with Trace these days. Man she's got you so under the thumb you're nearly squashed. Why do you put up with that crap?"

He sighs, shrugs his shoulders and admits, "Yeah she's been a bit more demanding lately, but what can I do? Maybe she's going through the change, you know, chicks her age can get early menopause."

I look at him like he's from another planet. "How the fuck do you know that? I wouldn't have a clue about any of that shit."

Scratching his balls he says, "Listen Davis, I'm forty eight, I've got two older sisters who are always talking about that stuff, it drives me mental. Every time we catch up they're crapping on about night sweats and being in a shitty mood, so I figure Trace might be starting to go through it too. I just cut her some slack, that's all."

"Isn't she too young?" I ask. "Don't they have to be older to go through that shit?"

Bruce straightens up. He's all Professor Know-it-all now. "Actually some women go through menopause in their early forties and then you've got peri-menopause which can kick in in their thirties."

I'm watching him with a look of shock on my face. I'm shocked at two things. One; that he knows so much about all this women's business, and two; that Claire might turn into a lunatic in a few years' time if this peri-menopause thing kicks in. She's twenty eight now so I may only have a few more good years until she loses the plot. Luckily my phone rings and breaks my train of thought, I don't want to contemplate what Claire could turn into. I answer the phone and it's Jonno from work. I ask him to hang on a mo, then I tell Bruce that I'll come over to his place later and we'll go to Eric's together. I wander back into the house, glad that Jonno's called.

"Saw ya on telly last night spreading that respect shit, good onya Davis. Me and the Mrs had a good laugh at your getting fired clip," he chuckles.

A pang of guilt hits me. Shit, I forgot to invite him and the boys to the launch. They were the last thing on my mind with all of the build-up. "Mate, I should have gotten you and the boys to come. Sorry, I didn't think of it."

"No worries Davis, it's no drama, I couldn't give a shit. But I was ringing to tell you that Mitch and Scott are making waves. They're getting up themselves about you getting famous, I think they might be jealous."

"Whaddaya mean? What have they done?" I demand.

"Well, I saw Mitch up in Beaker's office on Thursday after you got fired. I asked him what he was up to and he said he just wanted some of your shifts. Now we all know that's bullshit, 'cos who do you see about any change of shift?"

"You, the production manager," I answer.

"That's right, you don't go hobnobbing with the big boss for that now do ya?" I murmur my agreement and he continues. "Anyway I know something's up, I'm just not really sure what it is. Beaker didn't go back to Sydney yesterday like he normally would."

"Didn't he? Now that is kind of weird." This *is* beginning to sound a bit suss. Beaker hates Melbourne, he's always telling us how much of a hassle it is to come down each month and how he can't wait to get back to his beautiful Sydney.

"Yeah, he was in his office yesterday. Davis, he's never here on a Friday, and I spotted Mitch up there with him again."

"So ya reckon they're jealous? That's a laugh, considering how Mitch bagged my idea of becoming a celeb." I'm getting a bad feeling about this though. Mitch is such an arse licker to Beaker he could be up to anything.

"Yeah," booms Jonno, "I reckon they're cooking something up. I know Mitch has been in Scott's ear too, 'cos he was badmouthing ya yesterday. You know Scott, he wouldn't normally say boo, but Mitch's got him all fired up about ya for some reason. And the only thing I can come up with is that they're bloody jealous."

This doesn't make much sense to me, but who knows how other people's minds work. Especially someone as warped as Mitch, whose Mr Negativity personified. "Thanks for the update Jonno, I appreciate it mate."

"No worries Davis. Look there's probably nothing to worry about, I mean ya don't even work there anymore so they can't do nuthin to ya can they?"

"Yeah, I guess you're right, but it is kind of weird."

"Don't worry about it too much mate, I'll keep ya posted if anything else happens. I'll keep me eyes and ears open for ya," he promises.

I laugh. Jonno's a good bloke. "Thanks mate, I'll invite you to the next big thing I do, although at the moment who knows what that'll be."

"Yeah, I saw that chick get her top off on telly last night, I would have liked to see that!" he growls.

We say our goodbyes, I'm glad Jonno called to fill me in. If only I knew what Mitch was up to …

Chapter 7

It's now mid-afternoon and I'm at Eric's office with Bruce. The first thing Eric asked when we arrived earlier was, "What the hell happened to your family last night Davis?" He wanted to know why they turned into a bunch of lunatics. Buggered if I know what got into them, too much excitement and too much finger food is all I can come up with. Eric's question leads into a heated debate over the two grans, are they really carpet munchers or was it all an act? We're all still in shock over their disgusting behaviour. I shudder at the thought of them doing more than kissing, but I wouldn't put it past them. Eric and Bruce reckon they just did it for show, but I'm not so sure. With those two anything's possible.

We've been brainstorming for the past few hours, and I must say that Eric has outdone himself. He reckons he was so pumped up from the launch last night that he couldn't sleep, so he got busy designing my website, whoisdavisspanx.com. It's bloody awesome!

There's a banner up the top of the landing page with my picture on it. He's used the same design that we agreed would go on the billboards, and it looks great. It's got the lime green backdrop, on the left is the question 'Who is Davis Spanx?' and a cool photo of me is on the right. The photo is showing me from the mid-thigh up, so you can easily read the slogan on my t-shirt, which I'm pointing to in a rapper kind of way. I want to know if we can put light bulbs around the border to jazz it up a bit, give it a bit of bling. Within minutes Eric's got it sorted, and we all agree that it's a good look.

Also on the landing page are both of my YouTube videos, he's made them look really professional, and below them he's written a small blurb about me. Bruce points out that we need an *About Davis* page, which takes us a while to do, but Eric once again comes up trumps.

There's a page for upcoming events, which is blank for now, but hopefully will soon have heaps of stuff on it. As will the page for past events, so far it's just got last night's launch on it. There's even a page called *Invite me to an event* with an order form on it, so people can fill in their details, and the details of the event they want me to attend. It's totally cool!

Eric points out, "Yeah, I included the *Invite me to an event* page so it's easy for people to get a hold of you. Once they fill in the form it'll be emailed to your new email address. Pretty cool eh?"

"Fuck yeah. Aah, what's my new email address? Am I gonna have trouble remembering it?" I ask.

Chuckling to himself Eric says, "Not unless you forget your name dickhead, I made it nice and easy for you. It's just davis@davis-spanx.com, reckon you can remember that?"

I grin at him. "Yep, you're a legend, thanks mate." But my grin soon turns to a groan when I see the blog page.

"Oh come on Eric," I whinge. "Isn't it enough that I'm tweeting and soon I'll be doing the Facebook thing? Do I really have to do a blog as well?"

Bruce chips in, "Oh yeah, ya gotta do a blog Davis, otherwise ya won't be plugged in."

"Bugger being plugged in," I scowl, "what the hell am I meant to say on all of these things?"

"Who cares, just make stuff up," Eric says. "If you want to be a celebrity then this is the price you gotta pay."

"Well I wouldn't want to make stuff up, that's not right. But will people really want to know what I'm doing all day every day?" I complain.

Eric nods. "You better believe it buddy, they're gonna want to know everything, from when you take a dump in the morning to when you brush your teeth at night."

"Oh Jeezus," I groan.

Bruce has got his fists up near his eyes, and he's motioning them back and forth like he's rubbing away imaginary tears. Sticking his bottom lip out he says, "Oooh poor lil' Davis, having to do so much social media stuff just because he's a celebrity. Oooh, poor little cry baby."

Of course this cracks me up. "Thanks mate. It's just overwhelming having to do all this new techy stuff, that's all. You guys know it's not my thing."

Eric snaps his fingers. "I've got it. The solution to your techy problem is to outsource it!" I look at him blankly, what he just said doesn't make any sense to me.

"Ok let me explain," Eric says. "But first answer this question honestly. Do you think you might get to like this social media stuff, or are you always gonna hate it?"

"That's easy. I'll always bloody hate it, it's pointless, I couldn't give a shit about it."

"Even though this is a great way to get your message of respect out there to everyone?" Bruce inquires.

"Well I hadn't thought of it like that before. Sure it's important to get my message out there, but spending ages each day doing all those updates is gonna bore the crap out of me. Not to mention do my head in."

Eric's nodding and bouncing in his chair excitedly. "That's why outsourcing would be perfect for you. You just pay someone in India or the Philippines a few bucks a day, and they can do all of your posts for you. No worries."

"But…," I start to say.

Eric puts his finger up to his lips, shakes his head at me and says, "Just shut up a minute Davis and hear me out. I've used heaps of outsourcers over the years and they're great, they do anything you want them to."

"But how are they gonna know what to put on there?" I query. "It's not like they're watching what I'm doing all day, so how are they gonna know what to say?"

"Details details, don't worry about all that, just answer the question. If someone *could* do it for you, would you let them?" Eric pushes.

"Hell yeah! Why wouldn't I. That'd be awesome," I reply.

"Good, I'm glad we've got that sorted. We'll get onto the outsourcing soon, but for now why don't we concentrate on the rest of the website?"

For the next couple of hours we muck around getting a photo page and online shop sorted, this is Bruce's idea and I think it's brilliant. Eric takes some candid photos of me and Bruce, and immediately uploads them to the site to kick things off. He's also got some great shots of last night's launch on his phone, which he puts up as well.

Then we brainstorm some product ideas for the shopping page. I've already spoken to Tai and he can supply everything I need, man I can't believe I've got my own online shop now, how good is that! We settle on a few t-shirt designs with different logos, for now we've decided to keep to the same colour scheme, red writing on a black t-shirt. There's still the original one with 'respect yourself and respect other people' on it, but there's a couple more. One just has 'respect' on the front and back, and another one has 'I'm bringing back the respect' on the front and back. We've also got sorted some caps, water bottles, stubby holders and mugs, all bearing the respect logo in its various forms. It's quite a good range and we're pretty happy with everything, although I've got my doubts about the mugs, they seem a bit crappy, but the other guys reckon we should just get a hundred made up and see how they go.

Tai advised me earlier that he can manufacture everything at short notice, but since he's not set up for distribution I'll have to handle that myself. Bruce suggests using a fulfilment company that looks after sending all the orders out, which is a life saver, the thought of stuffing things into envelopes and toddling down to the post office just doesn't appeal to me. I love this outsourcing shit, I don't have to lift a finger!

I suddenly have a great idea. "Hey, we should have a page where people can vote for the products they want. We could have a list and they just select what they want, then when we get enough requests we can get 'em made up to sell."

"Nice one Davis," Eric says. "Yeah, let the people vote for what they want, give 'em the power of choice. I like it." Drumming his fingers on the table he adds, "The best bit about it is that you're pre-selling your products, you've got instant profit coming in."

I clear my throat. "Speaking of profit, I think we should all continue putting the same amount of capital in, then split the profits on the sales later, like we did with the t-shirts." I eyeball them, "What do you think? Do you guys want in?"

They both look at each other, then Bruce says, "Nup. Eric and I talked about this last night. We both reckon that the best thing is for you to do this on your own. It's your thing ok?"

"Yeah," agrees Eric, "we helped you get the ball rolling, but Davis this is *your* mission. Besides, from the profit you made last night you can easily fund the new merchandise yourself, so *you* should keep any future profit. End of story."

Eric then suggests that I set up a company to keep everything sorted and legit, which is a great idea. I tell them that I'll see if Danielle can do that, or at least put me onto someone else who can. Jeeze we've totally blitzed it today. I now have my own bloody business sorted. Wow!

Leaning back in my chair I stretch my arms up above my head, and my stomach lets out an almighty grumble. Looking over at the clock on the wall, I can't believe it's nearly five o'clock.

"I'm starving too," says Eric. "We've got everything sorted though, good work gentlemen." We all snigger and give each other a high-five.

Bruce yawns and asks, "Wonder how the girls are going?"

Suddenly my phone rings. Speak of the devil, its Claire. She wants to know if we're still at the office and if they should drop by. I ask the guys what they think, and it's agreed that the girls should get the limo to drop them off here, because we all want to go and get something to eat. I tell her I'll see her soon and hang up.

Then I ask Eric, "So what sort of time frame are we looking at to get the billboards up?"

Rubbing his hands together he tells me, "They'll be up Monday morning, I've fast tracked it, can't wait to see you up there. Oh yeah that reminds me, I want to try out the mobile billboards with you on them too. What do you think?"

"Sounds awesome," I laugh. I knew he'd agree that I should be on those things!

Grinning like The Cheshire Cat, he thumps the table with his hand, then stands up, stretches and says, "Yeah well this'll be a perfect platform for me to see how well they work, before I buy that company and merge it with my own. And it'll cost us nothing, which is a total bonus. I'll just insist it's part of my market research, they shouldn't have a problem with that."

"So how does that work, do we need to do different artwork for it?" I query.

Doing some Merv Hughes stretches he replies, "Nah, I'll just use what we've got, I can resize it easily to what we need no worries. It's a pretty cool setup actually, Spyder three wheeled trikes tow trailers with billboards behind them. The ads are all three sided and backlit so you can see the picture really well - even at night."

I can't wait to see my face being driven all over town! I look over and see that Bruce's trying really hard to stay focused, but he's losing the battle. He's gotten all fidgety, a sure sign that he needs something to eat. I ask Eric if we can get some bikkies to munch on, and maybe a coffee. He moves to go and get some, but the front door buzzer goes off, indicating the girls' arrival.

I tell Eric that he's gotta come out and see the Hummer limo before it takes off. The girls are standing at the glass door, waiting for us to let them in. Claire's laden down with what seems like dozens of shopping bags. Tracy's holding just one. Something seems a bit wrong with this picture, then I figure that Tracy's probably asked Claire to carry all of her bags for her. Typical.

Scooping Claire into my arms I give her a bear hug, but she can't hug me back because of all the bags she's holding. "Did you have fun?" I whisper in her ear.

Grinning, she says excitedly, "Just you wait till you see all the goodies I got, I scored big time!"

Taking some of the bags off her, I hear Eric squeal like a kid in a candy store. Turning around, I see his big arse disappear inside the limo. This should be interesting, I wonder how he's gonna squeeze in there, the big bastard. Bruce is oohing and aahing over the open bag Tracy's showing him. I ask Claire "How many of her bags are you carrying?"

Raising her eyebrows at me she answers, "None, these are all mine. Trace only got one thing. She spent all her money on a new Gucci handbag."

"You're fucking kidding me!" I snort.

"Nup, I knew you'd freak out. I'll fill you in on all the goss later. I want to see if Eric's gonna fit in there." That's my girl, on the same page as me.

We climb into the limo to find Eric sprawled across one of the many seats. He's already got a glass of champagne in his hand, and is demanding that we go for a spin around the block. I agree, so Tracy orders, literally *orders* the poor driver to take us to Taxie in Federation Square. Us blokes all look at each other, is she nuts? Bruce must be thinking the same thing because he mutters to me, "Why does she want a taxi when we're in a bloody limo?"

$$$$$$$$$$

Well it turns out that Taxie isn't a taxi, but a restaurant; a very schmicko restaurant in the heart if the city. Tracy insisted that we go there because it would be the perfect ending to *her* shopping spree. We all go along with it, because why the heck not. The looks this limo is getting are priceless. At one point Eric got the full disco pumping, it was freaking awesome, but the smoke machine fog was suffocating us, so I had to put the window down to get some fresh air. As we pulled up at a red light, smoke billowing out the window, we were the centre of attention. That's when people started to recognise me. They started pointing and shouting out, "Hey Davis!" It was totally freaky but in a good way. As the limo took off from the lights Eric raised his glass at me and shouted, "Man you gotta tweet this, get it out there dude."

Rolling my eyes at him, I realise I really need that outsourcer on the job, I don't want to stop having fun in order to send a bloody tweet. Claire sees the look on my face, put's out her hand and says "Give me your phone." I happily hand it over and she has the tweet done in seconds. She must have the fastest fingers in the west! Hmmm, something to think about there, maybe I should outsource my stuff to her! I'll have to run that by her later.

When we pull up at the restaurant, I give the driver a nice tip, thank him for putting up with Trace all day, and tell him to go home. Bruce and I make sure the girls have grabbed all of their shopping bags, our lives wouldn't be worth living if they lost any of them. A small crowd gawks at us as we make our way from the limo to the restaurant. The girls get up the stairs and head inside, but I'm lagging behind, taking a last look at the Hummer as it pulls away into the traffic. Man that was some sweet ride. Suddenly someone recognises me and the shout goes out, "That's Davis Spanx!" The small crowd push closer and I feel hands patting me on the back. One guy shouts out "Wanker," but then someone else yells, "Hey, bring back the respect!"

When I'm on the steps of the restaurant I turn around and point to the guy who made the respect comment and say, "Thanks mate, I appreciate that a lot. You rock. Keep spreading the respect." I swallow down the lump in my throat. I'm spun out that a total stranger would stand up for me like that, and that he'd use my own message to do it. That's pretty bloody cool.

I continue on, addressing the group. "I'll let you guys in on a secret, my website has *just* gone online, so you guys will be the first to see it. Check out whoisdavisspanx.com." A few people look at me like 'who gives a shit,' but most of the chicks whip out their phones to have a look. Again I point to the guy who stuck up for me.

"What's your name mate?"

"Bradley Lincon," he says shyly.

"Listen Brad, as my way of saying thanks I want to give you a respect t-shirt, ok? So go to my website, fill in your details on the *invite me to an event* page, and I'll send it to you." He looks pretty stoked at this, and now that I really look at him I notice he could do with a new t-shirt, he looks pretty grotty.

Giving the crowd a cheery wave goodbye, I stride into the restaurant where the others are waiting for me in the foyer. They're all checking out the photos of celebs on the wall of fame. Claire grabs my hand and tells me that was a nice thing to do, giving a t-shirt away. I'm mentally saying Bradley Lincon over and over in my head, I don't want to forget his name, I figure I'll write it down once we get to the table.

The restaurant is all chrome and glass, it's very very snazzy. Even though it's only five-ish the place is pretty packed, I comment on this and Tracy informs me that "It *is* a Saturday and it *is* the best new restaurant in town!"

The maître d' asks me, "You are Davis Spanx yes?" I affirm that I, am and he asks if we wouldn't mind waiting a moment. Bruce and I are elbowing each other in the ribs. This place is way out of our depth, Bruce and I are seriously under dressed. Eric looks cool calm and collected though, he's radiating his usual self-confidence. Soon a short fat guy comes over and introduces himself to us. Turns out he's the owner, Lawrence. He's kind of all gushy, and insists that we're seated in the VIP area.

I raise my eyebrows at everyone and Claire gives my hand a squeeze. Eric and Bruce snigger, but Trace says haughtily "That will suit us fine." Good one Trace, for once her attitude suits the occasion.

We all follow Lawrence through the main part of the restaurant, everyone seems to be staring at us. I can tell Trace is lapping it up, she's flicking her hair around and has her tits thrust out. She'll topple over if she's not careful. I'm afraid Claire's gonna crush my hand she's holding it that tightly, she's never really liked being the centre of attention. As we pass a nearby table, a man shoves a napkin and pen at me and asks for an autograph, so I stop and sign it. Wow, someone wants my autograph, that's wild!

What's even wilder is the VIP area. I thought the rest of the restaurant was snazzy, but the VIP area puts it to shame. It's a separate room on the second floor, with just one huge glass table and twelve chairs around it. The whole room seems to be made of glass, and is jutting out of the main building. It seems to be hanging in mid-air. Parts of the floor are glass as well, so you can look down onto the street below. Even though we're only two floors up it's pretty freaky. We all ooh and aah over it, then Lawrence snaps his fingers and a fleet of waiters appears, each pulling out a chair for us. Man, I could get used to this kind of service!

At first the table looks way too big for us, but within moments the fleet of waiters have delivered multiple trays of canapés and jugs of cocktails. *Jugs* of bloody cocktails! I can't believe it. Taking the huge glass that one of the waiters has poured, I have a sip and close my eyes in bliss. I deserve to celebrate and what a way to do it.

The waiters quickly vanish, leaving us all sitting there holding our massive cocktail glasses, grinning our heads off at each other. Lawrence informs us that after the canapés and aperitif cocktails he would like to serve us a degustation dinner with matching wines, would that be to our liking? We all just nod at him, everyone seems to have lost the power of speech.

Gesturing towards the door, Lawrence tells us that if we need anything we should ask Mr Jacobs and he'll look after us. Mr Jacobs is an imposing looking guy. He's well-built and very good looking in a rugged, James bond kind of way. The snazzy dark suit he's wearing adds to his charm, but I sense he's not a man to be messed with. He's standing at a little podium kind of thing outside the entrance to the VIP area. Turning, he inclines his head towards us, so we all nod back at him. Lawrence then tells us that it's part of Mr Jacobs' job to keep the riffraff out of the VIP area. Then he wishes us an enjoyable evening and glides away, a satisfied smile upon his face.

As soon as he's gone the spell is broken, and we return to our normal loud selves. We all start talking at once saying how awesome this is. Then Eric wants to propose a toast. He stands up and says, "To Davis, his respect mission and his t-shirts!"

I laugh, but he's got a good point. I couldn't afford to eat in a place like this without having that launch last night. So once they've finished toasting me I stand up and say, "Well I'd like to raise a toast to you, gentlemen, I couldn't have done it without you. And also to you ladies, for being so supportive." Bruce chokes a bit on his cocktail. Eric thumps him on the back and we proceed to get stuck into the canapés.

Claire suggests that we should invite Paul, to say thanks for last night, so I give him a ring. He says he'll be here in ten minutes. Then Eric and Bruce have a mini dispute over who gets to go up and tell Mr Jacobs that we're expecting another guest. Rock paper scissors ends the arguing, Eric wins and makes a big show of waving him over.

When Mr Jacobs gets to the table Eric says "Yes Jacobs, we're expecting a Mr Paul Ryan to be joining our party shortly. Be a good man and inform the chef of the change of numbers would you?"

Mr Jacobs again inclines his head - it must be his signature move -and replies, "Very good sir, is there anything else you require?"

Eric informs him that nothing else is needed at the moment, and off Mr Jacobs glides, back to his little podium. We see him hold his left wrist up near his mouth and speak into his cuff, just like a secret service guy. I give Eric a high-five.

"Love your work," I quip. "Nice one dropping the Mr and just calling him Jacobs. Very suave."

"Yeah that was fun, I felt like I was in a movie!" Eric gushes.

Bruce pipes up, "Yeah especially the bit where he talked into his cuff. That was freakin awesome."

"These canapés are bloody good," I say with my mouth full. Us guys are cramming them in like there's no tomorrow.

I notice that the girls aren't eating very much and I want to know why. Claire loves a good feed, so I'm a bit suss. She informs me that she's saving herself for dinner. I just look at her blankly, so she asks me if I know what a degustation dinner is. I don't. So I'm shocked to hear that there's probably fifteen courses to come.

"No way!" I splutter, and a piece of canapé flies out of my mouth and hit's Tracy, who's sitting opposite me. She squeals in disgust and stands up, madly brushing off her boobs and giving me a killer death stare. Sitting back down, she calls me a "dirty dog" and takes a big gulp of her cocktail.

At this moment Paul is escorted in by Mr Jacobs. Paul's laughing and I detect a smirk on Mr Jacobs' face.

Paul comes over and shakes my hand. "How are ya filth bag?"

I slap him on the shoulder and tell him I'm doing great. Once the other greetings are done a waiter appears from nowhere again, holds out Paul's chair for him, then pours him a drink, tops up all of our glasses, and glides away. Paul watches him as he leaves and shakes his head, a look of amusement on his face.

"This place is unbelievable, have I stepped into the twilight zone?" he asks. We all murmur our agreement, then he adds, "Nice to see you indulging today Davis, you deserve it mate."

I raise my glass towards Paul in thanks. "Hey I just want to say a big thank you for last night. You're a champ for letting me use the pub for the launch. I really appreciate it mate."

"No worries. As I said last night, I had the biggest takings ever, so I'm rapt."

We chew the fat for a while on everything that happened last night. Tracy takes herself off to the loo, I get the vibe she's still not happy about missing out on all the fun. While she's gone I tell Paul that under no circumstances can he reveal how much money we made from the t-shirts. Bruce fills him in on what happened this morning, how we had to send her on a shopping spree with Claire to make up for last night.

It's been bugging me since we met up with the girls earlier, I've got to know what happened on the shopping spree, so I ask Claire to spill the beans. Turns out that Trace was a total diva all day. Surprise surprise. Apparently she was using *my* name to try and get free stuff from all the shops, which totally backfired on her. She bought her Gucci bag within the first hour of shopping, then spent the rest of the day getting pissed, being belligerent to the shop assistants, and pouting.

"But I had the last laugh," says Claire, "every time she name dropped you in a shop the sales girls would recognise me - so *I* was getting all the attention and freebies, which was driving Trace nuts. I ended up getting *heaps* of free stuff, they just kept giving me things. It was awesome."

"Was she drinking all day?" Bruce wants to know.

"Pretty much, she got quite pissy at one stage."

Bruce has got his elbows on the table, he groans and puts his head in his hands. "That's just what I need. Two hangovers in one day is not gonna make Trace happy." He sighs. "Or make me happy, fuck why does she drink so much, the silly cow?"

He's still got his head down so Claire, Paul, Eric and I look at each other and grimace. This isn't what we need right now, although that's the first time I've heard Bruce call Trace a silly cow, maybe she's finally pushing him too far.

Bruce looks up at me. "Mate, I'm sorry she used your name to try and get free shit, that's really uncool. I'm gonna have to have a word to her about that." Then he looks at Claire. "I'm sorry she pulled that crap with you there Claire, it's out of order."

So that's what's pushed his buttons, the injustice of Trace trying to get something by using my name. I tell him not to worry about it, no harm's done. But for his sake I hope he stands up to her on this, she's treating my mate like shit and I don't like it. It's about time someone stood up to her.

The waiters return whisking away the canapé trays and cocktail jugs and glasses, replacing them with a cornucopia of dishes. By the sixteenth course we're all feeling no pain. I don't normally drink wine, but the ones they matched with each course go down a treat, especially those dessert wines, never had them before. I feel like I'm gonna burst, and no wonder - Claire ran out of oomph on the tenth course, so I've eaten all her other courses as well. Man that means I've had a twenty two course dinner! No wonder I'm not totally pissed, all the food is soaking up the grog.

It's been a hoot, the whole night people have been slowly walking past our VIP door, trying to peek inside. Jacobs, as we now call him, does his thing and just ushers them along. It's a crack up. One guy begged to have an autograph, but Jacobs hushed him and moved him along. I look at my watch, it's only eight thirty but it feels much later. I have a little laugh to myself. God, twelve hours ago Trace was banging down our door. Now here we all are sitting in the best restaurant in town, in the VIP room no less, having just enjoyed the most incredible dinner of my life. Yep it's been a big day. I'm thinking how great it feels to have the website sorted, and know that come Monday I'll be splashed on billboards across the city. I must have a goofy look on my face because Paul wants to know if I'm ok.

"Mate I'm better than ok," I say, giving him a wink.

"Good, just checking, that's all," he winks back at me. God I love Paul, he's such a great mate. Jeeze I must be more pissed than I thought!

We all agree that it's time to head home. Trace wants to go somewhere to party on, but none of us are up for it. God, I'm not quite thirty yet and I've turned into an old fart. I ask Jacobs for the bill and he gives me the imperceptible nod thing again, which cracks us all up. Then Lawrence comes back in and tells me that there is no bill, dinner is on him. Fuck me, that's unbelievable. I ask him if he's sure, and he insists, then his face suddenly lights up and says he knows what he'll charge me for our dinner. I'm all ears.

"A photo of you and I is all the payment I require for the pleasure of your company tonight," he says pompously.

He's a strange one, but that sounds fine by me. "Sure, no problem have you got a camera?" I ask.

Has he got a bloody camera! Jacobs brings a tripod over with a big professional digital camera perched on top. I can't help myself, "Nice camera, just had it lying around did ya Jacobs?"

"We always have a professional photographer on hand for our clients, sir." As if on cue, the photographer appears and starts fiddling with the camera. "It's important to capture the magic moments that take place here at Taxie," Jacobs says rather drolly.

Yeah, well that does make sense. Of course a swanky place like this would have a professional photographer on hand for the celebs to remember their amazing evening by. Once the photo is taken I shake Lawrence's hand and genuinely thank him for an amazing experience. He tells me that we'll have to come back to see my photo on the wall of fame, then he informs us that he has a car waiting outside to take us where ever we want to go. I ask him if someone could put the ladies shopping bags in the car for us as the girls aren't up for it, and I'm thinking that I'd better keep my hands free in case I have to sign some more autographs. I wish! Lawrence assures me it's no problem at all, the bags will be waiting for us in the car. I like this being a celebrity thing - you get treated with respect - it feels bloody awesome!

As we are leaving I hear Bruce ask Jacobs how much a dinner like this would normally cost. "Oh about three, maybe four thousand dollars sir," Jacobs says nonchalantly, "You *have* enjoyed the very best of everything." I see Bruce's eyes bug out of his head in shock, and I'm there with him. That's blown me away, you can buy a half decent car for that for that amount of money.

I turn and walk back to Jacobs. Putting my hand on his shoulder, I thank him for his excellent attention to detail tonight. I say that without him, the night wouldn't have been as fantastic as it was. It's true, he really added to the whole experience. Now it's his turn to look shocked. I don't think many people thank him for what he does. He inclines his head and wishes us a good evening, but I can see that he's trying to hide a smile.

Everyone stares at us again as we make our way to the door, another small crowd has gathered outside the restaurant. Lawrence is on it, he snaps his fingers and Jacobs is by our side in a flash. He's talking into his cuff again, and I notice he's got an earpiece in. He asks us to wait just a moment before exiting the restaurant. Within seconds there are four more dudes dressed just like Jacobs surrounding us. Jacobs gives his little nod and tells us that it's now safe to exit.

Eric, Bruce and I are nearly pissing ourselves as we're escorted through the crowd, surrounded by the Jacobs clones. Jacobs of course is leading our funny little procession, an air of extreme haughtiness is radiating from him, it's like he's almost daring someone to try and thwart our walk to the car. The crowd parts and lets us through, no dramas or hassles, just people calling out my name and lots of mobile phones held aloft filming and photographing our exit. Then just as we are about to get in the car, which is a black stretch limo, a guy with a professional camera calls out, "Over here Davis, give us a smile would you."

Fuck me it's the paparazzi! I can't help but laugh, this is unreal. So we all strike a few quick poses for him, get blinded by the flash then clamour into the limo laughing our heads off. Jacobs shuts the limo door and gives us a half salute in farewell. Quickly lowering the window, I grin and give him a proper salute back. His face lights up with a full blown smile and he waves us off.

We're all giggling and carrying on like pork chops as the limo moves into the traffic. "God, this is the best night ever – I thought last night was good, but this is even better," I shout. I do tend to shout when I get excited. Everyone whoops their agreement, even Trace is happy, so it must have been an amazing night.

We drop Paul off at the pub, Eric gets out there too, he reckons he may as well have another beer. Trace tries to talk Bruce into going to the pub as well, but for once he won't budge, he wants to go home. Then he whispers something in her ear, and she swats his arm and starts giggling. Claire and I look at each other. We certainly know who's going to be noisy tonight! I'm feeling cheeky, giving them a wink and a nod I say, "Gonna get the spa fired up tonight guys?" They both just laugh at me. "Better get your ear plugs out tonight babe, I think you're gonna need them," I murmur to Claire as I give her a nudge.

We're half way home when Trace lets out a squeal and sits up in a panic. "Our shopping! Shit, we left our shopping at the restaurant Claire."

Claire was nearly asleep, she had her head on my shoulder, eyes closed. I could feel her begin to nod off a few times, but with this she snaps to attention. I stroke her hair to soothe her.

"Hey, calm down Trace, don't worry. It's all in the boot, Lawrence took care of all that. It's sorted," I tell her.

Both girls visibly relax, and by the time we get home both of them have fallen asleep. I'd love to be a real manly man and pick Claire up and carry her inside, but that just isn't going to happen at the moment, I'd probably break my back. I need to work out a bit before I can do that shit, so I nudge her awake and guide her inside, then go back for the treasured shopping bags. I wave to Bruce and Trace, thanking them for a great night. No doubt I'll be hearing them later. Before I go to bed I make sure all the phones are switched off, I want a bloody sleep-in tomorrow, I need it after all this excitement. I creep into the bedroom, stupidly hoping that maybe Claire will have woken up and be horny, but I'm dreaming, and so is she. She's sound asleep in bed already, the wine must have gone to her head. Oh well, there's always hope for some Sunday loving tomorrow.

Chapter 8

Ouch! The makeup lady at Channel Six just poked me in the eye with her mascara wand. Man, I still can't believe I'm going on *Good Morning Today* with Kirk and Leeza. At the moment I look like a bloody clown though, my face is covered in shit and now, thanks to the eye poke, I've got tears streaming out of one eye, leaving streaky lines running down my cheek. It's not a good look. I can tell the makeup lady's not happy, and neither am I.

I thought I'd blitz this TV thing, I thought it'd be a walk in the park. I mean all I've gotta do is sit there and have a chat right? It's not rocket science. But the reality is I'm nearly shitting my pants I'm so nervous, the underarms of my respect t-shirt are soaked with sweat. Maybe I need to have Botox injected into my underarms to stop sweating, I've heard that it can help, because even if I fake some self-confidence here, the sweat's gonna give me away.

Jeezus, I've got to get a grip, gotta stop thinking this crap and concentrate on what I'm going to say. I've been trying to prepare in my head a bit, so that I don't look like a complete dick, but it's all so exciting I can't concentrate on any one thing for long. "Focus Davis, focus," I tell myself.

Dad and I had a pretend interview in the car on the way here, to help get me in the zone. Oh yeah, Dad worked his magic on me again. He rang me while I was driving on the freeway, said he should come with me for some moral support. He had a whole big spiel prepared, he rattled off all the pros and cons of me going alone. God he's good. Before I knew it I was making a huge detour to Carlton to pick him up. Lucky it was so early, otherwise the traffic would have been a bitch.

He's in the Green Room now, he just texted me saying that he's scoffing the free coffee and muffins. No surprises there. I could go a muffin myself, I'm bloody starving.

The makeup chick asks me to close my eyes while she does my mascara *again*, she says the again bit with some attitude. I'm positive she's trying to give me a guilt trip for fucking up her work, but what's a guy supposed to do when someone shoves something in your eye? It's only natural for your eye to leak in protest. I knew TV people wore makeup, but stuff having to go through this shit every day, it'd totally do my head in.

It's nice having my eyes closed though, I feel myself begin to relax a bit, and my mind starts to wander again. Claire and I had a great day yesterday, we did nothing much, it was awesome just to chill out and enjoy a lazy Sunday together. She tried on all of her new clothes and gave me a fashion parade. She even bought me a new jacket, which I was stoked about. Channel Six played a repeat of my launch from Friday night, so we cozied up on the couch together and watched it. I must say, it was pretty good viewing, we both had some major laughs.

After it finished we had a really good chat about this whole celebrity caper, she said she loves the message I'm trying to get out there, and that she'll support me one hundred percent. I asked her again how she feels about me having other, famous or semi famous chicks on my arm at events, and she said she was cool with it. In fact she was happy that she wouldn't have to escort me everywhere because she really doesn't like being the centre of attention. I picked up that vibe on Saturday, when we were all at Taxie, I could tell she was uncomfortable with the crowds and stuff. So I got really serious with her, and picked her brains about her not wanting any attention. I mean being a celebrity is all about being the centre of attention, right? That's pretty much the whole point to it. She said she was cool with *me* getting attention, she just didn't want any for herself. So I tried to dig a bit deeper to see if I could uncover any possible dramas that might arise from this, but she just kept insisting that she loves me and trusts me. She reckons that everything will be fine and there's nothing at all to worry about. So I'm glad that's all sorted.

Damn, I must have dozed off and had a power nap in the makeup chair, because I'm rudely awoken by a very loud, very gay, male hairdresser cursing at me. He says in his loud screechy voice that my hair is a disgrace and it's beyond his power to fix it. That's fine with me because I don't reckon it needs fixing at all. He's got a tin of something in his hand. Scooping out a blob he rubs his hands together then puts them up near my hair like he's ready to put some of that crap on me, but I stop him at the last minute. I tell him that I've already got some wax in there and that I'm quite happy with how it looks - thank you very much. Putting his nose in the air he sniffs at me, then flounces out of the room in a huff.

I'm left on my own, so I check my phone - may as well send out a tweet while I'm waiting. I asked Claire yesterday if she wanted to be my outsource blogger, tweeter, Facebook girl. Unfortunately she turned me down, she said there's no way she was going to do that all day and I can't say I blame her either. I even offered to pay her, to try and sweeten the deal, but it was still a no go. I might have to look into that Indian outsourcer Eric mentioned on Saturday. I don't really feel comfortable getting someone from another country to do it though, it just feels weird.

Giving myself the once over in the mirror again, I decide that I look ok, there's nothing else to do but wait until I'm called. I've finished my tweet but it's still too early in the morning to ring anyone - I'm bored. Grabbing a nearby hairdryer I turn it on and start drying my underarms, trouble is it's making me hot. I can see my face is turning red even through the bloody makeup, and I feel a dribble of sweat run down my spine. Bugger. Trust this to be the time when someone comes to get me. Now I look like shit. I ask if I can wait a minute to cool down, but the guy says we have to go right now.

He leads me through a labyrinth of corridors until I'm standing just to the side of the *Good Morning Today* set. I can see Kirk and Leeza. Wow, it's certainly a different view to the one you see on telly. Kirk finishes up the segment by plugging my upcoming interview. The cameraman calls all clear, and Kirk gets up and comes over to me, giving my sweaty hand a shake. I can see he's a bit grossed out by it, because he quickly rubs his hand on his trousers. Then he claps me on the shoulder and tells me to follow him onto the set. It's a different setting to the one he was just with Leeza on. We settle into a couple of comfy chairs, it's just me and him. My mouth is bone dry, I'm hoping my tongue doesn't stick to the roof of my mouth, so I take a sip of water. Oh God this is the worst feeling ever. I feel like crap. Kirk senses my nervousness and tells me to relax, that everything will be fine. Then the cameraman counts us in and we are on live morning TV. Holy shit!

Kirk leans towards me, smiles and starts the interview. "Welcome to the show Davis, you're quite a sensation." Then he turns to the camera. "Just in case you haven't heard of Davis Spanx, he's the latest

YouTube sensation. He became an overnight hit because he got fired and got someone else to tell his girlfriend he lost his job. In fact you had it sung to her by a mariachi band didn't you Davis?"

I try to swallow but can't, so I croak out a "Yes, that's right Kirk." Then the bit of spit I'd been trying to swallow goes half down my throat and gets stuck, so I end up having a coughing fit. Oh fuck this is all I need, my face will be neon in a minute. Taking another a sip of water I notice that Kirk's trying not to laugh. Shit, it must be old neon face here that's got him going. The water helps. I figure I may as well just fess up to how crap I'm feeling.

"Sorry about that Kirk. God I'm just so nervous, it's crazy. I'm normally pretty cool, calm and collected." Actually, just talking is suddenly making me feel a bit better.

Kirk clears his throat. "Well you certainly seemed cool, calm and collected last time we saw you at your launch. You had the crowd at The Watering Hole in the palm of your hand." He winks at me. "Apparently you were fired because you allegedly had *something else* in the palm of your hand while you were at work that day," he says chattily.

Here we go, I'm never going to live down this wanker thing. "Yeah, well I was fired unfairly Kirk. My boss accused me of doing something I didn't do. All I did was read a magazine Kirk. But he wouldn't listen to my side of the story, so he just sacked me. And he got away with it because he put all of us on casual rates a while ago."

"That's pretty rough, you'd worked there for a while hadn't you?" Kirk asks.

Nodding my head I answer, "Four years Kirk. That's why I felt I deserved a bit of respect. I was a great worker for him and he treated me like sh.., garbage." Phew, I just saved myself from swearing on national TV. I give myself a mental pat on the back.

Now Kirk's nodding. "I believe he said that you'll never be famous, that you're a nobody. Is that correct?"

I grin and reply "That's right. But I guess he was wrong eh!" Uncrossing my legs, I sit up in my seat. "That's why I'm on a mission, to spread my message of respect. I want to bring back respect. There's not enough of it around these days and I plan on changing that. That's why I want to be a celebrity Kirk."

"Well it looks like you're doing it. I checked this morning and you've now got over five million hits on YouTube, and that's just your first clip. Your getting fired clip, the one that you launched on Friday night, has gotten even more. It's had six million hits. Davis you're a star!" he tells me.

"It's insane isn't it?" I take another sip of water then say, "I guess people just like to see an idiot get himself in stupid situations. But as I said, as long as my message gets out there that's the main thing. I don't really care how stupid I look."

Kirk leans in towards me, he gives me an intense look then says, "Well, we'd like to help you get your message out there Davis. How would you like a weekly segment here with us on *Good Morning Today*? Where *you* get to spread some respect?"

I'm speechless. I'm sitting here on national TV like a stunned mullet, the only thing that's moving are my eyebrows, they're doing their own little dance. Finally I splutter, "Are you for real?"

Kirk's doing his funny head bobbing-laughing thing. "Absolutely brother, we want to help you spread the word, so how about it?"

My mind is racing, why are they asking me this on live TV, what's in it for them? I feel pressured. Now I wish I had an agent or manager, so I could get some advice. Taking a deep breath I twiddle my fingers for a second to buy myself some time. The bottom line is that I can make more of a difference if I take them up on the offer, and hopefully it will also skyrocket my celebrity status, which would be majorly cool. I make a snap decision. But I have to know one thing first.

"Will I have to wear this disgusting makeup each week Kirk?"

Kirk can't help himself, he totally cracks up. "I'll be honest with you. You're probably going to have to. But it's not every day that we offer this sort of thing. We like you Davis, and we like what you're trying to do, so we want to help you."

Holding out my hand for him to shake I declare, "I'm in! Of course my manager will have to ok everything. I guess having to wear this crap makeup isn't so bad after all!" Jeezus, I'd better get me an agent or manager quick-smart. Damn it, did I just said crap on TV? I'm gonna have to get a grip on my swearing now that I'm a TV personality!

We shake on it and Kirk smiles into the camera. "There you have it folks, now that's something to really look forward to. Tune in and see how Davis is going to spread some respect. You won't want to miss it!"

The penny drops, now I get why they want me. They want my millions of YouTubers to become *their* viewers! That's cool with me, I reckon it's a win-win situation. I wonder if I'll get paid. The camera pans back onto me and I say my catchphrase while pointing to my t-shirt. "Don't forget to respect yourself and respect other people, and don't forget to check out my new website, whoisdavisspanx.com!"

And there it is, my proper TV debut is done and dusted. It really wasn't that scary after all, I'd just whipped myself into a frenzy over nothing. I'm absolutely stoked to be walking away with my own weekly segment on morning TV. That's just un-fucking-believable!

Dad nearly squashes me in a bear hug when we meet up in the corridor. When he lets me go he cackles, "I was watching in the green room, Jeezus Davis this is incredible. You're going to be a bloody TV star! I'm so proud of you son. Now, I've been thinking. About this manager of yours. Who'd you have in mind? Have you got anyone lined up yet?"

I look him in the eye, trying to read his face, see what he's up to. But he's got the blank canvas thing going on - he's impenetrable, although I have a sneaking suspicion of what he's up to. Narrowing my eyes at him I lick my lower lip and am about to say something, but I'm interrupted by the makeup lady wanting me to come and 'take my face off'. She leads me down the corridor, and Dad follows me.

Once I'm back in the makeup chair I'm a captive audience, and Dad takes full advantage of the situation. He launches into the pitch of the century. So far he's selling me on the reasons *why* I need a manager, and why I need one *right now*. He's using every persuasion tactic he's got, and believe me, he's got a pretty big repertoire to choose from. It's lucky I was kind of ready for him, because, here it comes. He locks eyes with me and I'm trapped in his baby blues.

"Listen Davis, luckily I just happen to know the perfect guy for the job. Someone who has your best interests at heart. Someone who'll *fight* to get you the best deals out there, and who'll give one hundred percent of themselves to you. They've got outstanding charisma, they're a negotiation expert, which is important in doing great deals, and they're also honest, so ya won't get ripped off." I'm still transfixed by him, how does he do this shit? He continues on.

"And the best bit is Davis, at the moment this guy's got time to take a client of your calibre on." Running a hand through his short grey hair he gives me a cheeky grin and continues, "Because we all know you can be hard work mate, and this celebrity stuff can be challenging. But not for the guy I've got in mind. He'll blitz anything and anyone. No challenge is too big for me." Dad immediately realises that he just mentioned himself. "Shit, I wasn't planning on revealing that bit yet."

Chuckling I tell him, "Don't worry, I figured you were talking about yourself."

A look of surprise spreads across his face. "You did? When did you figure that out?"

"Only right at the start, I was onto you from the beginning."

He frowns, and plays with the dimple in his chin, "Jeezus I must be slipping up. So why'd you let me continue on like that eh?"

Closing my eyes so the makeup lady can get the mascara off I say, "Just wanted to see what you've got, hear the spiel, that's all."

The makeup chick chimes in, "Well I had no idea you were talking about you. I was thinking to myself that Davis here would be an idiot not to get this guy on board and signed up to him right away. Heck, I'd want that guy playing on my team."

Dad perks up at this. I smile and say to him, "Yeah Dad, I want you on my team too, you've got the job." Opening an eye I squint at him and smile, then hold out my hand and we shake on it. Dad looks rapt, he's beaming.

"Mate this is great," he says excitedly. "Since the heart attack I've been at a bit of a loose end, what with handing the agency over to Doug to run. I miss the buzz of real estate. Thanks again mate, just wait till you hear some of the ideas I've got for ya."

I nod but wonder, have I done the right thing here? I mean Dad *is* the master influencer, and I do want him on my team. I just hope he doesn't talk me into doing any stupid stuff like he did when I was a kid. He once talked me into a meat pie eating contest when I was twelve. I loved pies, and Dad figured I could win the prize of two hundred bucks and buy myself the BMX I wanted. I ate so many pies I spewed up all over the competition table. I didn't win, but I nearly died of embarrassment. I've never been able to eat a bloody meat pie ever since. Even the smell of them makes me want to chuck. That's just one example in a long list of stupid things he's made me do over the years. If he's my manager, I'll need to keep an eye on him.

"Ok Dad, I think we should have some ground rules right from the start. *I* have final say over anything you want me to do. You can't just say yes to something and then tell me about it later ok? I have to approve of everything that happens. Respect ok?"

"Sure, sure," he says while rubbing his hands together, "I'll run everything by you no probs."

I thank the makeup lady and we make our way out. As we're walking to the car park, a guy in a suit runs after us calling out my name. Turns out he's the assistant producer on *Good Morning Today*, and he wants my manager's details so that they can go over the contract and make arrangements.

Dad and I look at each other and smirk. Dad stands tall and proud. "*I'm* Davis's manager, give me your card son and I'll get in touch. We've got another important appointment this morning," Dad makes a display of looking at his watch, "which we're running late for."

The assistant producer whips out a card and smiles at us while he re-adjusts his tie. "We're very excited to have you coming on the show Davis," he pants.

"I bet you are," says Dad. "With the pulling power Davis has got your ratings are gonna go through the roof aren't they?" He eyeballs the assistant. "I think we both know that's the reason you want him on board, and that's fine with us. Just be prepared to pay him an outstanding fee for bringing you all this new business ok? That's only fair."

The assistant producer's face drops a bit. It's now obvious to him that we're switched on and won't be taken for a ride. Dad turns as if he's about to walk away. I've seen him do this heaps of times, I know the drill. So I thank the guy and I take a few steps with Dad, who promptly stops, turns and asks the guy casually, "How many weeks will Davis's segments run for? What have you got in mind?"

The poor guy looks totally flustered, Dad's done it again. "Well, we were thinking initially a six month contract, at ten k per segment which will run for about five minutes."

Dad furrows his brow while fingering his chin. "Nah, I can tell you right now that that's not going to work for us. Tell your boss that we'll only sign a three month contract and that we want fifty k per segment. If he baulks, tell him to do his numbers. He'll see it's still a win-win for both of us ok?"

The assistant producer looks shell shocked and just nods. "Right then," says Dad, "we've gotta shoot through. Let me know about those terms ASAP, I've got a meeting with another TV channel this arvo ok? So if you want to lock Davis in you'd better move fast." Again he goes to walk away then stops and says, "Have you got a pen? It's probably better if you call me when you decide. Our meeting with the other TV lot is at one thirty, you'll probably want to secure Davis for yourselves before then."

The guy eagerly hands him another card and a pen. Dad writes his name and mobile number on the back of the card and hands it back. "Talk to you soon mate. Cheers."

We both give him a wave, and off we strut to my beat up old ute. Both of us are trying not to crack up. Dad's muttering, "We gotta keep it together Davis, they've got cameras everywhere in the car park. We've gotta look professional."

We do keep it together, but only until we're out of the Channel Six car park gates. I pull up a bit further down the road and we go crazy, woo-hoo-ing and high-fiving each other. Dad and I are on cloud nine. He keeps saying "My son the TV star!" and I can't help grinning like an idiot.

I pull back out into the traffic. I want to take Dad home via the city and see if my billboard on St Kilda road is up yet, and see if I can spot any mobile billboards doing the rounds.

"Where the hell did you get fifty k from? That's unreal," I shout.

"Dunno, just pulled it out of me arse. The good thing is that we've got room to bargain with. They're probably not gonna go for the fifty k, but even if they drop it to say thirty, or twenty k, how bloody good is that?!" he says excitedly.

"You're a goddamn legend Dad." Although I take note that he's already steamed ahead with something before running it by me, but in this case I don't care too much, he's making me a fortune. But I know that it'll happen again, it's just his style. He gets too caught up in the moment.

He looks at me with a cheeky grin on his face. "Aren't you glad I talked you into letting me come with you today?"

"Yeah Dad I'm stoked, but you've still gotta run shit by me ok?" I give him a stern look.

"Course I will, the deal's not done yet and you'll get the final say, don't you worry," he says wagging a finger at me.

"Good. I loved how you said we were busy and had a meeting with another TV channel. You're such a top bullshitter."

Thumping the dash board for effect he says, "I'm *not* a bullshitter Davis. It's called creating scarcity. It's a technique, an art form, and it'll make us a shit load more money. I guarantee that Channel Six'll call us back by lunchtime with an offer. They'll be scared shitless that you'll go with the competition if they don't snap you up right now."

He's right. We're having coffee in a café on St Kilda road when he gets the call, and it's only eleven o'clock. We've both been admiring the view of my picture plastered all over the huge billboard opposite us, I look awesome! We both snap to attention when Dad's phone rings.

Dad gives me the thumbs up as he takes the call. I'm all ears trying to listen in, but I can't hear anything so I'm relying on his facial expressions. He's nodding, that must be a good sign. Then he disagrees with something, and says, "Nah, that won't work for us." They must come back with a counter offer, because he soon grins and says, "That sounds more like it." Fuck I wish I knew what was going on. He ends the conversation by saying that he'll run it by me and get back to them.

When he hangs up he just sits there staring at me with a goofy look on his face. He's trying to hold out on me! I casually take a sip of coffee, two can play at this game. Then I take a big bite of my ham and cheese toasty and chew it slowly. Jeezus the suspense is killing me. Bugger it, I can't hold out any longer, I've gotta know what happened.

Screwing up my face like I'm in agony I beg, "Aw c'mon Dad, spill, tell me what happened."

He suddenly explodes from his chair with both arms up in the air, letting out a loud "Yes!" He quickly sits back down again and leans in close to me. "Good news son, they've offered you a six month contract, at forty k a bloody week! They tried for thirty at the start, that's when I said that wouldn't work. So they said they'd up the price but wouldn't budge on the length of contract, it has to be six months."

My mouth's open and a bit of toastie falls out onto the table. "Fuck me! Forty k's unbelievable! And six months is fine, nice one Dad."

For a moment he's looking like The Cheshire Cat, then he gets his serious face on again. Angling his head a bit to one side, he takes a deep breath and says seriously, "Ok Davis, I'm officially asking for your approval on this. Is it ok for you to sign a six month contract, at forty thousand dollars a week, to have your own weekly segment on *Good Morning Today*?"

I laugh, "You smartarse!" But I appreciate the gesture, "It's a definite yes. I will happily sign a contract to that effect. Thank you very much Mr Spanx for negotiating an awesome deal for me." I offer him my hand and we shake on it, then we both crack up laughing.

There's something I don't get, so I have to ask him. "Why did you want a shorter contract?"

"So we could negotiate for more money sooner. You're locked into forty k for six months - now that's a fantastic deal - but who knows how much you'll be worth in a few months' time. The way you're going mate the sky's the limit," he replies.

I can see his point. He really is switched on, none of that would have occurred to me, but I'm still stoked with what I've got. He's staring at my billboard, I can see his brain's ticking over, what's he up to? "Anything I should know about? What are ya cooking up now?"

"I was just thinking that I should make sure that this contract isn't exclusive, that way you can still do interviews with other channels. Probably no other segments or shows though, but I want you to be able to do interviews and stuff with other channels. What do you reckon?"

It makes sense, I think it's a great idea. "Yeah, I don't want to be tied down to these guys, I still want my freedom."

We've been lucky, so far no-one's recognised me in the café, but that all changes when a group of teenagers comes in. There's about seven of them, they're all probably around sixteen or seventeen years old. They sit down, then one of them spots us sitting near the window.

A chick squeals out my name and they all come charging over. They're all asking questions at once, and a few are shoving napkins in my face, asking for autographs. Standing up I hold up my hands to quieten them down.

"Hey, how about a bit of respect please guys. I'm trying to have some time with my Dad here."

They all shut up and a couple of them apologise. Then they're all saying how sorry they are and that they didn't mean to be rude. I tell them it's no problem, but next time just be more respectful. "Now, would anyone like a photo with me?" They all nod and whip out their phones, so we get a waiter to take photos for us, which makes them all happy.

Some of them must have texted their friends, because by the time Dad and I are ready to go there's a crowd inside the café that's starting to spill out onto the street. I know they all mean well, but it's a bit freaky being surrounded like this. We try and make our way to the counter to pay our bill, but the crowd starts pushing and shoving.

"Hey, hey, give us some room here guys," I shout.

Someone calls out, "Davis is a wanker." Well that starts up a chant of wanker calls, which turns into a tussle between two groups of kids. Some of the kids are into the respect thing, and try to shush the wanker callers, which doesn't go down so well. I'm at the counter when the waiter says he's going to call the cops. I hope they get here quick, this could turn nasty. I'm not sure whether to try and get Dad behind the counter to keep him safe, or if we should just make a push for the street. The door isn't that far away, but it's blocked with people.

Fuck. I don't know what to do, but being called a wanker repeatedly is really pissing me off. I'm starting to see red.

"Oi!" I yell. "Stop carrying on like a pack of dickheads and let my Dad get through." This shuts them all up. All eyes swivel to me, so I continue, "Right. I don't give a fuck if you think I'm a wanker, but my Dad had a heart attack a few months back and this is *not* a good situation for him to be in. So I'd like to walk him out to my car, ok?"

There's a murmur from the kids. Not waiting to see if they agree, I start to push my way through the crowd, dragging Dad after me. A few kids put up their hands for a high-five as we pass and I give them one. But I also notice a group who, by the looks of them, would like to throw a few punches. It's still a tense situation. We make it safely to the ute which is parked right outside the café, and I see that the crowd has gotten even bigger. I open the door for Dad and he gets in, just as a police car pulls up.

Turning back to the kids I say, "Good onya guys, thanks for bringing back the respect here today. I really appreciate it. Thanks again."

The cops come over and ask what's going on. "Everything's cool," I assure them, "and it's cool because these kids decided to bring back some respect and not get in a fight. They should be proud of themselves." I eyeball the group that did the wanker calling, the guys that wanted to start a fight. "It takes a lot to show respect for yourself, and take a step back. Does anyone have their phone handy?"

Some kids shove their phones at me. I point to one and ask him if he'll jump up onto the tray of my ute and film the crowd. He nods eagerly. I ask him his name and whisper some instructions in his ear before he jumps up. I tell him that I want him to get a shot of the whole crowd first, then zoom in on the wanker callers who are now crammed outside against the window of the café. It looks like they tried to make a break for it but couldn't get through the crowd. I also ask him if he can upload the video to my website. I check that he's ready and he gives me a nod. I'm about to address the crowd, but I can't really see the guys at the back near the window, the troublemakers, so I jump up onto the tray of my ute, and start speaking to everyone.

"Ok, Bailey here is gonna film this and then upload it onto my website and YouTube for everyone to see, ok?" There's a few bewildered faces, but a lot of the kids look stoked.

"Why I want this filmed is because you guys," and I point to the trouble makers at the back, "could have really caused a lot of trouble here today, but you didn't." The group of trouble makers cringe against the window, trying to make themselves invisible.

"Look," I continue, "I just wanted to acknowledge publicly how great I think you are for bringing back the respect here. You guys stopped yourselves from hurting others with your fists, and from hurting yourselves by feeling crap about it afterwards. That takes courage. I wish there was more of it out there." Now they realise that they're not in trouble, the group of wanker callers puff out their chests and stand tall.

"So good onya guys, as I said before, you should be proud of yourselves. I know I'm proud of you - even if you did call me a wanker. You're a great example of how guys should conduct themselves, well done," I say, giving them a thumbs up.

Then pointing at the crowd I announce, "Now I'd like to do something new here with all of you guys. Ladies, this is for the guys only today, sorry. We're a brotherhood, and we're all about bringing back the respect. I want to honour that today, so guys, I want to hear you all yell respect as loud as you can after me, ok?

Pumping my fist in the air I shout as loudly as I can, "Respect."

The guys in the crowd follow my lead, all punching the air and shouting "Respect" in unison. We repeat it five times, it feels fucking awesome! I can see the excitement and power in their faces as we're doing it. When we finish I say, "Wow, you guys rocked that. I know that felt great for me, but how did you guys feel doing that?" Everyone screams their approval.

"You know that was so good I want to do it again," I shout. "But this time everyone can join in, and this time I want to get my Dad up here with me, is that ok?"

The crowd screams "Yes."

Then I say that I want the cops up here with me too. "Should I ask them?"

The crowd screams yes again, so I ask the cops if they'll jump up on the ute with me. They look uncertain, but then decide to do it.

So we go for it again. Me, Dad and the cops all lead the respect chant, punching the air as we do it. Cars are tooting as they drive past, and I notice that heaps of people are filming it with their phones. Bailey is still filming us as well. When we finish I tell the crowd that I want them each to give away five hugs. I give the cops, Bailey and Dad a hug. I'm so caught up in the moment that I jump down and start high-fiving and hugging people in the crowd. The troublemakers push their way through towards me. They're all grinning and telling me I'm awesome. Giving them all a hug, I thank them again and tell them to spread some respect. Then I have a quick chat to the cops, who are happy to have been part of it. Giving Bailey another high-five I thank him for his help and wish him well.

$$\$\$\$\$\$\$\$\$\$\$$$

Once we've driven off Dad turns to me and says, "As your manager I advise you to get a security crew put together as soon as possible. That could have turned very nasty Davis."

"Yeah I know. We're lucky it didn't."

"Crowds are funny things Davis, they can turn either way at any time. Better to be prepared and get yourself some protection eh?"

"Yeah, I'll have to get on it. Now I'm making money I can afford to get some people on the payroll."

Dad agrees, then asks "Where the hell did you get the idea to do that respect chant thingy? That was unbelievable, you gotta do that again."

"No idea," I say, cheekily flicking my eyes his way, "just pulled it out of me arse I guess. You must have taught me well." Thumping the steering wheel I shout, "I fucking love being a celebrity!" Then I say in a normal voice, "Yeah I think I'll make that my signature thing, get everyone to *feel* the respect."

Dad laughs and gives me a nudge, "You've finally found your true calling son. Jeezus you rocked that crowd. You were amazing."

I take Dad home and we fill Mum in on our crazy morning. She watched me on *Good Morning Today* so she knows they offered me my own segment, but she literally drops her cup of tea when Dad tells her how much money they've offered me.

"Forty thousand a week! I don't believe it," she squeals.

Dad preens and gets his smug face on. "Well you'd better believe it, because that's the fantastic deal *I* negotiated as Davis's *new manager*."

Mum's eyes are darting back and forth as she looks at each of us. I think she's trying to suss out if Dad's pulling her leg. She puts her hands on her hips, taps her foot a few times then says, "All my instincts are telling me that you're not lying David." Then she looks at me "But

I just don't believe they'd pay you that much, it's an insane amount of money." Placing her hand on my upper arm, her eyes widen and she blurts, "Not that you're not worth that Davis, it just seems like a lot of money for you not doing much, that's all."

"And good on him for bagging a killer deal like that eh love?" booms Dad. "Let's celebrate. I reckon a Virgin Mary'll hit the spot nicely." He strides off into the kitchen to make them.

Mum gives me a hug. "Oh Davis, I don't want you to think I'm not happy for you, I am, it's just…."

I cut her off mid-sentence. "I know. It's crazy is what it is. But what a ride Mum, wait till you hear what else happened."

So over Dad's Virgin Marys, which are excellent, I tell her about the café and my respect chant. She's just shaking her head, a goofy look is plastered on her face. Dad takes her hand.

"I know love, it's taken him a while, but he's finally found his calling alright. You should have seen him with the crowd today, he was magnificent!" They gaze lovingly into each other's eyes.

I kind of feel like I'm intruding, but with these guys I'm used to it. As kids we always knew where we stood. Mum and Dad were there for each other first and foremost, us kids came second. Not in a horrible way, we always knew that we were loved and that they'd do anything for us, but we also knew not to interrupt their special moments, which could be just a look, like the one they're giving each other now, or something more intimate.

This became especially true when Doug caught them going for it once. He was ten and I was only four, but I still remember it. Mum was horrified, I remember Dad just laughed it off, but from that moment on they had a code. If we came home and ABBA was playing on the stereo, we all knew not to disturb them in the bedroom, because it was Mummy and Daddy's 'special time,' as they called it.

It cracks me up that they still do it - not shag, but put ABBA on during their sexy time. I know they still play it because I dropped around a few weeks ago and *Dancing Queen* was blaring out. I decided the best thing to do was catch up with them the next day, and boy did I rib them about it then.

Dad's now stroking Mum's leg. I'm getting toey, it's time to make a move and leave these guys to it. I want to catch up with Eric if he's about. I want to congratulate him on how unreal the billboard looks, and I also want his advice on some website stuff. While Mum and Dad are canoodling I give him a quick call, but his receptionist Marissa tells me he's in a meeting and probably won't be available for the rest of the day. Bummer.

I ask Dad if we can catch up tomorrow, I want to get my contract with Channel Six sorted. He tells me he'll give the station a call later and let me know. He points out that we'll have to wait a while.

"We're supposed to be having a meeting with that other channel at one thirty, remember? So I'll call Channel Six later this arvo - make em sweat for a bit eh?"

Mum asks if I'll ring the grandmas to tell them the good news or should she. I tell her I'll give them a call later and fill them in on everything myself. They usually watch *Millionaire* together each arvo, so I'll give them a call then.

That reminds me, I still need to ask them about that pash on Friday night, I've got to get to the bottom of that. I ask Mum what she reckons, she agrees with Dad that it was just a publicity stunt, nothing to worry about. But I'm still not so sure, I have my suspicions about those two.

Getting up, I wink at Dad and say, "Must be time to put on some ABBA eh Dad?"

He lets out a loud "Ha!" slaps his leg and replies, "Off you go ya cheeky bugger, I'll catch ya later."

Chapter 9

I was going to surprise Claire and visit her for lunch, but after the café fiasco this morning I reckon I'd better get onto that security posse. I'm sitting in the ute, still parked outside Mum and Dad's, at a bit of a loose end. I just need some time to think things through.

Man, I've only been a celebrity for a few days, I can't believe I need a security crew already. Jeeze, what a trip. It's exciting, but a bit daunting. One thing about this celebrity caper is that it teaches you to think on your feet, I've experienced so many new things already. The dinner at Taxie was a blast, and I really liked that Jacobs guy.

Bingo! Snapping my fingers I say to myself, "That's it," I want cuff talking Jacobs to head up my security crew. He'd be perfect, he'd rock it! But how the heck do I contact him? He's already got a job in the best restaurant in town, he might want to stay there. "But that's a pussy job," I say out loud. Yeah, what guy would prefer to work in a boring restaurant when he can get heaps more action working for me? It seems like a no-brainer to me, I hope he sees it the same way. I toss around some ideas as to how to contact him. I could go in and have lunch, then ask him in person. But that doesn't feel right, I'm a straight up guy, I don't like underhanded behaviour. So I decide the best plan of action is to call his boss Lawrence, and ask if he'd mind me poaching Jacobs.

I call the restaurant straight away. Oh man, being a celeb really has its perks, the chick who answers tells me that Lawrence isn't available. So I name drop *my own name* - how cool is that! I tell her that this is Davis Spanx, and I'm sure Lawrence would be pissed off if he missed my call.

This gets immediate action, she apologises for the delay and I'm put straight through. Lawrence comes over all smarmy, he kind of gives me the shits the way he sucks up to me. I immediately ask him if he'd mind me offering Jacobs a job.

"Mr Jacobs is a free agent, he can do as he wishes. Although I'd be very sorry to see him go," he tells me.

Then I ask if I can get his contact details. Lawrence gives a brittle little laugh and insists that he put Jacobs on the line directly. Apparently he's working the VIP area this lunch time. Before I know it Jacobs is on the line.

"Hello Mr Spanx, how can I assist you?" he asks.

"Hi Jacobs, I've got a proposal for you. I've already asked Lawrence and he's cool with it, so there's nothing to worry about." I pause, waiting for some kind of response, but there's just silence.

"Are you still there Jacobs, can you hear me?"

"I can hear you loud and clear sir. You were saying something about a proposal?"

I clear my throat. He really reminds me of an English butler the way he carries on, but I love it.

"Yeah, Jacobs, I had a little incident this morning with a crowd that nearly got out of control. It made me realise that I need a security crew, and I'd like you to be the head of that crew. That is if you do full-on security stuff."

I pause again, waiting for a response, but there's nothing. Shit, maybe he doesn't want to change jobs.

"What I'm trying to say here Jacobs is that I want you to quit that pussy VIP lounge job and come work for me. I reckon a man like you needs a bit more action in his life. What do you think?"

He gives a slight chuckle then replies, "I couldn't agree with you more sir. When would you require my services?"

"Immediately Jacobs. I nearly got mobbed this morning, I need me a protection posse ASAP."

"Then a protection posse is what you shall have. It would be my pleasure to head up your... protection posse sir." I'm sure I detect a smile in his voice as he says protection posse again

"Ripper! You little beauty," I excitedly shout, "I knew you were the man for the job." I suddenly realise that I don't know anything about him. "You have had more experience than just looking after a VIP area in a restaurant, eh Jacobs?"

He coughs slightly and replies, "Yes sir, my experience is vast. Shall I send you my resume?"

"Nah, just give me a quick run down."

So he informs me that he's been in the protection business, as he calls it, for a long time. He's worked for various top class hotels all around the world. He's also had a celebrity client before, but he won't tell me who. He says that working at the restaurant was a step down for him, but he enjoyed the slower pace. Then he totally cracks me up by agreeing that it is a pussy job, and that he's looking forward to getting back in the action.

"Can you still use the cuff talking thing Jacobs? It's pretty cool."

He gives another slight chuckle. "Yes sir, I can continue using the *cuff talker* as you call it."

"Good. Now there's another guy I'd like on our protection posse - I really like that name Jacobs - that's what I'll be calling it from now on. Is that ok?"

"Very good sir."

"Anyway, do you think you can train a guy up? I've got someone in mind who wouldn't have a clue about any of this shit, would that be a problem?"

Clearing his throat he replies, "No problem at all sir. Just as long as the entire *posse* knows that *I'm* the expert and in charge of operations, I can't see it being a problem. Can he follow directions sir?"

"Yeah, that shouldn't be a problem," I assure him. "Now we need to discuss terms and stuff, I'll leave most of that up to my manager. But to start with I can only offer you a six month contract, is that ok?"

"Perfectly fine sir," purrs Jacobs.

"And as for what you charge, can you give me a ballpark figure?"

"Normally fifteen hundred a week sir."

"Ok, well let's make it two grand, you're worth it Jacobs."

This time there's a real smile in his voice as he says with enthusiasm, "*Very good* sir, I appreciate that."

"Right, now go and tell Lawrence he can give his pussy job to someone else. Tell him that you've had a better offer!"

"I look forward to doing that sir!"

We exchange numbers. I give him Dad's mobile number as well, and tell him to take tomorrow off. He can start with me on Wednesday, unless there's an emergency.

I'm grinning from ear to ear, this is so cool. Wait till I tell Bruce that I've got Jacobs on board, he'll love it. I make another call. It rings and rings. Come on, pick up, pick up, I mutter to myself, and it finally gets answered.

"Hey Davis, how are ya mate?" Jonno yells. He must be standing near one of the extruders, I can hear it in the background.

"Go into the tea room, I gotta talk to you properly," I yell back.

"Mate I'll call you back in five, this fuckin' machine is playin' up again. I can't talk right now," he snaps.

"No worries but make sure you call me back, it's important."

Just as I hang up ABBA music starts blaring from Mum and Dad's. Oh man, I've got to get out of here. I quickly decide to head home.

I'm on the freeway admiring the awesome billboard of myself that's coming in to view, when my phone rings. Fuck, I should pull over. Luckily Maccas is just up the road, so I answer the phone and ask Jonno to wait a sec while I pull off the freeway into the Maccas car park.

Switching off the ute I grab the phone and say, "You took your time, having a shit day are ya?"

Jonno groans. "That's a fuckin' understatement, look I can't talk long. What's goin' on?"

"Jonno how would you like to get out of that shit-hole. I want to offer you a job."

"Huh? Course I wanna get out of this bloody dump. What sort of job?" he demands.

"I want you on my protection posse."

"What the fuck's a protection posse? You in the mafia or something?" he cackles with laughter.

I laugh too. "Nah it's just my dicky name for a security team, I reckon it sounds cool."

"Let me get this straight," he says, "*you* want to offer me a job doin' *security* for *you*. Is that right?"

"Yep, you'll get trained by one of the best. The guy I've just hired as my head of security is awesome, he really knows his shit. He reckons he can train you up no worries."

"Well fuck me," Jonno shouts. "Is this for real Davis?"

"Yeah! Come on, you'd be perfect. You're an ugly bastard, you won't have to do much 'cos your ugly mug'll scare most of the punters away!!"

He cracks up at this. "Mate it sounds un-bloody real. This place is driving me nuts."

"The only thing is, at the moment I can only guarantee six months work. Would that be a problem?"

There's silence for a second or two. "Aw fuck it, I'm in. When else am I gonna get a chance like this eh?"

"Good onya Jonno. What's Beaker paying you?"

"A grand a week."

"Well how about I give you fifteen hundred, that way you might be able to squirrel some away for a rainy day eh?"

"You're havin' me on right?"

"Nup, I want you on board Jonno. I miss your pervy ways."

He cackles again, and I fill him in on how Dad's now my manager. Once I give him Dad's mobile number I cheekily order Jonno to go and give his notice.

"Fuck yeah," he yells. "And they can't do shit 'cos I'm casual. Suck on that Beaker! Jeezus Davis, you've made my bloody day!"

I tell him to take tomorrow off, adding that I'd like to get together for a meeting on Wednesday so that he can meet Jacobs and get everything sorted. I hang up feeling awesome, I've just changed two people's lives and it feels fan-fucking-tastic. I'm looking at Maccas, might as well have something to eat while I'm here. I wonder if the same chick's on who served me the other day? Pulling into the drive-thru I'm surprised, there's no other cars in the queue, it seems a bit strange for lunchtime.

I place my order over the intercom and drive up to the window. There she is, it's the same chick. I can't remember her name, but I know it's something exotic. She's standing at the window doing something with her mobile phone, it looks like she's texting. She quickly pockets her phone, then she recognises me.

"Davis! It's so good to see you again, in person that is. I can see you every day now you're up there," she says, pointing to the billboard on the opposite side of the freeway.

Taking a quick look at it I say, "It's amazing how quickly your life can change."

She nods. "Yes, you are very lucky."

She has no idea this could be her lucky day too. Looking at her name tag I smile and say, "Ajala, that's a very pretty name."

"My family is from India."

I wouldn't have picked her as being Indian, her skin's reasonably fair and she's got blue eyes. Her plat of long black hair is a bit of a giveaway though. "Really?" I say, "Wow. Do you work here full time? Hey, I'd never have guessed that you're Indian, you don't look it."

"I only work here part time. I'm a casual because I'm studying at uni. My family is from Pushkar in Rajasthan, but my grandfather was English."

"Noticed you texting when I pulled up, are you good at that? Do you like doing it?"

She looks at me strangely, it is a bit of a weird question, but she answers happily enough. "Yes I enjoy texting, I don't know if I'm good at it. I just do it." She looks over her shoulder and takes the bag of food that's passed to her, and hands it to me with a big smile on her face.

Taking it, I quickly look in my rear view mirror. Good, there's still no cars behind me. Cool. Smiling at her I ask, "Ajala, I'm wondering if you can help me. I need someone to do my tweets, Facebook posts and blogs for me. Do you think you could be that person?"

She looks stunned, but her smile is firmly in place. "You want me to work for you, to do your social media stuff?"

"Yeah, that's it. Be my social media coordinator. What do ya reckon? I'll pay you a grand a week, then you can say goodbye to this shit-kickers job. You're worth more than this Ajala."

Her eyes widen. "Really? Are you really asking me to do this?"

I laughingly reply, "Yes I'm really asking you to work for me. Put these numbers into your phone." I give her my personal mobile number, and Dad's as well.

"Call me when you make up your mind ok?"

She starts jumping up and down excitedly, yelling, "Yes, Yes, I want it, I want to work for you!" We're both laughing now.

"Cool, well tell your boss that you can't fit them into your busy schedule anymore. Tell them you're working for a celebrity now ok! I want you to take tomorrow off, but I'll be having a meeting on Wednesday that you need to come to, ok?"

Her eyes are shining, she nods, "Yes, yes, ok, ok."

I'm about to drive off, but I've got another idea. "Hey, you don't know anyone who's really good with websites do you?

"Oh yes," she gushes, "my brother Suraj is a web designer, he can help you."

"Ok I'll need to talk to him. Text me his number and I'll give him a call. Welcome to the team Ajala."

She waves after me as I drive off. Unreal. I love the term social media coordinator, it sounds professional. I should have found out what she's studying at uni. Never mind, I'll ask her on Wednesday.

I'm stoked to have Ajala on board, it'll sure take the pressure off me to do all that techy shit. I reckon a grand a week is a bargain to get that all taken care of. Woohoo, I've now got my Indian outsourcing sourced! It'd be a bonus if her brother's any good, I don't want to keep having to ask Eric to do stuff for me, he's busy enough with his own business.

$$\$\$\$\$\$\$\$\$\$\$$$

I head home and pop over to Bruce's. He's on the phone but lets me in, then he heads back down to his office. I make myself a coffee, turn on the telly, and get comfy on the couch while I wait for him. He seems to take for ever.

God daytime TV is crap, I've been channel surfing for the past ten minutes.

"Hey, hey," Bruce calls as he comes into the room, "how's Mr Celebrity today?"

Plonking himself down on the couch next to me he says "Saw you on *Good Morning Today*, sweet deal to land a segment with them." He holds up his left hand and we high-five each other.

"Mate that's just the start, guess what they're paying me each week."

Bruce scratches his balls, stares off into space for a second, then eyeballs me and says, "Two grand!"

"Higher," I reply with a huge grin on my face.

"Five grand."

"Much higher."

"Ten grand!"

"Higher," I shout.

"Fuck Davis, you got more than ten grand? Jeezus, what did you get?" he demands.

"Guess," I repeat.

"Fuck guessing just tell me!"

"Forty grand!"

He looks at me blankly, then blinks rapidly a few times, a look of shock spreading across his face. "What the, they offered you forty grand *a week*?"

"Yep," I nod, looking smug. "Pretty cool eh? *And* it's a six month contract."

"Fuuuuck," he breaths, "that's incredible"

"I know, it's a bloody miracle. I was thinking about it earlier - I've only been a celebrity for three and a half days and I'm getting paid the same as Kim bloody Kardashian."

Bruce jumps up off the couch. "Mate, I so didn't believe you when you told me you were gonna become a celeb. But look at you now." He suddenly frowns at me and adds, "It's all happening a bit quick though, don't you think?"

I get up and take my mug into the kitchen. Bruce follows me. "Yeah, but it is what it is. I don't want to stop it."

"Must be one hell of a ride," he laughs.

"It is mate, and I want you, my best mate, there with me every step of the way. Ok?"

We grin at each other and I slap him on the shoulder. "Wait till you hear what else has happened. Got anything to eat? I'm still hungry"

So we settle down at the kitchen table with some supplies, and I fill him in on everything that's happened. He pisses himself when I tell him about Dad becoming my manager. "Trust your old man to get in on the action. Mind you, he'd be bloody good at it."

But he nearly has a fit when I tell him how much I'm paying Ajala. "Jeezus Davis, a grand a week's too much. Why'd you offer her so much?"

"She's worth every cent if she makes that bloody social media shit disappear for me," I explain. "It's a total head fuck for me. I can't be bothered with that crap."

Bruce looks wary. "Yeah well, you'll want to keep an eye on her, check the stuff she puts out. She might put total crap out there about you."

I sigh and shake my head at him. "Don't have much faith in people do ya? Mate she'll be right. I've got a really good vibe about her, she's real nice."

Bruce still isn't convinced. "Sometimes you're too trusting, Davis. Just keep an eye on her ok?"

"I will, now drop it alright?" We stare angrily at each other. It's not often that we piss each other off, thank God. Raising my glass of coke to him I offer a truce, which he accepts.

Then I fill him in on what happened at the café, and my decision to get a protection posse sorted. I ask him to guess who I've got to head it up, but he shakes his head at me, telling me to get on with it, he's not in the mood for any more guessing games. He's in a bit of a cranky pants mood today, I dunno what's got into him, but he perks up when I tell him that I've got Jacobs on board.

His eyes light up. "Is he gonna do that cuff talking thing?"

I knew this would get him excited. "Yeah, I asked him if he could, and he's cool with that. I've asked him to train Jonno up as well."

Bruce narrows his eyes at me. "Are you talking Jonno from your old work?" I give him a nod and he rolls his eyes at me. "Why do you want *him* on board? *He'll* be no bloody good to you," he snaps.

This does it. His negativity is really pissing me off now. Crossing my arms I answer defensively, "I want him because I like him. He's an older guy who could do with a break. That's why, not that I need to explain myself to you! What the fuck's wrong with you today? What's your problem?"

Bruce stands up and puts his hands on his hips. "Mate the only problem I've got is watching you make some dumb-arse decisions, that's all. You're already throwing your money away, ya dick. What are you gonna pay Jonno?"

Setting my jaw I stare him in the eye. Fuck what he thinks of me. "Fifteen hundred a week, five hundred less than Jacobs."

Bruce shakes his head at me. "Un-fucking-believable. You're gonna pay a uni chick a grand a week to do jack shit. Now you're telling me you're gonna pay these other two clowns a shitload each a week to be your *protection posse*." He sneers the 'protection posse' bit at me. Still looking up at him I start shaking my head, he just doesn't get it.

"That's already four and a half grand a week Davis, are you an idiot?" he snaps.

That's done it, he's gone too far. Standing up to face him I snap back, "Since when is it any of your fucking business what I spend my money on? And no, I'm not an idiot Bruce. I just believe in sharing some of my good fortune around ok? I don't see anything wrong with that at all."

He seems to deflate in front of me. Rubbing a hand over his face, he looks at me sheepishly and says, "No you're not and idiot, sorry mate. Dunno what's wrong with me today."

"Can you see where I'm coming from with all this though?" I ask him.

"Yeah, yeah, I'm just not used to you flashin' a lot of cash like this, that's all." He sighs, "Look, I do see where you're coming from, ok?" He moves around the table and holds out his hand, we shake and then hug it out.

"You're a good bloke Davis. Just keep an eye out is all I'm saying."

"I hear you buddy. But don't question me again on what I spend my money on alright? It's not cool."

He assures me he won't do it again and I head home.

It feels so strange to be home during the day, I roam around the house feeling a bit out of sorts. That run in with Bruce was weird. They say that money changes people, but fuck that, the only thing I want it to change about me is my bank balance. I look at the time, it's only one forty. God today seems like the longest day ever, it'll be forever until Claire gets home, what am I gonna do with myself? I feel like I need to let off some steam. I've got it, I'll go and take out my frustration at the pistol club. Perfect.

That gets me thinking of the two grans. I may as well invite them along too, then I can ask them about that kiss the other night, and fill them in on all my goss. I call Grandma Drummond. She says there must be something in the air, because blowing something away is just what she feels like doing. She happily chats to me while she pops next door and asks Grandma Spanx to join our little shooting party. Grandma Spanx is up for it, so I tell them to get a taxi to my place, and I'll fix it up when they get here. I also ask them to hurry, because I'm bored shitless.

Once I hang up it hits me that I've only got the ute. Bugger. Usually I borrow Claire's car when I take the ladies with me, what am I going to do? I could ask Bruce if I can borrow his four wheel drive, but after our earlier run in I don't really want to. Getting a taxi there seems to be the only solution. To fill in time I jump on the computer and check out how many hits I've got on YouTube. Holy shit, the mariachi video is just under ten million. Ten million! And my getting fired one has gotten even more, it's up to a bit over twelve million. Bailey has already uploaded the café vid from this morning; and it's had half a million hits so far. Shaking my head in disbelief, I pick up my phone and send out a tweet, thanking all the fans for viewing my stuff. Then I jump on my new Facebook page and do the same. It takes me ages to do this, but just as I'm finishing there's a toot from the driveway. I quickly dash outside, I don't want the taxi to leave. But I needn't have hurried, both grans are gas-bagging to the driver, they love a captive audience. Sticking my head in the front passenger window, I give the ladies a wave and ask the driver if he can take us to the range. No worries he says, so I run inside, grab my keys and phone, then off we go.

I'm sitting in the front of the taxi. After our hellos the first thing the two grans do is launch into a report of what they had for lunch. Apparently they enjoyed a nice Mediterranean focaccia, which they pronounce as *fuckarchia*. I can't help but laugh at them, I'm sure they do it on purpose. Note to self, take them out to lunch sometime soon and make sure they order a fuckarchia! We get to the club in a jiffy. That's one good thing about living in Melton, the pistol club is so close.

The two grans are still chattering away excitedly as I escort them in, one on each arm. We all have to turn sideways and shuffle to get through the door, it's a strange ritual that we've been doing for as long as I can remember. Somehow it wouldn't be quite the same, coming in like normal people.

Gary the manager hoots at us as we come in. He bustles out from behind the counter to greet us. Both ladies receive a kiss on the cheek, which they make a big fuss over, and I jump at the opportunity to rib them.

"Hey I thought you two were into each other. Old Gary here doesn't stand a chance anymore, eh?"

They both giggle and look shifty. "Ooh we might swing both ways Davis, you never know," says Grandma Spanx.

"Eww that's so gross," I say, screwing up my face up in disgust.

"Yeah," pipes up Grandma Drummond, "we'll take any kiss we can get." And they both start giggling again.

Gary grabs my hand and starts pumping it. I ask if he saw their shenanigans the other night, and he tells me that he saw *all* of our shenanigans! He's got a good grip, it's like he doesn't want to let go.

"Great to see you Davis," he says excitedly. "Wow, I saw you on Channel Six this morning. Can't wait to see your new segment." He finally let's go of my hand. Giving it a rub I walk over to the counter, lean against it nonchalantly and remark, "Yeah it should be fun, I'm looking forward to it."

The two grans have moved over near the pistol display case. They're whispering to each other. Gary leans in and asks me, "Are they really lezzos?"

"Who knows mate, you heard them. They'll take any kiss they can get. Why? Got the hots for one of them have you?" I joke.

He goes bright red. Gary's probably somewhere in his sixties, I'm not really sure. He's a good bloke, and a top notch shot. He gets all flustered and quickly moves back behind the counter. Grandma Drummond comes over, opens her purse and plonks her pistol down on the counter in front of him.

"Gimme some sugar," she purrs at Gary, giving him a saucy wink. He goes even redder, then places a box of ammo in front of her. I don't have my own pistol anymore, so I hire one, grab some ammo and head out to the range.

Fuck me there's nothing like blowing off a few rounds, it just feels so bloody good. Grandma Spanx settles herself on a seat and watches us go for it. We both practice for a while, then it's show time. Grandma Drummond and I always have a bit of a competition, gotta keep it interesting. I get off to a good start, much to Grandma Spanx's disgust.

"Aw come on Pearl," she shouts from her seat, "don't let him win, we'll never hear the end of it."

"I'm doing my best Ella, the little shit must have been practicing," she retorts.

I laugh. "Yeah right, as if I've had time to practice lately." But she's distracted me, I miss the next shot and they both laugh.

"Right, I'm not talking to you two anymore, I've gotta concentrate." I squeeze off another round, this time hitting a bullseye. That'll show them!

We spend a very loud but fun hour blowing the targets away. I feel great, this is just what I needed. Grandma Drummond wins our competition, again, so I hand over her prize money. I'll have to invest in that video game she's got at home so that I can get some practice in. Grandma Spanx says she's gagging for a coffee, so we have afternoon tea in the clubhouse.

I've just stuffed a whole cupcake into my mouth when my phone rings. I can't answer it, there's too much cake in my mouth, but I can see who's calling. It's Dad, so I hand the phone over to Grandma Spanx so that she can answer it for me.

While they're chatting, Grandma Drummond leans over to me and tells me how much she enjoyed the launch last Friday night, and how nice it was of Paul to put on the party food. Bingo, it's time for The Grandma Report. Sure enough, she gives me a rundown of her favourites. Apparently the prawn spring rolls were the winner, closely followed by the mini Dutch meatballs. I finally swallow my cupcake and take a slurp of chockie milkshake to wash it down.

"How do you know the meatballs were Dutch?"

"Well that's what the cheffy man told us. Mmmm, the tomato relish dipping sauce was divine," she gushes.

I'm about to zone out, there's only so much food talk I can handle, but she suddenly leans in really close to me, and looks left and right, like she's making sure no one will overhear her. She beckons me even closer, our foreheads are nearly touching.

"About Friday night," she whispers, while taking another look around us, which is totally unnecessary as we're the only ones in the café area. "About Pearl and me having that kiss." She pauses again. I'm nodding like a crazy man, trying to egg her on. The suspense is killing me.

"Yeah, c'mon you gotta tell me," I beg.

She takes a deep breath. "Well..."

But she's cut off by Grandma Spanx, who's holding my phone out to me. She snaps at Grandma Drummond. "Uh uh, you said you weren't going to say anything, not yet. Davis, your *manager* wants a word with you," Grandma Spanx says with a giggle.

I take the phone off her, but before I answer it I say, "Oh come on you two, spill the beans." Grandma Drummond is looking sheepish, but Grandma Spanx shakes her head in defiance, then takes a sip of her coffee.

"Bugger," I say to Dad.

He laughs. "Yeah I heard that, they won't say anything to me either, except that it was a publicity stunt. I think they're trying to take the piss out of you."

I eyeball them both as I ask Dad, "So you're sure they're not lezzos?"

Both of their eyes widen. Grandma Spanx chokes on her coffee and exclaims, "That's no way to talk about your elders."

As I'm rolling my eyes at her, Dad continues, "Nah, as if they'd be lezzos. They're just pulling your leg Davis. Anyway enough about that, we gotta talk business for a sec."

We organise to have a meeting at his place tomorrow around lunch time, just the two of us. He's got an appointment with Channel Six scheduled for two o'clock, they want to get my contract sorted. He also tells me that they want me to do an interview on *Tonight's Current Affairs*. You little ripper!

The two grans are duly impressed with this when I tell them. I fill them in on the protection posse and what happened with me and Dad at the café. I also tell them about Jacobs and where I met him. They spend the entire taxi ride home picking my brains about the sixteen course dinner we had the other night, they want to know every last detail. So I promise to take them there sometime, but warn that they won't want to eat for a week beforehand so they can fit everything in. Maybe I can get Lawrence to rustle up a *fuckarchia* for them. Ha, that'd be a pisser. We kiss each other goodbye when they drop me off home. They still won't elaborate on their pash and its driving me mental. Maybe I can bribe them.

$$$$$$$$$$

I'm cooking dinner. The kitchen looks like a bomb's gone off, there's mess everywhere, not a single surface is left clean. I'm only cooking curried sausages and mash for God's sake. I dunno how Claire does it, the place never looks like a tip when she cooks. We have a thing, who-ever cooks doesn't clean up, but by the state of things she'd throw a hissy fit if I left all of this mess for her. I hear the garage door open, and quickly set the table, complete with candles. Gotta have the mood right, I've got so much to tell her. Damn it, I haven't had time to clean anything up.

She's faffing around in the laundry, and the first thing I hear from her is, "Darl that smells wonderful!" When she comes into the kitchen she just stands there, a look of disbelief is on her face. She surveys the scene of carnage, shaking her head at me. "What are we having?" she sighs.

"Curried bangers and mash," I say with a flourish of my hand.

"Wow," she starts to laugh. "You sure are a creative cook Davis. How the hell did you manage to make all this mess?"

I just stand there, trying to look helpless, with my hands upturned and a goofy look on my face. It works. She comes over and kisses me.

"I'm bloody starving and it really does smell great, how long till we eat?"

"Enough time for you to have a quick shower, off ya go." Pushing her off down the hall I give her bum a slap, then dash back into the kitchen and check on dinner, don't want anything burning. I have a quick clean up while she's in the shower. Oh man, that's racking up a few brownie points!

Over dinner I fill her in on everything. She didn't see me on *Good Morning Today*, and lucky for me no one's told her about my segment yet. She asks how I can afford to pay the security posse and Ajala, pointing out that while the t-shirts have made me some money, it won't be enough to cover staff expenses for long.

I've been saving the best till last. I excitedly tell her about Channel Six hiring me for a weekly segment, then ask her to guess how much she thinks they're going to pay me. Taking a deep breath she starts at a thousand, so we play the guessing game until she gets it right.

"Are you kidding me Davis?" she shrieks. "They're going to give you forty grand a *week*?"

"Yep."

"I don't believe it, why would they do that?"

"'Cos they want to turn my YouTube fans into Channel Six fans," I explain.

The penny drops, she gets it. "Wow, that's fantastic! Oh my God, you'll be a *real* celeb."

Narrowing my eyes at her I ask, "What do you mean a *real* celeb?"

"Oh you know. The whole YouTube thing would have petered out pretty quick, but this, this means you've really made it Davis. Wow."

I'm getting a funny feeling here. "Didn't you think I'd do it, didn't you think I'd become a celeb like I said I would?"

Putting her knife and fork down she says guiltily, "Well to be honest, not really. Of course I agreed with you, you'd just lost your job. I wanted to be supportive."

"You didn't believe in me," I breathe. "You lied to me Claire." I'm shocked, blown away by her confession. I take a sip of water to give myself some time to think. "You should have told me what you really thought. We never bullshit each other Claire, at least I thought we never did." I get up quickly, causing my chair to screech on the tiles, and take my plate over to the sink.

She rushes over to me and puts her arms around me, resting her cheek on my back. "I was only trying to be supportive Davis."

Turning around I push her away from me, I need to see her face clearly. "What about that big chat we had on Sunday, about me becoming a celebrity, about how we'd cope with it all? You said you were for it one hundred percent."

She won't look me in the eye, she tries to hug me again but I won't have it. Reality dawns on me. "So that was all just a crock of shit eh? That's why you were cool about me having the famous chicks on my arm. You weren't worried, 'cos you never believed there would ever be any other chicks. Is that right?"

She doesn't answer so I ask her again, this time raising my voice. "Is that right Claire?"

She nods her head and says, "You've always been a bit of a dreamer. I just thought this would all blow over in a week or two. Then you'd find another job and we'd be back to normal."

Rubbing my hand over my face I explode, "Fuck Claire, you never believed in me at all. That fucking hurts!" It's like my guts are being twisted into knots inside me.

"You're blowing this out of proportion Davis."

"Am I? I've just found out you've lied to me. I've never lied to you about anything. Ever. I thought we were solid."

She's got a funny look on her face, and starts to say something. "I'm sorry, I…"

But I cut her off. "Is there anything else you've lied to me about? Anything else I should know about?" She's looking guilty as hell. "What is it?" I demand. "You'd better tell me now."

"That jacket I got on Saturday and gave to you, it was a freebie," she blurts. "I didn't pay for it." Then she bursts into tears.

Oh fuck, not the bloody water works. She'd better turn them off quick smart. Part of me want's to hug her, tell her that it's alright, that everything will be ok. But the other part of me want's to shake her and yell at her for lying to me, for not believing in me. So I just stand there trying to keep control of myself.

She's hiccupping, gulping for air, and she just keeps saying sorry over and over. I can't hold out any longer, and wrap my arms around her while stroking her hair. We gently rock back and forth for a while. I love her so much, but she's hurt me badly.

Finally we pull apart. She blows her nose and wipes her eyes and we move over to the couch, holding hands.

"Well I guess we need to have another talk, now that you know I'm going to be a *real* celeb. How do you feel about the fame, the chicks and everything?" I ask tentatively.

Looking at me with bloodshot eyes she wails, "I don't know! I'm not sure if I can handle it."

Now I'm in shock, but for a different reason. What the hell, this could change everything. "What do you mean? Why couldn't you handle it?"

"I don't want to see other girls on your arm," she wails, and then starts sobbing again.

"Well *you* can be on my arm then," I say soothingly. "I only came up with that idea to get me noticed more. Now that I've got the Channel Six deal everyone's gonna know me. It was just an idea babe."

"But I don't want to be in the spotlight like you do, it scares me."

Giving her hand a squeeze I admit "It scares me too babe, but it's all part of being a celeb."

Suddenly her face hardens and she almost spits out the words. "You should just stop it all now Davis, before it really takes off. That way things can go back to how they were. We can get back to normal."

"Fuck that shit,' I explode, "there's no way I'm going back to working for a bastard like Beaker. I'm not working my guts out and getting jack shit for it ever again."

I can't believe she's just come out with this. Jeezus, I've got an opportunity of a lifetime here and she wants me to throw it away, just because she doesn't want to be noticed. I tell her this, which leads to more tears. I get up and get a box of tissues for her.

Trying to lighten the mood I say, "What happened to the adventurous chickie babe I met overseas? She was up for anything, this would have been a piece of piss for her."

She looks at me and nearly snarls, "Life, that's what happened Davis. I'm locked into everything I always said I'd never do. I hate my job, I hate living here. I have no choice in anything anymore."

Shaking my head in exasperation I state, "But don't you see that with me becoming a celeb, life can become an adventure again. This will give us the freedom to choose what we want to do. We can live wherever we want. You know I hate this shit-hole too. Babe, you can quit your job and do whatever you want. It's all there for us, ready for the taking babe."

"Yeah but I'll just be tagging along after you. I still won't be doing my own thing," she says blowing her nose.

I can't believe she feels this way. "There's just one thing that really matters here Claire. Do you still love me?"

She fiddles with the tissue in her hand. "I think so, but I'm not sure."

I feel like she's just punched me in the guts. All the fight has gone out of me. Slumping in the seat I say resignedly, "Well there's no point in talking about anything else. Not if you don't know if you love me or not. Fuck!"

I put my head in my hands. My world has just been turned upside down. Now it's my turn to cry, I can't help it. She rubs my back, which makes me feel even worse. "I think we should have a break Davis," she whispers.

My head snaps up and I eyeball her, "So you can get your shit together and see if you still love me?" I sniffle.

"Yeah, it's probably a good idea babe, don't you think?"

I don't know what to think, so I just nod. Tears are now streaming down my face, I can't believe this is happening. I'm so pissed off with her. I can't believe she never told me any of this. But the truth is I love her, and hopefully by giving her some space she'll sort herself out. This is all happening so fast, one minute we're fine, the next it's all falling apart. She's not sure if she loves me. Fuck. She doesn't believe in me. Fuck. Maybe it's better I've found all this out now.

I look at her. "Babe, you're killing me here. But I want you to know that I love you, and if you need some time then I guess you'd better have it."

Part of me is feeling like a pussy, I should just tell her to fuck off, tell her that I never want to see her again. But I can't do that, this is the girl I want to marry. Well I thought I wanted to marry her, now who bloody knows, I'm so confused.

She hugs me and we both sit there crying for a while. I tell her that I'll probably move back into Mum and Dad's, she can stay in the house rent free until the lease is up, which is only a couple of months away. There's no way I can stay here another minute, so I pack a bag, jump in the ute and head for the city. I'll stay in a hotel for the night rather than landing on the folks' doorstep. I don't feel like talking to anyone about this yet.

Chapter 10

Mum and Dad are staring at me with their mouths hanging open in disbelief. We're in the kitchen, and Dad just commented that I look like shit, that I must have been partying hard last night. I wish, I spent the night in a crappy Formula Two hotel in the city. It was shit, but at least I was anonymous. So I've just told them about me and Claire 'having a break'. They're as shocked as I was. Dad recovers first, finally saying, "Well I didn't see that one coming. Are you ok about it?"

Shaking my head I burst into tears. Fuck, I'm acting like a two year old, this is bullshit. They move either side of me and both start murmuring that it'll be ok, while rubbing my back and shoulders. Oh God, this makes me really turn on the water works. I sob out the fact that Claire doesn't believe in me, that she doesn't know if she loves me anymore. The murmuring and rubbing abruptly stops, I look up and see them staring at each other. I can see the pain on Mum's face, and Dad's shaking his head in astonishment. I cross the kitchen to grab a paper towel, and blow my nose noisily into it. There's copious amounts of snot coming out of me.

"Oh Davis," says Mum, but I put up my hand to stop her from continuing.

"Can we wait for a bit to talk about it? I've got to get my shit together."

They both absolutely agree. Mum declares that this is an emergency, so she rummages around in the pantry and pulls out a packet of Mint Slice biscuits. We all stand there, hoeing into them. I'm trying not to make any eye contact with Mum and Dad, but it's useless. I can feel their concern radiating out towards me. Shoving another bikkie in my mouth makes me feel a bit better, so I give them a small smile. Dad pats me on the back and tells me that he's been contacted by *The Weekly Star* magazine, they want to do an article about me. This perks me up a bit. I raise my eyebrows in question, signalling him to elaborate. I seem to have a conveyer belt of biscuits going into my mouth now, so I can't talk at this point.

"Yeah," he says, "remember the paparazzi guy that caught you lot at Taxie restaurant the other night? He's sold his photos to them, so they're all fired up about getting you in the next issue. They want to do a four page spread on you."

I'm trying to swallow the biscuits, but they're not going down too well. Mum shakes her head at me and asks if I want a glass of juice to help wash them down. I give her a full on grin, which must look pretty gross because she flinches and rushes to the fridge to get the juice. Dad laughs and claps me on the shoulder.

"That's my boy, you'll be back to your old self in no time. Now *The Weekly Star* originally offered you twenty grand to do the spread. I told 'em that for four pages they could expect to pay double that. So they've agreed to forty grand. Whaddaya reckon of that?"

Taking a chug of juice I reply, "Good onya Dad."

"Yeah, forty grand seems to be the flavour of the week eh!" he chuckles. "Now do you want to talk business yet or wait? I want to run through a few things with you before our meeting with Channel Six."

I agree that now's a good time, so we head into his study. I give him the lowdown on bringing Jacobs, Jonno, and Ajala on board. He's already touched base with Jacobs and Ajala, he reckons they sound perfect. When I tell him about how much I've offered to pay them all, he looks at me and says, "Smart move Davis. If you look after those closest to you, they'll always look after you."

I'm glad Dad gets it. "Yeah that's what I reckon. Bruce thought I was a bloody idiot for paying them so much."

"Sounds like you've been copping it from all sides, son."

I sigh and reply, "You're right about that."

Dad's sitting opposite me in his office chair. Using his feet he rolls himself towards me, then puts his hands on my knees and looks me in the eye. "Mate, your life is about to change in a very big way, and a lot of people are gonna feel threatened by that. It's only natural. Generally we all hate change. Especially if someone's moving up in the world, others might feel left behind. Try not to take it too personally eh."

I roll my eyes at him. "Well it's a bit bloody hard not to, especially when it's your girlfriend and your best mate. What the hell are you meant to do then?"

He pats my knee gently while saying, "Stay true to yourself and what you believe in, that's all you can do son." Then he pushes himself back to his desk.

I get what he's saying, but… "Why can't they just be happy for me?"

"Because deep down they wish it was them," he says.

I can't argue with that, it makes too much sense to me. "Thanks Yoda," I joke, and we both laugh.

"I know you feel like shit with what's happened with Claire, that's only natural, but it'll work itself out. Now, about this Channel Six meeting," he rubs his hands together, he's got a cheeky grin on his face, "I reckon we might be able to squeeze a bit more out of them. Let's try for forty five k per segment eh?"

$$$$$$$$$$

The meeting at Channel Six is a breeze, Dad easily gets the extra five grand out of them for my *Good Morning Today* gig, and they want to pay me another twenty grand for the interview on *Tonight's Current Affairs*, which will be shot early Wednesday arvo.

Dad said to me afterwards, "Mate, if they want to throw their money at you, you'd better be prepared to catch it!" I reckon he's spot on.

Turns out they've got a small team set up for my weekly 'respect' segment, which is totally cool. All I have to do is tell them what I want to have happen, and it'll get done. They also said that if I have trouble coming up with ideas each week they'll help me with that too, which is unreal, I was a bit worried about that side of things.

We're now in Dad's car, driving back to Carlton from the studio. "What are you gonna do about living arrangements?" he asks. "I take it that you're not going back to Melton."

"I was kind of hoping to move back in with you and Mum," I say shiftily.

He looks at me like I'm nuts. "Jeezus, why would you wanna do that?"

"I've got nowhere else to go, what do you expect me to do?" I retort.

He pulls up at a red light and looks at me. "Not bloody move back in with us. You're a cashed up celebrity. Get yourself a groovy bachelor pad in the city or somewhere. Anywhere but with us. I love ya son, but honestly, your Mum and I enjoy our space these days." He gives a dirty chuckle at the end of this.

I can't help but smile. "Yeah you're right, I'm still not used to this celebrity caper. I keep forgetting I'll be rolling in it soon."

"You're already rolling in it. Have you checked out your online sales lately? You're killing it. You'll have to order some more stock real soon."

Man, with everything that's been happening lately I'd almost forgotten about all that. Just as well Dad's on the case. The car takes off and I nod to myself, "Yeah I like the idea of a place in the city, maybe an apartment."

"Forget the apartment, go for the bloody penthouse!" he cries.

"Yeah that'd be pretty cool, I'm gonna miss not having Bruce next door though. It'll be weird not seeing him every day, he's a good mate."

Dad gives me a sideways look, "Even though he gives you the shits sometimes?"

"Yeah, well who doesn't give you the shits now and again?" I counter.

Dad thumps the steering wheel and says excitedly, "Hey we should drop into the office, see what Doug's got on the books. He might be able to point you in the right direction. Give him a call and see if he's in."

I do, and he is, so we head there straight away. I haven't been to the office in ages. When we rock up, Holly's busily painting her nails at the reception desk. Dad is not impressed. "Oi, put that away, that is *not* a good look for the agency," he thunders at her.

She shoves the bottle of nail varnish into a drawer, then jumps up and comes around to give him a big hug, while simultaneously holding her fingers out at a weird angle and gushing about what a nice surprise it is to see us.

"Sprung bad" I say.

She glares at me for a second then says, "It's not my fault, nobody told me that you were coming in."

Dad just hmmphs at her and strides off to Doug's office.

Holly wants to know all the goss, so I give her a brief rundown on everything. She grabs my arm in sympathy when she hears about Claire, smudging her nails on my shirt. So now I've got hot pink smudges on my sleeve - she's less than impressed, and tells me she'll just have to redo them as soon as Dad leaves. Yeah, he'd just love that.

Dad must have quickly worded Doug up about why we're here, because he grasps me in a hug as soon as I walk in, telling me solemnly "I'm here for you bro. Let's find you the best bloody bachelor pad in Melbourne, that'll show her!"

Dad and I exchange a look, Doug's a funny one.

"I don't want to show her anything," I state, "I just want a place to live."

"Yeah right," he says, giving me a wink as he slides behind his desk. "We might be able to find something that's up to your calibre, I assume you want all the bells and whistles right?"

Dad takes over. "Davis needs something that oozes style, don't you Davis."

I sit down on one of the chairs and cross my legs. "Guys, I don't know what I want."

"That's perfect, leave it to us," Doug shouts. We both have the same habit of shouting when we get excited. He and Dad are nodding to each other. I'm not sure if this is such a good idea.

"I don't want a pimped up place, just something central with garage space and…."

They're not even listening to me, they're completely engrossed with the computer screen. Doug mumbles something into Dad's ear and both their eyes light up. "Perfect," says Dad.

A few of the office girls put their heads around the door and say g'day, they want to know what Doug's all worked up about. They heard him shouting from their cubicles, at this rate the whole bloody world will know I've split up with Claire. I should probably send out a tweet about it.

I fill the girls in. They ooh and aah, and say how sorry they are to hear about the breakup. I tell them that we're looking for a place for me to live. Both Doug and Dad are oblivious that there's another conversation going on in the room. Cheryl, who's been with the agency for years, looks fondly over at them both and says, "It reminds me of old times, seeing them sitting there with their heads together like that."

Suddenly Dad and Doug say, "Yes!" at the same time and give each other a high-five.

"I'll ring him now," says Doug excitedly.

I stand up. "Hey, hey, you might want to run it past me first, guys. See if I like it."

They're both grinning at me. "Oh I think you'll like it," says Dad.

"Yeah, you'd have to be a bloody dickhead not to," quips Doug.

"Which one is it?" Cheryl asks.

"The penthouse at Paradise Towers," they say together. Well, Doug actually shouts it.

Cheryl looks at me. "Trust them on this one Davis, you're gonna love it. That place is wild." Then she ushers the girls out and leaves us to it.

I make a move towards the desk, but Dad holds up a finger and stops me. "Take a seat Davis, Doug and I will give you the lowdown on the joint."

I take a deep breath and can't help but laugh, here comes the sales pitch. Bloody hell, with two of them on the job I don't stand a chance!

"Come on then, hit me with it," I encourage.

Dad steeples his fingers, then he's off. "Imagine a place where everything's at your fingertips. The city is your playground, and your penthouse is your sanctuary. A sanctuary equipped with a state of the art Bose sound system. Your own games room, complete with billiard table and arcade games. A rooftop spa and barbeque area. Total security is guaranteed. You've got your own concierge cum security guard on duty twenty four seven."

Dad looks at Doug. They give a small nod to each other, then Doug takes over. "But wait, there's more. You've got your own twelve seat movie theatre, state of the art office, and three luxurious bedrooms. The complex also has a twenty five metre lap pool, sauna, conference room, and fully equipped gym. But we're saving the best till last. Do you want to tell him Dad, or should I?"

Dad waves his hand indulgently at Doug. "Oh you go for it mate."

Doug sits forward in his chair and shouts, "It's got its own car lift and double sky garage, you can park your cars in your bloody living room on the thirty second floor!" He sits back in his chair looking at me smugly.

I'm having trouble processing this concept, but they both immediately understand my look of incomprehension. Man that's the good thing about family, they really get you. So Dad smiles and starts talking to me like I'm a five year old. He explains that you park your car on the underground turntable, put your thumb print on the keypad, and the car is taken up via a car lift to the penthouse on the thirty second floor.

"It's the first one in Australia mate, you'll be blown away," Dad assures me.

"Ok I get it now, yeah it sounds pretty awesome," I agree.

Doug wants to know if he can ring the guy now. I'm a bit worried about how much it'll cost, but Dad tells me not to worry, he knows the developer, and he reckons he'll be stoked to lease it to a celeb like me. Apparently it's fully furnished, all good to go.

$$\$\$\$\$\$\$\$\$\$\$$$

Oh my fucking God! We're all standing on the outdoor terrace of the penthouse at Paradise Towers. The view is amazing, the penthouse is unbelievable. I feel like a kid in a candy shop, there's so much to explore. The car-lift-sky-garage thing is just incredible. We put Doug's Beamer in it, and were all just gobsmacked as we watched the car ascend to the penthouse from the street outside. The car lift is all glass, so you can watch it go up and down.

The developer's name is Neville, he's come to meet us onsite and says he's happy to show us around. He says he's a big fan of my stuff so far, and that he'd love for me to live here. He reckons a six month contract will work well for him. Dad and Neville mosey off inside to talk shop, leaving me and Doug alone on the terrace together.

"Pretty cool eh?" Doug asks.

"Cool's not the word, magnificent comes closer. Still doesn't do it justice though."

"Told ya you'd like it. C'mon, let's check out the games room again," he says excitedly.

We muck around in there for a bit, there's plenty to keep us occupied. It's got full on proper arcade games. There's one called *Street Racer Pro* that's got seating for two players, and there's another one called *Thrill Shooter*, which has got two rifles ready to blow the baddies away with. The pinball machine is awesome, as is the full sized pool table. There's even a fully stocked bar. It's the ultimate man cave. We have some fun for a while, then figure we'd better find out what Dad's up to.

We spot him and Neville sitting in the rooftop spa sucking on a can of soft drink each, they're laughing and clowning around. Jeezus, you can't take my Dad anywhere. Doug and I look at each other and both groan.

"I didn't know they were that good-a mates," Doug says.

I just shake my head. "Un-fucking-believable. C'mon, we'd better go and get him."

As soon as he sees us Dad tells us to get our gear off and jump in. There's no way I'm doing that.

"Oh come on you two, don't wimp out on me," he coaxes.

Doug's already kicking off his shoes and dropping his jacket on a sun lounger. He mutters to me out of the corner of his mouth, "Just do it Davis, if Dad's in there it's for a good reason. Get your gear off."

He's probably right, but fuck me, this is madness. I know I'll laugh about this later, but at the moment I feel like a bloody idiot. Here goes nothing. I strip off, leaving my jocks on. Doug's done the same. We approach the spa together, but Neville pipes up, "Lose the jocks, boys."

Doug and I look at each other then look at Dad. He gives us a nod, then stands up - his family jewels are on display for all to see.

"Come on boys," he chirps, "I thought I brought you up not to be shy."

I don't want to look at his cock, but I can't help it, my eyes are drawn to it. Dad gives his hips a shake, causing it to flop back and forth. Doug and I both go "Eww" at the same time, he must have been looking too! But we do as we're told. How the hell does Dad do this to me? I notice Neville checking out Dad's bum while he's standing up. Oh Jeezus he must be gay. Now I feel really uncomfortable, so I put my hands in front of my dick while we take the final few steps to the spa. But that's where any dignity stops, there just isn't a way to get into one of these things without showing your meat and two veg.

Doug quickly jumps in and I follow his lead. Sure enough Neville's eyes follow our every move, he's copping a good old look. Just as we've sat down, Neville asks if one of us boys can get him another can of lemonade. Oh Jeezus. I'm filled with horror. Doug and I stare at each other, neither of us makes a move, so I tell him point blank that I'm not doing it. Poor Doug scowls at me and clamours out of the spa, which is *not* a pretty sight, at least not for me and Dad. Neville seems to enjoy it though.

Dad calls out, "Bring a few more out for us too Doug," then he gives me a wink. At least Dad's got a heart, although he probably doesn't want to see Doug's hairy arsehole again.

Neville prattles on about the penthouse and I try to look interested for a while, but he keeps droning on and on. I let Dad and Doug do all the talking and just zone out for a while. Man this is an incredible experience. I'm sitting in a spa on the thirty second floor of the wildest apartment block I've ever seen. No wonder it's called Paradise Towers. The penthouse terrace wraps around most of the building, and from the spa area we've got a perfect view of the bay. Lucky it's a nice spring day. The ocean is twinkling at us, boats are bobbing about. I close my eyes for a minute, just enjoying the moment.

But I'm rocketed out of my nice relaxing daydream when I feel a hand on my thigh, creeping its way up towards my dick. My eyes snap open and I do a mad scramble kind of move to try and get away, splashing water everywhere. Doug pisses himself laughing and pokes me in the ribs. "Got ya," he smirks at me. Bastard!

Dad rolls his eyes at us and says to Neville, "You'd think with them being adults and all that they'd behave themselves, but oh no."

Neville gives a slimy grin. "There's nothing wrong with boys being naughty. I like it when they're bad."

"I bet you do," booms Dad, clapping Neville on the shoulder. Then he skulls the rest of his can of drink and tells Neville that this has been beaut, but Doug's got an appointment soon so we'd better make tracks. Thank God! Now we've all got to get out of the bloody spa. Neville waits till last. I swear I can feel his beady little eyes on my arse as I scramble out.

As Dad's getting out he lets off a massive fart. "Whoops, must be the lemonade," he says with a laugh. Doug and I crack up, but Neville looks a bit grossed out. Good, welcome to our world mate! Nice one Dad.

On the way out of the building Neville introduces me to the concierge/security guy who's decked out in a uniform, including a hat. He looks pretty buff, you wouldn't want to mess with him. His badge says Mr Porter, Jeeze it's weird how some people's surnames are like their jobs. Lucky mine isn't, I wouldn't want to be an S&M dude spanking people for a living!

Mr Porter welcomes me to the building and assures me that if I require anything at all I just need to contact him. I have my thumb print and a head shot taken and entered into the computer, allowing me access to the building and sky garage. This biometric security stuff is a total spin out, I feel like I'm James-bloody-Bond.

In the car on the way back to the real estate office, I ask Dad what the hell he was thinking by getting us all naked in the spa with Neville. He turns round from the front passenger seat to look at me. "Only getting you the bargain of the century boy."

"But why did we have to get naked, huh?" I whine.

"Because I'm a genius, *I* suggested it!" he says happily.

"You what!" Doug and I both shriek together.

Dad shakes his head at us. "You two have got so much to learn. Of course I bloody suggested it. What's the best way to get what you want? Make the other person think it's their idea, of course."

"I'm not following you here. Please explain."

"Jeezus Davis. The fact that Neville's as gay as a Mardi Gras is as plain as the nose on your face, right?" Doug and I both agree with him, and he continues. "Well, what poofter doesn't like to be surrounded with good looking virile men, preferably naked in a spa? Answer me that." Doug and I have to agree with him on that one as well.

"So I'm a genius, because I casually mentioned having a naked spa together early on in our conversation, then moved onto something else. But the seed was sown, right?" Dad taps his nose, Doug and I nod again.

"Then I told him about wanting the penthouse for six months at fifteen hundred a week. Lucky I just happened to have a rough lease agreement with me, as well as a confidentially agreement, eh!" Doug looks at me in the rear vision mirror and raises his eyebrows.

Dad continues on, "Davis, Neville would do anything for bragging rights about getting you naked in a spa. So, because I've already sown the seed, *he* brings it up. He says it's a great day for a spa, and if we all join him in it naked he'll be happy to sign a lease today." Dad laughs, "He was thinking with his dick, not his head. So *we* get a great deal, and unfortunately for him he can't say anything to anyone, otherwise we can sue him! Howzat!!"

Doug and I crack up. "Yeah you're a fucking genius Dad, just don't make me get naked for anything else ever again ok?' I deadpan.

"And don't make me show my arse to a poofter ever again," adds Doug.

"Sorry boys, but it was worth it. You get to move into your new penthouse *today* Davis, how good is that!"

I'm suspicious though. "Did you have this planned before we came? How did you get the lease and confidentially stuff."

He shrugs, "Look, I had a rough idea of what I wanted to have happen. You've always gotta know your outcome right? I knew Neville was gay and that the penthouse had a spa, so I grabbed the lease and confidentially agreement from Cheryl before we left the office. I *always* used to make sure she had some on hand." Giving Doug's hair a ruffle he adds, "You never know when a great deal's gonna show up, do ya Dougie!"

"Unbelievable," I mutter, then say to them both, "Well thanks for helping me out with this guys, although I'll never be able to get in that spa without thinking of slimy Neville, and you farting in his face Dad," which cracks us all up.

Doug weaves in and out of the traffic, we're coming up to another set of lights and the traffic is moving pretty slowly. Suddenly a three wheeled Spyder passes us, and there I am plastered all over the billboard it's towing. We all start pointing and jabbering like monkeys. I whip out my phone and take a picture of it, this is so cool. I'll have to give Eric another call and tell him how good it looks - I still haven't caught up with him yet.

"You're gonna have to get a new car Davis, you don't want your shit heap of a ute parked in your living room," Doug snorts.

"Too right," I agree. "Maybe I can hire something for now, until I can afford my dream car, my Porsche. The Cayman S Black Edition."

"Sounds snazzy," says Dad.

"Yeah, they only made five hundred of 'em. That's what I'd have if I could have anything. They're hot."

Doug wants to know how much they are, so I tell him that they start at a hundred and fifty thousand and work their way up, depending on what optional extras you want. They both whistle at the cost.

"Maybe I could work that into a contract somewhere in the future," Dad mutters to himself.

But I hear him and say, "Nup. I want to buy one myself, then I'll know I've really made it."

Doug takes us back to the real estate office where Holly is now busy reading a trashy magazine. She tries to hide it, but Dad's already spotted it. "Jeezus Holly, don't you do *any* work? You're meant to be the face of the business."

She sits up straight. "Exactly!" she says, smiling winningly at him. "That's why it's so important that my nails are done and that I know all about the latest fashion trends. So I can look good and make a great first impression with our clients."

Dad shakes his head at her. "Not good enough princess. C'mon Davis, we'd better go and pick up all your stuff."

I decline his offer of help because I've only got some clothes, some CDs and a few DVD's that I want to take with me. The penthouse is already set up with everything else I could possibly need. As Neville proved today, it's even stocked with towels and drinks. You name it, it's there.

$$$$$$$$$$$

Just as I haul the last garbage bag full of stuff into the back of the ute Bruce pulls into his drive. He gives me a wave and saunters over, raising his eyebrow at what I'm doing. So I tell him about Claire and me having a break. He immediately turns pale, and apologises for being such a prick yesterday. There's no harm done, I try to brush it off, we all have our bad days. He wants to know where I'm going, so I tell him about Paradise Towers. He's gobsmacked, his eyes are nearly bulging out of his head, especially when I tell him about the car lift and sky garage. He asks when he can come over and check it out, so I invite him over tonight - adding that I'm not up for any other company, is it ok if he comes by himself. He's up for that, thank God. I couldn't be bothered with Trace today, I'm not in the mood to put up with her crap. I tell Bruce I'll see him later, and head back inside to make sure I've got everything.

The house seems so quiet, so empty. I'm pretty sure I've got everything packed now. I never thought it would come to this, I always imagined that Claire and I would get married and live happily ever after. I know it sounds corny, old fashioned even, but that's the way I wanted things to be. To have that dream blown to smithereens is going to take some getting used to. I'm still mixed up about how I feel. She's a fucking bitch for doing this to me, but on the other hand, I'd do anything to turn back time. Yeah, I'd like to turn it back to when she still loved me, when she still believed in me. Now I'm getting upset again, I slam the bedroom door shut. Fuck it, I don't know what's going on in her head. I thought I did but I was obviously wrong. Clenching my jaw I take one last look around the lounge and slam the front door behind me. Jumping into the ute, I burn some rubber as I leave. Man I can't get out of there fast enough.

On the drive into town I'm trying to focus on the positives. I hate feeling like shit, and if it's one thing that Dad's taught me, it's that what you focus on gets bigger, whether it be good or bad. So choose what you focus on carefully, because you'll get more of it coming your way. Unlike Claire, I believe that you *do* have a choice in life. Yeah you might have a shit job, but if you hate it that much then change it. I never realised that she felt so powerless, that's something only she can work on.

I'm starting to feel a bit better, getting a better perspective on things. At least I've attempted to make a change in my life. Sure I got fired and that's gonna change things, but I didn't fall in a heap and whinge about it, or become a victim of circumstance. I had a vision. Admittedly a crazy vision, but everything in life starts with an idea. The car next to me toots their horn, some kids in the backseat wave at me, so I roll down the window and give them a big wave back. This puts a smile back on my face. Fuck me, life is one hell of a ride! Before I know it I'm in the city, next stop Paradise Towers.

I'm parked over the road, Paradise Towers is looming above me. I wanted to stop and watch a car go up the lift again. Don't think I'll ever get sick of seeing that. My ute's gonna look pretty funny compared to the Lotus I just saw going up. Pulling into the garage driveway, I place my thumb on the biometric control pad. My face immediately comes up on a screen and 'access granted' flashes before me, activating the security roller door which opens, allowing me to drive into the car lift area. This is *so* cool. I slowly inch the ute forward, onto the turntable. I think I'm in the right spot but I'm not sure. I don't want to stuff it up and decide it's probably best to go and grab Mr Porter.

I should have taken a photo of his face when he cops a look at my crappy ute sitting there. Shocked is an understatement, but he doesn't say anything. He advises me to pull forward a bit more, which I do. Then I jump out and put my thumb on another biometric control pad. The turntable springs into action and the car turns and slides into the glass car lift. I can't stop smiling. This is just awesome, it's like magic, I can't wait to show Bruce!

Mr Porter asks if I'd like him to show me up to the penthouse and I readily agree. Who knows what other techy things I'll encounter up there? I didn't take much notice earlier today when Neville showed us around. The lift requires my thumb print to get it going, then we're whisked up to the penthouse. The lift opens in the private foyer, and this time I notice two cameras above the entry door, as well as another security thumb pad. I comment on the amount of security, and Mr Porter informs me that this establishment is only for the most 'discerning clients.' I give a snort at this, and notice him give a bit of a smirk.

Once we're inside he shows me how the security system works, and how to contact the front desk, which is done via a video phone. I'm to inform them of anyone who will be visiting, and my guests will have their photo taken on their first visit, which will then be added to my visitor directory file. The front door of the building has facial recognition technology, so once they're in the data base I won't have to call reception to let them in, the door will automatically open for them as well as for me. He informs me that as a backup there's always someone on duty at reception.

We wander into the lounge and there she is, my crappy old ute is sitting there looking totally out of place in this sleek modern environment. I have to laugh, it looks so bloody ridiculous. I whip out my phone and take a photo.

"Bet you've never seen anything like that before eh!" I joke.

Mr Porter laughs. "It is a bit of a sight," he agrees.

I wallop him on the shoulder. "Good, I'm glad you've got a sense of humour. Mate, if I'm going to live here can we not be so formal?"

Mr Porter immediately relaxes his stance. "That's fine with me. Some clients like to keep it impersonal, others are more relaxed. I'm happy to fit in with what works for you sir."

"Well you can drop the sir and call me Davis. There's only one person who calls me sir, and that's Jacobs my security chief. You'll probably meet him tomorrow if you're on duty."

Mr Porter's eyes bore into mine. "That wouldn't be Joseph Jacobs by any chance would it?"

I shrug my shoulders. 'Dunno, I just know him as Jacobs. He used to work at Taxie restaurant till I poached him."

Mr Porter nods. "Yes, I'd heard he was having a change. Well you've certainly bagged yourself the best of the best there."

"You two know each other then, do ya? Oh and by the way, can I drop the Mr and just call you Porter?"

Mr Porter shuffles his feet a bit and replies, "Yes, Joseph and I know each other, we worked on a job together years ago. And certainly *Davis*, you can just call me *Porter* if you wish."

He spends some time showing me how to use all the gadgets. You need a barista degree to get the coffee machine working. The sound system's awesome. Everything is available at the push of a button, including the curtains, the mood lighting - both inside and out, and the pop-up TV that's built into the end of my bed. Jeezus this place is even better than I first thought. As soon as he leaves I call Bruce.

"Maaate, fuck waiting till tonight, can you get your arse over here now?"

"You bloody bet, I'm on it. See you soon maaate."

I give Eric a call, I really want to catch up with him, but Marissa tells me that he's had to go to Perth for a few days. Maybe I can get him on his mobile. So I try his number, but end up having to leave a message. Then I call down to let Porter know that Bruce is coming. Spewing Eric's in Perth, it would have been great to get him over to check out my new pad too.

$$$$$$$$$

"Fuuuuck!" Bruce is standing in the living room looking at my ute. He's been saying fuck over and over for the past few minutes. "This is in-fucking-sane Davis, how did you find this place?"

"Dad n' Doug got onto it for me, it's unreal eh?"

He moves over towards the windows, shaking his head. "Oh mate, talk about landing on your feet. You should *thank* Claire for wanting a break, otherwise you'd never have found this place."

Well I hadn't thought of it like that before, but he's right. "Come and check out the spa," I urge.

So we traipse outside, the wind has picked up a bit and it's quite blowy now. We chuck a lap of the terrace, both of us laughing and carrying on. I tell him about Dad making Doug and me get in the spa naked with Neville, and how Dad farted in his face. This totally cracks him up, he has to hang onto the back of one of the loungers to steady himself. Then he screws up his face and tells me that I'd better put an extra shot of chlorine in the spa to kill off all the nasties.

Bruce oohs and aahs at the theatrette and the huge movie screen, and we settle ourselves in the recliners for a bit, and discover that between each seat is a mini fridge. Oh happy days!

I've saved the best bit of the tour till last, I ask him to close his eyes before I reveal the games room to him. I even put my hands over his eyes so he can't peek.

"Mate are you reverting to your childhood or something?" he asks. "Yesterday you're asking me to guess shit, today you've got me blindfolded."

"Yeah well if I'm gonna be a kid again this is the place to do it." I steer him into the room and take my hands away. He looks at me first, then surveys the room.

160

"Oh you've got to be kidding me, far out," he says excitedly as he trys to take it all in. "These are the real deal. I don't believe it!"

"Yep, they're all proper arcade games, none of that namby-pamby crap here."

"Fuck me, this is the ultimate," he bellows.

"What do you want to play first? *Thrill Shooter* or *Street Racer Pro*?" I shout.

He starts jumping up and down screaming at the top of his lungs, "Shake-n-bake baby, shake-n-bake!" Bruce rushes over to *Street Racer Pro* and says with a manic look in his eye, "Which car do you want?"

I bounce over after him, I'm shouting with excitement too. "Doesn't matter, just pick one." He chooses the car console on the left and eases himself down into the seat. I take the right one and we grin at each other like lunatics. He whips my arse, three games in a row, but I get my own back when we move over to the *Thrill Shooter*. Ha! The two grans better watch out now, I'll be able to whip their arses too!

Man this is the ultimate. We play for hours, finally calling it quits at ten o'clock when Trace calls, commanding Bruce to get his butt home.

Chapter 11

The conference room in Paradise Towers is way cool, just what I'd expect after seeing the calibre of luxe the rest of this place has got. It's on the twentieth floor and has a great view over the city. Everyone's here. Jacobs did a double take when he first met Jonno, I should have warned him that Jonno's a full on bogan. He's currently kitted out with a Tigers' beanie shoved onto his balding head, teamed with a nice red flanno shirt worn open, over a super tight black Harley Davidson t-shirt. Tight black jeans clad his skinny chicken legs, pushing his beer gut up over his belt. It's not a good look – he looks bloody pregnant. I'll definitely have to do something about a uniform, and soon. Maybe I'll get him into a nice navy blue suit and crisp white shirt like Jacobs is wearing, it oozes sophistication and professionalism.

Clapping my hands to get everyone's attention, I ask them to take a seat. There's only five of us and the conference table's way too big, it could probably seat twenty, so we all sit clumped together at one end. I'm about to start my welcome speech when the door opens and a tiny Asian lady, in what looks like a maid's uniform, wheels in a trolley that's laden with drinks and nibblies. Dad rubs his hands together and Jonno licks his lips in anticipation, but I'm a bit confused, I didn't order this. So I stand up and go over to her, asking what's going on. Apparently any conference that's held in the building is always catered for, it's a complimentary service. Cool! I was wondering why Porter wanted to know how many people to expect when I asked him about using the conference room last night, I thought it was because he'd have to take everyone's photo for my security file. Nice one, Paradise Towers sure knows how to look after you.

Dad must have heard that the food's complimentary, Jeezus he's got good hearing. He urges the others to help themselves, saying that it's on the house. Ajala gives a little giggle, but I notice her licking her lips too. What the fuck is it about people and free food? You'd think they hadn't eaten for a month. I tell the trolley lady that she can just leave it there, there's no need to serve us, and she smiles, gives a tiny bow, and makes a fast exit. As soon as she's gone there's a stampede for the trolley. Jacobs remains seated, but the other three are already crowding around, shoving cake into their mouths. I look over at Jacobs and he gives a small shrug, so I tell him to get his arse over here if he wants anything to eat, otherwise he'll miss out. I've gotta say it's a pretty good spread, the petite triangle sangas are now disappearing at a rapid rate. I'd better grab some quick smart.

After we've all gorged ourselves I get down to business. First, I make sure that everyone's met each other and knows what their role is. Then I ask each of them to stand up and tell us all a bit about themselves. I know it's a bit wanky, but I feel it's the right thing to do. Ajala starts off, telling us she's doing a bachelor's degree in accounting at uni. She keeps gushing that she's just so happy to be here, she can't wait to start working as my social media coordinator.

Dad stands up and shares a bit about himself, then it's Jacobs's turn. He's just introduced himself and given us all a bit of a run down on how he likes to keep a tight reign of all things security wise, when Jonno interrupts him, he wants to know what Jacobs is going to teach him.

Jacobs gives Jonno a steely look and tells him, "You'd be surprised at how much goes into coordinating a safe environment for a celebrity. I can teach you everything you need to know in order to be an *exceptional* 2IC."

Jonno looks at him blankly. "What's a 2IC then?" he demands.

Jacobs takes a deep breath and says calmly, "It means second in charge, that will be your role, you will answer to me." Jacobs looks at me, "That's what we agreed upon, is it not sir?"

I stand up and place my hands on the table, so that I'm leaning forward slightly. "That's right Jacobs, you're the head honcho of our security posse. What you say goes," I swivel my eyes to Jonno. "Alright mate?"

Jonno nods his agreement as a smile slowly spreads across his face. "An *exceptional* 2IC, now I'm up for that!"

I sit back down to let Jacobs finish, but unfortunately he doesn't elaborate much on his past, he just skims over the same things that he told me. It seems that Jacobs is a bit of a dark horse.

Then it's Jonno's turn. He tells us all how stoked he is to be here, and what a blast it was telling Beaker to stuff his job because he was coming to work for me. He's just telling us how he's only ever worked in plastics, and that this is the chance of a lifetime for him, when there's a discreet knock at the door.

I call out, "Come in," and in Porter strides, looking very pissed off about something. Shoving a newspaper at me, he tells me that I need to see this.

Oh shit. There on the front page of *News of The Day* is a naked photo of me clambering out of the spa, with Neville in the background ogling my arse. The photo is very grainy, but you can definitely tell it's me. The headline reads, 'Naked spa romp, is Davis gay?' Fuck me, I'm speechless. I quickly hand it over to Dad. He groans when he sees it and says, "Oh mate, oh shit." It then gets passed around to the others. Jonno cracks up laughing, but Jacobs looks like he'd like to murder someone.

Porter's still standing there. "I'm so sorry about this Davis," he laments, "someone must have taken it with a telephoto lens from a nearby building. It's totally unacceptable. Paradise Towers sincerely apologises for this."

Jonno's still sniggering. I look up at Porter and say, "Hey it's not your fault, shit happens. Admittedly this is embarrassing shit, but what can you do?"

"You can sue them Sir," Jacobs growls. "It's slander, a very serious matter. Your reputation is at stake here."

Now it's my turn to snigger, "Well I wouldn't go that far."

"I would," Dad declares, and everyone else agrees with him.

A mobile rings, it's coming from Porter's jacket. He answers it and says to me, "Mr Horton is on the phone, he would like to apologise to you personally."

I have no idea who Mr Horton is. Dad whispers to me, "It's Neville."

So I take the call. He's in a steaming rage over the whole thing, and rants on for a good five minutes about it, saying that our privacy has been invaded and that he wants to take action immediately. Thanking him for his concern, I tell him he should talk to Dad about it. He assures me that if there's anything I need, or that he can do for me, I just have to ask and it's done. I happily hand the phone over to Dad, I'll let them sort it out between them.

Porter and Jacobs have moved over to the bank of windows and are having a quiet chat, I'd forgotten that they know each other. Jonno and Ajala are still engrossed with the newspaper.

Ajala says to me, "I'm thinking that we will need to do some social media damage control for this, Mr Davis." Her eyes are gleaming with excitement, "There will be a lot to attend to."

I nod and agree with her, "I'm glad it's you not me who's gotta do it all. Just tell me what you need to know."

She whips out her phone and asks me exactly what happened yesterday, she wants to record it so she can transcribe it later. I'm not sure about this, I don't know if I want her recording me. Shit, I've got bloody Bruce's voice in my head telling me to be careful, so I tell her that Jacobs and Jonno need to know the full story as well, and that I want to wait so that I can tell everyone together. She does a funny little Indian head waggle and plays with her phone. I'm not too comfortable with this whole recording caper, I want to run it by Jacobs while Dad's still on the phone.

I mosey on over to the windows where he and Porter are whispering. I catch the phrase 'Operation Zinger' as I approach, and they quickly shut up. What the fuck's Operation Zinger all about? Now's not the time to find out, I'll save it for later. Porter moves away, leaving Jacobs and I to it. So I ask Jacobs what he reckons about Ajala recording my conversation, and he immediately balks at the idea.

"Under no circumstances should you ever do that sir. She seems like a very nice young lady, but we really don't know much about her yet. She could use it against you in the future. Just tell her to take notes for now." Man, he and Bruce will get along together beautifully.

As I turn around Porter's about to close the door after him. He nods in my direction, then he's gone.

Dad's sitting there with a smug look on his face. I hate to think what he and Neville have come up with, luckily I don't have to wait to find out. He's bursting to tell us all. "Davis this is great, it's massive free publicity. I know it's not the kind of publicity you want, but it is what it is, so let's ride this wave."

I slump in my chair, I just know he's going to hit me with something, I can feel it. "Ok" I sigh, "What have you two got planned?"

Fingering the cleft in his chin he says, "Well Neville and I both agree that we should sue the newspaper, he's really wound up about this. He insists on paying all the legal costs." Dad stops playing with his chin and steeples his fingers, he's eyeing me off.

"And?" I ask.

"And what?" he casually asks. "That's it, we're gonna sue the bastards, end of story. No one calls my boy a poofter and gets away with it." He quickly looks at the others and adds, "Not that there's anything wrong with that of course, each to their own. But they're not getting away with sticking that label on my boy!"

My phone rings. It's Doug, he must have seen the paper too. I answer and there's hysterical laughter on the other end. Calling him a bastard I quickly hang up.

Right, it's time to get this meeting happening. I stand up and take charge. First I tell Ajala that we won't be recording anything that's said today due to confidentiality rules. Moving on, I inform everyone that there's a couple of things I need to fill them in on, namely my having a break with Claire, and what really happened yesterday in the spa. They're all sympathetic about the Claire issue, but Dad looks guilty as hell when I tell them it was his idea for us to get in the spa naked. He tries to defend himself by saying that he did it for me, to bag me a great deal, but the withering looks that the others throw his way are good enough for me. He seems duly chastised for a minute or two.

Next we move on to security details, we need to figure out how this is going to work, with the TV stuff, public appearances, etc. Jacobs suggests that he and Jonno accompany me to any TV interviews, my weekly segment at the studio, and any other public appearances. The best way to achieve this he says, is if I get a sedan style car, where he and Jonno can double as my drivers and bodyguards.

This sounds like a workable plan to me. I look over to Dad, who gives a nod and agrees it's a very sensible idea, he doesn't want me to get mobbed again like at the café the other day. Jacobs raises an enquiring eyebrow at me, so I fill him in on what happened. Ajala asks if I've seen the clip on YouTube yet. I tell her I have, but the others haven't, so we all watch it on her laptop. Man it's getting heaps of hits, it's now past seven hundred thousand. The respect chant is awesome and the power of it comes across in the video. Bailey did a great job filming it, he's captured the lot. Jacobs is horrified, and tells me that we were very lucky that things didn't turn nasty.

"That's exactly what I said," Dad quips, looking very pleased with himself.

Jacobs then explains that for larger public appearances he will need to hire more security for the event, and asks how would I feel about that? I can't see anything wrong with it, Dad gives the thumbs up too.

Ajala wants to know how the social media side of things will work. I've given this a lot of thought, I don't want to mislead people, that's not my style. So I've decided to be up front about having a social media coordinator working on my behalf, keeping the fans up to date with everything. I'll also send out my own tweets and posts, but only occasionally. I want to see what she thinks about this. When I share my thoughts, there's complete silence around the table for what seems like ages.

Maybe I've got this all wrong, but then Ajala grins, does her head waggle thing and says, "I like it Mr Davis. I was worried about how we could coordinate everything. But do you think the public will like the fact that it's me doing a post, not you?"

Folding my arms across my chest I answer, "I don't care what they think, I'd rather be honest than bullshit them. I'm sure other celebs outsource this shit but they just don't tell anyone. Respect, that's what it's all about."

Next I explain how I envision us working this social media system. I'll call Ajala each morning to get her up to speed with things, and I'll touch base with her throughout the day to keep her updated when stuff happens. For me, talking is heaps easier than typing, so calling her a few times a day is no problem at all.

"Does that work for you?" I ask her.

"Oh yes," she gushes, "that is an excellent plan."

I tell her she must introduce herself to my fans, and position herself as my personal eyes and ears, so to speak. She wiggles in her seat, sitting up proudly, full of importance. She wants to know if she should send me her posts first, so that I can approve them before she sends them live. Giving her a grin, I tell her that it's an excellent idea and I'm lucky to have her on board.

Turning to Jacobs and Jonno I say, "I guess I'll have to do the same with you two, let you know what's happening each day eh?"

"Yes, it's normal practice to have a daily briefing sir," Jacobs agrees.

Jonno's taken his beanie off and is scratching his head. Now seems the perfect time to broach the subject of a uniform. I ask him if he'd wear a suit like Jacobs. His eyes light up. "Fuck yeah, that'd be shit hot *sir*."

I laugh, "Cool, but you don't have to call me sir, Jonno. It sounds weird."

"Well get used to it, 'cos that's what I'm callin' ya from now on. Gotta show some respect, eh!" and he gives me a wink.

Next I ask Jacobs if he can get Jonno sorted with a suit. He looks relieved at the prospect.

Then I ask Dad if there's anything else that we need to cover now, and he mentions my products and how we need to keep an eye on the stock levels. I raise my eyebrows at Ajala and ask if she'd be interested in looking after that side of things as well. She jumps at the chance to do it, so I tell her to keep me updated with the results from the special webpage where people vote for the respect products they want. Last time I checked people wanted respect ashtrays, go figure. She assures me she's onto it, then slides over a card with her brother's name and website on it. She tells me that he hasn't contacted me yet because he wants me to check out his website first, to see if his services are what I'm after.

I decide that we might as well have our first daily briefing right now. The Channel Six interview is coming up this arvo, and I'll want my security posse with me. This raises the question of what car we'll use. Dad says we can use his Mercedes if we want, till I get something sorted, which sounds good to me.

Ajala's been busy typing for a few minutes, she swings the laptop round to face me, asking if her first post is ok. I read it, it's great. She's positioned herself as my personal reporter, on the job to keep everyone updated because, unfortunately I'm too busy to give them the time they deserve, and yet I don't want them to miss out on any of my news since my fans mean so much to me. It makes me look good, gives her importance, and makes the fans feel needed. It's perfect! I push it over

169

to Dad. He gives a chuckle as he reads it and then he gives her the double thumbs up.

Standing up I say "This meeting is now officially over." Smiling at them all I add, "I just want you all to know that I can't do this without you guys, I really want to thank you all for coming on board to help me out."

There're all grinning at me, then Ajala starts a little clap and the others join in. I'm a bit embarrassed, but it's nice of them to do it.

"Now let's all go upstairs, I'll give you a guided tour of my penthouse."

The reason I had the meeting in the conference room instead of in the office in the penthouse is because I wanted to set a standard right from the beginning. I wanted them to get the feeling that we're all doing a job, not just hanging out. If I'd had it in the penthouse it would have been too relaxed, too informal. But now that the standard has been set, I want to share my incredible home with them all.

Man, the penthouse has the same effect on everyone. It's jaw-dropping, eye-popping, sensory overload. Dad's made himself at home in the kitchen, he's whipping up some coffees while I give the others a tour. Everyone bursts out laughing when they spot my crusty old ute parked in the lounge. When I lead them out onto the terrace and show them the spa area, Ajala wants to know where exactly I was sitting in the spa. I flash her a worried look, and she explains that for her report she needs to be able to paint the picture correctly, so I point out to her where I was sitting.

Then we all check out the buildings nearby, the secret snapper could have taken the photo from any number of different places, depending on how good their telephoto lens was. Jacobs is tut-tutting and murmuring to Jonno, who's nodding his head to everything he's being told. I knew those two would get along, they're as different as chalk and cheese, but united in the desire to serve and protect. I chuckle to myself as I think this. Serve and protect, Jeezus, it makes 'em sound like New York cops!

It's weird being driven around. Jacobs and Jonno are in the front of Dad's Merc, and I'm sitting here in the back feeling like royalty. It's late afternoon and we're heading to the studio later than was first agreed. *Tonight's Current Affairs* called Dad and asked if we could do a live show tonight because they want to air it as a special. He ran it by me and I agreed that it was cool, it makes no difference to me.

Don't know how Jacobs managed it so quickly, but Jonno is already decked out in his new suit and it's totally transformed him. He's standing tall and has an air of menace about him now. He's had his head shaved, and a pair of wraparound shades completes his outfit. He looks awesome, definitely not someone you'd want to mess with. Jacobs has certainly worked his magic on him, it's amazing what a new set of clothes will do for a man. I really must get onto some new clothes for myself, gotta maintain a snappy image. Today I'm in my new, regulation black respect outfit, which consists of black jeans and Converse runners, and a long sleeved black tee under my respect t-shirt. I'm nervous about the interview because it'll be much longer than the one I did on *Good Morning Today* with Kirk.

This time having my makeup done doesn't seem as tedious as before, I still don't enjoy it though. It's a different chick, and I think I like this one better, she seems a lot nicer. Her names Bria, and she's happily chatting away to me as she does her thing. At least she doesn't poke me in the eye like the other lady did. The time passes quickly.

I've got my security posse stationed outside the makeup room, one man on either side of the door. It's quite comical really, Jonno's still got his sunnies on, he's a classic.

Unfortunately the same hairdresser is on duty. He flounces in, hands fluttering everywhere, and screeches that he just doesn't know what to do with me, that I'm a mess. Then he puts his hands on my shoulders, looks at me in the mirror and says, "You're such a naughty boy Davis! I know what I'd *like* to do to you!" Giving my shoulders a squeeze his hands move up and start massaging my neck. Bria, who's in front of me working on my final coat of mascara, snorts with amusement and carries on with her job. Oh fuck, no way, he's coming on to me! I just glare at him in the mirror, trying to stare him down, but this doesn't seem to be working. Maybe in gay land this is taken as a come on, because his hands start massaging my neck a bit harder, and he starts breathing heavily. I can't move my head or poor Bria will kill me. I hear sniggering coming from the door, and notice that Jonno's peeking around, listening to the conversation. I will him to do something, to stop gay-boy, but he doesn't. Luckily I'm saved by a chick who comes rushing in announcing that we've got three minutes.

Glaring at gay-boy I admonish, "Mate you shouldn't believe everything that you read in the papers ok, I'm not gay."

Bria rips off the protective paper around my neck and I'm hustled out, with gay-boy blowing me a big kiss as I go. Jonno sees it and totally cracks up. As we walk down the hall I tell him his behaviour's not very professional. Looking at Jacobs for some support, I notice that he's got a smirk on his face, but at least he's not laughing like Jonno. Giving them both a stern look I tell them that we'll discuss this later, then I walk out onto the set.

Tanya Gilmore, a stalwart of Aussie TV journalism, stands up and holds out a manicured hand for me to shake. I've been watching her on telly for years, she's been around forever and is known for going for people's jugulars, making for great TV viewing. She tells me to take a seat and make myself comfortable. I can't believe I'm about to be interviewed by her, I'm so bloody nervous. There's even a small studio audience here, which is pretty cool. What's cooler are the respect t-shirts I can see out there. I give the audience a wave and they clap and cheer for me.

I get comfy on the couch, and Tanya starts the interview off by immediately bringing up todays newspaper story. There's a big screen behind us, and another two on either side of the set. Plastered across them all is the picture from the newspaper, with its blaring headline, "Naked spa romp, is Davis gay?" Great, this is *not* how I wanted the interview to start, but I'll have to go with it. I promptly deny being gay, adding, "Not that there's anything wrong with that, if you're that way inclined," and explain the real circumstances of the spa fiasco to her.

She doesn't respond to my explanation at all, instead she drops the Claire bomb. She leans towards me and says, "Sources tell us that you've split up with your long-time girlfriend Claire. And now, with this photo as evidence, we're guessing it's because you're secretly gay, but now you're ready to come out."

The audience goes "Ooh."

I can't believe I'm hearing this, taking a deep breath I puff up my cheeks as I let the air out. I tell her that she's got it all wrong. "Claire and I are having a *break*, we haven't split up for good yet, and I'm not bloody gay!"

Tanya pounces on my comment. "I couldn't help noticing that you said the word *yet* Davis. That you haven't split up *yet*. To me that suggests it's only a matter of time until you do?"

This interview is already doing my head in, I'm now regretting saying yes to doing it live, but there's nothing I can do except plough on. "Look, Claire needs some time to work some stuff out, that's all. I'm happy to give her that time. Me being gay has nothing to do with it."

She pounces again. "Ha! So you are gay! You just said so!"

I look at her like she's mental, talk about twisting your words. "I obviously need to spell this out to you Tanya. I. Am. Not. Gay. I have never been gay, and I never will become gay, ok? Claire needs some time out, that's all."

"Why? Why would she want time out?" Tanya demands.

I rub my hand through my hair in exasperation. I really don't want to divulge our personal life to the nation, but considering the situation, it's probably the best thing to do. The posse are standing at the side of the set in the background, they're in my line of sight. I notice Jacobs doing a slashing action with a finger across his throat. He does it over and over again, mouthing the word 'Stop,' but I decide to press on.

Recrossing my legs, I take a deep breath and confess, "Actually Tanya, the reason Claire and I are having a break is because she doesn't know if she loves me. She didn't believe I'd become a celebrity, she thought it was all a joke, that I was a joke."

Leaning in closer to me Tanya retorts, "Well between you and me, I thought this celeb thing of yours was a bit of a joke as well! But you're proving us all wrong aren't you. So the break up's got nothing to do with you being gay?" she pushes.

"I'm not bloody gay!" I shout. "I got naked because Dad asked me to!" Oh fuck, I probably shouldn't have said that. Jacobs is now waving an arm to get my attention, while he continues the slashing thing across his throat. I probably should stop, that would be the smart thing to do.

Tanya licks her lips, she's about to ask me something, but my phone starts ringing. Shit, I forgot to turn it off before coming onto the set. I slip the phone out of my pocket, and I'm about to turn it off when I notice that it's Claire calling. I tell Tanya's that it's Claire and that I'd better take it. She shakes her head at me and says in a disgusted tone, "You do realise that you're live on national television, don't you?"

Nodding at her I answer the phone, and Claire tells me that she's watching the show and is horrified that Tanya's been grilling me like this. She wants to talk to Tanya to set things straight. A grin spreads across my face. I tell her to hold on a tick, then I put her on speaker phone. Claire angrily lays into Tanya straight away, telling her and the nation that I am *not* and have never ever been gay. She says that she's shocked at the total lack of respect Tanya's showing me. Then she goes on and says that it is only a break, we haven't split up for good, and it's *her* fault that we're not together. She informs Tanya that my Dad is always getting me to do stupid things, and this getting naked in a spa caper is just another one to add to a long list. Finally she snaps at Tanya to start treating me with some respect, tells me that we'll talk soon, and hangs up.

The studio audience goes wild, cheering, clapping and calling out Claire's name.

Glaring at Tanya I say, "Right, so have we cleared everything up now? All the facts are straight? I am officially not gay!" Blowing a kiss into the camera I tell Claire, "Thanks babe, I love you."

Tanya looks totally pissed off that her interview hasn't gone to plan. She takes a sip of water, then turns and says to me with a bit of a sneer, "Well, I guess it's time to bring on our special guests then."

Nodding at the camera she begins to clap. I have no idea who they're bringing out, it's probably Dad. He's probably talked them into letting him come on, the cheeky bugger. The couch is quite comfy so it's easy to relax into it. I'm idly thinking that I'm glad the worst of this interview is over, it's panned out pretty well, all things considered. I'm pleased with the way things have turned out. Claire's a bloody lifesaver for getting me out of that sticky situation, but I think I've handled myself well.

I notice that Jonno's now doing a strange arm waving action and pointing to me. What is it with those two? Tanya gives me an evil grin, and stands up to welcome the next guest. I don't bother turning around because I'm sure I know who it is, so I'm totally shocked when Beaker and Mitch lean across and shake Tanya's hand, then sit down next to me. Mitch mutters "Wanker" at me while in the process of sitting down.

Fuck! This is the last thing I expected, what the hell are *they* doing here? Tanya looks like the cat that's got the cream. She's absolutely loving watching my discomfort and surprise.

I say g'day to both of them and offer my hand for Beaker to shake, but he just puts his nose in the air and ignores me. So I offer to shake Mitch's hand and he also refuses, then openly calls me a wanker to my face. The studio audience gasp at this.

Looking out at the audience I shrug my shoulders with my palms upturned, and shake my head, then say to Mitch, "Oh come on mate, there's no need for that." He just glares at me, giving me a death stare.

Eyeballing him, I demand, "What's your problem?"

"You Davis, you're my problem," and he continues with the death stare. I must say it's working, I'm feeling pretty uncomfortable here.

Then Dad's words echo in my head. "Stay true to yourself and what you believe in, that's all you can do son."

So I sit up in my chair, lift my chin, look at Tanya and tell her to "Bring it on. Show me what you've got."

My comment causes her to blink rapidly a few times, I think my change of attitude here has surprised her alright. I'm not gonna let these guys make me feel like shit, I deserve better than that. She clears her throat and looks down at her notes.

"Mr Brooks, let's start with you," she says confidently. "Is it true that you caught Davis coming out of the toilet with a girlie magazine?"

Beaker puffs up his chest importantly and smiles at Tanya. "First of all please call me Roland, and yes that's exactly what happened. My office manager and I caught him red-handed exiting the toilets trying to hide the magazine behind his back – he was looking guilty as hell."

175

"That must have put you in a very awkward situation Roland," Tanya coaxes.

He nods vigorously. "Yes it did. My office manager, a woman, was absolutely horrified by the situation, and begged me to take immediate action, which I did." He turns and smirks at me.

Tanya's all sympathetic towards him. She's trying to look innocent by opening her eyes wide, and enthusiastically nodding to everything he says. It's really pissing me off. "Well you can't have that sort of behaviour going on in the workplace now can you?" she says while looking down her nose at me.

Beaker bristles with importance. "If it wasn't for my supportive new production manager here I wouldn't have come on your show tonight. But Mitch has opened my eyes to what Davis is *really* like, how he's been trying to disrupt the rest of my workers. Tanya, he's even poached one away from me. But it's no great loss, Mitch does a *much* better job than Jonno ever did!"

I can see Jonno in the wings, he looks like he's going to explode with anger. Tanya perks up, "Maybe you'd like to fill us in on your side of things Mitch."

Mitch rubs the palms of his hands on his jeans, I notice that he's quite sweaty. "Davis is a born trouble maker," he sneers, "but he does it in a subtle way. He used to deliberately ignore me." He hangs his head then continues, "He used to make me really depressed, and I know he tried to make the other guys feel bad because they still smoked. He was always all high and mighty 'cos he'd given up."

Beaker pats him on the shoulder to comfort him. Mitch looks up and says, "As soon as Davis pulled his little stunt I went and told Mr Brooks that he'd done the right thing in firing him, that Davis has disrespected not only him, but the whole company. All of us blokes have to use that loo, and I find it really difficult going in there now, after what he did in there." He rubs at his eyes, as if to wipe away tears.

Tanya's onto it. "Oh you poor thing Mitch, I really feel for you. You must feel kind of...violated by all this. Do you?"

Oh great, now she's feeding him lines, I don't believe this! I also don't believe the crap that's spurting out of him. Mitch peeks up at Tanya and says with a sniff, "You're right Tanya, I *do* feel violated. We all do. That's why a couple of us are ganging together and we're going to fight this. We're going to sue Davis for the emotional damage he's done to us."

The studio audience goes 'Ooh' and Beaker's bug eyes are nearly popping out of his head, this is obviously news to him.

Tanya's eyes swivel to Beaker. "Are you going to sue Davis as well Roland? After all, he *has* traumatised quite a few of your staff by the sounds of it."

Beaker squirms around in his seat, then blusters, "Well I must say that I hadn't thought of it before. I wish Mitch had discussed this with me earlier." He gives Mitch a disapproving look, "But I understand where he's coming from, I really only wanted to come on tonight to share my side of the story, not get involved with any lawsuits."

Ok I've had enough, this is bullshit and I'm not going to sit here and take any more of this crap. I jump in before anyone else has a chance to sling more shit at me.

"Are you aware that you three are bullying me Tanya? That's what's happening here. I'm sitting here being falsely accused of something I haven't done - *again* - in front of the whole nation. You should all be ashamed of yourselves!" The studio audience claps as I continue, "Look, I came onto your show as a sign of goodwill, and all you've done is run me down and try to make me look bad. First with the gay accusation, which thanks to Claire was cleared up immediately, and now with this other crap. I thought interviewers were meant to be impartial, but it's clear that you're all for Team Mitch here, not Team Davis. That's not only unethical, but it's plain rude for a person in your position."

The audience claps louder. Tanya jostles her notes on her lap. Her crossed leg is bobbing up and down manically, I've clearly unsettled her.

Turning to look at Mitch I tell him, "Mate just *try* and sue me, you haven't got a chance in hell of getting anywhere with it. I happen to have one of the best lawyers already working for me because of the false gay accusation in the paper today. You know damn well you've got absolutely no evidence, not a leg to stand on. Emotional damage my arse! You're just an opportunist that's trying to get some money out of the situation." The audience suddenly stands up and starts clapping and cheering for me.

Mitch is now blushing, I bet he feels like a dickhead, and so he should. He spits the words at me, "You're a wanker Davis and I *will* sue you, and so will Scott, you loser." He folds his arms defensively across his chest.

Suddenly there's a kerfuffle in the wings and Jonno stomps onto the set. Jacobs is trying to hold him back, but Jonno's like a bull at gate. He shakes Jacobs off and stands facing the four of us. He's got his back to the audience, so a cameraman quickly moves around behind us to capture what's about to happen. Jonno stands there, legs apart, hands on his hips. He's pushed his sunnies up onto the top of his newly shaved head. He looks plain scary.

"Enough," he bellows, "I can't believe the shit I'm hearing here. I've known Davis for four years and I've never known him to hurt a fly. He hasn't got a bad bone in his body. Whereas *you*," and he points his finger at Mitch, "have always had a bloody big chip on your shoulder. *You're* the trouble maker here, not Davis. *I* should know, *I* put up with your dodgy sick day phone calls, and your constant whinging and bitching about everything and everyone. Pull your head in and get real Mitch, if anyone's a wanker here it's you."

Tanya tries to regain control of the interview and asks Jonno who he is.

"I used to be the production manager for Roland here, until Davis was good enough to offer me a job with him." He looks at Beaker and shakes his head. "Good luck having Mitch as your production manager, he couldn't organise himself out of a paper bag!" Then Jonno put's his arm out towards me and motions me towards him with his hand. "C'mon Davis, this interview, if you could call it that, is over. These joker's are showing you a distinct lack of respect, you deserve better than this mate."

Standing up, I address the three of them. "I agree. I *do* deserve to be treated with more respect. This is *exactly* why I want to spread the message of respect. You three have just given a perfect example of what's wrong with the world today. You're all small-minded, insensitive, and have a total disregard for anyone else except yourselves." I shake my head at them. "Thanks for a great interview Tanya, thanks for showing the folks out there how *not* to behave." Looking right at the camera I point to my t-shirt and say, "Don't forget to respect yourself and respect other people guys."

The studio audience is going crazy, they start stamping their feet and chanting my name. I give Jonno a nod, give the audience a wave, then we walk off the set together.

Chapter 12

On the way back to the makeup room Jonno's livid, a stream of foul language is spurting from him. He angrily intersperses it by telling me I should have walked out of the interview much earlier. Jacobs isn't much better, he keeps repeating that I need to have some media training. Immediately.

The posse position themselves outside the door of the makeup room again, and when I enter, Bria, gay-boy, and a few others that I've never seen before start clapping. Plonking myself down into the chair, gay-boy tells me that it's such a waste I'm not gay - he has a *huge* crush on me.

Grinning at him I ask him his name. It's Ricki, so I tell Ricki that I'm flattered that I'm crush-worthy, and that if I *was* gay then he'd be the first one to know about it. I give him a saucy wink and he giggles and simpers, then asks if we can get a photo together, all his friends will be so jealous! Bria takes a photo with Ricki's phone, and I ask him to upload a copy to my website. His eyes widen and he squeals, "You've got it you hottie!"

I can't help but blush. Bria starts removing my makeup and congratulates me on putting Tanya in her place, she sums it up nicely by stating that "She's a complete bitch."

Ricki pouts and says, "Yeah she treats us all like trash, she's unbelievable. But you sure showed her!" Snapping his fingers he quips, "Don't mess with spunky Davis!" He blows me a kiss, then grabs the other two girls and ushers them out, leaving me alone with Bria.

She beams at me. "Isn't he *fun*? He so like, cracks me up."

"Yeah he's growing on me," I admit. "Maybe I should request to have you guys do my hair and makeup permanently."

Bria's eyes light up "Really? That would be way cool. Oh my God, Ricki's gonna love you forever!"

$$\$\$\$\$\$\$\$\$\$\$$$

In the car on the way home my phone's going bonkers. Dad's already rung and he wants an emergency meeting tonight. He's already asked Danielle if she's free, so they're going to meet me at the penthouse when I get there. The two grans call to offer me their support. They're sharing the phone and both of them are trying to talk to me at the same time, so there's a lot of "What did he say's" and "Let me talk to him's" going on throughout the conversation. Those two are as mad as a cut snake. Grandma Drummond says that it's ok if I really am gay, they'll both still love me. I hmmph at them, and they both cackle back at me. Jeezus!

Doug calls too, he's as bad as the Grandmas. He just yells "Go Team Davis!" and hangs up.

The posse and I haven't even had a chance to talk about anything yet, I've been too busy on the phone, so as we swing into my street I invite them to the meeting with Dad tonight.

Jacobs suddenly pulls the car over to the curb and stops. I lean forward, about to ask what's going on, but I can see for myself. Ahead outside Paradise Towers is a mob of people. They're chanting something and holding placards high above their heads, they're a bit too far away to make it all out, but it looks pretty full on.

Jacobs whips out his mobile, hits speed dial, and immediately starts conversing with someone. Jonno and I look at each other, then at Jacobs. He says into the phone, "Affirmative, that's a code red," then snaps his phone shut. He informs us that he's just spoken to Porter, alerting him to our imminent arrival.

Apparently the demonstrators are for, get this, 'Team Mitch.' And they're shouting out "Spanx is a skank!" "Spanx wanks!" and "Down with Davis!"

As we watch, a TV crew pulls up. Fuck me, I've had enough of their shit for one day. Jacobs' phone rings, he mutters a couple of quick "Ok's," then snaps it shut again. Turning round to face me he announces, "Porter's standing by to have the garage door ready and open for us, so we won't have to stop for verification. Given the circumstances, I think a meeting is definitely called for this evening sir. Are you ready?"

"Let's do it," I nod, then ask "Jacobs, what's a code red?"

Putting the car into gear, he looks at me in the rear vision mirror and replies, "It means that backup has been called for sir. In this case, Porter's alerted the police."

I nod at him again, but my mouth's hanging open in astonishment. Jonno turns around to give me slap on the knee. "Ha! You've officially reached celebrity status mate. Good onya!"

I've got butterflies in my tummy, this is pretty freaky shit. God Mitch is a dickhead. As we get closer I notice there's about twenty demonstrators, and that Scott is their leader.

"Little fucking shit!" explodes Jonno when he sees him. "Mitch must have put him up to it. I bet they've cooked this up together." He angrily thumps the dashboard and starts to open his window.

Jacobs nearly has a fit and orders him to put it up, NOW.

"But I want to have a go at the little bugger." The window starts to go back up and Jonno whines, "Hey, that's not fair, who's doing that?"

"I am," growls Jacobs. "It's a security threat to have it down. For all we know they might throw something at us, we need to be prepared."

"Oh, sorry, didn't think of that," Jonno admits demurely.

Porter's got a security crew standing across the entrance to the garage, keeping the demonstrators at bay. Jacobs whisks us towards them as a TV camera is shoved in front of the windscreen, but Jacobs doesn't stop. Some of the demonstrators hit the car with their signs and hands as we pass, while screaming out their slogans at us. I can't help but cower in the seat a bit, its plain scary. I notice that Scott's now lurking in the background, he's not actually in amongst the action. The security crew lets us through, then they're immediately mobbed by the demonstrators. The last thing I see as we head underground is all of them clashing together, then I hear the sound of police sirens. Bloody hell, I'd better warn Dad about this.

Now that we're safe we all sit in the car for a minute. I'm really shaken up, and so is Jonno by the looks of things, his breathing's gone kind of funny. Jacobs is cool, calm, and collected. He takes immediate control of the situation and orders Jonno to open his door, swing his legs out, put his head between his knees and take some deep breaths. I ask if he'll be alright and Jacobs confidently says that he's only hyperventilating, he'll be right in a few minutes.

Jonno's about to open his door when it's suddenly yanked open by someone outside. Jonno and I both scream, but it's only Porter, thank God.

"Jeezus Porter, you scared the shit out of us, don't sneak up on us like that!" I snap. Porter and Jacobs smirk at each other, I'm sure they find our wimpy behaviour amusing.

Jonno does his breathing thing like Jacobs instructed, and I take this opportunity to call Dad. He's only five minutes away, and actually sounds excited at the prospect of having to fight through a demonstration. I ask Porter if his security team can do the same for Dad as they just did for me, and he gives me the thumbs up.

Before we know it Dad comes to a screaming halt next to us in the underground car park. He's driving Mum's red Hyundai Getz. It's hardly a cool getaway car, but he's beaming at us. Danielle's sitting in the passenger seat, looking as shocked as I was a few minutes ago. She's as white as a sheet.

Sure enough, as soon as Dad gets out of the car he's bouncing up and down, saying how much fun it was, and that he's always wanted to do something like this. We all glare at him, and he realises that now's probably not the best time to show so much excitement about a pack of demonstrators. He coughs into his fist, regains some composure, and assists Danielle out of the car. As soon as she clambers out she punches him on the arm, calling him a bloody maniac. Unfortunately this brings back his crazy grin.

Porter suggests that Dad put his car on the car lift up to the penthouse.

"Have you still got your shit heap up there?" Dad asks me.

"Yep," I answer suspiciously.

"Yeah well I definitely want a photo of *that*!" he beams at me.

Dad wants to put the Getz on the turntable himself, so he mucks around getting the car positioned just right. I'm about to put my thumb on the control pad, but Dad stops me and asks Porter if people are allowed to ride up in the car. Porter narrows his eyes at Dad and tells him that no, it's not normal protocol, but Dad pursues it. He wants to know if it *could* be done.

Porter sighs and resignedly admits, "Well yes Mr Spanks it *could* be done, but we don't normally encourage it."

Rubbing his hands together Dad exclaims that this isn't a normal day now, is it? He's got a wicked glint in his eye. Then he asks me if I feel like a little ride. I don't really see the point and tell him so.

"Jeezus Davis," he retorts. "Don't you wanna give your fans out there a final wave for the night?"

Jonno stops his breathing exercise and stands up with a huge grin on his face. "Oh yeah, c'mon Davis. Scott and Mitch would just *love* to see ya do that!"

I turn to Danielle, she seems to be the only sane one left here. "What do you think, should I do it?" I ask.

Shrugging her shoulders she says cheekily, "You've had a pretty insane day so far, why not cap it off with this eh?" Then she gives Dad a high-five. Man, all my family are crazy motherfuckers!

I balk at the idea of going up in the Getz though, the crowd would never see me in it anyway. I suggest that ideally we need a convertible, with the top down.

"Or a ute," offers Dad.

"Yeah that would be perfect," I agree, so we send the Getz up on the lift, and a few minutes later it returns with my rusty old ute. Jumping onto the back I give everyone a salute, Porter activates the car lift, and up I go.

Porter alerted the security team outside as to what's happening, so they will point me out to the crowd. Sure enough, as soon as the car lift reaches the first floor I've got a perfect view of the crowd spread out below me. The camera crew is filming, and there's some paparazzi on the scene as well, their cameras are flashing as I ascend. The protesters are yelling and waving their placards at me, while I just grin and wave back to them all. I immediately spot Scott, so give him the old 'I'm watching you' signal, by pointing to my eyes with a couple of fingers then aiming them at him. He tries to melt into the crowd, which has now grown larger than its original size, someone must have put the word out. Shaking my head I do it to him again, I want Scott to know I'm onto him and Mitch, that I've got them in my sights.

As I arrive at the penthouse the others are just coming through the foyer. I've got to admit that Dad was right, this is a pretty cool stunt to pull, but I won't fess up to that just yet. Don't want his head getting any bigger than it already is. Well that was the plan, but when I see the look of excitement on his face I give in, and we hug it out. I confess to him that it's the coolest thing I've done in ages.

He wants to know if he can have a go sometime, but Porter instantly quashes the idea by telling him it was absolutely a one-off. "Aw bugger," Dad laments, then he whips out his phone and takes a few snaps of me standing in the back of the ute, with the little red Getz next to it. It's a bloody classic, both cars look completely out of place surrounded by all this luxury.

Dad insists on having his photo taken standing in the back of the ute as well, which means everyone wants one. Well everyone except Jacobs, who declines the offer. Then we all head out onto the terrace to peek over the side and watch the action down below. The cops have arrived and some of the protestors seem to be dispersing, but there's still a good crowd down there. Man the wind up here is freezing, so I nominate the office as the place to do this evening's business.

I give Ajala a quick call, and she tells me that she was watching the coverage on TV and saw everything that happened. She was just about to send me some posts to authorise. Ideally she should be here with us tonight, so I ask her what she's up to. She squeals that she can be here in fifteen minutes; she'll get a lift on her brother's motorbike. I just love her enthusiasm, but I warn her about the protestors and tell her to be careful. I insist that she use the garage entrance for safety reasons, but she balks at this.

"No one's going to know who I am, I'll use the front door Mr Davis."

So I call downstairs to inform Porter that we're expecting her, and that she insists on using the front door. He groans but tells me that it's fine.

$$\$\$\$\$\$\$\$\$\$$$

Danielle starts the meeting off, she wants to address the *News of the Day* article first, so I pass her over to Dad, telling her that he's got that all sorted with Neville. She says she's up to speed on all that, what she really wants to know is if I want them to retract the article. I have no idea what she means, so she explains that if an article is published that's either false or misleading then I have the right to ask them to retract it. They withdraw their opinion so to speak.

"Why would I bother to do that if we're already suing them?" I ask.

Grinning at me she replies, "To rub their noses in it, so they admit publicly that what they did is wrong. That's why."

"Right, well shit yeah! Let's ask them to do that!" I shout.

Dad's looking at us both with a goofy look on his face, his eyes are watery. "What?" I ask.

"I'm having a proud parent moment here ok? Jeezus I love how smart you are Danielle, isn't she smart everyone?" We all agree with him. Danielle's turned bright red but Dad continues, "It was just a great moment there watching you two together, wish your Mum could have seen it." He leans over and pats my hand. "I'm real proud of you too Davis, you handled yourself exceptionally well in that hideous interview. That Tanya should get the chop. Claire saved your bacon tonight alright."

I tell him that both Jacobs and Jonno had tried to get me to stop the interview earlier, but I hadn't listened to them and I'm glad I didn't. At least the public can now see Mitch for the slimy piece of work that he is.

Danielle agrees that from a litigation point of view it was a very smooth move, even though I hadn't planned it at the time. She reckons that because he was openly hostile to me, he'll have a very hard time trying to make anything stick. I want to know if she can represent me if it comes to that stage with Mitch. Slamming her fist down onto the table she says passionately, "Just watch me smash him Davis. No one messes with my little brother and gets away with it!"

Fuck, I sure wouldn't want to be on the wrong side of her, Mitch better watch out alright.

Porter rings, announcing that Ajala's on the way up, and that she's caused quite a commotion. I go to let her in and she's all bright eyed and rosy cheeked, I'm not sure if it's from the ride over here or the crowd she's just dealt with.

"Oh Mr Davis they know who I am! They recognised me as your social media reporter!" she says excitedly.

Ushering her along towards the office I ask, "What's with this Mr Davis shit? You can just call me Davis, Ajala."

She waggles her head at me. "No no no. You don't want me to call you sir, and I think that just Davis is far too informal. So *Mr* Davis is perfect, I am showing you the respect that you deserve."

I raise my eyebrows at her. "Well, if it makes you happy, then I'm happy too ok? Mr Davis it is then."

We enter the office and I introduce her to Danielle. She says hi to everyone, then I ask her what happened outside. Her eyes light up and she cries, "It was so exciting! The TV people wanted me to say something but I just told them *no comment!*" She claps her hands with glee, "Those pesky protesters were yelling nasty things about you Mr Davis, but I just pushed my way through them into the building." Waggling her head, with a smile on her face she says, "I am Indian, crowds do not intimidate *me*!"

We all give her a little clap, her enthusiasm is infectious. Wow, her and Dad'll get along like a bloody house on fire, they're loving all this excitement.

Next we move into damage control for the interview. Danielle suggests that we approach the head honcho of Channel Six and demand an apology from Tanya. Dad snorts at this, he reckons we've got Buckley's chance, there's no way that's ever going to happen. But I like the idea, surely it can't hurt to ask, so I jot it down on my to-do list.

Jonno wants to know what the plan of action will be regarding Mitch and Scott. He calls them a couple of dumb arses and says that they're totally out of order. He reckons he knew they were up to something, just not something as big as this.

"I'm afraid we'll just have to wait and see if they cause any more trouble," Danielle informs him.

At this, Jonno sits up in his seat and drums his fingers on the table. "But isn't causing a demonstration harassment against Davis?" he growls.

Danielle eyeballs him. "Well yes and no. The fact they did it in a public place means that, unless they physically assaulted Davis, we can't press any charges. It's within their right to demonstrate their opinions freely."

"But they hit the Merc with their fists and signs. Doesn't that count for anything?" Jonno demands. He's looking very pissed off.

"Only if they caused some damage," counters Danielle. She looks to Jacobs, Jonno and me, then asks, "*Did* they do any damage?"

I shrug my shoulders, so does Jonno. We all look to Jacobs. "I haven't had time to properly inspect the car, but from the cursory glance I had, no major damage was inflicted," he admits.

Jonno's fingers drum the table louder. "That's bullshit! Surely we can get them on something?"

Danielle shakes her head at him, "Sorry Jonno, unless there's some damage to the car, and you know exactly which person did it, we've got nothing."

"Yeah, I noticed that Scott stayed well back from all of the action, he was just egging everyone else on," I add.

Jonno's mobile rings, he gets up and takes a couple of steps away from the desk to answer it. As soon as he says hello he turns round to face us all, he's pointing to his phone. His face goes beetroot red and he says loudly, "Yeah whaddaya want Mitch?"

He listens to his phone for a sec, then says very loudly while eye-balling Danielle, "Oh you just wanted to rub it in a bit more, did you? You wanted to see if we enjoyed the welcoming committee you organised for us, eh?"

One of Jonno's eyes has started twitching, and his fingers have gone white he's gripping the phone so tightly. He listens intently, then starts to yell down the phone, "You little....," but before he can say anything else, Danielle leaps out of her chair and wrestles the phone off him. It goes flying across the floor and there's a mad scuffle as they both try and grab it. Jacobs springs into action and grabs Jonno from behind, twisting his right arm up behind him. Jonno lets out an astonished "Oi!" then realises that it's Jacobs. He shakes his head and lets out a big puff of air.

Danielle's sprawled on the floor clutching the phone to her chest. She must have put it on speaker phone by accident, because we hear Mitch give a manic laugh, then he spits out, "Spanx wanks, you're a fuckin' wanker Davis," and hangs up.

Danielle's breathing heavily. She stands up and smooths down her skirt, she's still in her work suit which is now rather crumpled.

Jacobs releases Jonno's arm, and Jonno immediately begs for forgiveness. He says he had no intention of hurting Danielle, he just saw red when Mitch was taunting him, and desperately wanted to call him "A little fuckin' bastard."

Danielle sits back down and glares at Jonno. Dad's fussing around her making sure she's ok. Shrugging him off she states, "I'm fine!" Then she places Jonno's phone on the table and says, "Look, how we handle this situation with Mitch is critical." She looks over at Jonno, who's still standing. "We don't want to call him a little fucking bastard here, we need to be keeping our cool." Her voice softens and she smiles at Jonno. "Even though that's what he deserves, it's better if we don't ok? This way we can build a better case against him."

Jonno grunts, then heavily sits back down. I can tell he's still not happy, but we've all just got to bide our time on this.

Dad wants to know when I'm going to get a car sorted, he wants his Merc back, and he's not too happy about leaving Mum with nothing to drive. I wave a hand at him, telling him that I'll get onto it tomorrow.

"You'd better. *The Weekly Star* want to come and do the photo shoot tomorrow arvo." He looks at me sheepishly, "I might have forgotten to mention that to you, sorry mate."

Shaking my head at him I say, "Don't sweat it Dad, it'll be fine."

"Yeah, well ya want to make sure that you get rid of the ute and get something a bit more respectable, ok?" He scratches his chin and looks at Jacobs and Jonno. "In fact if it's alright with you boys, I'll drop both of you off, then take the Merc back home with me. Danielle, can you drive Mum's car home for me?" She nods and Dad continues, "Good, this way Davis will *have* to get off his arse and get some cars organised, nothing'll happen otherwise."

"I like your style Mr Spanx," says Jonno.

Dad inclines his head to him and replies, "Thankyou Jonno, I appreciate that." And they both chuckle.

I jot down 'get cars sorted' on my to-do list, then ask Dad, "When am I starting my segment on *Good Morning Today*? I can't remember if it's this week or next week."

Apparently they want to do a live segment this week, but after Tanya's live interview I'm not so sure it's a good idea. And Friday is looming, it's already Wednesday, that means I've only got tonight and one full day to decide what I want to do. Shit! I say as much to Dad and he says, "Pull your head in and get your thinking cap on mate."

Then he offers to help me, in fact the whole team does, but I decline, saying that I appreciate their offer but I really want to do this myself. They all look a bit crestfallen, so I add that in the future I might have to call for assistance, which seems to perk them all up again.

Danielle warns us all that tomorrow's papers will most likely be running a story on me, and that I should expect the worst. Yeah, I wonder what they'll come up with, there's plenty of ammo for them to choose from given the shenanigans of the TV interview and the protesters.

Jacobs wants to go through some security issues and he'd like to discuss the car thing with me again. I really value his opinion, so I ask if he can come over tomorrow morning and we'll get it all sorted. He assures me that "He'd be delighted to."

Next I ask Ajala to make sure we touch base first thing tomorrow morning, once we've sussed out all of the papers. She suggests that it would probably be a good idea for me to send out a personal tweet and do a couple of posts tomorrow, just to keep the fans happy. I fully agree, I need as many people on my side as possible. She quickly checks her phone, and squeals that my YouTube vids have gone insane! The mariachi clip has now had fourteen million hits, and my getting fired one has had fifteen million. She pauses dramatically, and tells us that we won't believe how many hits the one outside the café with the crowd chanting respect has had. We all stare at her, the silence is deafening. Then she shouts, "Twenty two million hits!"

"Fuuuck," I yell.

I start jumping up and down on the spot, laughing manically. Everyone's ecstatic, even Jacobs is grinning from ear to ear. Wow, twenty two million hits, that's in-fucking-credible! I high-five them all, announcing that the meeting's over. It's great to end it on such a high.

Dad asks if I want him to stick around for a while, but I notice Danielle's looking at her watch. Giving him a hug I tell him we'll catch up tomorrow. He's about to get in the lift with the others, but I quickly pull him aside and whisper, "Do you and Mum wanna be in the photo shoot tomorrow?"

He spins around to face me, eyes gleaming, and asks if I'm for real. I give him a nod and he lets out a whoop of delight. "Just wait till I tell your Mum, she'll be beside herself. *The Weekly Star's* one of her favourite mags!"

Pushing him into the lift, I wave everyone goodbye. Dad starts blabbing to the others about being in the photo shoot as the lift doors close. I send the Getz back down in the car elevator, then stand there for a minute, breathing deeply. Ah, silence at last. Bliss.

$$$$$$$$$$

Grabbing a Sexy Juice from the fridge I decide to enjoy my new home, and settle down in one of the lounge chairs looking out over an awesome view of the city. Time to do some brainstorming for Friday's segment, gotta get my head around it all. I whip back into the office and get some stuff, then get comfy again. My pen is poised but no ideas are coming to me. Tapping the pen on my bottom lip I let my mind wander for a bit. I'm stoked that the café crowd video has had so many hits, I really didn't expect that. Doing that respect chant was freakin' awesome. I'd love to do it again, it was so powerful. It probably sounds weird, but I felt like a real man as I was doing it. It was kind of like in Braveheart, when William Wallace gives his speech and gets them all fired up. Bingo. I now know one thing I want to have happen more often, so I jot it down on my notepad.

Next I start thinking about what I want to achieve with my segments. The whole purpose of them is to get my message of respect out there, that's why I wanted to do this celeb thing in the first place, and spreading the respect is still my main mission. I want to show people that it's ok to show respect. In fact I'd like to be able to create a culture where it's a cool thing to do, which is a pretty big ask, considering how fucked up our society has become. When did it become ok to king-hit or bash someone? Why have we let manners and basic respect for other people go out the window? We all just seem to accept that that's the way it is nowadays, which is totally fucked up.

I mean sure, I've done shit in my past that I'm not proud of. I've been in fights, admittedly only a couple, and they were because someone else had a go at a mate or a girlfriend and I was trying to protect them. But if I'd really had my shit together and not felt the urge to prove myself, I guess I would have found another way to deal with the situation. On the whole I think I'm a pretty decent bloke, I don't take shit from people, but I don't go out and look for trouble either. So it really pisses me off that you can't go out safely at night anymore – because there will probably be a fight or some other bullshit. I mean I'm still a youngish bloke, I'm only twenty nine, and *I* don't feel safe going out in the city late at night. It must be crap for older people, they must be shit-scared.

Thinking these thoughts is getting me angry, I'm pissed off that society's like this. But then I smile to myself. Jeezus, I'm so lucky to be in a position to maybe make a difference here, even if I can just get the ball rolling with this respect thing.

Hmmm, I tap my pen again. How the hell am I gonna do this? Right, that's given me an idea, maybe I'll organise a.., but nah, that won't work, not for the first segment anyway. I jot something down on my notepad under a subheading for future segments, then start the pen tapping again. Man this ideas thing is harder than you'd think. It's taking me ages to come up with…nothing! Fuck. Now I'm starting to stress out, what if I can't do it? I know I've got my own dedicated crew at Channel Six to help me, and my own posse all jumped at the chance, but I really want to do it myself. This is *my* thing, and I want to feel a sense of accomplishment with it.

I need a mental break, so I wander out onto the terrace and peek over the side. It's quiet down there now, all the protestors have gone home thank God. That was one weird experience, one I don't especially want to repeat. I chuck a few laps of the terrace, I need to clear my head.

Holly went through a hippy stage when she was a teenager and got into meditation and stuff. I'm sure that's when she experimented with free love and became a bit of a ho. But regarding the meditation stuff, she was always saying that you had to clear your thoughts in order to let new ones in. I can hear her voice now loud in my head. "You need to be like a vase Davis, an empty vase, so that new thoughts can be poured in. If your vase is full you can't put anything else in, so that's why you always need to make sure you empty your mind regularly." At the time I didn't really get it, but strangely tonight it's making sense to me. I haven't thought about this stuff for years.

Standing with my hands gripping the balustrade and the wind whipping my face, I try to let it carry my thoughts away, I try to empty my mind. The wind is freezing, but feels great. I notice how noisy the city is and I suddenly experience a sense of calm within. Fuck this shit works! But as soon as I think it it's gone, I've lost the inner calm. It disappears in a flash. Bugger. It felt pretty good though. I'll have to ask Holly if she still meditates, get some pointers off her.

Wandering back inside, I sit down and immediately have a fantastic idea, then another one. It's like the floodgates have opened. I write as fast as I can, going with the flow of ideas. I don't know how long I've sat here scribbling, but I've now got two pages of stuff. I review what I've got, cross some things off and give everything else a star rating. One star meaning it's not urgent, up to five stars meaning that I want to do it now. There's three things with a five star rating, so I ponder on which to choose first. After a while I'm totally happy with my decision. I can't help but laugh, my Channel Six crew won't know what's hit them when I tell them my ideas. I hope they're up for it!

Suddenly my tummy lets out a massive rumble. Shit, I forgot to have any dinner tonight. I also forgot to ring Claire, I wanted to thank her for saving my arse. I'm missing her like crazy, it's so weird being on my own. In fact I've never lived on my own before, this is a totally new experience for me. In one way I'm loving the freedom, but it's a bit freaky not having anyone to talk to. Before I lived with Claire there was always someone home at Mum and Dad's. Man, I used to wish for a bit of peace and quiet when I lived there.

I mumble to myself about this being a new start for me. Shit, I'm already starting to talk to myself. I used to think people who did that were nutters, but now I can see why they do it.

Getting up, I go into the kitchen to grab my mobile, and I'm shocked to see that it's one in the morning. What the hell happened to the time? I'll have to call Claire tomorrow, but I send her a text telling her I love her. I know I should hit the sack, tomorrow's gonna be a full on day. But I make some toast and head into the games room, *Thrill Shooter* is calling me. I can pretend I'm blowing Mitch and Scott away, awesome! I'll just have one game...

Chapter 13

"Happy anniversary!!" Bruce bellows, as he thrusts a small bouquet of flowers at me while waving a six pack of beer around with his other hand. He's also got a wad of newspapers tucked under one arm. Rubbing a hand across my face I grin, and open the door wide to let him through.

"Maaate. Nice flowers, you're spoiling me!" I joke.

Bruce bustles into the penthouse and I trail after him. Man I feel like shit, bloody *Thrill Shooter*. I got totally sucked in and played until four in the morning. I was just scoffing my third coffee when Porter announced that Bruce was on his way up.

Dumping his stuff on the dining table, Bruce turns to face me. "You've officially been a celeb for a week Davis! We need to celebrate!"

He's right. "Shit yeah, it's Thursday isn't it? Man I can't believe I was fired only a week ago."

Bruce grabs the flowers out of my hand, goes over to the kitchen and rummages around for something to put them in. Settling on a glass jug, he fills it with water and stuffs the flowers in while saying, "Yeah congrats buddy. I picked these up at the servo on the way over. Jeeze you've packed a lot in the past week eh? Saw you on the telly last night. That Tanya was a complete bitch, and how cheeky is that Mitch dude? I couldn't believe what I was seeing." Placing the jug on the table he asks, "Is he really gonna sue ya?"

"Not if I can help it, I've got Danielle on the case. Mate, she was all fired up about it last night, especially with that other stunt Mitch and Scott pulled."

I've got the huge flat screen TV on, and perfect timing, just as I've said this *Good Morning Today* runs some footage of last night's protest again. I've been glued to the box while I was having my coffees. I can't get enough of watching myself go up in the car lift, they've played it four times already. So pointing to the TV, I steer Bruce over to the couch and we both sit down to watch the show. He's gobsmacked. His eyes keep swivelling back and forth between me and the TV, and his mouth is hanging open in surprise.

When the clip ends he slaps his knee and exclaims, "Fuck! I can't believe my best mate's got bloody protestors out after him. That's a classic!" Shaking his head he says, "Oh mate, you've hit the big time now alright!"

We both crack up at how crazy this all is, it really is ridiculous. We channel surf for a while, some other programs are running footage as well, and some are even playing bits of last night's interview with Tanya.

Jumping up I grab the papers Bruce brought with him, better check out if I'm newsworthy again. Sure enough I've made it onto the front page of *News of the Day*. There's one photo of me cowering in the backseat of the car, and another one shot from further back, showing the car and the angry protestors waving their placards. The headline screams; 'Davis ignites protest!' with a sub heading of 'Is Spanx a skank?'

The Daily Herald has a photo of me waving from the car lift while the protestors hold their placards high. It's also got a smaller photo of a guy holding a "Down with Davis" placard. The headline for this one reads, "Is Davis going up or down? - Vote today and make your opinion count!" I read the article and at least it's not as trashy as *News of the Day's*. They want readers to vote whether they like me or not.

I hand it over to Bruce who peruses it, then says, "Who gives a shit what they think? Good publicity for ya though."

"Yeah, but I'd be spewing if Mitch got more votes than me, he's such a prick."

"Can't argue with that," Bruce replies while adjusting his balls. "Mate, if I was you I'd be straight onto Twitter and shit, getting the fans to vote. You should round up your troops Davis, and whip Mitch's arse!"

God that's done it, I'm fully awake now. I punch Bruce on the arm and shout, "Fuck yeah. That's a brilliant idea!" I quickly reach for my mobile, which is on the coffee table. I'm about to send out a tweet, but realise that I don't want to seem like I'm begging my fans for their votes, I want the decision to come from them. So I send out a tweet simply saying that they should check out *The Daily Herald*.

I've just finished doing my Facebook update when Ajala rings me. She's an early bird today, I wasn't expecting to catch up with her until later. She tells me that she just got my tweet but hasn't seen Facebook yet, so I fill her in on my latest post, and she agrees that letting the fans decide if they want to vote is a smart thing to do. But she tells me that she has no problem with unashamedly plugging the need for them to vote. "*You* don't want to suck up to them Mr Davis, but there's nothing wrong with *me* asking them to vote is there?"

She's got a good point. I quickly ask Bruce what he thinks and he reckons Ajala's onto something, so I agree that she should go for it, plug it heaps. We agree to check in with each other later on. Man, today's already shaping up to be a crazy one, and it's not even nine o'clock yet!

I explain to Bruce that today's gonna be mental, what with having to get some cars sorted, doing the photo shoot, and who knows what else. I'm worried that he'll be bored because I won't be able to spend much time hanging out with him. Giving me a sneaky look, he tells me that he's more than happy to while away a few hours in the games room.

Ha! I rib him that the only reason he came round to see me is to play, but then I tell him, "Go for it mate, I gotta grab a shower. Jacobs will be here soon and I've got some calls to make." Bruce gives me a wink, jumps up off the couch and nearly sprints to the games room. Can't say I blame him, my games room rocks!

After scrubbing up a bit it's time to hit the phone. God I hate being put on hold, the music's always crap and it gets stuck in your head for ages afterwards. I'm hoping that I'll be able to erase *Islands in the Stream* from my memory banks, but I don't like my chances. I've been humming along to it for the past five minutes and it's pure torture. I'm trying to get through to Malcom Blewitt, the head honcho of Channel Six, and so far I've been given the run around. The first response is that he's unavailable, but when I tell them that Davis Spanx wants to have a word with him about last night's show the scrambling begins.

First they put me onto the producer of *Tonight's Current Affairs*, who apologised for Tracy's behaviour last night but told me there's no way I'd be able to talk to 'Big Mal,' as they call him. So I told him that I'd get hold of Big Mal one way or another. He just laughed and said good luck before hanging up on me. So I'm on bloody hold again, while the receptionist at Channel Six is probably throwing a hissy fit about me demanding a personal contact number for Big Mal.

Maybe if I get up and walk around I can distract myself from this insane song, I've progressed from just humming it to singing along. Shit. I've gotta get a grip. I'm about to wander into the games room and see how Bruce is going, but I'm stopped in my tracks as the security video phone beeps for attention. Porter informs me that I have a visitor.

"Who is it?" I ask.

Porter winks and says, "The gentleman wants to remain anonymous, so that he can surprise you."

"Is he legit? Does he get your approval Porter?"

Porter smirks and assures me, "The gentleman is indeed a gentleman Davis, I approve. Shall I send him up directly?"

"If it's good enough for you, then it's good enough for me. Thanks Porter, yeah send him up."

Within seconds the lift in my foyer opens and a guy in a pinstripe maroon suit steps out. I can't see his face because he's holding a huge hamper up in front of it.

"Hey, today's my lucky day, everyone's bringing me prezzies," I joke as I hold open the foyer door for him. I try to get a look at his face as he comes in, but he strategically moves the basket around, effectively blocking my view. This is starting to get a bit weird, who is this guy? I'm still on hold, I've got my mobile held up to my ear and I can't help myself, I start humming along to the shitty song again.

Once the mystery man's inside the penthouse he puts the basket down, turns to face me, and holds out his hand for me to shake. "Nice ta meet ya Davis, I'm Mal Blewitt. Hope I'm not disturbing ya, but I wanted to deliver this in person."

I look to the phone and then to him. Wow, it's like I've teleported him here! I must still be humming because he says, "Still on hold with reception eh? As soon as I heard ya wanted a chat I got over here quick as I could. I told Rhonda the receptionist to delay you for as long as possible. Looks like it worked!"

We shake hands, after all it's the polite thing to do, but I'm still spun out though. This guy is meant to be as tough as nails, and here he is grinning like a clown, shoving a gift basket at me. He claps me on the back and says, "Not many people know this Davis, but I *love* surprising people, it gives me a real buzz. Nice place ya got here alright." Moving over to where my ute is parked, he lets out a massive whoop of laughter.

"Now *that's* a sight for sore eyes! Jeezus son, you've gotta get yourself a decent set of wheels. I know ya can afford it, *'cos I'm payin' ya!*" he booms, laughing at his own joke.

At last the power of speech returns to me. I walk over to where he's standing and say, "Yeah it's actually on my list for today. Hey, thanks for dropping in, this beats a crappy phone call any day." Putting my mobile in my pocket I add pleadingly, "Mr Blewitt, you've gotta do something about your on-hold music."

Turning to me he states, "It's just Mal to you ok Davis. And no, I don't need to change the music," he chuckles. "That's the whole point of it, it works like a bloody charm. No one can stand being on hold for long, so we don't get as many complaints, alright."

I'm puzzled by this so I ask, "But who hassles you?"

Shaking his head slowly he sucks his teeth and replies, "You'd be surprised at how many whinging, bitching people there are who want to complain about all sorts of shit. It's a total waste of our time. So this way, we put them off before they can whinge or bitch to us."

I'm getting it now, "But won't that make them whinge and bitch even more? Because the music pisses them off?"

Big Mal roars with laughter and claps me on the back again. "Who cares mate? As long as they're not whinging and bitching to my staff I couldn't give a shit!"

I like him. He's not as big as I imagined, actually he's kind of short and pudgy, and he's got a bloody good double chin going on. His dark hair's balding, and he's got big bushy eyebrows, with brown eyes that bore right into you. His voice makes up for his size though. He's loud. And even though he's not that tall, he gives off an aura of pure male power. I can understand why a lot of people would be shit-scared of him, but strangely we seem to have hit it off.

"Wanna come and blow some shit up?" I ask.

He narrows his eyes at me, "You're not a fuckin' terrorist are ya?"

Pissing myself laughing, I assure him that I'm definitely not a terrorist, and explain that I've got an awesome game called *Thrill Shooter* in the games room. His eyes light up and he says, "I'm in, let's go!"

Bruce is playing *Street Racer Pro* and yelling, "Move over motherfuckers, I'm coming through!" as we enter the room.

Big Mal takes in the set-up, whistles, then says "Niiice!" while nodding his approval.

I take him over to meet Bruce, whose eyes nearly pop out of his head when he sees who I've got with me. He immediately apologises for his language.

"Hey, no apology needed here," Big Mal affirms, "you lap those mother fuckers!"

They shake hands and we move over to *Thrill Shooter*. I figure I should take it easy on him for the first few games. He's having a ball and is a pretty good shot, but half way through the second game he asks if I'm going easy on him, so I fess up and he laughs. "Jeezus I like you Davis, there's no bullshit with you is there? I gotta say it makes a nice change."

I try to look at him without turning my head too much, don't want him blowing my brains out and getting too many extra points. "Yeah well, I like to keep things up front," I say. Damn it, I must have taken my eyes off the game for a sec, because he gets me a beauty.

"Gotcha!" he booms. "Eat shit and die Davis!" God he cracks me up, you just don't expect to hear that sort of stuff come out of him. He looks so conservative, and he must be in his sixties. "Don't go easy on me son, I'm a crack shot with the clay pigeon shooting, been doing it for years."

We keep playing and I get him to talk about himself a bit. Man he's an interesting bloke, a self-made billionaire, I could listen to him for hours. But he soon turns the conversation back to me, so I fill him in on how I've been shooting pistols since I was a kid, thanks to the two grans. He wants to know more about them, and loves the fact that I still take them shooting with me. "Are they gay?" he asks.

Squeezing off a couple of quick shots I reply, "Dunno, they keep avoiding the issue. Mum and Dad deny that they could be, but I've got my suspicions."

"Well they certainly went to town at your launch the other night, those naughty naughty girls!" There's a bit of a break as the game moves onto the next level, then he adds, "I'm still tossing up the idea of putting them on the box, giving them their own show. The audience loved 'em, they could be a real winner."

I groan, "Mal, if you put them on telly you'll never get rid of 'em!"

Conversation stops as we concentrate on the game for a while. Finally after four more levels Big Mal wins and runs a victory lap of the games room, his arms spread out like aeroplane wings as he goes. Bruce and I both crack up at his antics.

When he finishes he declares, "You boys have gotta come on me boat, I've got laser clay pigeon shooting all set up, you're gonna love it!"

We all high-five each other, then Big Mal and I head out to the kitchen. I retrieve the hamper and put it up on the bench. It's crammed full of luxury goodies, my mouth's watering just looking at it all. While the coffee machine's doing its thing I whip a box of chockies out of the hamper, rip off the lid, and cram one onto my mouth. Then I push the box over to Big Mal who does the same.

"Fuck Davis, I feel like a kid again, playing games then stuffing me face with chocolate. I gotta do this more often!" He quickly shoves another couple of chocolates into his mouth and gives me a chocolatey grin.

I get the coffee sorted then pull up a stool next to him. Suddenly I'm not so sure of myself. Talking on the phone seems much easier than being face to face with one of the richest and most influential men in Australia. But I decide to just dive in and tell him what's up.

"I wanted to talk to you about the show last night Mal, Tanya really pissed me off."

He takes a sip of coffee and looks at me intently, while slowly putting his mug down. God I feel like he's looking right into me, it's very intimidating. Then he smiles, and his eyes are immediately full of warmth again. How does he do that? "Why the hell do ya think I wanted to come over here myself? Last night I watched one of my best journalists treat my newest star with total disrespect. She didn't just piss *you* off Davis, she pissed me off as well alright."

I relax a bit. Cool, at least he's on the same wavelength as me, this is good. Picking up another chocolate he examines it, then drops it into his coffee. Stirring it around he continues, "There's only one problem here Davis."

"What?" I ask.

"Last night we got the best ratings of the year." He thumps the counter top with his hand. "We smashed it! It was bloody brilliant!"

Now I'm a bit confused, is he happy about Tanya treating me like shit or not? I ask him, and he tells me that in a perfect world he'd be on my side one hundred percent and Tanya would be toast - he would have fired her last night, end of story. But....

"TV's *not* a perfect world Davis, it's a shit fight. Every day ya scramble to try and make it to the top of the heap. And last night we not only made it to the top, we went sky high. Now I feel for you I really do, but can you see my dilemma here?"

I certainly can, I tell him that I realise that Tanya was just doing her job, and I respect that. What I have a problem with is the way she went about it. She was underhanded, pushy, rude and plain disrespectful. Big Mal tells me that that's journalistic TV, it's the way things are done, and that Tanya always pulls an opinion, which gets the viewers to watch.

"I'd like an apology from her Mal," I state.

He looks at me and scoffs, "It ain't gonna happen Davis, sorry mate."

I'm not going to let it go that easily and say, "What if I could get an apology out of her so *I'd* be happy, and you guys would have your ratings go through the roof again, so *you'd* be happy. Would that work for you?" I then cross my arms and lean back on the stool.

This is one of the brilliant ideas I had with my brainstorming session last night. I think it's a winner, and going by Big Mal's reaction he might think it is as well, because he's suddenly stopped chewing and is giving me that spooky penetrating stare again.

"What are ya thinking? Hit me with it," he demands.

So I explain that tomorrow I want to start my first segment on *Good Morning Today* by introducing myself to the viewers. I want to tell the audience what respect means to me, then have Tanya come on and *I'll* interview *her!* I'll ask what respect means to her, and if she feels it's appropriate then she can apologise to me for her lack of respect on the show last night. Then I can finish up by giving a brief outline of what will happen on the weekly segments.

Big Mal is transfixed as I'm telling him all this. When I finish he pumps the air with a fist and shouts, "Hell yeah! That's bloody brilliant Davis!" Sandwiching my face between his pudgy hands he kisses me on the forehead, then slides off the stool and dances around a bit, before telling me, "You're a bloody legend! You little ripper! Tanya'll apologise to ya alright, if she knows what's good for her."

I thought it was a good idea, but I wasn't expecting this sort of reaction. Big Mal's still twirling around when the security video phone bleeps again. Jacobs is here. I excuse myself for a minute and go to let him in. He spots Big Mal doing his thing and raises an enquiring eyebrow. Shaking my head I murmur, "Sugar rush," and tell him I'll explain it all later, shooing him off to the games room.

$$$$$$$$$

Big Mal's calmed down a bit when I get back, he sure is full of surprises. The first thing he tells me is that he doesn't know what's gotten into him today, he doesn't normally act like this.

"Doesn't worry me," I say cockily. "You can do what you want, I don't give a shit." He roars with laughter and tells me again how much he likes me, so I take the opportunity to ask if Bria and Ricki can be my stylists whenever I'm at the studio.

He immediately agrees, booming that I can have whatever I bloody want, all I need to do is ask. I'm wondering if now's a good time to run through some other ideas I've got for my segment. Some of them are pretty out-there, they'll definitely take longer than the five minutes that's normally allocated to me.

Big Mal flicks his eyes at the hamper and back to me a few times in quick succession. I notice that the box of chockies in front of him is empty and he's gagging for more. So I act all polite and ask in a toffy nosed way, "Would you care for some more refreshments before we continue sir?"

He chuckles and says in a very bad British accent, "Ooh I shouldn't, but why not be a devil!" I tell him to help himself and he pounces on the hamper. Within seconds the bench top is littered with plastic wrappings as various packages are opened. He's a captive audience now, he can't talk because his mouth is stuffed full of chocolate, so I spill the beans on what I'd like to see happen on my segment. He's nodding along, a dreamy expression on his face. I'm not sure if it's because of my ideas or the copious amounts of chocolate he's ingesting, either way he's a happy man.

Suddenly he puts up a hand to stop me, swallows his mouthful and roars, "We'll have to do some specials!" His eyes are gleaming with anticipation. "There's too much content for a piddly little five minute segment."

Hopping down from the stool he starts pacing. "This is just what we need. Jeezus Davis, you've got more ideas than my so called professionals." Then he whips around and eyeballs me. "I'm paying ya forty five grand for the weekly segments right?" I nod. "Well you'll have to get more for your specials, how 'bout we make it a hundred grand for each one you do. Ya should be able to get an even better new car with that lot. Whaddaya reckon?"

Grinning, I tell him that I'll have to run it by my manager. Big Mal's onto me though. "Forget that shit Davis, I've heard all about your bloody Dad, he drives a hard bargain. So let's cut out the middleman and the bullshit, and make it a straight one fifty alright?"

I'm trying to keep a straight face here, I don't want to give away that this is in-fucking-credible! But he takes my silence as reluctance to accept, so he throws his hands up in the air, sighs and shakes his head at me.

"Alright! Jeezus you're worse than your old man! I'll make it two hundred grand per special, but that's as high as I go. Are ya happy now?"

Who would have thought that keeping my mouth shut would make me more money? I'll have to remember that little trick. I can't keep quiet for any longer though, a grin plasters itself on my face, I hold out my hand and we shake on it. "Fuck me, that's unreal," I gush, "yeah, I should be able to get my Porsche pretty soon now. Thanks Mal."

He claps me on the back again. I'm sure I'll have bruises after all this backslapping, but for two hundred grand I couldn't give a shit!

"Better make it official like, have ya got a pen and paper Davis?"

I nip into the office and grab them, just as Dad announces on the video phone that he's arrived, asking me to open the door. Oh man he's gonna go ape-shit when he finds out about this deal!

Sure enough Dad's jaw drops when I introduce him to Big Mal, he can't believe that I've got the bigwig here in the penthouse. As soon as they've shaken hands Big Mal asks for the paper and pen. He scribbles something on it and signs it, then pushes it over to me. I read it and sign it, then I show it to Dad. His eyes nearly pop out of his head. "What the hell have I missed out on here?" he demands.

"Your boy's got his shit together alright. I like him and I support what he's wanting to achieve, he's a good bloke," says Big Mal. He straightens his tie and adds, "God I haven't had so much fun in ages."

Dad looks at us both, I can see his mind working, trying to figure out what we've been up to. "Mal and me played some *Thrill Shooter*, he's a pretty good shot!" I say flippantly, like we hang out all the time together.

"Right" breathes Dad. I know he's desperate for more.

"Then I pitched my ideas to Mal for my segment, we're gonna turn some of them into specials," I'm so excited that I shout "and he's gonna pay me two hundred grand per episode Dad, howzat?"

"Is that right?" Dad asks in astonishment. I think he's having trouble comprehending all of this, especially the fact that Big Mal, the untouchable TV tycoon, is hanging out with his son and throwing money at him.

Big Mal looks at Dad and says, "Davis drives a pretty hard bargain, I started at a hundred grand and he got me up to two. You've taught him well."

Dad visibly preens at the compliment. "Yeah he's a chip off the old block alright." He gives me a high-five, "You got yourself a great deal, good one son!"

Big Mal gives Dad a wink and says, "Mate, *I'm* the one who got a good deal here. Davis, you're gonna breathe some new life into Channel Six, and to me that's bloody priceless! I would have paid ya more if you'd asked though!"

"Bugger," I mutter.

"Shit," says Dad.

Big Mal laughs at us and says that lucky for me it's only a six month contract, so I can re-negotiate everything then. Waving the bit of paper we just signed he adds, "But until then I've got ya locked in! Ha! Happy days, alright!"

I can't wait to tell Bruce, he probably won't believe me. All this excitement is too much, I've been holding on to a big piss for ages but now I've really got to go. Excusing myself, I rush off to the loo, leaving Dad and Big Mal together. When I come back out they're nowhere to be seen. Then I hear something coming from the terrace, so I poke my head out and there they both are, standing next to the spa pissing themselves laughing. I stalk over to them, Dad better not have invited him to take a dip.

Big Mal's got tears streaming down his face. He splutters to me that Dad's just filled him in on what really happened with Neville.

"Did he tell you that he farted in Neville's face as he was getting out of the spa?" I ask.

It's payback time, Dad embarrassed me so much with that stupid stunt it's only fair to try and get back at him a bit. Unfortunately it doesn't have the desired effect I was looking for, because Big Mal shakes his head and erupts into another fit of hysterics, he can hardly breathe he's laughing and wheezing so much. Spluttering he says, "That's fucking gold!" He claps Dad on the back, "You've gotta come on the boat with the boys. No if's or *butts* alright." He cracks himself up even more, even I've got the giggles now, it's bloody contagious.

We all settle down a bit and Big Mal looks at his watch and says that he's got to go, he's already cancelled one meeting this morning so that he could drop in, and by the looks of it he'll be running late for another one. Throwing his hands up in the air he booms, "But I'm the bloody boss, what are they gonna do, sack me?" This sets him off laughing again, Jeeze the guy's a comedian.

Then he gives me the intense stare again and says seriously, "Now listen Davis, I'm personally gonna be on set tomorrow morning to make sure Tanya apologises alright?"

I nod and he claps me on the shoulder again. Yep, I definitely felt a twinge that time, it could be a health hazard to be around him for too long. Reaching into his jacket he brings out a small gold case, he pushes something on the side of it and a lid pops open, revealing some very snazzy business cards. He hands me one and tells me to call him on his private number whenever I want.

"We're mates now Davis, so don't be shy alright?"

I thank him again and see him off in the lift. Just as the doors are closing he makes a clicking noise with his tongue, points his finger at me like a gun and he tells me he's voting for me in *The Daily Herald* poll today. Cool.

As soon as he's gone Dad and I just stare at each other for a sec, then start jumping around screaming like lunatics. Jacobs comes sprinting out of the penthouse demanding to know what's happening, and to see if we need assistance. I shout, "The only assistance I'm gonna need Jacobs, is in spending the TWO HUNDRED GRAND that Big Mal's gonna pay me for each of my TV specials!"

Bruce appears just as I'm saying this. He asks if I'm bullshitting and I shout that it's true, Dad's nodding as well to back me up, so Bruce lets out a shout and chest slams me, nearly sending me onto my arse. Jacobs is smirking at us all, but he's maintained his cool composure. The video phone in the foyer goes off and Jacobs answers it, confirming that everything's under control, and that this is normal behaviour for the Spanx brigade.

I'm puffed, so I ask him what's up, and he informs me that because we're in the lift foyer building security can see us, and were worried that the situation may have been dangerous. I give the cameras a wave, then a thumbs up, and we all move into the penthouse. Nice to know security's got my back if I ever need them. Also nice to know that I'd better wait until I'm in the penthouse to ravish Claire, I wouldn't want them seeing *that* little show. That reminds me, I've gotta ring her. She'll be blown away when I tell her about this new deal, maybe this will change her mind about everything and we'll get back together soon, I bloody hope so. Whipping out my phone I give her a quick call, but it goes straight to voicemail, so I tell her I miss her and hang up.

$$$$$$$$$$

Jacobs is itching to get the car situation sorted, and he suggests that we hire something for now, he's got a new Range Rover in mind. I agree with him, and Dad gives the thumbs up too. This way I can get the cars I really want later on when I get cashed up, there's no need for me to rush into anything. God Jacobs is on the ball, being able to fit lots of people in the car is a sensible idea. Me being me, I would have gone for looks rather than suitability. Jacobs knows where we should go and wants to leave immediately, he's champing at the bit to get it sorted, but I'm not sure about what to do with the ute. Bruce suggests giving it away, then Dad suggests that I flog it off in a charity raffle, raising some money to give to something I believe in.

Sounds good, "But who the fuck's gonna pay anything for my piece of shit ute?" I ask.

Dad taps his nose and says, "Mate, you're best buddies with one of the richest blokes in Australia now, I'm sure he or his mates'll fork out a bit to support the charity of your choice."

Jacobs pipes up, "In these circumstances sir it's not about the *piece* being auctioned, it's about the *cause*."

Bruce adds, "Davis, you should have a housewarming-cum-being a celebrity for a week party, and auction it off then." He and Dad are both nodding their heads at me.

"Hey you should have it tomorrow night," Bruce adds, "to celebrate a week since having your launch. That'd be perfect."

"Maybe, but tomorrows pretty short notice isn't it?" I ask.

Dad grins and says, "That's half the fun, it's a surprise party as well, what more could ya want. I think it's a great idea. Why don't you and Bruce talk about it while you're getting the hire car sorted?"

But now I'm confused. Do I need a new car for myself today, as well as Jacobs' hire car, and do I get rid of the ute now or do I need to hang onto it. The whole point of getting rid of it today was because of the photo shoot this arvo. I'm standing there looking off into space, probably looking like a dickhead while I'm trying to process all of this.

Dad chuckles. "Bit lost are ya son?"

I admit that I am, so he tells me 'as my manager' to just get Jacobs' hire car sorted today, and not worry about the ute, he'll get that sorted himself. I ask him what he means. He looks shifty and tells me that I should just leave it for today, it doesn't matter if it's in the shoot, he's got it all sorted.

I'm getting a funny vibe here, but maybe it's just because my brain nearly melted trying to work all this shit out. Usually I'm a smart guy, but this car switch totally did my head in. Maybe I've got a sugar come down. If the stuff gives you a rush, then you've gotta come down from it, right? Yeah that must be it. I ask Dad if he wants to come with us, but he looks shifty again and tells me that he's going to do some styling on the penthouse, to get it ready for the photo shoot later.

$$$$$$$$$$

This car hire place is freakin' amazing, they've got heaps of luxury cars lined up all good to go. The hire dude seems disappointed when he can't talk me into a Lamborghini or a Lotus, but when I explain *again* that it's really only going to be used as a security shuttle, he finally asks me to come into the office and complete the paperwork, which takes no time at all. He asks for an autograph for his daughter which I happily give, and we zip out of there in the new Range Rover.

One of my mobile billboards passes us as we're heading back home, and I realise that I still haven't gotten hold of Eric. He's gotta be back from Perth by now. I give him a ring but it goes straight to voicemail again, so I leave him a message saying that I'm probably having a party tomorrow night and I want him to come, we've got heaps to catch up on. I couldn't help but name drop Big Mal in the message. Eric would do anything for a chance to meet him, he's one of his man-idol s. When I hang up Bruce swivels around from the front seat and asks what's up with Eric. I explain that the last I heard he was in Perth for a big business meeting, but I haven't heard from him in days, which is kind of weird.

I'm gobsmacked. We're back at the penthouse and Dad wasn't kidding when he said he was going to do some styling for the photo shoot. There's people swarming all over the joint putting up fairy lights, placing huge potted trees out on the patio, doing all sorts of stuff. He's even put some big fake palm trees in the foyer and lounge room. Bruce is pissing himself laughing, but I'm scanning the joint, trying to take it all in.

Then my eyes spot what's sitting next to my ute. Oh my fucking God, it's my dream Porsche, the limited edition Cayman S Black. It's sexy, black, and oozes sophistication. The contrast between it and the ute is staggering. I must have let out a squeak of surprise because Bruce asks me what's wrong. I just point at the Porsche. He's as shocked as I am and starts choking and coughing, so I give him a thump on the back.

We're mesmerised by the vision before us, and glide over to inspect it more closely. I feel like I'm in a dream, this is so surreal. The rest of the penthouse disappears from existence, I only have eyes for the black beauty which is now within touching distance. Placing a hand on the bonnet, I lovingly caress the Porsche badge with my fingertips. Bruce lets out a groan. He's crouched down and is examining the front wheel. Our eyes lock, neither of us can talk yet, we're still too enraptured. As if in slow motion we both turn back to the car, Bruce puts a hand on the wheel and lets his fingers stroke the spokes, while I run mine down from the badge to the air intake grill. Our eyes meet again, this time we slowly smile at each other.

The spell's broken when Dad says loudly, "You two should get a bloody room! That's car porn!"

Standing up, I turn around and am blinded by a flashing camera. It's gotta be industrial strength, no phone or normal camera could nearly blind someone like that. Shielding my face with a hand I ask Dad what the hell's going on, and he happily informs me that *The Weekly Star* got here a bit early and wanted to capture my surprise car moment.

"Mission accomplished!" I shout. "Can they stop for a minute?"

The blinding flashes stop as quickly as they started, and it takes a few seconds for my eyes to adjust properly. When they do, before me stands the hottest chick I've ever seen. She's the one pointing the camera at me, and Dad's whispering something in her ear which gives her the giggles. Jeezus, I've got the hottest car and the hottest chick in the same room, what am I gonna do?

I'd like to think that I'll be cool calm and collected, but I know myself better than that. If I can just focus on stringing a sentence together then I'll be doing ok. Dad introduces us, her name's Bambi. Of course it is, what else would a goddess like this be called? I tell her that

I'm Davis. Fuck that was a stupid thing to say, what did I say that for? Now I'll look like an idiot!

"I think Bambi here already knows who you are son. Now, are ya gonna get in the car so she can take some snaps?"

Giving Dad a death stare, I turn around and see that Bruce is staring at Bambi with his mouth slightly open. Hmmm, so it's not just me then, this chick has got super powers of hotness going on. I think Bruce might actually be dribbling, so I nudge him with my foot and whisper, "I think I've died and gone to heaven."

"Me too," he drawls.

"C'mon, we gotta keep our cool, get in the car with me," I mutter to him. Bruce doesn't budge, so I give him another, bigger nudge with my foot. Unfortunately this causes him to lose his balance and he topples over sideways like a bowling pin, but he quickly scrambles to his feet, does a couple of springy jumps, then shakes himself out.

Dad shakes his head at us and says to Bambi, "That other clown's Davis's best mate Bruce. Seems he mightn't be able to introduce himself just yet, give him a bit of time and he'll come round though."

Bambi nods solemnly, as though she's used to seeing this kind of behaviour from guys. She gives Bruce a little wave with the tips of her fingers and he bounces himself around to the passenger door, opens it, and falls inside. I manoeuvre myself into the driver's seat, and as soon as we're both in I ask him, "What the fuck was that? Why'd ya keep jumping like that?"

"Fucked if I know," he pants, "I think I even forgot how to breathe for a minute there. She scorched me mate, her hotness scorched me. I can't believe how hot she is!"

"She's a vision," I agree, and we both nod together, then say at the same time, "and her name's Bambi!" Bruce puts a knuckle into his mouth and bites it, he looks like he's about to burst into tears. I know how he feels. We just sit there for a bit watching her, I feel relatively safe now that I'm in the car. Raising her camera she starts taking more photos. Dad wanders off, chatting to one of the decorators.

"At least you're single now. Me, I've got no chance. Life is sooo unfair!" Bruce wails.

"Hey, I'm not bloody single, we're just on a break ok?" I point out.

"Yeah well that's as good as single, at least you've got more chance than me," he moans.

Bruce and I finally get the guts to exit the car. Well we don't have a choice really, Bambi wants us to do some different poses. This leads to having a chat, which totally breaks the ice. Turns out that Bambi isn't scary at all, she's a sweetheart. Bruce is still licking his lips a lot, but at least he's standing upright. Before I can stop him he's invited her to my party tomorrow night. I babble something, trying to explain that I haven't even organised it yet, but she's welcome to come if she's free and doesn't have anything else on. This comment makes Bruce elbow me in the ribs. I think she caught on to the innuendo because she gives us a funny look and says that she's free, and that her best friend is an event organiser, so if we need any help getting things sorted she's positive her friend can help.

"Actually, she's not only my best friend," Bambi simpers, "she's my identical twin. You can hardly tell us apart." Bruce groans and I immediately blush, I'm sure I've turned crimson. But I just can't help getting a mental picture of two Bambi's nakedly frolicking together before me. By the sounds of it Bruce has got the same idea.

The best I can come out with is, "Wow, that's great."

Bruce is nearly giving himself whiplash he's nodding so frantically.

Shaking out her mane of long blonde hair, she runs a hand down the thigh of a slim black leather clad leg and tells us that they often work together, they make a good team. Bruce and I are now breathing heavily, as we intently watch the hand that was just on her leg move up to the shoestring strap that's holding her silky red top up. I notice she's not wearing a bra and that her nipples are on patrol, they're nearly piercing the thin fabric they're so erect. Lowering her hand she lazily brushes it over a nipple, while staring at us with a slight pout on her glossy pink lips. Bruce and I let out a gasp. Oh my fucking God, this woman has got us on the edge, I could shoot a load easy, and she's still dressed!

That's when I realise that my cock is as hard as a rock, and I'm sure she can clearly see it. Shit! Should I try and hide it? Should I walk away? I wish I could, but I can't move. I decide that fuck it, it's only normal to have this sort of reaction. I'm a hot blooded male in the prime of his life, what does she expect? But the other part of me is saying that I'd better move away, or at least cover myself, I should show her some respect. I'm in a dilemma, she's so out of my league.

Suddenly she wags a finger at us and says with a cheeky grin, "Ha-ha, sucked in! Sorry guys, I'm just messing with you."

I notice that Bruce has put his hands in front of his dick. "You mean you don't have a twin?" he whimpers.

Shaking her head she admits, "Nup, I just couldn't resist torturing you two."

Letting out a sigh, my cock deflates like a balloon, phew. She's looking at me steadily, her gaze flicks briefly down to my dick. "I sure had you going though, didn't I Davis?" she says flirtingly.

So I eyeball her, then flick my eyes to her tits and back while saying, "You sure did Bambi, you sure did."

Suddenly there's a shout from the terrace, so I excuse myself, grab Bruce by the arm, and we stumble away.

Jeezus! Dad's got a Hawaiian theme going on out here, there's even more fake palm trees out here, with a bar set up underneath them. It's totally kitsch but totally cool. He's put sand around the spa like a fake beach, and there's also giant carved Tiki statues dotted around. Plastic pink and red hibiscus bushes complete the scene. Dad's rubbing his hands together as he approaches us, a grin plastered from ear to ear.

"Why Hawaiian?" I ask.

"Why bloody not eh? The Bali theme's been done to death. Ya need to be a trendsetter Davis, and I reckon this is just the ticket."

I have to agree with him, it's bloody awesome.

Bruce has positioned himself behind the bar and is rummaging around underneath. He comes up with a couple of coconuts and plops them down on the bar. "Who's thirsty?" he asks. I tell him to forget that shit, after the ordeal we've just been through we deserve a beer. Dad wants to know the goss, so I run inside, grab him a coke and some beers for Bruce and me. Then I raise a toast to 'Black Beauty' the Porsche. I want to know how he managed to get his hands on one, but Dad refuses to tell me anything unless I tell him what happened earlier. So we fill him in on how Bambi 'tortured' us.

He pisses himself laughing, before saying, "A gentleman should always shield a ladies eyes from an offending penile protrusion, Davis. As much for her sake as for his own." Clearing his throat he adds, "Some women can't control themselves. Now you don't want them throwing themselves at you, do you? So next time cover it up eh!" He gives Bruce a wink then takes a gulp of his drink.

It turns out that Big Mal and Dad cooked up the idea of getting me the Porsche while they were out on the terrace this morning. Big Mal had asked what sort I wanted, and Dad told him the make, model, and that there were only five hundred of them made, so I probably had no chance of getting my hands on one. Apparently Big Mal had said, "I just happen to have one sitting in me garage at home." To which Dad joked that it'd be perfect to have one in the photo shoot today. Big Mal insisted on sending it over right away, and the deal was done. So I've only got it on loan, but how cool is that!

$$$$$$$$$$

The photo shoot and interview go off without a hitch. The journalist that interviews me is nice. Lucky for me she's very plain, which is just as well, I couldn't have coped with another Bambi today. I was surprised at how quickly it all went, it seemed to be over in a flash. She even asked Mum and Dad for a few comments.

Mum's stoked. She's dolled up to the nines, and makes Bambi take some extra photos 'just for the family'. Bambi's a good sport and says she'll drop them in at the party tomorrow night. Whoops, I forgot to mention the party to Mum, she doesn't have a clue what Bambi's talking about, so I quickly update her on everything. Mum immediately wants to call the grandmas and let them know, and I can hear their shrieks of excitement as she talks to them. The usual three way conversation takes place, with Mum conveying their questions to me. They want to know if I'm putting on any food, which I hadn't even thought of, but of course I should. So I give Mum the thumbs up, which sets off more shrieks of delight.

Bambi sidles up closer to me and says that her best friend Kaylee really *is* an event organiser, and by the looks of things I could use some help. She slips me a card and tells me to get onto it now. She's right, I do need help. The only parties I've ever thrown have been your average backyard barbies, which called for plenty of chops, snags, and beer. This is a whole new ball game.

So I give Kaylee a call. She says she's free tomorrow night and she'd love to help me organise things. I ask how much she charges and she says she'll waive her fee as long as I pay for the hired help, and as long as she can bring some friends. I want to know why she's willing to waive her fee, and she tells me that it'll look great on her website, her business will explode. She also wants the kudos of doing my party, and adds that I probably couldn't afford her fees right now anyway. I smirk to myself. If only she knew that as of today, I'll be making two hundred grand per TV special. I can afford any bloody thing I want!

Kaylee wants to come over immediately, she wants a visual as soon as possible to see what she's working with. Given it's such a small window of time she's got, I tell her to get herself over here right away.

Fuuuck, Kaylee's as hot as Bambi, but in a redhead-ish, shorter-legged way. Bruce does a double take when she comes in, and makes a quick exit to the terrace again. Guess he doesn't want any more embarrassing moments, and I can't say I blame him. Jeezus, now I've got to get through another meeting keeping it together. Great.

I needn't have worried too much, Kaylee's like Bambi in that she knows she's hot, but she's approachable. No wonder they're besties. A vision of them dancing together in miniscule bikinis flashes into my head, but I erase it quick smart. So far I haven't disgraced myself at all, I've held it together really well.

We're wrapping things up, Kaylee's got everything sussed. She's exceptionally organised and seems to understand what I want perfectly. She's happy to go with the props that Dad's brought in today. She loves the Hawaiian theme, but she'd like to add a bit more pizazz to it. She finishes jotting something in her notebook, then looks at me with the greenest eyes I've ever seen.

"Shall we do a walk through so I can show you where everything's going to be?"

"Sure." I follow her out of the office and into the main open plan living area, keeping an eye on her tight little ass as she minces along in front of me. High heels sure do some magic to chicks' bums, it's poetry in motion watching her arse orbs undulate beneath that tight mini skirt she's wearing. Man I've got it bad, I can feel a stirring in my pants again. Shit! I was doing so well.

Dad sees us coming and ushers Kaylee over to the kitchen bench for some refreshment, asking her how it's all going. He looks pointedly at my dick and gives me a frown, then jiggles his head a few times in the direction of the terrace, like he's urging me to go outside. I don't need to be told twice. I make a break for it and collapse on a sun lounger next to Bruce.

"Fuck, I got another hard on. I had to come out here to get away from her," I declare.

A female voice asks from behind me, "Having a *hard* day today, Davis?" I whip my head around and Bambi's grinning at me cheekily.

"What are you still doing here, I thought you'd gone home," I whine.

Moving over to Bruce's lounger she perches herself on the edge and says, "Oh I thought I'd keep Bruce company for a while." She strokes his hair and he swats her hand away, giving me a guilty look.

"Besides, I thought I'd wait for Kaylee, she's cute isn't she? Bad luck she's got a boyfriend."

I just hmmph at her, I was hoping for a bit of space. There's only so much in-your-face-hot-chickies I can handle in one day, and I've had my quota.

It's like she can read my mind, the next thing she says is, "You'd better get used to hot chicks Davis, the world you're getting into is full of 'em, and they're gonna want to gobble you all up!" She snaps her teeth together sexily at the end of her sentence.

Bruce sprays beer out of his mouth and starts choking on it. I lean over and thump him on the back again. This is getting to be a bit of a habit today.

Bambi stands up, wipes some beer spray off her tight leather pants and says, "I think you need a wing-girl to help steer you through the oncoming babe bonanza, Davis. I can help you with that." She leans over and her top gapes open, giving me an eyeful of her pert naked titties. She fishes around in her back pocket for what seems like ages, then casually hands me a card.

I really try not to look down her top, I really do, but her boobs are nearly in my face. I quickly look at the card instead and mumble that "I'll think about it."

Kaylee and Dad come out. Kaylee wants to run through her vision for the terrace with me, but Dad's giving me a disgusted look. He cuts her off, and tells her that as my manager, he already approves of what she's got planned, and he's happy to walk me through it himself later. He's sure Kaylee's got heaps to do, so she'd better get on it. Bruce and I both flinch at his choice of words and Dad stifles a smirk, insisting that we stay here, he'll see the girls out himself.

When he gets back he stands in front of us with his hands on his hips, staring down at us disapprovingly. It makes me feel like a naughty kid. "I don't bloody believe you two, you acted like a couple of horny little teenagers today. Hope you're proud of yourselves, you're a couple of dickheads!" Shaking his head at us he lowers himself onto a lounger.

"Bambi reckons I need a wing-girl, to help steer me through the bonanza of hot babes that are coming my way," I tell him.

Dad lets out a sigh and closes his eyes. "And let me guess. Bambi's up for the challenge, eh?" Then he chuckles and says, "Ya lucky bastard!"

Chapter 14

I smashed *The Daily Herald* poll! I whipped Mitch's arse, which is freakin' awesome. According to the paper, a whopping one and a half million people have voted for me, compared to a measly three hundred and sixty two for Mitch. But as Jonno said in the car on the way to the studio this morning, it's a worry that he's even got that many supporters.

Some of them are waiting outside the studio gates, waving their Team Mitch signs at us as we drive in. There's only about fifteen of them, and they look like they're freezing, the poor buggers. They're pretty bloody dedicated seeing as it's five thirty on a frosty Friday morning. Channel Six have got their own camera crew on the job covering the action, which is nice and convenient for them. Jonno reckons the studio might have organised for the protestors to be there, to get some activity and drama happening, stirring things up for my segment. He could be right. It'd be a pain in the arse if these dickheads turn up wherever I go. Dunno if I could handle that.

Bria and Ricki are over the moon about becoming my permanent stylists, they're even more excited when I invite them to my party tonight. Ricki squeals with delight and tries to give me a kiss, which luckily I deflect just in time – turning it into a hug instead.

"Strictly no kissing," I snap at him afterwards. Pouting at me he says that as long as he can have a hug then it's ok. Bria giggles at his antics as she starts smearing my face with the disgusting foundation shit.

Suddenly I hear a commotion coming from the hallway, there's shouting and what sounds like a scuffle. Jacobs' voice rings out, ordering whoever it is to "Stop it!"

Bria, Ricki and I all stare at each other, then it's a mad scramble to the door. We all peek out and see a single protestor's sign bobbing up and down. Jacobs and Jonno are blocking the person from getting any further down the hall, and I notice that Jacobs is talking into his cuff.

A camera crew with a reporter chick appear out of nowhere, and I step out into the hall behind them, which is a bad move. The protestor immediately spots me, and he starts screaming, "Die Davis Die."

I'm shocked and stunned, but he really shouldn't have said that, not in front of my posse. Jacobs grabs the placard out of the guy's hand and tosses it over his shoulder, it nearly hits the camera crew but they duck just in time. Then in a smooth move, he and Jonno grab the offender, and within seconds they've got him face down on the carpet. Some other security guys push past me and the camera crew, but my boys have already got the situation under control.

Ricki grabs my arm and clings on tightly to me. His fingers are digging into me, and when I swat him away he says in a dramatic voice full of awe and terror, "They want to kill you! They want to kill you!" Then he buries his head on my shoulder and starts sobbing. Fuck me, he's unbelievable.

"Stop being a bloody drama queen Ricki, Jacobs and Jonno are onto it."

He peeps up at me and wipes away an imaginary tear. Then he gets a gleam in his eye, "Jacobs is hot! I like a man who's in control," he says while licking his lips.

Bria tuts and pulls him away, back into the makeup room.

The protestor is still sprawled on the floor and the cheeky camera crew move in. The reporter shoves a microphone in his face and asks him why he did it.

"Because Davis is a capitalist wanker!" he yells. "He should die!"

The guy looks vaguely familiar, I'm trying to work out if I know him. Jonno must have been thinking along the same lines because he pushes the camera crew aside, kneels down, and takes a good look at him. "Are you related to Mitch by any chance?" he growls.

The protestor looks defiant and spits out, "He's my cousin! I'll defend our family honour to the end!"

Standing up, Jonno turns to me and shakes his head. The reporter chick pushes the microphone back in the guy's face and asks what the story is about the family honour. I'd like to know too, so I step forward, but Jacobs holds up a hand and orders me to keep my distance.

The guy snarls into the microphone, "Davis disrespected my cousin. He's tainted his workplace with his *filthy* behaviour. He's a capitalist wanker!"

The security guys have a quick word with Jacobs before they haul him off, and the camera crew immediately turns their attention to me. The reporter asks me how I feel after receiving my first death threat.

Man I must look a sight with my makeup only half done. I admit to her that I'm a bit shaken up, I certainly didn't expect this to happen. I tell her that I've got no further comment for now but I'd like to address it on my segment this morning.

They switch off the camera and she asks me if I'm really ok. I don't want to seem like a wimp, so I joke that it's the makeup that's making me look like shit and I'll be fine. I want to know if they can show the footage on my segment today. She says that she'll ask Charlie, the show's producer. I'd like to have a word with him too, so I tell her to send him in to see me if he's got time.

Jacobs and Jonno come over to me. "You guys rocked that!" I say. "Good job boys, well done."

Jonno puffs up at the compliment, "Me first proper security situation." He looks at Jacobs, "Was that a code red or blue?"

Jacobs actually grins at him and replies, "I believe that was a code blue Jonno, if there had been more of them we would have moved to a code red. You did an excellent job, well done."

Wow, I thought Jonno looked puffed up from *my* compliment, but with this praise from Jacobs, he's flushed with happiness and self-importance. I tell them that I'm impressed with how quickly and smoothly they *both* handled the situation, they really worked remarkably well together as a team. I'm proud of them for looking after me so well.

Jacobs inclines his head to me, Jonno rubs his hands together and says, "Wonder if there's any more crazy cousins we gotta worry about."

A door slams somewhere further down the corridor, and Big Mal stomps towards us with a trail of people following along behind him. He's bellowing at the top of his voice, "It's not bloody good enough! I will *not* have my stars harassed like this." He turns his head as he's still walking and barks at a girl, "Get on it NOW, I want some answers. Security should never be breached like this. Someone's heads gonna roll alright."

Coming to a halt in front of me he shakes my hand, then urges me into the makeup room, he wants to have a chat. He pauses in the hallway, pointing at Jacobs and Jonno and praises them for doing a good job. "At least someone round here can do what they're meant to! If you boys ever want a job there's one waiting for ya with me alright?" Then he turns to the rest of the group and tells most of them to piss off, except for Charlie, he wants him to wait in the hallway, says he'll call him in in a minute.

Big Mal slams the door of the makeup room shut behind us. Bria and Ricki are cowering in the corner. He looks over at them and suddenly his thunderous expression is completely transformed into Mr Happy. He says to them very nicely, "Would you two mind waiting outside for a sec? I want to have a private chat with Davis." They both nod and are about to exit when he adds, "Davis speaks very highly of you two, keep up the good work alright."

Ricky simpers at the compliment while Bria looks stunned, but they both mumble their thanks as they walk out with their heads held high.

I tell Big Mal that that was a nice thing to do, and he says, "Hey I've got no problem giving praise where it's due. I also have no problem tearing the shit out of someone if they've done a crap job." Tapping his nose he gives me a wink. "The secret Davis, is to always do a good job, plain and simple. Now, about this security issue."

Taking a seat in one of the makeup chairs I ask, "Should I worry about getting a death threat? It's pretty bloody freaky Mal."

Big Mal remains standing, casually resting his bum against the counter. He eyeballs me and replies, "Nah, don't worry about it mate. I get 'em all the time, that's what we've got security for." Somehow this doesn't make me feel any better.

He then apologises profusely, telling me that his security team here at the studio are meant to be top notch - for this very reason. "I'm a man who's got a lot of friends Davis, but just as many enemies. I need the security to not only protect my stars, but me as well."

He goes on for a while in this vein, then suddenly changes the subject and asks me if I like the Porsche. I can't help but grin and answer excitedly, "Hell yeah, it's freakin' awesome!"

"Well ya can keep it, as my way of saying sorry alright?"

I just stare at him blankly, then tell him that he doesn't have to do that.

"You're right," he booms, "I don't. But I *want* to, so accept it gracefully. I'll get the plates personalised for ya as well alright."

"That's un-fucking-real," I shout. "Thanks Mal, you're a god-damn legend."

Clapping me on the back he happily says, "That's more like it!"

I quickly take the opportunity to ask him to my party tonight, and tell him about auctioning off the ute.

He cracks up laughing and says, "Count me in, do ya want me to spread the word among some of me cronies. I can get some uber-rich mates to lob up, whaddaya reckon?"

I nod enthusiastically, telling him it sounds perfect. Putting up my hand up for a high-five, he looks at me for a sec, then grins and gives me one. Fuck, he nearly breaks my wrist, the guy's as strong as an ox. Then I pitch my idea for putting what just happened with the protestor on my segment today. He gives the all clear and tells me to run it by Charlie. As he's leaving he congratulates me on winning the newspaper poll. Giving me a cheeky wink he says, "I knew you'd bloody win." Once he steps out the door he bellows to Charlie to get his butt in here and to "Run with whatever Davis wants, alright."

$$$$$$$$$

My first respect segment is going really well, God I was so nervous at the start. I've introduced myself and told the viewers what respect means to me, how it can range from picking up your dog's shit when you take it for a walk (I don't have a dog, but if I did I'd pick up its shit) to holding a door open for someone. There's opportunities throughout every day to show it in small, thoughtful ways. It doesn't always have to be about big, grand gestures. And that's one of the things I'll be doing on my weekly segments, I'll be showing the viewers some smaller acts of respect, as well as including some bigger things too.

Next, they show footage of the protestors outside the studio this morning, and what happened in the hallway earlier. The camera crew captured it all perfectly. The guy comes across as a complete loser, especially when he says I should die and calls me a capitalist wanker. They beeped the wanker bit, but you could still tell what he was saying.

When it finishes I say, "This is a perfect example of someone showing a lack of respect. I'm now getting a death threat about something I didn't do in the first place. It's crazy!"

Then I lead into my interview with Tanya by saying, "I felt a distinct lack of respect from her, I wonder what respect means to Tanya, I'd really like to ask her." Staring into the camera I ask the viewers, "Wouldn't you like to know too?" then I act all surprised when she comes out and sits in the chair next to my desk. "What a wonderful surprise," I exclaim, I'm deliberately hamming it up for the camera. Then I ask her what respect means to her.

She quickly lists various things, like letting someone in in traffic, or giving someone a wave if they do let you into the traffic. I nod my head and she continues, she rambles on for a while then looks thoughtful. "Giving older people respect is important to me," she says.

So I jump in and ask her about younger people. Do they deserve to be shown some respect too? I can tell she's blushing, even through her caked on makeup.

She eyeballs me, then looks directly into the camera and says, "I'm really glad that you asked me that Davis. Yes, it *is* important to show younger people respect. And I'd like to officially apologise for not showing *you* enough respect on my show. You said that we were bullying you, and you were right. I'm sorry I did that. I could have gone for a different angle, but I was trying to create great viewing for our audience - at your expense."

Taking a deep breath she continues, "One thing I'm learning about you Davis is that you don't need any help in causing a sensation, you can do that all by yourself. But you treat other people with respect and I've got to say, I respect you for that. So, I'm sorry. I hope you can forgive me." I immediately accept her apology, then she adds, "I've got to admit, Davis, you've made me re-think my whole interview technique. And congrats on winning *The Daily Herald* poll, you really blitzed it!"

Standing up I ask if we can hug it out, which we do. Then I tell her that I really appreciate her apology, and there's no hard feelings - I realise she was just doing her job. Then I advise the audience to tune in next week. Pointing at the camera I say, "Respect yourself and respect other people." Then it's over. Phew!

As soon as we cut to the ad break clapping erupts from the set. Big Mal, Kirk and Leeza all crowd around, telling me what a great job I did. Big Mal's stoked, he keeps telling me I'm a natural, and makes a snap decision to open the phone lines, allowing the public to call in and give their opinion on my segment. Then he tells Kirk and Leeza to get ready for the onslaught. It's easy to see he's absolutely loving this, rubbing his hands together he booms, "This is gonna go berserk! Get ready people."

The atmosphere on set is electric. Big Mal gives Tanya a hug and tells her that she did great. She's obviously happy with how everything went because she's beaming at us all. Kirk gives me a high-five, then he and Leeza quickly take their places on set and announce to the viewers, "We want to hear from you, give us a call and tell us what *you* think of Davis's new segment."

I hang around for a bit, just watching the magic of television take place. I'm also curious as to what people will say. Big Mal's standing next to me, and so far they've taken six live calls. The viewers are rapt with my segment, they like my style. Most were horrified that I got a death threat, but all are thrilled with Tanya's apology. The consensus is that they can't wait to see what I'll do next. Kirk and Leeza cut to the news, and Big Mal claps me on the back. I wasn't expecting it, and nearly fall flat on my face - which cracks him up.

The cops are waiting for me in the makeup room when I get back. Apparently the protestor had a knife on him, so they're going to lay charges. Jacobs and Jonno are in the room as well, and Jacobs says that's why he didn't want me to get too close to the guy.

I ask the cops, "What about Mitch, can we charge him with anything? He's the ringleader here."

They inform me that unless he personally, physically harasses me they can't do anything. Jonno tells them about the phone call with Mitch, but again they say they can't do anything. Bummer.

As the cops are leaving Dad calls. I've had my phone on vibrate since before going on the set today, and it didn't stop vibrating the whole time I was on air, which was very distracting. Next time I'll give it to one of the posse to look after. I notice that there's heaps of messages.

Dad's nearly hysterical. He shout's that he saw everything on the show, and demands to know if I really am ok. I can hear Mum in the background asking him if I'm alright. I reassure Dad that I'm fine, then suddenly Mum comes on the line. She's nearly incoherent with panic, she's jumbling all her words together. I quickly try and placate her, but I'm not sure it's getting through. In the end I tell her that the cops are onto it, it's a one off situation, and it won't happen again. This seems to finally calm her down, and she passes the phone back to Dad. He says he loved my segment and can't wait for the party tonight, the whole family's coming, and they'll be arriving early.

After I hang up I check my messages. One of them's from Claire, she's worried about me too. Bria's nearly finished with me now, so I tell the posse that I want to go and visit Claire at work, I really need to see her. Jacobs and Jonno have a quick pow-wow, then Jacobs asks me how many exits there are to the building.

Staring at him I say dryly, "Only one. It's a café mate, not a department store."

Jacobs looks a bit miffed by my answer and explains that, after my death threat this morning, I need to take my security a lot more seriously. He advises that it's probably not a good idea to visit her today. But I don't care, I want to see her face to face. We've still got so much to sort out, to talk about, and I don't want to do it over the bloody phone.

Jonno snaps his fingers and says, "We could get you a disguise! You could go incognito."

Jacobs sighs, "You're certain you have to see her today sir?"

I nod, and he inclines his head to Jonno. "In that case, Jonno's idea is an excellent one sir."

Jonno smirks and adjusts his lapel.

Bria pipes up, "Hey I can give you an awesome disguise. Me and Ricki'll get ya sorted, won't we Ricki?"

Ricki had been lounging in one of the other makeup chairs, idly flicking through a trashy magazine. He immediately jumps up, they both look at each other and shout together, "The props department!"

Clapping his hands together with excitement, Ricki sizes me up and says, "You're gonna love your new look, Davis!"

An hour later I hardly recognise myself, they've turned me into a hippy! I'm sporting a long flowing blondish wig and tinted John Lennon glasses. Bria's given me a moustache and short beard, which are the exact same colour as the wig. They've even got me kitted out in a groovy paisley shirt and fringed black suede jacket. I've kept my own black jeans and converse runners on though.

Jonno and Jacobs had been banished from the room while the transformation took place. Even I couldn't see what was going on, because Ricki had swung the chair around so that my back was to the mirror. Taking another look at myself I whoop with glee, it's freakin' awesome!

Ricki opens the door for the big reveal. Jonno and Jacobs take a look at me and at first are shocked into silence, then Jonno cracks up. "That's bloody amazing." He looks at Bria and Ricki, "You two should be doing movies!" he gushes.

Jacobs has a funny expression on his face, he's doing something weird with his lips, they're sort of pursed, a bit like a cats bum. Suddenly he bursts out laughing and exclaims, "That's the best disguise I've ever seen! Jonno's right, your talents are definitely wasted here you two."

Ricki nearly swoons from Jacobs compliment. I guess his crush has now fully transferred itself from me to Jacobs - he'd better watch out or he'll be plastered with hugs. As if on cue, Ricki holds out his arms towards Jacobs and takes a few steps in his direction, indicating a hug is on its way. But Jacobs shakes his head, crosses his arms and narrows his eyes into slits. He gives Ricki a look that stops him in his tracks, causing him to pout. I can't help but chuckle.

"No hugs, no touching at all, thank you Ricki," Jacobs orders.

"That's right mate, keep your hands off him if you know what's good for you," I quip.

"Not fair," mumbles Ricki, who's still pouting.

I thank Ricki and Bria, and tell them I'll see them at the party tonight. The posse and I make a quick exit. In the car on the way to Claire's work, I decide that I'd better warn her that I'm in disguise, don't want her blowing my cover. The shop phone rings out - they must be flat chat, so I try her mobile but it goes straight to voicemail. Bugger!

227

$$$$$$$$$$

We get a parking spot right out the front of the café, which is a bit of a fluke, it's normally impossible to get a park here. We debated on the way over whether one of the boys should go in first and approach her, but I decide against it. I'll take my chances and go in alone.

It's not a big café, only about ten tables fit into it, and sure enough the place is packed. There's only one small table free, so I quickly grab it. It's so cool being in disguise. I just don't want Claire to freak out when she discovers it's me.

I spot her at the register; she's fixing up a bill for some people. She looks over at me and … nothing. She doesn't have a clue it's me sitting here. She must feel me watching her though, because she keeps shooting me quick glances while she does her thing. Bessie, one of the other waitresses, is delivering some food to people at a nearby table. It looks and smells delicious. Even though I'm sitting at one of Claire's designated tables I don't want to get Bessie's attention, so I busy myself with the menu. I know Claire will come and take my order when she's got a minute. I'm actually pretty hungry - getting a death threat and doing your first TV segment certainly builds up an appetite.

Finally Claire comes over, and she's all smiles - her pen and pad are poised ready to take my order. We make eye contact and I watch her expression change. She frowns a bit then shakes her head, and asks me what I'd like. I've just had a great idea, a way to guarantee that she won't blow my cover.

I ask if I can borrow her pen and pad for a sec, but she tells me no, she needs it. Fuck! So I beg her, plead with her, and she tells me that I'm creeping her out, and she'll call the cops unless I leave. For fuck's sake's, I'm only asking for a pen and paper, not a million bucks here. Then it suddenly dawns on me that she's probably already freaked out about my death threat this morning. She's on edge, and a hippy dude repeatedly asking for her pen and pad *is* a bit out of the ordinary.

Raising her voice she asks me to leave, I notice a slight tremble to her voice. Damn, I *have* freaked her out. But now she's aroused the curiosity of people at the neighbouring tables, they're all staring at us.

Shit. This was meant to be a covert operation, not an attention grabbing exercise.

Taking a deep breath I whisper to her, "It's me, Davis!"

She squints at me and snaps, "I'm warning you, you'd better leave now."

So I try again, a bit louder this time. "It's me Claire. Davis!" I flip up the John Lennon glasses so she can see my eyes properly, and bingo, recognition dawns on her.

"Shit Davis, what are you doing here?" she hisses at me.

Giving her my best puppy dog eyes I say, "I had to see you, I miss you babe."

Unfortunately someone at the next table heard my name, and now I can hear "That's Davis Spanx!" being spread from table to table. Standing up, I give the boys in the car a wave. They immediately jump out of the car and move into position, blocking the door to the café so no one can go in or out. This is so not what I wanted to happen, but I'm glad that Jacobs insisted we have a backup plan in case I'm recognised. I'm quickly realising that Jacobs is worth his weight in gold, he's on the bloody ball alright.

The whispering of customers quickly turns into a hum of excitement. Claire's looking pissed off with me so I plead, "I just wanted to talk to you babe." Then I address the café patrons. Taking off my glasses I admit to them that yes it's me, Davis Spanx, and I'm in a disguise because I thought it would be a good way for me to see my girl without being hassled. Some of the punters nod and whisper to each other.

I continue, saying "As some of you probably know, I had a death threat this morning." There's more nodding and whispering, "So I really wanted to reassure Claire that I was ok." Putting my arm around her waist I kiss the top of her head, which causes a chorus of ooohs to erupt from the customers. I smile at all the faces if front of me and say, "Would it be ok if I buy you all a coffee while I have a quick chat with my girl here? You've probably noticed that my security team are guarding the door." All heads swivel to the door. "For security reasons it's best if we all stay in here and don't let anyone else in or out. I know it's a lot to ask but is that ok with you all?"

There's a general murmur of agreement, but one old lady raises her hand and tells me that she has to meet someone and needs to go now. I tell her that's fine, I'll have to buy her a coffee another day, which makes everyone laugh. She asks me for an autograph for her granddaughter, tells me that it's nice to see some manners, and walks out with a smile. I ask if anyone else is in a hurry. Everyone shakes their heads, so I tell them to enjoy their coffees.

Taking Claire's hand I move over to the counter, fish around in my wallet and deposit a few fifty dollar notes next to the register. Then we both retreat to the small kitchen, I don't want our conversation overheard. Sally the boss gives us a wink and hustles out, telling us to take as long as we need. Once we're alone I try to pull Claire into my arms but she pushes me away, saying that now's not the time for that.

Taking a step back from her I say, "Thanks for saving my arse on *Tonight's Current Affairs*, Tanya was giving me a proper grilling 'til you called in."

Claire shuffles her feet and crosses her arms, "Yeah well, it wasn't right, she was treating you like shit. I couldn't believe she apologised to you today though, that's all everyone's been talking about. That and your death threat."

"Do ya miss me babe?" I'm kind of scared to know the answer.

She smiles, then reaches out to take my hand. "Of course I miss you. Part of me thinks I'm a complete nutter, but the other part needs some space." She looks deep into my eyes, "I'm still really confused darl, but yeah, I'm missing you like crazy. The house is so quiet without you."

Pulling her towards me again, I put my arms around her, nuzzle her ear and murmur, "The beds quiet too eh!" Then I give her bum a squeeze. Probably not a good move, because she immediately squirms away from me.

I want to know how long this 'break' is going to last for, I need to know what's going on. I don't want to be in limbo like this for too long - it'd be too painful. So I ask her what's going on.

Shuffling and looking down at her feet she replies, "I don't think you're going to like this Davis, but I think we should have a complete break for a month or two, and then re-evaluate things."

I rub a hand across my face in frustration, this isn't the answer I was expecting. "Jeezus Claire, you make it sound so bloody clinical. Re-evaluate my arse! We're not a bloody budget, this is our life!"

"Exactly," she snaps, eyeballing me, "and I need to re-evaluate mine, ok?"

"Actually, no. It's not bloody ok. I know exactly how I feel about you. I love you, deeply, madly, passionately. I don't have to re-evaluate anything, and its bullshit that I should have to wait around for *you* to decide what you want! But if that's what it takes then I'll do it." Shaking my head at her I add, "It's just not fair, I hate this not knowing. It's doing my head in Claire."

This is not how I pictured our conversation would go, I thought everything would be cool. I was secretly hoping that she'd missed me so much that the stupid break would be over and we could get back to normal. The party tonight would have been the perfect opportunity to celebrate our new togetherness. I was hoping to wow her with it, as well as the news of how Big Mal's gonna pay me two hundred grand a pop for my TV specials.

We move to opposite sides of the kitchen, sizing each other up like we're prize fighters. I feel like she's just given me a left jab to the heart. I don't want a bloody break, I just want her. This is so fucked up. Why can't she just be happy with the awesome new life I've created for us? Why can't she just love me?

She's got her arms crossed again, which isn't a good sign, "Maybe we should just break up then, finish it properly," she retorts angrily.

Oh fuck. I glare at her and blurt, "Maybe we should."

"Fine," she snaps.

I can't believe she just said that, I can't believe she'd throw away our five years together like this.

"Fine!" I snap back at her. "Just remember, this was *your* idea Claire. So that's it then, we're breaking up?"

She nods defiantly, "That's it Davis, we're over."

I'm so pissed off and hurt I could explode. Fuck her, fuck the life we could have shared, fuck everything. Slamming my fist down on the bench top I growl, "Thanks for breaking my heart Claire!" Then I stomp out of the kitchen. I'm trying not to cry, I want to keep it to-gether, so I quickly put my glasses back on, hopefully they'll camouflage my eyes.

As soon as I'm out in the café all eyes are on me. Shit. Putting my head down, I try to hide behind a curtain of hair. Suddenly one of the punters stands up and says, "Let's give three cheers for Davis, to thank him for the cuppa."

But instead of cheering they all stand up, punch their fists in the air, and chant "Respect" a few times at the top of their lungs. They must have all worked this out while Claire and I were out the back.

It's too much for me, I can't control myself any longer. Letting out a ragged howl I promptly burst into tears. The room goes deathly quiet, the only thing you can hear is me sobbing. Fuck! Then a lady stands up next to me, and puts her arm around my shoulders to com-fort me.

She actually looks like a *real* hippy, she smells of patchouli and everything. Patting my shoulders, she nods and says authoritatively, "I know, chanting together is *so* powerful. I think we were all moved by that weren't we?" There's a general murmur of agreement, then she continues, "Thanks for sharing your outpouring Davis, it's beautiful."

Oh Jeezus, that's done it. Burying my face on her shoulder I really let rip, I howl it out. More of the punters get up and start embracing me from all sides. Soon I'm the nucleus, everyone's clustered around me in a group hug. Other people have started crying too. The hippy mama tells us all to "Release it guys, let it all out, set yourself free." I have no idea how long we all hugged and cried it out, but the group naturally seems to disperse after a while.

Giving hippy mama's hand a squeeze, I thank them all for sharing this moment with me. "Your respect chant really touched me guys, but the real reason I'm a blubbering mess is because Claire wants to split up for good.....we're over." The punters all gasp. I sniff a few times and let out a couple of hiccups. "I just want to thank you all for your support just now, you guys are great."

A chick stands up on her chair and says, "She mightn't love you Davis, but *we* do!" Everyone agrees with her, and I get teary again.

Hippy mama hands me a business card which reads, 'Destiny Harmony: meditation and spiritual teacher.' She tells me to call her if I need her. Giving her a final hug, I make my way to the door.

As soon as I'm safely in the car Jonno asks what the hell happened in there. Jacobs was worried that he might have needed backup, and tells me that he wants me to wear a personal alarm from now on. I reveal that Claire's broken up with me, then promptly break down again.

"Oh fuck, you poor bastard," says Jonno. I'm so glad the car's got blackout tinting so that no one can see me. "Do ya wanna go to your folks place?" he asks me.

"Nah, just get me home. I need some space," I sniffle.

Jonno grunts and looks over to Jacobs, who nods his head and puts his foot down on the accelerator.

$$\$\$\$\$\$\$\$\$\$$$

I've been sobbing all the way home, intermittently filling the guys in on what went down in the café. My fake moustache and beard are gradually sliding off my face from all of the tears, but I don't care. When we get close to Paradise Towers, Jacobs lets out a groan and mutters to himself, "Not again." Sure enough there's a throng of protestors lurking around the entrance. Jeezus, with the mood I'm in they better not try anything.

Jacobs must have been keeping an eye on me in the rear view mirror, because he clears his throat and says, "Given everything that's happened so far today sir, it's quite understandable that you're feeling a bit out of sorts. But I must advise you against any outward displays of aggression at this point."

I don't say anything, so Jonno pipes up, "What he's saying is don't stir the pot, even though you're probably bustin' ya guts to smash some of those shit heads. Just ta get it out of your system, like." He swivels around in his seat to look at me. Jacobs is now flicking his eyes between the road and me, they're both trying to gauge my reaction.

Letting out a big sigh I say, "I hear you loud and clear guys, but those fuckers better not try anything today, I might not be able to control myself."

Jonno and Jacobs exchange looks, and I hear a loud click. "What did you just do?" I demand.

"I've activated the door locks sir, so you can't exit the car," Jacobs states.

I try the electric window button, but nothing happens, the window doesn't open. "I've also locked the windows; it's for your own protection sir."

"Fan-fucking-tastic Jacobs, do ya want a bloody medal?" I know I shouldn't take my shit out on him but I can't help it. Jonno and Jacobs share another look. I huff, and angrily kick the back of Jonno's seat, which makes him snigger. "What?" I shout. "What the fuck's so funny?"

"Have ya had a look at yourself lately? Not only are ya actin' like a two year old, ya look like a freak, with your beard an' that half off ya face. Hey Davis, you're off ya face!" Jonno laughs at his own joke, and I cop a glimpse of myself in the window reflection. I do look bloody ridiculous. I can't help but crack a small smile.

"Sorry for being a prick guys. Fuck what a day. The last thing I want is a bloody party tonight."

For a change the protestors are on my side, their placards say "Respect!", "We love Davis" and "Team Davis." This throws a spanner in the works. We could have easily driven past an anti-Davis mob, but it seems wrong to snub these people who are out here to support me. I say as much to Jacobs, and he agrees that I can put the window down, but I'm still not allowed out of the car. Jonno swivels around in his seat again and motions for me to lean closer to him. When I do, he rips off the moustache and beard.

"Fuuuuck!" I screech, more out of surprise than pain. He cackles, and tells me to stop being such a baby. Then we're among the throng of supporters. I'm rubbing my face as the window goes down, and suddenly the crowd erupts into a respect chant. Giving them a wave I hear a chick ask her friend, "Why's he wearing a wig, and what's with his face?" Shit, I'd forgotten about the wig. Oh well bad luck, they'll have to take me as I am.

The chant subsides and a guy calls out, "Sorry to hear about you and Claire, we reckon you're better off without her." And they all whoop their agreement.

How the hell do they know about that already? It only happened about twenty minutes ago. So I ask the guy, and he says it's all over Twitter. Shit. I'll have to get onto Ajala about this.

It'll probably be in the tabloids soon, so I may as well confirm it now. I yell out the window that it's true, Claire's broken it off for good, and that I'm feeling like shit but I really appreciate their support - it means a lot to me - and right now I need to get inside and get myself together. The crowd parts and lets us through, there's no dramas at all. In fact a lot of girls are blowing me kisses as we inch our way forward into the garage.

$$$$$$$$$

The penthouse is like an ants' nest, it's teeming with people who are all being directed by Kaylee. Porter's sitting in the foyer keeping an eagle eye on the proceedings. When I ask him what he's doing, he informs me that the amount of things that go missing from apartments when you get this much outside help in is unbelievable. He must have seen my look of scepticism, because he elaborates and tells me all about a certain 'do', where the hired help openly pinched a statue and were never busted for it.

I'm not convinced, so I ask him how they could possibly get away with it. He assures me that it happened, that it's hard to keep tabs on everyone. That's why he's watching the lift and foyer - just to be sure no one rips me off.

"Or ruins your reputation, eh Porter?" I joke.

He agrees, saying that he's glad my boys are now here to help him. I wander off to have a quick chat with Kaylee. As soon as she spots me she rushes over and gives me a big hug.

"Oh Davis, you poor thing. Are you ok?"

"What, with being dropped or having a death threat?" I try and joke.

"Both, but I guess I was referring more to you and Claire."

"Jeezus, everyone's heard about me and Claire. Social media is un-bloody-believable."

"Have you seen the video yet?" she asks.

235

Narrowing my eyes at her I demand, "What bloody video?" She shifts uncomfortably from one high-heeled foot to another, telling me to hang on a tick, then she teeters off.

When she returns she's holding an iPad, and shows me the YouTube clip of me in the café. From the respect chant through to my breakdown, and the group hug, they've captured it all. Great, this is just what I need. Aah the life of a celeb, nothing is sacred anymore, especially having a meltdown. I look at the number of hits it's had and gasp, a hundred and fifty seven thousand already – and it's only been up for half an hour. Kaylee rubs my back and murmurs that everything will be ok.

Ripping the wig off my head, I throw it on the floor and run my hands through my hair, giving my scalp a good scratch. "Right, let's see what you've done with the place eh?"

"Are you sure? You don't want to have some time out?" she asks worriedly.

"Nah, I'll do a *walk through* first, then go and take out my frustration on *Thrill Shooter.*"

She takes my hand, which I'm not really comfortable with, and pulls me out onto the terrace, telling me that she's impressed with my lingo - I'm picking up this event jargon quickly. Remembering my need to contact Ajala, I quickly excuse myself for a minute and give her a call. It goes straight to voicemail, so I tell her to jump onto YouTube to get updated, then to ring me back.

I move back over to Kaylee. At the moment my heart's not really into all of this, but I tell her I love what she's done with the place, throwing in lots of oohs and aahs for good effect. She's pretty switched on, so she orders me to go and have some boy time, adding that we can go through stuff together later on. I quiz her on what we could possibly need to go through, and she runs off a list of things I never even thought of. Just as well I've got her on board, otherwise I'd be totally stuffed. She wants to know who else I want to invite, so I rattle off some names, then tell her to talk to Dad. He'll know who to invite if I've forgotten anyone. I can't deal with any of this just now, the party's meant to get started at eight, so I've got around seven hours to get my shit together. Whose idea was it to have a bloody party?

Grabbing a beer out of the fridge, I dodge a few decorators and head into the games room for some mind numbing fun. Escapism is exactly what I need right now, get me a fuckin' gun!

Chapter 15

The family all arrive early for the party, and immediately want to know how I'm feeling. They fuss around me, asking if I'm ok after everything that's happened today. There's lots of hugs and back rubs from everyone. I tell them all I feel like shit, but life goes on, what can you do?

"For a start you erase that Claire from your memory," Grandma Spanx declares, "How dare she break my Davis's heart like that?" Reaching up she holds my face between her hands, and planting a kiss on my cheek she adds soothingly, "Don't worry love, you'll get over her. One day *she'll* be the one crying over her stupid mistake."

"Yeah, well I'm just gonna try and get through tonight. That's my first plan of action."

Danielle tells us all to hang on a sec, and rushes out to the foyer. She returns carrying a large plastic bag. Everyone huddles around her and she hands something out to each of them, but I can't see what it is. Then they all turn their backs to me and lower their heads. Looks like their putting caps on their heads. They are, and when they turn back around, they're all wearing *I love Davis* caps. I can't help but laugh.

"Who the hell had the idea for these?" I demand.

Everyone immediately points to Dad, who's holding his hands up in surrender. He gives me a wink, "Guilty as charged, don't ya just love them?"

Dunno if I love them, but I'm still chuckling. God my mad, crazy family cracks me up.

"Mission accomplished," says Danielle, *"Operation Cheer Up Davis* is a success."

Doug smirks at me and leads everyone in a family high-five. As I high-five Mum I mutter to myself, "Yep, nice one guys."

Suddenly Danielle plonks a cap on my head too. Whipping it off I declare that I can't wear a hat that says I love me. "Why not?" several of them ask at once.

"Because it's dicky, that's why. I've dolled myself up enough for tonight already, I don't want to overdo it."

This seems to placate them because they all nod, and murmur that I look "Classy," "Hot," and "Schmicko."

I *have* dolled myself up for the occasion. I'm wearing shiny, snazzy, black pointy toed dress shoes, teamed with black tuxedo pants which have got a groovy satin stripe down the outside seams. I've got the regulatory respect t-shirt on, but have teamed it with a tuxedo jacket with tails. I think it's a good look for the evening. Jacobs had me sorted out within the hour when I asked him this arvo if he knew where I could get my hands on some formal gear. He's a legend.

Holly and the two grans still haven't seen the penthouse yet, so I give them and the family a guided tour. They're all blown away with the luxe of the place. The two grans keep poking and prodding at the leather furniture, asking if it's all 'real'.

"Of course it's all real," blusters Dad, "only the best of the best for our Davis!" He gives me a cheeky wink and nudge, then we continue on with the tour.

Kaylee really has outdone herself. The penthouse is pimped to the max, it's like something out of a movie. The Hawaiian theme that Dad started for the photo shoot yesterday has been interspersed with a Moroccan theme, which sounds bizarre, but it works amazingly well.

Most of the penthouse is off limits to guests, except the huge lounge cum dining room cum kitchen area which spills out onto the terrace, plus a couple of powder rooms.

Kaylee didn't want people wandering through the whole place, so she's made the terrace the hero, the twinkling lights out here just beckon you to come and party. She's somehow squeezed in a marquee on each side of it, so the spa area is now like a tented Hawaiian cave, with the tiki bar inside. High bar stools surround lots of little circular tables, which are all decorated with grass skirt fringing. Fake hibiscus flowers are dotted everywhere too. The Bar girls are wearing Hawaiian costumes of coconut bikini tops, pink grass skirts, and flower leis around their necks and heads - it's awesome. It's definitely a place you want to hang out in.

She's turned the marquee on the other side of the terrace into a Moroccan lounging pavilion, complete with hookahs - the type you smoke, not poke. The glass water pipes are sitting on low coffee tables, and the two grans immediately pounce on them, wanting a go, but Kaylee says they'll have to wait until later. They completely ignore her, and giggling like naughty kids they grab a mouthpiece each and suck, causing the water inside to bubble away. Mum tuts at them disapprovingly, but I notice Grandma Drummond's eyes are glittering with excitement. Man I hope those two behave themselves tonight!

The wait staff are all decked out in Moroccan costumes, it's like walking into another world. The guys are wearing turbans and flowy capes, while the chicks just look hot in what I suppose is traditional Moroccan costume. Unlike the Hawaiian chicks, there's no flesh to be seen, but they're still dead sexy. We all ooh and aah and Kaylee claps her hands with delight.

"So you like it?" she asks me.

I laugh, giving her a hug. "This is incredible! You're gonna be the event planner to the stars after this."

Pulling back from the hug she looks at me seriously. "I already am Davis - you're a star, and don't you forget it!"

"He sure is," interjects Mum, "Oh Kaylee, this is just fantastic."

Holly wants to wear one of the Hawaiian girls' outfits, and she wants to wear it now. It looks like she's gonna throw a hissy fit until she gets one, but Kaylee saves us all hours of hair pulling frustration by diffusing the situation quickly and easily.

"Holly, you wouldn't want to be mistaken for one of the barmaids would you. *Everyone* would be hassling you for drinks and nibblies all night. You don't want that, do you?"

Holly purses her lips and looks steadily at Kaylee. She knows when she's outdone, so demurely admits that she doesn't want that to happen. Then she asks in a little girl voice, "But can I have one to take home and wear later? They're really pretty."

"Of course you can," sooths Mum, "Can't she?" she asks, looking at Kaylee imploringly.

Kaylee raises her eyebrows in surprise. "Yes, I can make that happen". Mum leans over and whispers something in her ear, causing Kaylee to laugh and say, "Yes Mrs Spanx, you can have one too."

Mum nudges Dad in the ribs, then grins and winks at him. He grins back at her, giving her bum a saucy smack. Oh man, I did not want that image of my Mum dressed up like that for Dad during their sexy time capers, but it's already there in my head. I look over at Doug and he's wincing, we're obviously thinking along the same lines. Shaking our heads at each other, I usher our little tour back inside, I can't wait to show off the games room. The kids are already ensconced there, which is where they're gonna stay for the rest of the night. Kaylee's organised someone to keep an eye on them, which is great. I know the two grans are gonna go ape shit over *Thrill Shooter*. I take a quick look at my watch, we've got about an hour before any guests arrive, plenty of time to whip their arses.

$$$$$$$$$$

The party's in full swing and my face is hurting from smiling so much. As far as I can tell everyone's having a good time, and I'm blown away by the calibre of people that are here. Kaylee and Big Mal seem to have materialised the who's who of the social set. Everyone from actors, models, sports stars, TV and radio personalities, to the really big guns like Big Mal and his cronies, as well as my motley crew of family and friends. It's a real mixed bunch but it seems to be working. Dad's having a ball hobnobbing with all the top players, Big Mal's introduced him to everyone, telling them how Dad farted in Neville's face. Surprisingly Neville doesn't seem to mind, he's been flittering between groups, hamming up the whole spa incident to anyone who'll listen.

I nearly fall over when Warney and Liz Hurley come over and introduce themselves, saying they're big fans, and that they're rapt to meet me. Tracy, who's already half pissed, spots us and drags Bruce over. Butting into our conversation, she introduces herself and Bruce as my besties. Bruce looks like he wants to die he's so embarrassed, especially when Trace drags Liz off for a 'private chat'. God knows what she'll bombard poor Liz with, the poor love, but Warney takes it all in his stride. He's a top bloke all right.

I've been keeping a tight rein on my drinking, I really want to get smashed, but now is not the time. I don't want to make a complete dick of myself, which tends to happen when I get pissed. Wow, I must be finally growing up.

Ajala swans over, dragging a guy with her. She scrubs up really well, she's looking beautiful. Giving her a hug I tell her how good she looks, which totally embarrasses her. She gushes about what a great party it is, and how she's loving being my social media coordinator. She slurs the word social a bit, so I advise her to get some water into her, "And don't you dare send out any tweets or anything tonight, you'll be in big trouble if you do ok?" I tell her seriously.

She giggles, waggles her head at me and agrees that it's probably a good idea to steer clear of it for tonight. Then she introduces me to her companion, who turns out to be her brother Suraj, the web design wiz. I apologise for not getting in contact, but he cuts me off by saying that he understands how busy I am, and that he's a big fan. I ask him how tricky it'd be to add a page to my website where people can upload their videos, I need a page dedicated to it because the photo page has already been swamped. He assures me that it would be easy for him to do, so I promise that we'll talk soon to get it organised.

Bambi and a bevy of her beautiful friends join our little group, and Suraj's eyes nearly pop out of his head. I know exactly how he feels, so I introduce him to Bambi, who leans over and gives him a kiss on each cheek, telling him that he's a very handsome man. Suraj gets totally flustered, so Ajala drags him away, but he keeps looking back over his shoulder at Bambi. It looks like she's claimed another heart.

"Naughty girl, you turned him into a blithering mess," I chide.

She slips her arm around me and whispers, "I know, I'm *very* naughty." Then she looks deep into my eyes. "Do you think I need spanking?"

Pinching her bum I say dryly, "You wish baby cakes," and saunter off. I'm glad I know she's just messing with me. It's kinda fun mucking around with a hot chick, knowing full well that it's just a bit of fun.

I spot the grandmas giggling and milling around the buffet table together, so I make a beeline for them. Oh Jeezus, I've just spotted Grandma Spanx shoving something into her purse. I skirt around a group of people I don't know and gently take her by the elbow. Looking down at her I ask, "Having a nice time ladies?"

"Oh yes," they babble together.

"You've outdone yourself Davis," says Grandma Drummond. "You've even got smoked salmon vol-au-vents, they're just marvellous! Have you tried them yet?" Her blue eyes twinkle up at me, they seem rather bloodshot.

I realise that I haven't eaten anything yet, but I'm about to as Grandma Drummond pushes a vol-au-vent up to my mouth, if I don't open it she'll probably squash it into my face. I make some appreciative noises as I chew and swallow. When I open my mouth to say something about the purse, and to quiz them on whether they've been smoking anything, Grandma Spanx shoves a meatball into my mouth. They could probably stand there feeding me for hours, so after I swallow it I hold up a hand to stem the flow of incoming food. Grandma Spanx looks dispirited, and tries to sell me on the chicken drumette she's holding, but I insist that she have it, which perks her up a bit.

While she's chewing I take the opportunity to ask what they're putting into their handbags. Denial is their first reaction, but when I tell them that I clearly saw Grandma Spanx shove something into her purse they both cave in. Grandma Drummond opens hers up, and I'm disgusted by what's in there. It's a mash of assorted party food, it looks and smells totally gross. Raising my eyebrows at Grandma Drummond she grudgingly opens hers as well, the same revolting mess is in it.

Shaking my head at them, I then ask if they've tried the hookah yet. They both nod enthusiastically, saying that a lovely young man made up a special mix for them. I notice Grandma Spanx elbow Grandma Drummond in the ribs, and they both start giggling uncontrollably. Great, my two grans are stoned, I *knew* they'd be up to no good.

"You two are unbelievable! How about I get a tray of party food sorted for you both to take home, so you don't have to shove anything else into your purses. Would that work for you?"

Two sets of eyes open wide with surprise and longing. "Really?" says Grandma Spanx.

"You'd do that for us?" whispers Grandma Drummond.

Putting my arm around both of their shoulders I say, "Hey, you know I'd do anything for you two. Come on, let's hit the kitchen and get your munchies sorted."

$$\$\$\$\$\$\$\$\$\$$

Bambi's working the room, she's flirting outrageously while taking photos of everyone. As soon as *The Weekly Star* found out that she was invited they called Dad and offered to pay a ridiculous amount of money for exclusive photos of the bash. Fine with me, I'll pool the fee into a charity.

Who is Davis Spanx?

After a lot of umming and aahing as to which charity I should nominate for the auction, Big Mal of all people suggests that I set up my own. He throws back at me all the ideas I've shared with him about my TV segment, about the vision I have for bringing back the respect. He finishes by saying that not only will I be helping others, but by having my own charity, I'll also be creating a platform for other people to help me. And by allowing them to donate their money to my cause, this will also raise my credibility. At first I balk at the idea, but he's right, I do have big ideas for my respect segment which I'll somehow need to fund. So after a pretty good sales pitch from him I can now see the benefits, and setting up my own charity now seems like the logical thing to do. He's a very persuasive man.

Taking a slurp of his drink he says, "*I* know you're not a blow in Davis. *I* know that ya want to create some real change. By havin' your own charity you'll be able to do it on an even bigger scale. I'll get one of my finance blokes to help ya sort it out alright."

Clinking my drink against his I laugh, "You're on! Thanks mate, this is unreal."

Clapping me on the back he adds, "Now I'll go spread the word about it alright," and he swaggers off towards the tiki bar with not a care in the world. Fuck me, I know I've hit the big time now, I've got my own bloody charity going on!

It doesn't take long for Dad to hear about it. He comes rushing over and asks me if the rumour's true, have I got my own charity. When I explain that it's Big Mal's idea, and that he'll help me get it sorted, Dad quickly agrees that it's a bonzer idea. "What are you gonna call it, son?"

Shit, I've got no bloody idea. Chewing my bottom lip I look off into the distance trying to think of something.

"What about...," but I've got nothing, my mind is blank. All I can think of is Respect Inc. Dad doesn't seem too impressed with it, and neither am I.

Doug wanders over to join us, so I fill him in on what's happening. Taking a gulp of his drink he says, "That's easy, your charity name should be The Davis Spanx Respect Charity." Waving his glass at me he adds, "Gotta keep it simple mate, ya want people to know exactly

245

what their giving to. Don't want to bamboozle them with fancy named shit."

"I like it, good one Doug," I say, giving him a punch on the arm. Telling me to hold his drink for a sec, he whips out his wallet and hands me a fifty dollar note.

"Here, consider this your first donation. Jeezus, I can't believe you've got your own bloody charity. What'll it be next, your autobiography?" Chuckling at his own joke he asks me to introduce him to Bambi.

Dad and I look at each other, then Dad proceeds to tell Doug about her being my wing-girl.

Doug nearly chokes on his drink and splutters, "You're kidding! How'd ya get her to do that for you, ya lucky bastard?"

Mumbling that it was her idea, Dad interrupts me and happily elaborates, filling Doug in on the antics of my misbehaving dick yesterday - revealing how I turned back into a teenager.

"Don't bloody blame ya mate," Doug smirks. "She's hotter than a vindaloo. Come on, I want an intro."

Bambi doesn't disappoint, she insists on taking a photo of me and Doug. Then she turns on the charm. Within seconds Doug's jabbering on like an idiot, nearly stuttering in his inability to hold it together. Luckily he's saved by his wife Janelle, who's honed in on Doug and Bambi like a guided missile. I can tell she's pissed off, so can Doug, because he immediately excuses himself and asks Janelle if the twins are ok. Assuring him that they are, she coyly suggests that they'd better go and check on them in the games room, just to be sure. They make a quick exit and I can see Janelle's fingers digging into his arm. Jeeze she shouldn't worry so much, Doug's all bluff. There's no way he'd do anything to jeopardise their marriage, he knows what a good wicket he's on. They've been together seventeen years, since they were both eighteen, and are still rock solid. I envy them a bit, but I guess my time will come. Eventually.

Right, I mentally give myself a slap, gotta stop thinking that kind of shit 'cos it's making me upset about Claire again. Spotting Kaylee out on the terrace by herself, I nab her before she gets caught up in doing something or chatting to someone. I tell her about my new charity and she squeals with delight, saying it's awesome. Then she looks at her watch.

"We've still got an hour and a half until the auction. How about I get a 'Davis Spanx Respect Charity' banner made up so we can hang it near the ute. What do you think?"

Scratching my chin I boldly reply, "Bloody great, but its ten o'clock on a Friday night. You're dreaming."

"Do you want it or not?" she challenges.

"Yeah, course I want it. Just don't reckon ya can do it, that's all."

Putting her hands on her hips, her green eyes flash at me, "Just watch me." And she quickly teeters off, a woman on a mission.

Bloody redheads, I sigh to myself. But an hour later she's as good as her word. I'm out in the Moroccan tent chatting to Kyle Randiland, he's been trying to convince me to come on his radio show next week, when Kaylee grabs me by the arm, excuses me, and drags me away with her. Kyle yells out as I'm leaving, "That's it mate, drown your sorrows with a redhead, there's nothing better! See ya next week!"

The banner's way cool, it's not something she's just pasted together herself, but a real professional one, with 'Give to the Davis Spanx Respect Charity' plastered across it. There's even a photo of me on one end, with a bubble coming out of my mouth saying my catchphrase, "Don't forget to respect yourself and respect other people."

"That totally rocks," I gush, giving her a quick peck on the cheek. "I can't believe you got it done. How'd ya do it?"

She grins at me, "Ah Davis, all I can say is that I've got lots of friends in helpful places."

I notice a clear plastic barrel, the type you use for bingo and stuff, sitting next to the roped off cars. People are busily stuffing cash in it as I watch. Cool.

"Have you had a look at the guest book I set up yet?" she asks.

I tell her I haven't, so we wait while a woman finishes filling it in. When she turns around I realise that it's Jen Hawkins. She gives me a kiss, and gushes that she loves what I'm doing. Wow. I move over to the guest book and check it out. There's a sign stuck to the podium on which the book is resting, and it reads 'Don't be shy now, let Davis know if you want him to come to your next party or event. Make sure you leave him your contact details.' Turning the book back to its first page, I see that Big Mal's started it off by writing 'Davis is a star with a heart,' and that he wants me on his boat ASAP. He also writes that he's donating half a mill to get my charity started! Oh my fucking God!

Flipping through the pages, I discover a who's who of celebrities that have all given me glowing praise, as well as noting when they've got events on that I *must* go to. They've all included either mobile numbers or emails, or both. A lot of them have followed Big Mal's lead and disclosed how much they've donated, and the figures are absolutely astounding. It's mind-blowing.

Kaylee brings me back to earth, saying excitedly, "Davis, you are totally set up now. Look at all these A-listers that want *you* at their gigs. Pretty cool eh?"

"You're a fucking genius!" I shout as I pick her up and twirl her around. Lots of people turn our way and smile indulgently at us. They, like Kyle, probably think I'm gonna give her one. As if! But this *is* absolutely incredible. I now have my own personal book full of celebrity contacts, and the best bit is that I know they want a piece of me! Shit a brick! Wait till Dad hears about this. Then I have a thought.

Setting Kaylee back down I ask her, "What about privacy? Why aren't these guys worried about their details getting out?"

Rolling her eyes at me she replies, "Because everyone here's in the same boat. I guess you'd call it a code of ethics. It's about respect Davis - exactly what you're on about. These guys are all the top players of their game so to speak, so they wouldn't disrespect each other by pilfering someone else's details. It just wouldn't happen, so relax ok?" she assures me.

"Yeah but not everyone here's an A-lister, what about the bar staff and waiters. What about my family and friends? They're not A-listers either."

She points to a guy standing not too far away, a big burly security guy by the looks of him. "Trevor there is on duty not just to keep an eye on the cars, well the Porsche really, he's also posted there to make sure no one dodgy gets to your guest book, ok? It's all safe and sorted Davis. Your family and friends are cool, so he just has to worry about the hired help, and they wouldn't dare."

Excellent. I give her another hug and tell her I've got to go find Dad and let him know, he's not gonna believe this.

I find him propped up at the tiki bar talking to Molly Meldrum. I say g'day and am really tempted just to hang out for a bit, I mean Molly's a bloody Aussie legend, and I've got the chance to chew the fat. But my excitement gets the better of me, and after a brief exchange, where I tell him how awesome he is, I excuse us both. Towing Dad into the lounge with me, we make our way towards the guest book. Some people are lined up waiting to write in it, so I point out the banner to Dad, who gives a cheers with his stubby to it. Then he spots the barrel that's filling up with cash. His eyes bug open as I tell him that it's only the tip of the iceberg, and that Big Mal's donated half a million. He nearly drops his beer.

"Well that shits on Doug's fifty bucks eh!" he says, and we both crack up laughing.

The guy who was just signing my guest book turns out to be Nathan Buckley. Dad grabs his hand and pumps it, enthusing that Bucks is doing an ace job as coach. Dad's a mad Collingwood fan and so am I, although not to the extent that Dad is. He's a real one-eyed supporter, he was in tears when Collingwood lost the grand final to Geelong back in 2011. Bucks is a good sport, and tells Dad that he appreciates the support and that he likes what I'm doing. Patting me on the back he tells me it's bad luck about Claire, to which I just nod. Then he says that he expects to see us at a game next season, and wanders off.

"Jeezus, I shook his hand," breathes Dad.

"Check this out Dad," I say as I pull him over to the book. He blinks rapidly a few times, flips a few pages, then turns to me. A look of astonishment is etched upon his face.

"Either I've had too many beers and I'm hallucinating, or this is your own bloody Rolodex of VIPs ego-stroking comments, invites, contact info, and amounts of money they're throwing into your charity. Is this for real Davis?"

"Yep."

"Fuuuuck! You little ripper! Who set this up?" he demands.

"Kaylee, she's a bloody legend eh?"

"Oh mate, she's a bloody legend alright. This is your ticket to total celebrity acceptance." He grabs the top of my arm and gives it a squeeze. "Christ Davis, you know what this means don't ya?" I just stare at him and he says, "Your bloody experiment! The whole reason you wanted to do this was to reach celebrity status and put out a good message. Mate you've done it! In a bloody week! It's unreal! *You're* unreal!" he says excitedly.

Suddenly he turns a deep shade of red, and I realise that he's holding a beer in his hand. He shouldn't be drinking, God I hope all this excitement isn't too much for him, I hope he's not gonna have another heart attack. I shouldn't have worried though, because a second later he lets out a massive fart. Breathing a huge sigh of relief, he tells me that he's been holding it in for bloody ages. The smell is revolting. I gag and quickly move away from him, but he follows me, so I quiz him on how many beers he's had.

"Only two." Then his face lights up, *'That's* what's making me fart, bloody beer. Can't have anything carbonated anymore." He gives the offending stubby to a passing waiter and grabs a juice instead, just as Trace stumbles over to us, with Bruce trailing behind.

"Whash all the cash for Davish?" she slurs.

Oh great, she's really pissed now. God I hope she can hold it together for the rest of the night. I signal a waiter and grab a bottle of water off the tray for her, but she slaps it away, swaying on the spot.

"It's donations for my charity Trace. Everyone's been really supportive, I've got heaps of money for it already."

"Sgreat, betta have a lookshee," and she stumbles off towards the barrel, leaving us all staring after her.

"Hope she doesn't get too messy tonight mate," I tell Bruce.

"Nah, she'll be right, don't worry about her. I'll take her out to the games room if she starts playing up."

Bruce follows Trace over to the barrel. I swear he's got the patience of a saint, I don't know how he puts up with her. They both stare at the money for a bit, Trace wants to spin the barrel so she gives it a few turns, then she spots the guest book. She might be pissed, but she's still switched on enough to know what's going on within its pages. I'm busy talking to another group of people when I hear her screech at someone, "Give me back my fucking phone." I inwardly

250

groan and turn to see her trying to snatch her phone back off Trevor the security guy. She can't reach it because he's too tall, she's not a happy camper.

I immediately spring into action and rush over, the last thing I want is a scene, especially with Trace. Bruce is telling Trevor to just hand the phone back to her but he won't. I ask what the problem is, and Trevor informs me that Tracy was taking photos of the guest book pages with her phone.

Shit! This is not good, I don't want to piss off any of my VIP guests with a breach of their confidentiality, it could ruin everything.

In a nice soothing voice I tell Trace that she's not allowed to take photos of the book for privacy reasons. She just looks at me blankly, then denies taking any photos at all, saying that she didn't get a chance to before 'Bugalugs here' snatched it off her. So I explain that in that case, she won't mind if we just check her phone to make sure she didn't take any by mistake.

"No fuckin' way, thass a breesh of my privashy," she slurs belligerently, while swaying on the spot and glaring at me.

"Come on darl," pleads Bruce, "just show 'em there's no photos, then you can have another nice glass of champagne. Huh?"

"No!" she says, stamping her foot.

Jacobs materializes at my side and I explain what the issue is. He asks me quietly if he might assist in the situation, so I tell him to knock himself out.

Advancing on Trevor he pretends to bump into him, knocking the phone out of his hand onto the floor. Then quickly dropping to his hands and knees, Jacobs gropes for the phone, pretending to fumble it under the barrel stand, which conveniently has a curtain attached to the bottom of it. He darts underneath the curtain to retrieve the phone. Meanwhile Trevor is apologising profusely for his actions, he seems to be distracting Trace quite well. Suddenly Jacobs pops up, phone in hand. He inclines his head slightly towards me as he hands Trace the phone, apologising for any inconvenience, then he offers her a special champagne cocktail that's waiting for her in the tiki bar - if she should wish to go and get it. Trace grabs Bruce by the wrist and hustles him outside, muttering something about 'Privashy schmivashy'.

Jacobs reveals that she did indeed take photos, she'd gotten nearly three pages worth. Putting my hand over my mouth I exhale loudly in relief, man that sure was a close call.

"Thank God you and Trevor sorted that out without making a scene. I can't thank you enough Jacobs."

Giving me a small bow he says, "Just doing our jobs sir, glad to be of assistance."

"Did Trevor know what you were up to? He didn't seem surprised when you knocked the phone out of his hand."

Jacobs smirks and brings his left hand to eye level. "I believe it's called cuff magic sir."

"Ahh, the good old cuff magic," I nod, then quickly lean forwards and say into his cuff, "Nice work everyone, well done."

With this Jacobs cracks a smile, and I distinctly hear a tinny Jonno voice coming from his earpiece, "No worries sir!" He must have really yelled it in order for me to hear him, because Jacobs jumps with fright and then stalks off, to no doubt find Jonno and berate him. He probably nearly burst Jacobs' ear drum.

Soon after the Tracy shenanigans it's time for the charity auction. There's been quite a buzz about it, there's even a couple of telephone bidders, Big Mal told me earlier that a couple of his mates couldn't make it to the party but didn't want to miss out on all the fun, especially when they heard what they'd be bidding for. I never dreamt that my crusty old ute could be so popular!

Moving through the crowd towards the cars, I notice that the barrel's gone missing, my heart skips a beat and I begin to feel faint. What the fuck happened to the barrel? I hurriedly approach Trevor, and he advises me that my Dad's pinched it so that he can count the amount donated so far. Man, that's the second time tonight I've freaked out over nothing. First Dad's un-heart attack, now the mystery barrel disappearance. I knew I was on edge but this is ridiculous, I need to chill out and relax a bit. But looking at the time, I know I've still got a way to go before that's going to happen.

It's show time. Taking to the mini stage that Kaylee's rigged up, I thank everyone for coming, and express my heartfelt gratitude that they've all come to support me at such short notice. I tell them I'm completely blown away by all the stars and big-wigs that are here to-night, adding that I'm honoured by all their invitations, I'll do my best to attend each one. Then I affirm that before me is the most generous group of people ever assembled, judging by the amount of cash in the barrel and all the other pledges made tonight. I start clapping and ask them to give themselves a hand. A murmur of agreement spreads through the crowd and they all join in the applause.

Dad jumps up onto the stage with me. "It's official," he yells out over them all, "The Davis Spanx Respect Charity has made four point eight million dollars tonight!"

He's beaming out at the crowd, whereas I've got my jaw on the ground. Did he just say four point eight *million* dollars? The room erupts with the deafening noise of cheering and clapping, but I'm still standing there like a stunned mullet, it's a lot to take in.

I start to thank them again but Big Mal calls out, "Let's make it a nice round number. I'll donate the extra 200k to make it five mill, al-right."

Fuck me, five million dollars in one night. This is unbelievable! I'll really be able to get my charity rockin' and rolling with this sort of cash injection. "Wow," is all I can manage at the moment, so Dad takes over, giving me a few seconds to get myself together.

He gives a little speech about how proud he is of me, and how it's only a week since I had my launch at Paul's pub. I spot Paul in the crowd and raise my glass to him in thanks. Eric's standing next to him. Wicked, I can't wait to find out where *he's* been hiding. Dad continues on, referring to what he said to me earlier about how my goal was to reach celebrity status, and to spread a good message.

He pauses then says, "And with the help of all you good people, Davis has achieved that tonight. Next thing you know he'll be standing beside Hugh Jackman on the red carpet – that's his other goal."

I can tell Dad's about to get a bit teary, I can hear the catch in his voice. I cry at shit easily too, and it's all Dad's fault. As a kid he always told me that it's more manly to express my emotions rather than hold-ing them in, because if I hold them in for too long they can fester, making me unhappy in the long run.

Sure enough, a tear seeps out of one of Dad's eyes. Sniffing it back, he puts a hand on my shoulder and says, "*You* guys might have only known him for a week, and what a week it's been. But *I've* known him his whole life, and let me tell you, you ain't seen nothin' yet! I'm so proud of you son, we all are. Well done."

We have a hug, and I spot Mum and the rest of the family. She's crying, the two grans are crying, in fact most of the chicks in the room are crying too. It must be the day for it eh.

Big Mal clears his throat loudly, and announces that he's got something to say before we kick into the auction. Dad steps down off the stage to make way for him.

"It's no secret,' Big Mal booms, "That I think young Davis here's the best thing since sliced bread, alright."

Anyone that knows Big Mal knows that he ends pretty much every sentence with alright, it's a given, but there's still a few people who murmur their agreement to him before he continues on.

"I reckon his Dad's right." He taps his nose. "I'm a bit more in the know than you lot, and I know this for certain – you *ain't* seen nothin' yet alright. He may be the new kid on the block, but he's gonna be doing some pretty amazing stuff very soon. You'll all have to *stay tuned* to Channel Six to see it alright." He cracks up at this shameless plug for *his* TV station.

"Anyway I got a little prezzie for ya Davis. I told ya this morning I'd look after the plates for the car." From behind his back he reveals two personalised number plates. They're black with white writing, and the letters read RESPECT. Oh that is way too cool, I'm grinning from ear to ear.

"Alright?" he asks.

"Shit yeah! It's awesome, thanks Mal," I shout.

"Right then, let's get this auction under way. Where's Mr Dealer Drome? Come on out Andy, and get the boy some more money!"

Suddenly the lights go down, music blares, and strobe lights flash around the room. I move off the stage towards the family, clutching the number plates to my chest. Andy from *Deal That Deal* jumps up on stage and cries out, "Who's feeling lucky tonight? Who wants to drive away in this magnificent example of horsepower?"

Someone yells out, "Are you talking about the ute or the Porsche?" Everyone cracks up, and the auction begins.

Dad wants to know why Big Mal's giving me personalised plates to a car he's only lending me, so I explain that after the death threat this morning Big Mal decided to give the car to me, as a way of apologising. Dad just chews his bottom lip, shakes his head, and tells me that I've got the bloody Midas touch. I can't argue with him, especially when the ute reaches seven hundred and fifty thousand dollars. There's a bidding war between one of the phone bidders and a lady down the back who I can't see, but I can hear. In the end it goes for eight hundred thousand to the phone bidder. Unbelievable! That's nearly six million dollars all up. Hey, I'm nearly the six million dollar man!

Just as everyone's dispersing back to the bars to refresh their drinks, Jonno and Jacobs bustle over. I can tell by the looks on their faces that something's up.

"It's Mitch," Jonno snaps angrily, "he just called me again. This time he told me to get ready for a surprise."

"What did he say exactly, can you remember?" I demand.

"He said, 'Surprise, I'm gonna light up that bastard Davis's life', then he just laughed and hung up."

I look to Jacobs and ask him if he's got any idea what this means, but shaking his head he admits it could be anything.

Suddenly there's a loud whoosh outside, and what sounds like an explosion. People immediately scream, and all hell breaks loose. Oh fuck, what just happened? Jonno and Jacobs set off at a sprint, Jacobs is yelling into his cuff, calling for backup. I run out onto the terrace after them.

There's another whoosh and an explosion, and I now see what's causing all the commotion. Fireworks are being fired straight at the penthouse from a nearby building. So far they've missed the terrace and are exploding above it, hitting the large windows of the penthouse and showering sparks down onto everything below. Jacobs looks outraged, he yells something at Jonno and then runs back inside. The guests are over their initial shock, and now they're loving it. They probably think it's all part of the evening's entertainment.

I'm horrified, someone could get badly hurt from this. Whoosh, another one just misses the terrace, it looks like Mitch's aim is getting better. Shit.

Jonno's backup team arrives, and together they try ushering everyone back inside, citing safety reasons as the excuse. Most of the guests are putting up a fight though, they don't want to miss out on all the fun.

I'm really worried that someone will get hurt, so I call for everyone's attention and urge them to follow the security teams' instructions. This seems to work, and everyone grudgingly goes inside. Meanwhile, Kaylee leads a crew of waiters and waitresses out onto the terrace. They descend on the marquees and immediately start dismantling them, as I hear the wail of police sirens getting closer.

Whoosh, another firework hits the top window of the penthouse and explodes. Everyone inside oohs and aahs at the spectacle.

Neville comes rushing out with Dad, demanding to know what's going on. Neville sets his jaw and barks that it'd take more than a bloody firework to break the windows, they're cyclone proof, they're ultra-toughened, and nothing can break them. This at least makes me feel a bit better. Then Jacobs reappears and informs us that the police are onto it, if the idiot hangs around to shoot any more off they'll catch him for sure. Mitch must have known this, because the assault has stopped.

The Hawaiian tent is a shambles, half up, half down, and there's a smell of burning. Suddenly a lick of flame appears on one side of the tent and Neville shouts, "Leave it to me." He disappears round the corner of the terrace, reappearing a few seconds later with a fire hose. He gets into position, then shouts for Dad to turn the water on. Luckily he puts the fire out before it gets a chance to take hold properly. Thank god Neville was here and knew where the fire hose was, it could have been a disaster otherwise. A few guests have drifted outside again to watch the action, but no one seems to have realised that anything's wrong. Just as well they're all pissed.

Breathing a sigh of relief I go and get myself a beer, I bloody deserve one. Jacobs is talking to someone on his phone. When he finishes the call he tells me that the cops got the right building, but they haven't been able to nab Mitch. He got away. The police are now on their way over to talk to Jonno about the phone call he received.

256

Turns out the cops can't do a thing. Again. The only hope is to catch Mitch red-handed. Unless they can do that, nothing can be pinned on him. Apparently the phone call isn't incriminating enough, he didn't say anything that he can be arrested for. Fuck me, what's it take to arrest a nutter these days?

$$\$\$\$\$\$\$\$\$\$$

At last it's time to relax, today has just been mental. Everyone's gone home except for Eric, Bruce, and Trace who's sleeping it off in one of the spare rooms. After the guest book photo rigmarole, she tuckered herself out playing *Street Racer Pro* with the kids. Thank God, you never know which way it's gonna go with Trace. Luckily tonight she mostly behaved herself, although apparently she was livid that we'd deleted the photos from her phone. She told Bruce that she had a mind to say something, until he reminded her that she'd denied taking them in the first place - therefore it wasn't in her best interest to say anything or else she'd look like a liar.

Kaylee and I personally saw each guest off with a Respect Goody Bag in hand. I told her she'd better have put her own card in there, and she assured me that she had. She really deserves to get the best gigs in town after the amazingly slick production she put on tonight.

As Dad and the family were leaving he assured me that the weekend is mine to do with as I please. Mum even told me to give Sunday lunch a miss if I want, then Dad insisted that I take a couple of days off to get my head together and just relax a bit. Sounds good to me, it's exactly what I need.

So now it's just me and the boys, thank fuck for that. We've been chewing the fat, catching up on Eric's antics. Sure he went to Perth for a business deal, but it also turned out to be the hottest few days of his flamboyant sex life so far. That's why I couldn't get hold of him, he was all 'tied up'. He really puts Bruce and me to shame, the guy's an absolute stud.

We move on to talk of Claire and me. We all know not to diss an ex-girlfriend, there's always a minute chance of getting back together, so if you diss them it's likely to get uncomfortable. We've all done it, so we know not to go there, it's an unwritten man code. Eric says wisely that you never know what's gonna happen in the future, and tells me I should just enjoy myself right now. Yeah, well *I* know that Claire and I are history. I give them the lowdown on what happened in the kitchen at the café, about how callous she was. After a bit of head shaking Bruce snaps the conversation forward, saying that the YouTube vid of me crying and the group hug is gonna become another cult classic.

"The hippy mama was really nice, I liked her." I say.

"Well I liked the long blonde wig, you should grow your hair and dye it mate," jokes Eric.

"Today's just been one big bloody drama after another."

"Let me get this straight," says Bruce. "Today you've had a death threat at the studio from Mitch's crazy cousin, scored yourself your dream Porsche with personalised number plates because of said death threat, debuted your weekly TV segment, on which you got one of Australia's hardest hitting journos to apologise for bullying you. You've donned a wacky disguise and been dumped by your long-time girlfriend, while having most of it filmed for public consumption." As he's running through this list he's ticking them off his fingers. "You've also thrown the party of the century, which has enabled you to gain full celebrity status, as well as raising nearly six million bucks for your new charity - the charity that you decided to put together only a matter of hours ago. And last but not least, you've survived a bombardment of fireworks which could have caused a massive fire and total carnage." He looks at me and shakes his head. "Mate, you must be fucked."

"I bloody am! But you're forgetting the run in with your lovely wife that could have caused carnage of a different nature. If she'd gotten away with it I'd be totally fucked. And there's Dad's fake heart attack." Both of them lean forward with a look of concern, but I wave them away saying, "Nah it was nothing to worry about, he just needed a good old fart. But I thought the barrel with all the cash had been pinched at one stage too, which totally freaked me out." Taking a deep breath I add, "But there were also some of my own supporters outside Paradise Towers today, and that felt freakin' awesome. Not to mention hobnobbing with all the VIPs tonight, I can't believe how generous they all were. Today's been a bloody rollercoaster alright, but what a ride!"

Eric and Bruce look at each other, then Eric leers, "Mate if I was you, I'd be giving that Bambi chick the ride of her life, she's a goddess."

Yawning loudly, I tell them that she's only my wing-girl, that's all.

Giving each other a knowing look, Bruce shudders and says, "Whatever she is, you're a lucky bastard mate."

Yawning loudly again I say, "Guys I'm fucked, I've gotta crash. You two can do what ya want tho', there's enough spare rooms for you to crash too Eric." Standing up, I give my balls a scratch and bid them goodnight.

Eric cheekily calls out after me, "Have sweet dreams about Bambi won't ya Davis!" Giving them the finger I toddle off towards the bedroom, accompanied by the dulcet tones of their boyish sniggers.

Chapter 16

By mid-morning I just can't sleep anymore, so I drag myself out to the kitchen for a coffee. Spotting Bruce standing next to Black Beauty, I make a detour to the lounge area. He's gazing lovingly at her, a goofy smile is plastered across his face. Nodding his head in greeting, he tells me dreamily that Eric's already gone home, but Trace is still crashed out and he doesn't expect her to surface until after lunch.

"C'mon, let's take her for a spin, we'll go get some brekkie," I blurt.

Bruce's eyes light up and we both scramble into the car. We're giggling and bouncing in the seats like naughty kids as we ride down in the car lift. Luckily Porter didn't spot us. I'm still totally buzzing from last night, so this seems the perfect way to start the day.

The excitement level goes up a notch when I start her up and she roars into life. It isn't a purr, but a throbbing, awe inspiring roar. Pressing the accelerator a few times to hear the magic of the engine causes more bouncing and hoots of delight. This finally alerts Porter that something's going on, and he materializes next to my window, asking if I need any assistance with the car.

"No probs here mate, we're fine," I tell him nonchalantly. I shouldn't have spoken so soon because buggered if I can get it into gear. Shit. I forgot how tricky manual cars can be - my crappy old ute is an automatic and so is Claire's car - it's ages since I've driven a manual.

Porter stands there smugly, arms folded across his chest with a definite air of 'I told you so' about him. After a couple more embarrassing crunches of the gearbox I admit defeat, and ask him to show me how it's done. He says there's a few tricks, and shows me the ropes.

"They should come with an operating video or something," Bruce puts in.

Arching an eyebrow Porter says to me, "If I was you, I'd book into the Porsche driving school on the Gold Coast. Really learn how to master a machine like this – from the experts."

Bruce and I look at each other and shout at the same time, "Bring it on!"

I finally bunny hop out of the garage - much to Bruce's amusement, but soon get the hang of driving it. Oh. My. God. The amount of power is unbelievable, it's like we're cocooned in another world, a world of extreme driving pleasure. It surpasses all of my expectations. I think it's ruined me in a way, there's no way can I go back to driving an ordinary car after this, no way.

After the brekkie run, which turned into a hoon down the freeway just for the hell of it, Bruce and I Google the Porsche driving school. It's a man's paradise. A paradise where all of your driving fantasies are waiting to be fulfilled. We're both drooling over the website, desperate to get our arses there.

I call them immediately and book six spots for the following weekend. Dunno if Eric's even gonna fit in a Porsche, but I couldn't leave him out. Dad'll shit his pants over this little beauty, so will Doug, and I'm guessing Paul will be up for it too.

Giving Dad a quick call I fill him in, he's over the moon and suggests that I invite Big Mal as well, as a thank you for the car. Nice one Dad.

So I give Big Mal a ring, and he goes wild with excitement, he's in! I tell him that it's a two day course, and he immediately booms that he'll cancel everything he's got on, there's no way he's missing out. I have to hold the phone away from my ear, he's so loud. "Nothing's gonna stop me from comin' with you boys alright."

Paul, Eric and Doug all have similar reactions when I call to tell them my plans. As soon as I'm done with the phone calls Grandma Spanx rings.

"I hear there's a party on the Gold Coast and you haven't invited us gals," she accuses.

Shit, news travels fast. I do some quick thinking. "Yeah it's a boys weekend away, sorry, but it's boys only Grandma."

"Oh come on Davis, I could be dead in a month's time. Make an old lady happy eh, I've always dreamed of driving a snazzy car... and *you* can make that dream come true Davis."

Jeezus, she's throwing everything at me, the guilt trip and all. I'll try and hold out for a bit longer. "Yeah, but if I let you come then all the girls are gonna want to come as well, and that'd kind of ruin the boys only fun wouldn't it?"

There's silence, she's trying to freeze me into saying yes, but then I have a great idea. "Look, if all of you ladies want to do it, that's fine, I'll organise for all of you to go together. I'll even throw in accommodation and spa treatments at the Palazzo Versace. How does that sound?" I know I'm on a winner, Mum's always wanted to stay there, and what chick isn't mesmerised by spa treatments?

"What kind of spa treatment are we talking here? Just a massage, 'cos if that's all, well I don't know…" drawls Grandma Spanx.

I laugh. I've got her, hook line and sinker, now I've just got to negotiate the deal. "Nup, a massage is just the tip of the iceberg. You ladies will be getting the full VIP treatment, you can have the works. A full day of spa treatments ok? And I'll even throw in buffet breakfasts as well." Then I think of the ultimate deal sealer.

"Imagine the bragging rights you're gonna get over everyone at the retirement village. Not only are you gonna get to drive a Porsche, but you'll be staying at the swankiest hotel, having all the spa treatments you girls can handle, *and* indulging in the best buffet breakfast on the coast. It's gonna be amazing."

I hear heavy breathing from the other end as I'm giving her my sales pitch. I wouldn't be surprised if she's drooling as well.

"Sold!" she shouts. "When do we go?"

Punching the air I give a silent 'Yes!' Then I say to her, "I'll let you know, now go and tell the others what's going on."

She blows me a couple of kisses, says a quick goodbye and hangs up. This is great, the girls deserve to have some fun too, it's a win-win situation all round. I'm rapt that the sanctity of our blokes' only car experience has held up to the challenge though.

God it's a hot phone alright, it rings again almost as soon as I hang up. I answer thinking that it's Grandma Spanx again, trying to get an even better deal. So I answer the call with, "Ok, how about I throw in some shopping money so you can buy some new handbags, will that sweeten the deal enough?"

Loud, raucous laughter erupts at the other end. Shit, it's Big Mal! "Lovely thought Davis, but it's not my thing alright."

I chuckle and fill him in on what just went down with Grandma Spanx. He laughs, "So that's where ya Dad and you get it from eh? The old bargaining gene's been passed down to both of ya! Listen, I called to let you know that I've got the plane ride and accommodation sorted. Ya can also give your security boys the weekend off, I've got my own crew that I like to use when I'm up there alright."

I explain that the whole point of inviting him is to say thanks, and that I want to take care of everything, but he cuts me off mid-sentence and booms at me, "Look, we've established that ya love the car alright. Now do ya want a lift in my private jet or not?"

"Wow."

"Yeah, bloody wow. I've got it, I want to use it, end of story alright."

What am I meant to do, say no to the guy and piss him off? I don't think so. Oh bad luck, I'll just have to go along with it. "No worries Mal, that sounds awesome. Thanks mate."

"Good, I'm glad we've got that sorted. Now, we'll all be stayin' at my place on the water, you're gonna love it alright."

"Sweet! There's only one problem," I sigh.

"What?" he growls.

"Grandma Spanx'll go ape shit when she hears that we're going on your private jet and the girls aren't, maybe I'll upgrade them to first class. Is there first class between Melbs and the Goldie?"

"Course there is ya galah. But I'll save ya the trouble of having ya balls broken. They can use my plane as well alright. That should keep them happy."

"Jeezus Mal, ya don't have to do that," I blurt.

"This conversation is starting to sound like Groundhog Day Davis. We've been through this before. What do ya say when I offer to give ya something?"

"Uhh, thanks Mal, you're the best."

"That's better, that's what I like to hear. You're happy, I'm happy, it's as simple as that. I gotta go, but has Charlie talked to you about Friday's show yet?" I tell him he hasn't, so he gives me his number and tells me to call him ASAP.

I can't get through to Grandma Spanx, she's busy talking to the others, so I'll have to save the good news about the private jet till later. Bruce has been entertaining himself in the games room while this was all going on, so I give him the rundown and he squeals like a pig when I tell him about Big Mal's private plane and waterfront house. Both of us rush over to my laptop and Google it. Holy shit, this is gonna be the best boys weekend away ever!

$$$$$$$$$$

Bambi's a freakin' legend. She's been my wing-girl at various celeb shindigs over the past few days, and her insight for a newbie like me has been invaluable. She helped guide me through the mass of invites I received in the guest book, helping me prioritise which party or event to go to first, especially when there's more than one on at the same time.

She said that the basic rule of thumb is to go to the one you know you'll have the most fun at last, so you can party freely when you're there and not stress out about having to be somewhere else. Makes perfect sense to me. So we spent a good few hours trawling through the list, making our own list and action plan. She's not just a pretty face, she knows everyone, and everything about them too. I'm stoked she's my wing-girl. To celebrate I took her for a spin in the Porsche. At least I didn't embarrass myself with her in the car, like I did with Bruce on Saturday morning.

I'm wearing what's now become my regulation big-wig party out-fit, which consists of my tails and stuff from my own party on Friday night. It's great because I don't have to think about what to wear, which suits me just fine. Jacobs is currently inching the car through a crowd of anti-Davis protestors towards some huge wrought iron gates that are being guarded by a bevy of security guys. Jonno's grumbling about what dickheads the protestors all are, they should just go home and stop hassling us all the time. I've gotta agree with him on that one.

Jacobs lowers the window for the security team and they take a quick look inside, acknowledge who I am, and grant us instant entry to the mansion.

Suddenly there's a thud on the back window. I turn around and am faced with an egg running down the glass. Bloody protestors. Bambi comments that it's totally gross, and I murmur my agreement. These protestors seem to be gradually ramping things up. At first it was just thumping the car with their fists as we drove past, but this is the second time we've been egged. I feel like a sitting target, I just hope that this is the extent of their crappy behaviour and they don't do anything else to us. Jacobs assures me that if they cross this line and take it any further, then the cops will be able to nab them. But so far they've stayed within the so-called law.

I'm sure I spot Scott in the mob again, I've seen him a quite a few times now. He always appears on the fringe of the group, and seems to urge the others on while keeping a low profile himself. Bloody idiot, dunno what his problem is. We always got along at work ok, maybe I should ask him why he's helping Mitch, what he's got against me.

What I don't get is how the hell they know where I'm going to be all the time, it's really starting to do my head in. They always seem to be a step ahead of me, wherever I go, there they are. This week on Facebook, Mitch unleashed a verbal assault, I think he's trying to wear me down by posting disgusting, untrue things about me. Every day he comes up with more derogatory crap, it's endless. Buggered if I know how he comes up with it all, if I gave a shit I'd be shattered, depressed, and probably ready for suicide. Luckily I don't let him get to me. I don't even bother reading what he says, I just hear about it from Ajala, Dad, and Bruce, as well as the media. I'd have to be deaf and blind not to see and hear about it on telly every day. It's been plastered everywhere, and has been the main subject of discussion since the death threat and fireworks prank last Friday, which triggered it all off. Dunno what the media did before I came along.

Most of the public are outraged that Mitch is going this far, and that he's getting away with it all. I think it's pretty strange too, that the guy can publicly do all this shit and not be charged with anything. People are also up in arms about his whole Facebook bullying campaign. I've done a couple of interviews about it, one with Tanya on *Tonight's Current Affairs*, and the other one on radio with Kyle Randiland, which was pretty cool.

Kyle had quite a bit to say about Mitch. I hope to God he was listening, just for a bit of payback. A lot of people don't like Kyle. Sure he's got a big mouth, but he's ok – especially if he's on your side. Man he dissed Mitch in an awesome way, I was nearly pissing myself when he called him a "low down, slimy, attention seeking git." I couldn't have said it better myself!

I keep telling everyone that Mitch can only affect me if I *let* him. He has no power over me at all, unless I give him that power. Just because he writes shitty things about me doesn't mean I have to read them, or react to them. There's no way I'm gonna let him turn me into a victim. The fact I'm ignoring him is probably driving Mitch crazy, and if it is, well good, sucked in!

A lot of people want to know why I'm *not* affected by all this. I get asked all the time if I'm supressing any hurt and anger. The answer is simply no, I'm not supressing anything. As I keep telling them - I choose not to be affected by it, end of story. Just because he's fucked up doesn't mean I have to become that way too. Fuck that shit.

I never thought I'd become a poster boy for anti-Facebook bullying, but if that's what comes out of this then it can only be a good thing. I've heard that some people get really depressed, depressed enough to kill themselves over this stuff, which is such a waste. So if I can show people another way to handle it then I'm up for the challenge.

I still don't understand how Mitch's band of loyal protestors know my every move though. I mean Ajala tweets and posts heaps of stuff, but not personal info like where I'm going to be at certain times of the day, and for this very reason. These protesting idiots aren't just turning up to the VIP parties and stuff, they seem to know my every move.

Yesterday I finally went to get my hair cut at Silvio's in Carlton. He must be about seventy by now, he's like part of the family. Dad's been taking me and Doug there since we were kids, which is a bit scary, especially as he only seems to have about three different haircuts in his repertoire. But it's a habit I just can't break. Besides, I like how he cuts my hair, which is just as well seeing as it hasn't changed that much since I was a kid. Sure, I've asked for different styles over the years, but Silvio would always narrow his eyes at me, flick my ear with his comb, which bloody hurts, and say, "I am the master of the cut. An artiste! You leave it to me young man!" Needless to say I've always ended up with the same style, the twist is that sometimes he takes it shorter, sometimes he leaves it a bit longer. Now I just leave it up to him, there's no point in arguing with 'The Master'.

So when I rocked up for my haircut yesterday, there they were. The bloody protestors were waiting outside the barber shop waving their stupid signs and calling me a wanker. Silvio loved the attention. After discussing my party at length, which he'd attended and assured me was "Just as good as his wedding day"- which I think is cryptic for freakin' awesome - he wanted to know all the goss. So I filled him in. We discussed Mitch and all the shit he's doing to me, which really pissed him off. As we were talking about this stuff, one of the idiots outside banged on the window to get our attention. When we turned to look, he gave us the finger and waved his placard, which read 'Davis is a wanker.' Silvio's eyes and mine met in the mirror, and he offered to threaten them with his cutthroat, but I talked him out of it. Chances are he'd get done for it while the protestors get let off. Mitch's gotta be getting inside info from somewhere, but at this point I don't have a clue. Jacobs is working on it though, and with him on the case Mitch better watch out!

$$\$\$\$\$\$\$\$\$\$$

Back to the party. I'm getting more comfortable with this socialising stuff, I can work a room pretty well now. I don't get as star struck and tongue tied around all the VIPs as I used to. It's awesome walking up to a group of strangers and know that I'll be welcomed with open arms, that I'm part of the 'in' crowd. And the chicks love me! If I wanted to, I could probably get laid ten times a night, but that's not my style.

My own party is the only one I've been to so far that has been wall to wall stars, which makes me feel pretty damn good. Heaps of people have told me that it was *the* invite of the year. This one's being held by one of Big Mal's uber-rich mates who was at my shindig, and it's the second party we've been to tonight. The first one was thrown by an A-list movie star.

Yep, I'm learning the ropes pretty quick thanks to my wing-girl here. She seems to know everyone at every bash we go to, which comes in handy because remembering names isn't one of my strong points. But the old fall back of calling someone 'mate' or 'love' always works like a charm for me, I'm sure most people don't even realise that I have no idea what their name is.

268

We haven't been here for very long, but I'm getting toey already. It's only one am, but there's only so much small talk I can make. People seem to ask me the same questions all the time and it gets a bit boring. That's the bummer about nonstop parties, it gets a bit dull after a while, talking about the same old same old.

Man I crack myself up, here I am hobnobbing with all these amazing people, still in my first week of doing it, and I reckon I'm over it already. Fuck, I need to get a grip. I need to change tactics in the conversation department and start turning it back onto the person I'm talking to, deflect it all back onto them, because if I have to explain about me and Claire, or the 'Team Mitch' shit one more time tonight, I think I'll lose it.

I must be tireder than I thought, I'm not usually as cranky as this. Scanning the room, I recognise heaps of people from the other parties I've attended this week, everyone just seems to do the rounds. I've gone pretty hard at it this week, really thrown myself into the 'circuit' as Bambi calls it. I've been trying to distract myself, keep myself busy, trying not to think about stuff too much.

I take a swig of water, I've had enough grog for the night. I've got my show to do first thing in the morning, so I'd better keep a clear head.

Someone gently puts their hand on my bum and gives a long gentle squeeze – it's a very intimate gesture. Figuring that it's probably Bambi, I wiggle my bum a bit to egg her on, which works. The squeeze gets harder and I feel something in my pants getting hard as well. So I freak right out when I turn around and discover that it's not Bambi who's clawing my bum, but an older woman with so much makeup on she almost looks like a clown. My mind races, do I know her? Have I met her before? I draw a complete blank. Shit.

"Oh Davis," she simpers seductively, "*now* I see what Malcom sees in you, he's always been able to spot a star."

Cocking my head at her slightly, I realise that I can't fake it with this lady, so I ask if we've met before.

"No darling, I haven't had that pleasure yet. I'm Malcom's first ex-wife Denise, but you can call me Dee Dee."

"Riiight, lovely to meet you Dee Dee."

"I believe you call him Mal, that's quite an honour you know." She then proceeds to tell me all about her marriage to Big Mal, and what a top bloke he is. "He traded me in for a younger model years ago, we're still good friends though," she finally finishes with.

I pointedly look at my watch and tell her it's been a real pleasure talking to her, which it has - once I got over the horror of being felt up by an oldie. I inform her that I've got an early start with my segment tomorrow.

She leans forward and says, "I like you Davis, so I'm going to give you some advice. Now that you're in the position you're in, expect the unexpected sweetie."

Frowning at her I ask what she means, but she dismisses me with a wave of her bejewelled hand.

"Oh, just be aware of so called friends, that's all luvvie. It's a dog eat dog world out there my boy, so keep your eyes and ears open." I must look confused because she pats me on the cheek and tells me, "Don't worry sweetie, *I* wouldn't ever sell you out, and I had a damn good offer today to do so, which I turned down. But then I'm loyal, unlike some others."

I ask her again what she means, but she just gives me a mysterious smile, tells me that I've got a great arse, and that she'll be watching me tomorrow morning. Then she air kisses me and glides away.

Bambi comes over giggling. "So you've met the lovely Dee Dee then? Did she go for your bum or chest?"

"Bum."

"Ooh aren't you the lucky one! She only does that to very special people. She did it to me a while back, which was interesting."

"But you're a chick," I say surprised.

"Well spotted Davis!" she says cheekily. "Old Dee Dee goes for anything on two legs, male *or* female. She's not fussy. I think that's why Big Mal got rid of her. That's my theory anyway."

I fill her in on what Dee Dee just said. Bambi frowns for a sec, then asks me if I knew that Dee Dee not only owns *G'day* magazine, but has a big say in what goes into it each week.

Shaking my head I confess, "I had no idea, she didn't mention any of that to me."

"She probably assumes you know. Most people do. They were quite the power couple Big Mal and Dee Dee, what with him in TV and her in the mags. They *were* the media here in Melbourne years ago, a real force to be reckoned with." Bambi takes a sip of her drink, taps her foot for a sec then announces, "Bet I know what's going on, do you mind mingling for a bit longer? I reckon I can get some goss." And she heads off, leaving me standing there alone.

In the car on the way home Bambi finally spills the beans. Yes she got some goss, and the reason she didn't tell me at the party is because she wanted Jonno and Jacobs to hear it as well. Bambi's informant is one of her editors. It turns out that *The Weekly Star* has just paid someone for a story about me. Apparently it's an 'insider's guide' to Davis, and they paid big bucks for it too. I ask if she knows who sold out on me, but Bambi doesn't have a clue, her editor wouldn't tell her.

"That's what Dee Dee was referring to," she says excitedly. "They obviously tried to sell their story to *G'day*, but Dee Dee rejected it, out of loyalty to you and Big Mal."

"Fuck me, who the hell would do this?" I mutter to myself.

"Could be anyone, even someone you went to school with who you haven't seen for yonks," says Bambi. "As soon as people realise they can make money out of you they usually do, I'm sorry to say."

"My guess is that it's the same person who's tipping off Mitch." Jacobs states.

"Yeah," agrees Jonno, "I reckon you're right. Unless, unless it's Mitch himself the shifty bastard. I wouldn't put it past him."

Great, this is just what I need, a friend, or even a crazy ex-colleague selling out on me. I'm racking my brains trying to figure it out, but keep coming up blank. Maybe Jonno's right and it is Mitch. It could be anyone though, someone from disco bowling, the pistol club, man, the possibilities are endless.

Bambi pats my knee, "We'll just have to wait till next Monday to find out, that's when the next issue comes out. I'm guessing they'll fast track it for that issue, they won't want to sit on it for long."

$$$$$$$$$$

271

The studio lights seem to be scorching this morning, I'm sweating like a pig, I can feel the makeup trickling down my neck. Jeezus, that death threat here at the studio last week had more of an effect on me than I realised. As soon as we pulled into the studio car park this morning, it hit me. They had full on security at the gates to stop the anti-Davis mob from getting close to us, but as soon as I got out of the car I totally freaked out. A nearby car backfired, sending me and Jonno flying to the ground for cover. I thought someone had taken a shot at me. Jacobs kept his cool and led both Jonno and I inside as quickly as possible. Not a good start to a day I've been looking forward to all week. Today we go for our boys' weekend away, and I can't bloody wait.

Kirk asks me if I'm ok as we cut to an ad break. I admit that I'm a bit out of sorts today and he bobs his head in acknowledgment. I'm doing a very quick Q&A with him and Leeza before my segment starts. We pre-taped my segment earlier in the week, so Big Mal wants us to do a quick live chat to keep the punters happy.

For the past few minutes I've been answering a series of questions sent in by the viewers. So far we've covered the Facebook slander and my breakup with Claire, surprise surprise! There's only one more question to answer after the ad break, then we'll cut to my pre-taped stuff.

For my segment this week, we took to the streets and asked people what respect means to them, and how they'd like to see more of it shown. It was heaps of fun to do, I loved it. Some of the answers were quite surprising. One old lady said that just because she's old doesn't mean she's invisible. She wished people would respect older people by saying hello to them in the street sometimes, instead of ignoring them. A teenager told me he wished his mum would respect his choice of clothes, his mum then grabbed the microphone and said that she wished he'd respect her asking him to clean up his room. Yeah everyone loves to be on TV, get their fifteen seconds of fame!

Taking a sip of water, I try to compose myself by giving myself a bit of a mental pep talk, telling myself to be cool. So far these questions have been doing my head in, they're just so bloody predictable. I give myself a bit of a shake out to try and loosen up, but I probably look a bit manic because I notice Ricki fanning his face and pointing at me in the wings. The ad break finishes and Leeza asks me the final question.

"A little bird tells us that one of your friends might have sold a story about you to a magazine, is that true Davis?"

I give Leeza a squinty look and shake my head. I'm pissed off about this one, this isn't the question we ran through earlier, this is totally personal and I don't want to talk about it. I sigh and give her an answer.

"Well Leeza, your little bird seems to be *very* well informed, maybe *you* can tell me who's spilling the beans about me hmmm?"

Leeza gets flustered and looks to Kirk, asking him if she should say anything. He slaps his thigh and says jovially that if he was in my shoes he'd certainly like to know.

Kirk eggs her on, "C'mon Leez, put us all out of our misery here, who did it?" Then he turns to me and asks, "You really don't have a clue Davis?"

I'm fuming, but I tell him in a very calm, soothing voice that "No I don't have a clue, please fill me in." My voice might be calm, but I certainly don't feel that way.

Leeza licks her red lips and sit's up a bit straighter. "Well you all heard it here first, *allegedly* your best mate's wife Tracy Finch has given *The Weekly Star* an inside story about you. What do you think of that?"

I'm gobsmacked, I truly am, and before I can censor myself out it comes. "What do I think? I think she's a total bitch! That's what I think." Looking right into the camera I shout, "This is not only an act of total disrespect, but of betrayal. Trace, you should be ashamed of yourself!" With that I stand up and storm off the set.

Leeza and Kirk stare after me in shock. Kirk holds up a hand to his mouth, looks intently into the camera and says, "Whoops, maybe we shouldn't have told him, what do you all think? Call in, tweet, whatever, and let us know if we did the right thing." Then they cut to my pre-taped segment.

Man am I pissed off. I want some answers. My phone rings and its Big Mal. I have it out with him, but it turns out that he knew nothing about it either. So once I hang up I head back to quiz Kirk and Leeza. Apparently Kirk got the tip off and went with it, without running it by anyone else. Not a smart move buddy, not only am I not happy, Big Mal's not happy either. Kirk's put himself in the shit over this one. His

phone rings and I can hear Big Mal blasting him from where I'm standing, I even hear him scream at Kirk, "Where's your bloody respect?"

My phone rings again. It's Bruce, and he's not happy either.
"What the fuck, did I just hear that right? That my *wife's* dishing dirt
on you?"

"Too bloody right. Ya mean you didn't know about this?" I yell.

"Maaate, if I'd known about this I would have bloody told ya -
and throttled Trace already. She's out of order here. I'm really sorry
mate, I really am."

I calm down a bit, "Look, it's not your fault your wife's a bloody
dickhead. She treats ya like shit, now she's treating me like shit. It's
what she does, in case you haven't noticed."

There's a short silence on Bruce's end, then he says, "Yeah, well
it's one thing to treat *me* like shit, but she's got no right treating *you* like
shit. Sorry mate."

"Don't you dare apologise for her," I snap at him. Then in a gen-
tler tone I ask, "Now are you all packed and ready to go? I can't wait
to get out of this shit hole for a few days. You're still coming to the
Goldie, aren't ya?"

"Are you sure you still want me to?" he asks meekly.

"Hell yeah, this is just what we need. See ya at the airport at
eleven," and I hang up.

$$$$$$$$$$

Oh the joys of private jet travel. No queues, no waiting, no stress, no
drama, oh yeah I could get used to this. We all could. Of course at first
we're all trying to look cool, calm and collected, but stuff that! Dad's
the first to crack, the first to punch the air and shout, "This is what
I'm talkin' about! This is the life I was meant to live!"

Soon we're all chest slamming each other and carrying on like
dickheads on the tarmac. Big Mal missed the first bit of this as he was
running a bit late, but he cops an eyeful of us dancing around like
clowns in the aisle as he gets onboard. A big grin spreads across his
face and he claps Paul on the back, which sends him head first into
one of the seats, cracking us all up.

As soon as we've taken off, the hostess comes round with drinks and trays of canapés. "Got any of the duck legs love?" Big Mal asks, giving her a wink. She assures him she has and goes off to get them.

"Bit better than cattle class eh boys?" he booms at us.

Answers range from "Hell yeah!" to "You bet" to "Shit yeah" from me, Dad and Paul - to just open mouthed nodding from Eric and Doug. I think they've got man crushes on Big Mal, because whenever he talks to them they go suspiciously quiet, which is very strange for both of them. Don't blame them though, Big Mal rocks.

We thought the private jet was awesome, and yeah it was, but waiting for us at Coolangatta airport are two shiny black helicopters ready to whisk us away to Big Mal's place. Can this trip get any better? Oh yes it can. The choppers whisk us up the coast to Big Mal's place. Fuck me, he's got his own floating helipad on the water out the front of his mansion! He sure knows how to do things in style. The mansion is on the Nerang River, overlooking Surfers Paradise, and it's incredible.

A bevy of staff greet us on arrival and take our bags off to our rooms. Big Mal gives us all a guided tour. I've never seen such luxury, it even puts my penthouse to shame - which is saying something. Everything's big and in your face. We're all looking at each other in wonder. Talk about hitting the jackpot, this place shits on any hotel you could stay at. And Big Mal only uses it occasionally, maybe three or four times a year he reckons. Man if I had something like this, I'd never want to leave it. The indoor pool is incredible, and the main staircase is breathtaking - with a huge chandelier doing it justice. We wander from room to room, each one outdoes the last in opulence and luxury.

Throughout the tour Dad and Doug are nudging each other, the real estate bug in them is rearing its head. Dad can't help but ask a few questions about the property, which Big Mal is only too happy to answer.

Over a relaxing game of pool on the full sized pool table, I fill the guys in on what led me to the Porsche driving experience here on the Goldie. They all crack up when I tell them about my first go of trying to drive Black Beauty, and how Porter had to help me out. It's only because of Porter's suggestion that we're here today.

"Well here's cheers to Porter!" says Paul. We all take a swig of our drinks, Dad's on the tomato juice, the rest of us are indulging in a beer.

"Too bloody right, without him we wouldn't be here having our boys weekend away," I say.

"Now I just wanna say something here," booms Big Mal. "What happens here this weekend stays here alright. No dobbing, or telling anyone what we get up to alright."

"Here's to that!" Paul agrees, and we all clink glasses to seal the deal.

Everyone except Dad gets stuck into the grog immediately. We figure it's now or never, because we have to be completely sober for the rest of the weekend. Dad's nominated as our designated anti-idiot director. We all agree that since he's going to be sober he can pull rank, and keep us all in line if need be. Luckily he only has to exercise his anti-idiot capabilities twice.

The first time he puts his foot down is later that night, after the strippers Big Mal's organised have finished their show. And what a show it was. Doug's caught up in the moment and declares we should have a nude pool party with them, to see if they can do synchronised stripping. It's probably a good thing Dad talks us all out of it and stops it from happening, but at the time none of us are overly impressed with his decision.

The second time Dad puts his foot down is just before bed, when I'm feeling romantically inclined. I want to ring Claire, but Doug loudly dobs me in to Dad, who rushes into the room and wrestles my phone off me before I've finished dialling her number, saying that I'll thank him for it in the morning.

The Porsche driving experience is educational, but completely mad. On the first day we all piss ourselves laughing, watching Eric try and squeeze himself into one of the cars. It's like watching a sardine get into a can, but he quickly masters the art of getting in and out.

On the second day, just before lunch, Dad totals his car in a spectacular accident that he amazingly walks away from without a scratch. After his initial shock, and after we'd all watched the video of it about a hundred times over lunch, Big Mal crowns him the day's champ. So we all hoist him up onto our shoulders and run around with him, as Big Mal sprays him with champagne. Dad's in heaven, and announces that he'll happily smash up another car just for the kudos. Thank God we've got the all-inclusive insurance package!

One thing we decided, and discussed at length during the weekend, is that Bruce will be moving into the penthouse with me as soon as we get home. Over the course of the weekend he opened up about his marriage. He's come to the conclusion that it's time to walk away from it. Trace has been sucking him dry (in more ways than one) for years, but having her sell out on me is the final straw.

You can't blame a dude for sticking around for great sex, but as Big Mal pointed out to us on Friday arvo as we were playing Texas Holdem poker, "Sex is just one card in the pack guys. Unless you've got more than the ace in your deck you'll never win the hand."

Ok so he might have been a bit pissed when he said that and so were we, but it sure made a hell of a lot of sense at the time. Maybe not so much now, but it's still classic Big Mal.

The weekend flies by in a whirlwind of excitement, adrenaline, and fun. It's just what the doctor ordered. Yes, we got to drive some very cool cars, quite crazily I must say. Yes, we had some amazing female entertainment, all above board - just your average strippers and lap dancers, which I wasn't expecting. Jeezus, Big Mal's full of surprises! And yes I learnt a bit about my mates, not all good stuff, but they're my mates so who gives a shit. All in all I think I had the best bloody weekend of my life. We've all walked away as certified racetrack gods, I've even got the certificate to prove it, which is way cool. Man it's gonna be hard driving my car normally when I get home.

Before we know it we're back on the private jet, heading home to Melbs. The mood is a lot more sombre on the trip back. I think everyone except Big Mal is wondering if we'll experience anything quite as amazing ever again.

Suddenly Big Mal breaks the silence. "We need a code word for our man weekends away alright?" This grabs everyone's attention.

"You mean there's gonna be more of them?" Eric asks hopefully. He and Doug quickly got over their awe of Big Mal, it only took a burping competition on Friday night to break down their defences. Big

Mal won the comp, which is no surprise really, considering how bloody loud he is.

Big Mal grins at us all indulgently and booms, "Hell yeah, you boys are my party bitches now. I had so much goddamn fun this weekend it's criminal. We gotta do it again, and we need a code word for it alright."

We all look at each other, grins are creeping onto everyone's faces now, the hope and excitement is palpable.

"How about 'Operation Breakout'?" Bruce suggests.

Everyone looks at each other, then nods their agreement. It's perfect.

"Operation Breakout it is boys. Now, when are we all gonna breakout on my boat? We gotta get that sorted alright."

"Sweet Jesus, bring it on!" I shout.

Everyone high-fives each other, and certainty in the future of sacred man-partying is restored to all.

Chapter 17

I've called a full on meeting today. It's Monday morning and I figure it's best to have everyone together in the conference room at Paradise Towers, so we can see what Trace wrote about me in *The Weekly Star* and do some damage control if need be.

Dad's rocked up with Danielle in tow, she said that since she's my lawyer she's not going to miss out on it. At least she's got some good news for me. *News of the Day* have retracted their article about the rooftop spa incident and the gay accusation. Apparently they're going to give me a full apology and an out of court settlement, which is pretty cool.

Danielle grins at me, a cheeky gleam is in her eye. "Well we showed them not to mess with the Spanxs! Terry my boss is over the moon at the publicity our firm's getting for this." Launching herself at me, she engulfs me in a big hug saying, "Who would have thought you'd help me become partner! Davis you have no idea how much you've helped my career, my future is sorted thanks to you!"

Hugging her back I say, "Hey no worries sis, glad to be of service. You did an awesome job. Thanks."

Dad's baby blues are glued on us, he's watching our exchange closely. Before Danielle and I end the hug, he wraps his arms around both of us and says, "You kids are amazing. You make your old dad as proud as punch." With a sniffle he lets us go.

"What's goin' on? Is this a Spanx love-fest or what?" Jonno demands as he enters the room. Three sets of eyes swivel his way and we all start laughing. He's wearing a nineteen forties style hat with his suit today. He's got it tilted at a jaunty angle, it's very gangster-ish.

"Dude it suits you, where's the violin case with the machine gun in it?" I joke.

"Ha bloody ha," he growls at me. "I like it. I think it adds a certain depth to my outfit," he says defensively.

Jacobs comes in, rolls his eyes at me and announces, "I've informed Jonno that the hat can stay, provided he takes it off during certain *situations*. We don't want it distracting him from his duties." Giving Jonno a steely eyed glare he adds, "Security comes first, doesn't it Jonno? Our look comes second, got it?" Jonno agrees demurely and goes and sits down.

There's a certain level of excitement amongst the group. Dad distributes a copy of *The Weekly Star* to us all. He's got a pile of newspapers with him as well, which makes me feel a bit uneasy.

Trace is on the front cover of *The Weekly Star*, wearing a totally unsuitable outfit for a woman's mag. She's poured herself into a skin tight skimpy singlet, which is barely containing her huge boobs. And of course she's got her trademark leopard skin spray-on pants on, complete with hooker heels. She must have had something done to her lips because they're freakin' ginormous, it's a trout pout from hell. She looks perfect for a playboy mag, but it's not a good look for a weekly woman's magazine.

I hear Bruce gasp when he sees her on the cover. I invited him to the meeting too, I mean it's his wife here, or soon to be ex-wife by the sounds of things. "She looks like a slut," he murmurs to no one in particular, and Ajala gives him a comforting rub on the back. I've got her up to speed on the whole Trace situation, so she's probably feeling a bit sorry for poor old Bruce. Funny he should call Trace a slut now, she's always dressed like that. Guess his eyes have finally been opened to what she's really like.

Everyone goes quiet, the only thing to be heard is the rustling of magazine pages being turned, and the odd expletive from some of the group assembled around the table.

After a few minutes I can't help myself, I crack up laughing as I'm reading the article. It's not overly long, but they've managed to put it on a two page spread. Most of the space is taken up with photos of Trace striking unnatural poses — she's such a try hard. They've done the shoot outdoors. There's one with her holding a photo of me and her while she's reclining on a rug in a park. She looks totally uncomfortable, somehow I don't think this is the start of her modelling career. I know that photo well, we took it last Christmas at a BBQ. Bruce was in the photo as well, it was taken of the three of us, but she's chopped Bruce out of it, so it's just me and Trace. Un-bloody- believable! The cheek of her! There's another one of her on the pier at St Kilda, looking out to sea. I think she's trying to look wistful, but with those luber-lips she just looks stupid. There's another one of her in a bikini on the beach. Jeezus, now I know why Bruce hung onto her for so long, she really has got an incredible body. The tiny leopard print bikini shows it all off to perfection. Bruce must be looking at it too because I hear him groan, and Jonno clears his throat the same way he used to at work, when he was perving on the chicks in *Zoot*. I glance up at him, and sure enough Jonno's licking his lips, his eyes are glued to the page. God, what a motley crew we are. Glancing over at Ajala, I notice that her eyes are nearly popping out of her head as well.

None of them expected this, this blatant flaunting of Trace to all and sundry. Somehow I'm not surprised though, I should have guessed she'd turn it around so that it's all about her. Her 'article' is really just a plug for how great she thinks she is. She hardly even mentions me, which is a total crack up. All she says is that I lived next door to her and that we always went disco bowling together. She fails to mention that her husband was with us, as was my girlfriend Claire. Instead she's trying to make out like it was just the two of us. She's even quoted saying "It's no surprise that Claire broke it off. Davis and I are *so* close. It's amazing how well he knows me." I think she's trying to imply that Trace and I were having an affair, and that when Claire found out about it she broke it off.

Bruce must have just read that bit too because he looks over at me and says, "What the fuck's she trying to do? She's cut me out of the photo, and the vibe I'm getting here is that she wants everyone to think you two were shagging each other."

Running a hand through my hair I reply, "Yeah, and you know that's bullshit don't ya?"

"Shit yeah, she was always telling me how much you shitted her. She wouldn't shag you in a million years!" Bruce quickly realises what he's just said because he looks horrified. "Fuck, sorry mate. That came out wrong."

"No it didn't, it's the truth mate. She used to drive me mental, always crapping on about herself. It's a mutual dislike, don't worry about it ok?"

Everyone else at the table's been watching this exchange between Bruce and I like they're passing a car crash. All eyes are on us, glued to the conversation, no one can look away.

There's a lull, and Dad jumps in. "I think the important thing to focus on here is that Trace has shown her true colours. It's obvious she's only interested in looking after herself, and she'll do anything to achieve it."

Bruce has got his head in his hands, he looks deflated, like he's shrunk into himself. I get up and go over to him. Putting a hand on his shoulder I say, "Dad's right. Mate, you decided on the weekend that it was over between you and Trace. This just proves that you've made the right decision. We're still mates, nothing's gonna change that ok?"

He looks up at me with puppy dog eyes, then stands up, and we hug it out. "Do ya think she's right?" he asks. "Do ya think that Claire thought you two were on together, and that's why she broke it off with you?"

Sitting back down I snigger and confidently say, "Nah, that's all bullshit. Claire knows what Trace is like." I really want to add that Claire hated Trace's guts but I don't. There's no point in telling him that, not yet anyway. "Mate, Trace had nothing to do with us splitting up, it was all Claire's decision. So don't worry about it," I reassure him.

Damn, all this talk about me and Claire has made me feel like shit again. I nearly called her last Friday when I was pissed with the boys, but Dad grabbed my phone off me, which was probably a good move. I still miss her, you can't automatically wipe away five years, it just doesn't work like that.

As if sensing this, Danielle slams the magazine shut and tells us that legally I could sue Trace and *The Weekly Star* if I wanted to. They've run a misleading story and it's within my rights to defend myself. Good deflection sis, she's certainly got my focus on something else alright.

"Nah, think I'll let this one go. Trace'll get too much mileage out of it otherwise. And the last thing I want is for her to benefit from being a salacious, slanderous, sellout."

"Hey that'd make a great headline," quips Ajala. "My salacious, slanderous, sellout of a so called friend. Can I use it on the blog?"

This totally lightens the mood, nice one Ajala. I affirm that she certainly can. Once everyone's had their say about the Trace interview Dad hands out the next newspaper. It's *News of the Day*, and the head-line on the front cover screams "We're sorry Spanxie."

Danielle snorts and says, "Do you want to sue them for calling you Spanxie?"

All eyes swivel to me again. I *hate* being called Spanxie, it goes back to primary school and being teased mercilessly by the other kids. Some of Doug's mates still call him Spanxie, and he's fine with it, but with me it still hits a raw nerve. I hate it, end of story. And if anyone ever calls me that I immediately let them know I don't like it.

Dad crosses his arms, leans back in his chair and says, "You know what's gonna happen now, don't you? *Everyone's* gonna call you Spanxie. Unless you tell them otherwise."

So I tell Ajala that we need to get the word out ASAP. "Blog it, tweet it, Facebook it, the works. I won't answer to that name." Then I make a decision. "Ajala, I'll do it myself – with your expert help of course. But I want the fans to know NOT to refer to me as Spanxie, and I think they'll get the message if it comes straight from me." She agrees wholeheartedly, saying that the fans will totally listen to me, they'll respect my wishes.

Then Dad hands out *The Daily Herald*, which is running a story on the Tracy interview. At least they pepper their story with lots of 'allegedly's', and don't make any claims or elaborate on it too much, they just comment on Trace. It seems that she's now been categorised as a gold digging bimbo. Good, it's what she deserves. As we're all talking about the article, Dad's phone rings. He answers it and holds it out to me, saying that a Dee Dee wants to talk to me. Raising my eyebrows at him, I grab the phone and move away from the table to take the call.

"I told you to expect the unexpected and beware of so called friends, didn't I?" she purrs at me. "How about we blow this bimbo out of the water, expose her for what she really is. Do you fancy doing an interview with *G'day*? We could have some fun."

I instantly get a flash of Dee Dee squeezing my bum the other night. I'm not sure what kind of fun she's talking about, but from what Bambi told me she's a kinky old thing. As for doing an interview, I'm all for it, nothing would make me happier than raining on Trace's parade. I've got a great idea, but I need to ask Bruce first. Dee Dee says she's happy to hold for a minute, so I quickly tell Bruce who I'm talking to, and that it'd be great for him to get his side of the story out there as well - I point out that he may as well make some money out of it too. He gives me the thumbs up, so I tell Dee Dee I'd love to do an interview - and so would Tracy's husband Bruce.

"Oooh, goodie goodie," she purrs, "yes we'd love to hear Bruce's side of the story. When are you boys free?"

"I'll pass you onto my manager, he'll sort out when we can do it and what our fees are. Thanks Dee Dee, this is great." I hand the phone back over to Dad.

Bruce is gobsmacked when Dad tells him they're going to pay him fifty grand for his interview, with an option to make him even more if the story takes off and the public demand additional juicy info. They're happy to pay up as long as he's exclusive to *G'day* magazine. Patting him on the back I say, "Welcome to the madhouse mate. Life will never be the same again!"

With all the Trace stuff sorted, we can finally move on to what I'm really excited about. This week I'm starting preparations for my first TV special, which is happening live Saturday but will go to air the Monday afterwards. I've got less than a week to get it all sorted, it's a huge undertaking, but one I have no doubt about the success of. I might be just starting my preparation, but Big Mal's already informed me he's put together a special team just for this, and they've been on it for the past week, which makes me feel a lot better. There's a heap to do, so I'm happy I've got lots of backup.

My plan is to book out an entire hotel in the city, and put up a lot of homeless people for the night. I'll supply them with a new tracksuit, dinner, and breakfast at the hotel. Plus everyone will get their own Streetsmart Swag to take away with them afterwards, so they'll always have a dry, warm place to sleep wherever they are. The only thing I'll ask in return is that they help make their own breakfast, and then help the room attendants make up their room the next day. I reckon it's a brilliant idea. Being able to help these people out, and bring a modicum of self-respect back into their lives, gives me a real buzz. But when I tell everyone, there's dead silence around the table. They all squirm in their seats, not wanting to look me in the eye.

"What? Don't you think these guys need a break?" I ask incredulously.

Dad's the first to reply. "It's not that, that's not the issue at all, am I right guys?" Everyone nods their heads in agreement with him and he continues. "I think it's more to do with the *scale* of what you want to do. Aren't you biting off more than you can chew?"

"Yeah that's a pretty tall order mate," adds Bruce.

"Who cares if it's a tall order, I'm in a position to make a difference and that's exactly what I intend to do."

Jacobs clears his throat. "Well sir, if anyone can do it, it's you. You've already changed all of *our* lives. I don't see why you can't expand on that."

I give Jacobs a grin. "Thanks mate, I appreciate that."

Next thing everyone's talking at once, agreeing that anything's possible, and that I should be able to pull it off. When I tell them that Big Mal already knows about my plan and has given it a green light, the excitement level goes up a notch. Obviously if he agrees, then I'm onto a winner.

We spend a while talking about it, and I outline how I envision it all working. "The only problem that I can see is how to get the homeless people to know about it, and how to get them all together," I state.

"Yeah, that and getting them on TV- I bet most of them won't want to be seen on telly," adds Danielle.

$$$$$$$$$$

I've been invited to three different things tonight, but I'm not going to any of them. Instead I've decided to visit the two grans and share a bit of love with them. That was the plan, but it turns out that Grandma Drummond is out with some gal pals, and Grandma Spanx has gone into the city to listen to a lecture at the Adult Education College. Jeeze, it's only Monday night and those two have got a better social life than I used to have – before I became a celeb that is. When I didn't get an answer from either of their home phones, I called Grandma Spanx on her mobile. She whispered where she was, and said she'd love to meet me afterwards and have a coffee. Cool. I tell her that I'll be wearing a respect cap and I'll meet her at the main entrance.

I could walk from Paradise Towers but figure I'll get a cab. If Bruce was home I'd ask him for a lift, but he's gone to pick up some more stuff from his place, and have it out with Trace if she's home. I sent Jacobs and Jonno home earlier. I knew I wasn't going to go out partying tonight, so they may as well enjoy an evening off. And there's no point in taking the Porsche, there's not much parking on Flinders St, so it'd be too much of a hassle.

I'm feeling nervous and vulnerable. So far no one's recognised me, I've got my cap pulled firmly down shielding my eyes. For the first time in what seems like ages there were no protestors lurking around the apartment building when I left, which makes a welcome change.

I glance at my watch again, its eight fifteen. Grandma Spanx said the lecture finished at eight. I'm getting toey, so I try and amuse myself with my mobile phone, may as well play some more Angry Birds.

It's Murphy's Law, just as I start playing I hear a "Yoo hoo," and there she is getting out of the lift, rushing towards me. She looks so cute in her red beret. A grin lights up her face, and I can't help but smile too.

Giving her a big hug, I ask her what the lecture was about. She's always coming here and doing courses or lectures, her appetite for learning is still voracious. She looks up at me and says solemnly, "The meaning of life."

"Wow, that's a biggie. And you covered it all tonight did you?" I'm such a smart arse sometimes.

She playfully smacks me on the wrist and chides, "No silly, it's a three week thing. Tonight we covered religion, next week's all about your life purpose."

Linking her arm through mine we set off together. There's heaps of café's nearby, so we amble along deep in conversation towards her favourite one, which is a groovy little place at the end of Colley Lane. One of the things I love about Melbs is that it's got so many snaking laneways that are crammed with funky little shops and cafés, they're real Aladdin's caves. You feel a bit like an adventurer when you go down one, never sure what treasures you'll discover. She tells me that Dad's already told her and Grandma Drummond all about what's happening for my TV special.

She stops walking, reaches up and takes my face in her hands. Looking me in the eye she says, "You've got such a big heart Davis, you make us all so proud. What you're doing is wonderful, just wonderful." Then she plants a kiss on my cheek, re-links her arm through mine, and we set off again. I've got a lump in my throat, but I feel fan-fucking-tastic.

My feeling of elation soon turns to terror when, just as we've started walking up Colley Lane, someone abruptly pushes me in the back, forcing me against a closed shopfront. Grandma Spanx, who is holding onto my arm, stumbles, but I quickly put my arm around her waist to stop her from falling. Adrenaline immediately takes over, nobody's gonna hurt my Grandma Spanx - not on my watch.

Swinging around I place myself in front to protect her, and come face to face with a guy who's maybe in his mid-forties, it's hard to say. His hair's long and unruly, it's hiding a lot of his face, and he's wearing an odd assortment of clothing. Then the smell hits me, Jeezus the guy smells like a sewer, it's absolutely disgusting.

The laneway is fairly dark at this end, the only shop left open is the café, and it's right at the other end, a good distance away from us. We're the only ones here. The mugger takes a step back, pulls a knife out, and demands all of our money and our phones. His eyes are darting all around us, scoping everything out. "Keep quiet and hand everything over," he hisses.

My heart is going a million miles an hour, so are my thoughts, and I can't believe what I'm thinking. My fear has been replaced with something else. Excitement. Oh Jeezus why can't I be normal and just freak out. That's what most normal people would do in this situation, but not me. I'm thinking that this guy could be the missing link that I need for my TV special. I needed to find someone with the inside info on where to find homeless people, and here he is standing right in front of me! Admittedly having a knife in your face isn't the ideal way to meet someone, but hey you've gotta roll with the punches right? All this is running through my head at lightning speed. Mugger-man shuffles his feet and growls for us to hurry up.

"Are you homeless?" I blurt out.

He looks at me like I'm a moron. "Of course I'm fucking homeless, do ya think I'd mug people and sleep in the fucking park if I didn't have to?" he hisses angrily.

I'm a big believer in the right thing happening at the right time, be it meeting someone, experiencing something, or learning something new. So even though this guy has just scared the bejeezus out of Grandma Spanx and I, all I can see here is an opportunity. An opportunity to help this guy, maybe turn his life around in exchange for some info from him. I know I'm probably in for a hard sell though, and by the way he's acting he's probably high on something. He might be too proud and refuse any help I offer him, the only way I'm going to find out is to ask him straight up.

"How long have you been homeless for?" My question seems to piss him off even more.

"Who the fuck cares. Now give me your fucking money or I'll cut ya." He waves his knife at us threateningly.

I take a deep breath, here goes. "Mate you can mug us and steal some money off us, which won't be much - I don't carry much cash these days, do you Grandma?"

"No I certainly don't, and for this very reason!" she says haughtily.

I give her a wink, to try and instil some confidence in our situation, then I continue on. "So as I said you'll get a bit of money out of us, but not much. You'll probably blow it all tonight on whatever it is you spend your stolen money on. So you can do that, that's one option. The other option is, that in exchange for some information, I'll pay you what you'd consider a large amount of money- but I can't give it to you right now because I don't have it on me, we'd have to go to an ATM together and get it."

The guy is now bouncing from foot to foot, he's clearly agitated. "What sort of info and what sort of money are ya talkin?" he demands.

"First of all, do you know many homeless people? Do you know where they all hang out?"

He quickly looks up and down the laneway, scanning around us for something, then he puts two fingers in his mouth and lets out a piercing whistle. Grandma Spanx and I look at each other. I don't like this, maybe he's calling for backup, maybe we should just get the hell out of here, we might get bashed or even worse, maybe he'll kill us. I wouldn't put anything past him. Nothing is worth letting that happen so I whisper to Grandma Spanx that we should try and go.

Suddenly mugger-man points his knife at us again and snaps, "Fuck this shit. Just give me your fucking money. NOW!"

Grandma Spanx takes her bag off her shoulder and rummages around in it. I figure she's getting her purse out and so does mugger-man. I'm totally gobsmacked when she pulls out a pistol and points it at the guy.

"Drop the knife, and don't run away honey!" she commands. Now *he* looks like he's the one in shock. His knife immediately clatters to the ground.

"What the hell are you doing carrying that thing around with you?" I whisper. *I* know that it's actually a paperweight, a paperweight of a replica of a .357 Magnum revolver. I know this because I gave it to her for her birthday years ago. Normally it's got pride of place on top of her mantelpiece, not in her bloody handbag – or so I thought. She flicks her eyes in my direction for a sec.

"I always carry it with me at night. For protection."

"But it's illegal," I retort.

"So is getting mugged!" she replies while waving the pistol at mugger man, then ordering him to stand against the opposite shop front. When he's in place she snaps at him, "Listen to what my grandson's got to say. You'll be glad you did." Taking a step back, but still pointing the gun at him, she motions with her head for me to talk to him.

Jeezus she's a freakin' legend, this'll go down in Spanx family history as one of the most outrageous things anyone's ever done. It's right up there with having a pirate in the family, and those two having a granny pash.

I quickly explain to mugger-man that I want to get as many genuinely homeless people together for one night and give them a free tracksuit, dinner, a night in a hotel, and breakfast, as well as a Streetsmart Swag to take with them. All they have to do is turn up, enjoy being clean, warm, well fed and well rested. The only thing I ask of them is to make sure they help make their breakfast, and help clean their rooms – as a show of respect.

Turns out the guy's name is Fang, and it's clear that this wasn't what he was expecting to hear, especially when I mention that everyone's going to be on telly. I finish telling him everything, adding that

I'd like him to be my co-ordinating officer, to help me get the word out on the street, help me assemble everyone, that sort of thing, and that I'll pay him handsomely for his time. He's been staring at me open mouthed throughout my little speech, and now I notice a tear run down his cheek.

Putting out my hand to shake, I ask him if we have a deal. He sniffs and asks if I'm for real, which I assure him that I am. He takes my hand and we shake on it. Looking him in the eye I tell him that I can't do this without him, I need him to help me, and I believe he's the perfect man for the job. He blinks rapidly a few times, nods his head, then mumbles, "It's a long time since anyone believed in me. Thanks. Sorry I tried to mug you."

"So you're in?"

He gives me a shy smile, "Yeah I'm in."

Suddenly a group of three thugs run into the laneway, sliding to a halt next to us. They all check out Grandma Spanx and I, then ask Fang what's going on. One of the guys is peering at me. "Holy shit, it's Davis Spanx! Guys, check it out." They all peer at me. Fang asks them if they know me.

"Dude everyone knows Davis Spanx, he's the respect guy."

"Yeah, he's everywhere, he's way cool," adds another of them, and they all clamour around me, so I shake all their hands and introduce them to Grandma Spanx.

"Hey you're the lezzo granny!" one shouts.

"Don't piss her off," Fang warns, "she's got a gun."

"What this old thing?"

She whips it out of her bag again and waves it around, causing the three guys to freak out and scatter. Fang holds his ground though, and tells the others, "She's cool, you wouldn't shoot us now would you Mrs Spanx?"

She eyeballs him, "I like a man with manners, and you've finally shown some. Honey I couldn't shoot you even if I wanted to, this is only for show. It's a paperweight."

At this the group of three all crack up and tell Fang what a pussy boy he is, he's been done by a paperweight wielding granny. They pretty much treat him like shit. At first he just takes it. I get the feeling that this is normal behaviour, that he's the lowest ranking in their little group and cops shit all the time, even though by the looks of things he's probably the oldest. But suddenly Fang straightens his shoulders, stands tall, and announces that he's my co-ordinating officer.

They all snigger, throwing derogatory comments his way, so I step forward and tell them it's true. Fang's my right hand man for my upcoming TV special. This immediately shuts them up. Mission accomplished.

It's a real pleasure watching those three sucking up to Fang, once they realise he's not bullshitting them, that I really have enlisted him as a key member of my team. They all want in on the action, but I pull rank and tell them that for now Fang is the main man, although he *might* decide to recruit them later, if he wants to. At this, Fang pushes the hair away from his eyes, revealing a disturbingly gaunt face, but his eyes are bright and full of ambition - or maybe crack, it's hard to tell.

I ask if the other three will excuse us for a moment, Fang and I have got a bit more business to discuss. They all slink out of the laneway, but I can hear their excited chatter drifting back to us from around the corner.

"How do you feel?" I ask him.

He grins at me, showing a mouthful of missing and rotten teeth, he's only got about three decent ones left in his head. I try not to stare and cringe, but it's a big challenge. "I feel like I'm tripping man," he answers, "and that this is just a dream. A dream where I've got the chance of redemption."

Wow, that's pretty heavy stuff. I tell him, "Mate, I've got no idea what redemption means to you, but I appreciate you taking me up on the offer to help me out. Now I'm proposing that I pay you a grand for your help this coming week ok? That's what I pay some of my other staff. I only employ the best people, so I expect to pay for their expertise."

Fang's mouth is opening and closing like a fish. "But, but ... I'm not an expert on anything, I don't deserve that much," he stammers.

"How long have you been living on the streets for?" I quiz.

"Since I was fourteen."

"And how old are you now?"

"Twenty nine."

Fuck me, that's the same age as me. I can't believe it, he looks so much older. I'm trying to work out how many years that is. Grandma Spanx whispers 'fifteen' to me. God she knows me so well, it would have taken me bloody ages to work that out.

"So you've been homeless, living on the streets - or in parks - for the past fifteen years, is that right?" I inquire.

He nods at me and this time it's my turn to grin. I say, "Mate, if that doesn't make you a bloody expert I don't know what will! Trust me, you're the perfect man for the job!"

We talk about a few details, and I ask him how we'll stay in touch. Luckily he's got a mobile phone, which he stole yesterday. How convenient. So I give him my number and ask him to call me tomorrow, there's a lot to get organised, but if he wants to he can start getting the word out tonight about what's happening. I haven't got a hotel sorted yet, but I'm confident of finding one soon. He apologises again for trying to mug us, but I wave it off, saying that his timing was perfect, but he'll have to wait a bit longer for some cash.

The three of us walk out of Colley Lane together and are greeted by Fang's mates, who immediately start fawning over him. I'm taking Grandma Spanx home to my place for a stiff drink. Coffee won't cut it after this ordeal. As we're all standing at the kerb, with me trying to hail a taxi, one of my mobile billboards cruises by. Fang looks from it to me and back again a few times.

"Who is Davis Spanx?" he reads out loud. "He's a bloody legend, that's who," he breathes.

Chapter 18

As our taxi pulls up outside Paradise Towers a large group of Team Davis supporters cheer our arrival, which spins me out because there weren't any there when I left to meet Grandma Spanx earlier. One of Fang's mates must have tweeted about the attempted mugging, causing my supporters to flock to Paradise Towers to lend me some moral support. Bloody social media.

After her bravado in Colley Lane, Grandma Spanx broke down in tears on the taxi ride home, it must have been delayed shock. She's now busily wiping away her tears as we open the door of the cab. Supporters swarm around us, asking if she's ok, trying to comfort her. She admits that yes, we were mugged, but luckily no harm was done. Suddenly phones are flashing in our faces as people capture the teary moment. I quickly whisk her inside, giving everyone a wave as we make a hasty retreat. Porter demands to know if we're ok, which I assure him we are, before we head upstairs for that stiff drink.

Dad got a tweet about it and rocks up ten minutes later with Mum in tow, she's hysterical with worry. By the time they arrive Grandma Spanx has downed two hefty, neat scotches, and has regained her composure. She's back to her usual outgoing, feisty self, and can't help boasting to Mum and Dad about how she saved the day by pulling out her paperweight Magnum.

The look on Mum and Dad's faces is priceless. They must get an immediate visual of the scene, because Dad splutters and starts pissing himself laughing, which sets Mum off, which sets both me and Grandma Spanx off. After we all calm down I fill them in on what happened, explaining how it's actually been a blessing in disguise, because I've now got Fang on board for the TV special.

Dad's phone is going bonkers, he's being bombarded with calls. He can't ignore it for long, and soon starts checking his messages. They're all from the press, wanting to confirm if we really were mugged. They also want to know the legitimacy of a rumour about me putting up homeless people in a hotel. He quickly organises a press conference for the following morning, to be held in the conference room here at Paradise Towers. Once he's satisfied that both Grandma

Spanx and I are ok, Dad hustles the girls into the lift, saying that he'll catch me in the morning.

$$$$$$$$$

Wow, my very own press conference. This is a first, and it's pretty bloody cool. Grandma Spanx is the real crowd pleaser though, she jumped at the chance to do it with me when I asked her last night. She's milking our story real good, playing the heroine to perfection. She even brought her fake Magnum to show off to the press, so of course we have to pose for heaps of photos with it. At one point she strikes the classic Charlies Angels pose which she totally rocks - in a very senior way! I also confirm that the rumours are true, I'm doing a *Respect the Homeless* TV Special soon, where I'll be taking over an entire hotel to sleep them in. There's quite a buzz from the press about it.

Bruce and I do our interviews with *G'day* magazine in the arvo. It all runs smoothly and is pretty uneventful, which makes a nice change. Bruce totally gets off on the whole thing, it's given him a real confidence boost which is great. He reckons he could get used to this celebrity caper.

As we're wrapping everything up, Dee Dee calls and asks if I can possibly get Grandma Spanx to do an interview today. I tell her I'm sure she'll agree. Jeeze, Grandma Spanx is gonna have bragging rights for the rest of her life after this. When I call and ask her she shrieks with delight, joking that she'll have to get Dad to be her manager as well, then she insists that Grandma Drummond be included in the interview too.

They do their photo shoot out at the pistol club. Gary the owner is stoked, and manages to squeeze into the background of one shot, cheeky bugger. I can't wait to see next week's issue with them in it. We'll have taken over the whole *G'day* mag, what with their interview, Bruce's interview and mine all in one. Talk about a bumper issue!

Jacobs threw a massive hissy fit when he found out that Grandma Spanx and I were nearly mugged. He ranted on about me being an open target, and from now on insists that I have security with me at all times. He's right, so I don't have a problem with it, even though things turned out fine this time. I must admit that Fang gave me quite a scare, especially when combined with Mitch's death threats.

Mitch's gang of protestors might be lying low, but he's trying to make up for it with lots more vitriolic posts on Facebook. His comments are getting worse, they're a cesspool of antagonistic, scathing untruths. Lucky I've got a thick skin. Ajala rang me in tears yesterday after reading what he'd posted, so I told her to forget about him, he's not worth getting upset over. She wailed that it's her duty to read everything, seeing as she's my social media co-ordinator, so I've banned her from reading his posts, I won't have that sweet girl getting herself in a tizz over me. It just means that Mitch is winning his stupid war.

I finally got onto Ajala's brother Suraj, and he's done an awesome job of updating my website, adding the pages where people can upload their respect vids. He's rocked it. He's set it up similar to YouTube, in that the vids are categorised in such a way that there'll always be room for more uploads. I got him to do the same with the photo page too. The new look website only went up two days ago, and the amount of content that's already on there is insane.

Since I'm flat out getting the TV special organised, I'm going to air some of the fans respect videos on my segment this Friday morning to save myself a bit of work. I got Suraj to announce this on my website and things immediately went berserk. Big Mal's all for it, and Charlie my producer is rapt because it's a no-brainer, it'll save him a stack of work too, allowing him to focus on the TV special.

$$\$\$\$\$\$\$\$\$\$$

It's all systems go, I can't believe it's Wednesday already. The past couple of days have flown by in a flurry of activity. So far so good, everything's coming together nicely for the TV special. I'm having a meeting with the production crew this morning. Charlie's been tearing his hair out over how to book out a whole hotel, all the ones that his team's tried so far have had advance bookings, there's no hotel anywhere in the city centre that's totally vacant for the night we need it.

In a moment of brilliant insight I ask him which ones have the least amount of bookings, so he quickly gets a list together. There's one right in the heart of the city that's only got twenty two rooms booked for Saturday night, which is when it's all happening. So my solution is to see if we can upgrade the guests to a swankier hotel, and cover their costs. Who's gonna say no to staying at a five star hotel instead of a four star? You'd be a mug to miss out on that.

After much to-ing and fro-ing the Monahan Hotel finally agrees. They've given us a price for booking the whole hotel, which will sleep four hundred guests. It comes to $52,000, and that's including dinner and breakfast. Sweet, my charity can easily cover that. Oh how times have changed, once upon a time that would have been more than my salary for a whole year's hard slog - but not anymore!

With that sorted I leave Charlie to talk to them about the dinner and breakfast arrangements. I stress to him that I really want people to pitch in and help make breakfast and clean their rooms.

My next job is to get onto Tai, Eric's mate who's done all of my respect merchandising so far. He's done a brilliant job with the t-shirts and caps and other stuff, dunno if he does tracksuits though. I've decided that instead of the usual red writing that goes on everything I want it to be yellow, so it puts everyone who stays at the hotel into their own exclusive group. I'm hoping that by doing this, long after this has finished people will recognise that these guys were part of the TV special, and show them a bit more respect on the streets. That'd be really cool.

Turns out that Tai's up for the challenge, but he has a coughing fit when I tell him I need four hundred, in various sizes, emblazoned with my respect slogan, and that I need them in two days' time! Lucky he's a chilled out dude. After his initial shock, I explain what they're for and he starts jabbering with excitement, saying that he's happy to be part of the project. Getting a price from him, I then ask how much more it'd cost to have four hundred caps as well. He gives me another price which is exceptionally reasonable, so I tell him that if he gets it all done on time I'll give him a thousand dollar bonus. He's always gone the extra mile for me, which I really appreciate, so I reckon he deserves a bonus.

The final stage of prep is getting the Streetsmart Swags sorted, which is dead easy as I've already spoken to the manufacturers. I had them on standby for three hundred and fifty swags, so getting it up to four hundred shouldn't be a problem. Man I'm so excited, it's all coming together perfectly. Now I just need to get onto Fang and tell him where and when it's going to happen.

Easier said than done, he was meant to ring me but he hasn't yet. Hope he hasn't gotten cold feet. I have no idea how to contact him, so fingers crossed he'll call.

My phone rings and I grab it, hoping it's Fang. But it's Big Mal, he wants to talk about what he's referring to as 'Operation Respect'. Man he cracks me up, he's just a big kid really. I'm in the car on the way home from the studio meeting. The traffic's been a bitch, bumper to bumper for the last half hour. Big Mal asks if I've got time to talk and I confirm that at the moment I've got all the bloody time in the world.

"Good," he booms down the phone, "I want ya to fly to Sydney now, meet me there for lunch alright."

I tell him the traffic situation, and he advises me to get to the airport ASAP, his plane's waiting for me. "I'll have ya back by dinner time alright," and he hangs up.

I fill Jacobs and Jonno in on the new development. Jacobs is more than happy to change directions and get us to the airport. Jonno wants to know why Big Mal's flying me there. I just say that he wants to do lunch - which isn't a lie, but it's not the whole truth either. I haven't told anyone else about what I'm planning, apart from running it by Big Mal to see what he thinks. And with him whisking me up to Sydney, I'm betting that it's a goer.

'Operation Respect' has nothing to do with the TV special, it's a whole new thing. And it's big. If people thought I was being ambitious with the TV special then this'll blow them away. It all stemmed from Grandma Spanx and me getting mugged the other night. The streets just aren't safe anymore, it's plain scary out there. So what I want to organise is a 'Respect The Streets' rally, where hopefully I get stacks of people to march with me down Swanston St, ending with a free concert at the iconic Sidney Myer Music Bowl. If I can pull this off I'll be stoked. Besides getting the message out there for people to respect the streets and help keep each other safe, it's gonna be a hell of a lot of fun. There's already a couple of marches that deal with violence against women, and as a family we normally go to the 'Reclaim the Night' march each year. But everything seems to be focused on just women, what about us blokes? What about kids? What about older people? I want something that includes everyone. We all use the streets, so we should all respect each other on them.

It pisses me off there's such a lack of respect in society these days. Every day the media bombards us with the latest rapes, stabbings, shootings and bashings. It's become normal for people to get bashed, robbed, raped or killed. But it's not normal, and it's not ok. That's why I want to do something about it, try and instil a message, or ultimately, create a new culture where people want to look out for each other again. To bring back the respect. Dunno if my method will work, but something's gotta give, and I'm gonna a give it a bloody good go.

I've been dying to tell Dad and everyone about 'Operation Respect', this is the biggest secret I've ever kept. But until I know for sure that it's a goer I'll keep my mouth shut.

We finally rock up at the airport, the private jet's all set to go. Leaning forward, putting my head between the front seats of the car, I look from Jacobs to Jonno and ask, "Fancy a plane trip boys?"

Jonno's eyes pop wide open and he asks in a shocked voice, "What, ya want us to come with ya this time?"

Nodding at him I answer, "Don't see why not, Big Mal didn't say I shouldn't bring you two. Whaddaya say, are you both up for it?"

"Shit yeah!" shouts Jonno.

I turn and look at Jacobs, who imperceptibly inclines his head towards me and says, "Very good sir, Sydney it is."

$$\$\$\$\$\$\$\$\$\$\$$$

The restaurant is humming with murmuring voices. When Big Mal and I walk in all eyes are on us, and a ripple of excitement goes through the group of diners. Big Mal waves to a few people as we make our way to our table – we've got a bird's eye view of the harbour and Sydney Opera House. There's another guy already sitting at the table waiting for us and I instantly recognise him. It's Frankie Mellor, he's *the* guru of big event management, he's an Aussie icon. For the past forty years he's been bringing all the top bands to Australia, and not only does he get them here, but he organises the most incredible concerts ever. He must be nearly seventy by now, but if you hear that Frankie Mellor's putting on a show, you know it's gonna to be awesome.

We all shake hands, introductions are made, and we get straight down to business. Both Frankie and Big Mal are pumped up about my idea, and it soon becomes clear that not only is it a goer, but due to my saturation of the local media, which has apparently now spread overseas, we've got bands lining up to do the gig.

"This is gonna be huge," drawls Frankie. "Davis, as soon as I put my feelers out about this, me phone rang off the hook nonstop. You'll never guess who wants to be a part of it."

I raise my eyebrows in expectation, I have no idea.

"C'mon Frankie, put the kid out of his misery alright," coaxes Big Mal. The grin on his face is the size of the Sydney Harbour Bridge, he's obviously in the know already.

Frankie leans back in his seat and holds up both his hands in a gesture of surrender. "Get ready mate, I'm about to blow your mind." And he starts rattling off the names of top bands while counting them on his fingers. "Well of course you've got Jimmy Barnes and Angry Anderson, this is right up their alley. Billy Thorpe, Thirsty Merc, Mental as Anything, Kate Miller Heidke, Guy Sebastian, Jessica Mauboy, Tex Perkins, Pete Murray, Paul Kelly, The Church, Babba, Delta Goodrem, but it gets better. Hunters and Collectors want in, so do The Hoodoo Gurus and Tim and Neil Finn. Those guys *never* do shit like this, but the pièce de résistance is…" He does a drum roll with his hands on the table and announces, "Kylie!"

My mouth drops open in astonishment. "Really?" is all I can manage right now, I'm in shock. I mean he's just listed the most amazing array of Aussie artists, topped off by the princess of pop herself. It's no wonder I can't speak.

"Yeah, there's heaps of others but I can't remember them all off the top of me head. I'll give you a full list to peruse later on, so ya can pick which ones you want to have perform."

Oh my freakin' God, I get to choose who performs? That's insane!

"Jeezus," I shout, "I can't believe all these people want to do it. It's in-fucking-credible, this *is* mind blowing!"

A few people from nearby tables turn to see what the commotion is, but they don't gawk at us. Big Mal and Frankie are both looking at me indulgently.

"Mate, haven't you heard the expression 'if you build it they will come'?" Frankie asks.

Nodding I reply, "Yeah I've seen the movie Field of Dreams, it was great. I've always remembered that line from it too."

Frankie continues on. "Davis you've created this respect movement at exactly the right time, it's struck a chord with everyone. They're just as unhappy with the way people treat each other these days as you are. They admire what you're doing, and they want to be a part of it. Mate you have *no* idea what you've started, this is just the tip of the iceberg." He looks across to Big Mal and gives him a wink.

We're interrupted by the waitress bringing over the biggest seafood platter I've ever seen, it's so big that it's got its own bloody trolley. Big Mal's licking his lips and Frankie's rubbing his hands together in anticipation. All conversation stops as we devour the feast. Oh yes, life's good at the top.

I take a minute to just absorb and enjoy the surroundings I'm in right now, I nearly have to pinch myself. A few weeks ago I was a lowly factory worker, but now I'm having lunch with two of the biggest players in Australia, while looking down on the sparkling blue waters of Sydney Harbour. Fuck I love my life.

Big Mal must have gauged my mood, because he raises his glass and gives a toast. "To you Davis, enjoy it mate, you deserve it alright."

We're messily scoffing our lunch - and it really is scoffing, not a modicum of finesse is exhibited throughout the entire meal by any of us. I guess it's a bit hard to have manners when you're ripping legs off things and sucking the meat out of 'em. It's good to know that where a good feed is concerned, we're all on the same playing field. There's no time for talk as we busily stuff our faces, and it's nice to feel at ease in such esteemed company.

Finishing our feast, we resume the discussion. Big Mal and Frankie want to roll with the rally and concert sooner rather than later, there's a lot of talk about striking while the iron's hot. Hey, they don't have to convince me, I'm ready to rock'n'roll whenever they are. So I ask what sort of time is needed, how long does it take to get something like this organised?

Frankie and Big Mal look at each other, then both sets of eyes rest on me. I'm sensing a vibe here, I'm sensing…but before I can figure it out, they both say together, "Next Saturday night!"

Then they shut up. Both of their mouths are twitching, as they wait for my response. I can't believe what I just heard. Am I halluci-hearing? Did they really say next Saturday? I'm nearly wetting myself I'm so excited, I thought it'd take months to organise. Counting the days off on my fingers I shout, "Fuck off, that's only nine more sleeps!"

They both crack up laughing at my reaction, then Frankie fishes in his trouser pocket for something and hands Big Mal a crisp hundred dollar note. "You were bloody right *again*, I gotta stop making stupid bets with ya," he says to Big Mal.

Big Mal's looking smug. He explains, "I bet him that you'd say fuck in your first sentence and I was right!" He makes a big show of tucking the hundred dollar note into his shirt pocket, deliberately leaving some of it sticking out for us to see. Then he clears his throat, "Seriously though Davis, we can do it in this timeframe no worries."

I'm still shaking my head in disbelief. "Wow, that's unbelievable guys, I thought it'd take ages to get sorted."

"Not when you're working with the best of the best mate. We make shit happen," says Frankie. "Am I right or right?" he asks Big Mal.

"You're spot on alright."

Coffee is served and we talk some more. Frankie wants to know if I have any idea of how I want the stage to look. All I know is that I want my respect slogan visible, that's all I've got for now. He says that he'll get some stage mock ups done ASAP, along with the list of per-formers for me to peruse. Apparently they already know the date of the gig, and everyone's up for it.

"I'm gonna make it a TV special, that way none of the punters miss out if they can't come, alright," booms Big Mal, and he claps me on the back. Lucky I wasn't holding my coffee cup or Frankie would

301

have worn it. "It's gonna be bigger than bloody Carols by Candlelight alright!" he chuckles.

Remembering what Frankie said earlier, about this being the tip of the iceberg, I want to know what he meant. So I ask him.

"It means that Big Mal and I reckon your respect rallies and concerts are gonna go global, simple as that," he answers with a smile.

"You're a bloody worldwide YouTube sensation," Big Mal booms. "It's obvious that the whole world's ready for your respect message Davis. If I was you, I'd get ready for one hell of a ride son."

Fuck me. I'd never imagined *that* before, but suddenly in my mind's eye I see myself in different countries around the world. England, America, Asia. I'm at the head of a respect rally, and on stage in front of thousands of people, who are all helping bring back the respect. I must have completely zoned out for a minute, when I come back to reality they're both looking at me intently.

Frankie nods his head sagely, "He's seen it, he's stepped into it. Watch out world, here comes Davis Spanx!"

I look from one to the other blankly, and Big Mal declares "The first step to creating anything is seeing it, stepping into it. Hold that vision Davis, and run it like a film for yourself. Often. Before you know it mate, you'll be living it. Trust me, it's what's made me rich alright."

$$\$\$\$\$\$\$\$\$\$$

When I'm in the car heading back to the jet I give Dad a call, to see if everyone's free for an emergency family meeting. I'd like to take everyone out to dinner at Taxie, that way I can tell them about Operation Respect all at once. I insist it's a level ten emergency - I gotta have everyone there. He calls me back fifteen minutes later, everyone's in except Holly. Apparently she's got a hot date and doesn't want to cancel it.

"Her and Tobie broke up on the weekend, so she's on the pull again," Dad explains.

Enough said, I read that situation loud and clear. She'll be gaggin' for a shaggin', and not even her little celeb brother's gonna get in the way of her getting one. Bloody typical!

Apparently the two grans are beyond excited by the prospect of dinner at a fancy restaurant, they remembered it was where I had the sixteen courses, and they've asked Dad to ask me if that's what they'll be having. I tell him that yes, if it can be done then that's what we'll have tonight.

In a cheeky move I ask Jacobs if he can pullover for a sec, then I inform him and Jonno that I'll need them on duty tonight, is that ok? Both confirm that its fine, then I tell them that I'll be requiring their services at the dinner table. Two heads snap around from the front to look at me.

"I want you boys to have dinner with us tonight, your family as well, alright." Shit I'm starting to sound like Big Mal. Gotta watch myself, I don't want to get into the same habit as him and end every sentence with alright. I mean it's alright for him to do it, I got no problem with that, I just don't want to imitate him.

Eyeballing Jacobs I ask him, "How would you like to call Lawrence at Taxie and book us in?" Grinning from ear to ear I add, "I'm sure he'll be pleased to hear from you, I reckon he'll get a shock when you tell him *you're* one of the dinner guests eh!"

Jacobs grins back at me and chuckles with delight. "I'm sure he will sir. It would give me *immense* pleasure to make the reservation."

Jonno and I listen in as he makes the call, both of us are trying not to snigger too loudly. When he hangs up Jacobs is grinning from ear to ear, and admits that was the most fun he's had in ages.

"Just wait till dinner time," I quip, as he pulls back out into the traffic.

Jonno pesters me with questions all the way home on the plane. He knows me well enough to realise when something's up, but I manage to dodge him beautifully by saying, "All will be revealed tonight." Man, I'm busting a gut here trying to hold it all in.

$$$$$$$$$$

I pick everyone up from Mum and Dad's in a black stretch Hummer limo, which goes down a treat, everyone loves it. When I invited Ajala, I asked her to send out a tweet to let the fans know what I'm up to. I don't normally do this, but why not create a bit of a buzz eh? For maximum impact Dad makes us crank up the fog machine so that the cabin of the Hummer is engulfed in a thick cloud of smoke. It's getting to the point where we're all having trouble breathing, and everyone's making a fuss, demanding to open the windows. But Dad's commanding us like a general, shouting over the commotion 'Hold on, it's nearly time." He keeps repeating this for what seems like ages.

Kaci, Holly's little one, and Jack and Jill, Doug's twins, are in heaven. They're squealing and carrying on like pork chops, and they're not the only ones. We're all behaving like lunatics. Doug cranks the music volume up, turns on all the disco lights, and we all squirm around, boogying to the music.

When it finally comes time to open the door and get out, a massive cloud of smoke dramatically billows out, accompanied by loud doof-doof music and flashing lights. Thanks to Ajala's tweet there's a huge crowd waiting for us, and they all go mental, cheering and chanting 'Davis, Davis, Davis', while the paparazzi capture us all stumbling out into the fresh air, gasping for breath. Good one Dad, what a way to make an entrance! It's pretty bloody cool, especially the red carpet Lawrence has rolled out for us, complete with gold ropes to keep the crowd back. He's also stationed a few security dudes at various points along the red carpet.

I ask Jacobs if he recognises any of them, and his face erupts into a massive grin - the biggest I've ever seen from him. "Yes sir, a lot of them are ex colleagues. I'm sure seeing *me* on the red carpet will be quite the bombshell." His grin has now been replaced by a smirk. Good on him, he deserves to lord it over them all for a change, he's a top bloke.

Making our way up the red carpet everyone's striking poses for the paps. I honestly think my family were made for this shit, they've all taken to it like ducks to water. I notice the reactions of the security dudes to Jacobs. Their eyes are nearly popping out of their heads, and he gives each one his signature head inclination as he glides past. Meanwhile I sign a few autographs, pose to have my photos taken with some of the fans, and give out lots of high-fives. As I'm making my way up the steps I notice that Dad's already ushered the rest of the family inside.

Reaching the top of the steps with Jonno and Jacobs flanking me, I shush the crowd with a downward motion of my hands. I'm about to plug the upcoming TV special when suddenly there's a bit of a ker-fuffle. Someone's trying to push through the crowd. Bugger, I should have thought this out better, Mitch is probably up to something. I noticed a few 'Davis is a capitalist wanker' placards in the crowd earlier, but didn't think that much of it. The guy raises his face towards me and shouts something out which I can't understand. Jacobs and Jonno position themselves closer to me, ready for action.

Suddenly I realise who the guy is, it's Fang! So I tell my boys to go and escort him over to me. I hardly recognised him at first, he's spruced himself up. He's wearing a very badly fitting brown suit, and he's hacked off some of his manky hair. He looks like a reject from the Brady Bunch, but good on him for making an effort. When I shake his hand I notice that this time it's clean, and his nails aren't full of grime. He's also cleanly shaven, and the pong of piss has left him, thank God.

"Bloody good to see ya mate, you had me worried. I thought you'd done a runner," I say while pumping his hand.

"Nah, I just had to get meself clean. In more ways than one, if ya know what I mean," he says giving me a cheeky wink.

Wow. Putting my arm around his shoulders I tell him that he's awesome and that I'm really glad he's here. Then I turn back to the crowd and shout, "I'd like to introduce you to a very important man. He's my street guru, and my right hand man for the upcoming *Respect the Homeless* TV special. Everybody say hello to Fang."

The crowd dutifully chant, "Hello Fang." I feel him stiffen beside me, this has probably freaked him out a bit, but bad luck. I want everyone to know who he is.

When their done I shout, "Guys, if you see Fang out on the streets, make sure you say g'day and give him a hand if he needs it. He's gonna be helping me organise things, so he might need some assistance from all of you fans. Is that ok?"

"Yes!" they all scream back. Cool. I thank them and move to go inside. Fang seems to be rooted to the spot, so I move my hand from his shoulder down onto his elbow, indicating that I want him to come into the restaurant with me. The crowd are loudly doing the 'Davis' chant again, it sounds awesome.

"Come and have dinner with us," I ask him. I see a look of total shock and hesitation play across his face. "C'mon," I coax. "You've gotta come, you're part of the team now. I won't accept no for an answer." Putting my hand on the small of his back I give him a gentle push towards the doors.

He's still looking hesitant, but takes a few tentative steps, then Jonno pipes up. "Mate what the boss says goes, so get your arse in there." This does the trick and we hustle inside together.

The others are all clamouring around the wall of fame in the reception area. When Grandma Spanx spots Fang come in she rushes over and gives him a big hug, telling him how good he looks and how glad she is to see him here. With that I see him finally relax, and introductions are made to the rest of the family who all greet him warmly. We all admire the wall of fame for a few minutes more – my photo's got pride of place right in the middle. Then we head upstairs to the VIP area.

We've just finished off our fifth course, which consisted of slivers of Wagyu Beef with a mustard jus, and quenelles of truffle mash. Just as well Mum's on the case, I wouldn't have a clue what half this stuff is, only that it all tastes freakin' amazing.

The two grans are in ecstasy. So far each course has brought a hoot of delight from them both, followed by a dissection and discussion of the dish, before it quickly disappears into their mouths. A heated exchange erupted earlier between them, Mum, and Danielle, as to what the third course was. They were arguing that it was salmon, but Mum and Danielle were positive it was smoked trout. In the end I called a waiter over to end the dispute. Mum and Danielle won, trout it was, much to the chagrin of the two grans – it didn't stop them hoovering it up though. I've got a strict no handbag policy for those two tonight, I stashed their bags under my chair as soon as we arrived, so they can't pull their usual stunt!

I'm building up the suspense for my big announcement. When we arrived earlier, I asked Lawrence if we can have a short break between the fifth and sixth courses. He bowed and said that it was a perfect time for a palate freshener. I just agreed with him, buggered if I knew what he meant. The palate freshener that Lawrence suggested is now served, and turns out to be cups of lemony sorbet. Right, that means it's show time.

Standing up I tap my glass to get everyone's attention. All conversation abruptly stops and everyone looks at me expectantly. I fill them in on my lunch with Big Mal and Frankie first, just to set the scene. Then I divulge the plan for my Respect the Streets rally and concert - but I don't spill the beans about who's going to be performing at the concert yet. Throughout my little speech mouths have been dropping open in astonishment, almost in a domino effect.

"If Grandma Spanx and I hadn't been nearly mugged the other night, then I probably wouldn't have thought of doing this," I admit, raising my glass for a toast. "So here's to you Fang, thanks for setting all this in motion, without you this probably wouldn't have happened."

There's a stunned silence, the same as when I announced the TV special plans. Again Dad's the first to say anything. He gives a 'cheers' to Fang, and everyone else follows his lead. Sitting back down, I chuckle to myself.

"What?" demands Doug, "What else have ya got up your sleeve?"

Licking my lips I take a spoonful of the sorbet to delay things, and make a big show of how good it tastes. My family all know me well enough to know that I'm milking the situation. Mum has a quick pow-wow with the two grans who are sitting next to her, then states, "We reckon you've got a marching band on board, a good rally always has a marching band tucked in it somewhere."

I nearly choke on the sorbet, but quickly recover. "Close, but no cigar Mum. Sorry to say there's no marching band involved." Her and the two grans faces immediately drop, she's about to say something but I get in first. "No there's no marching band, but there *are* some of the biggest Aussie performers ever, lined up to put on the awesomeest show Australia's ever seen." I do as Frankie did, and run through the list, ticking them off my fingers as I go, finishing up with Kylie.

At the mention of her Doug shoots up out of his seat and punches the air - he's a big fan, a big fan of her hot pants clad arse! Janelle gives him a filthy look, but he's too busy singing one of her songs and dancing around to notice her dagger-eyes. The twins have gone ballistic, squealing with excitement. In fact, as I was reeling off the list of performers the enthusiasm within the group grew and grew.

307

Doug seems to have started something, because the two grans jump up and join him. Before I know it we're all dancing around like dickheads, even Fang, Jonno and Jacobs join in

We soon wear ourselves out and collapse back into our seats. Everyone's talking at once, jabbering on about how great it's gonna be. Then they all start asking me questions. I hush them and say that all I can tell them at this point is that Frankie and Big Mal are organising it, it's happening next Saturday, and I get to choose which bands I want to have play!

"O.M.G. Davis, that's only a bit over a week away," shrieks Danielle.

"I know!" I shout. "But Big Mal and Frankie are sure that's when it's happening. They've got it all sorted," I assure everyone.

Dad's grinning at me. "That's bloody incredible," he says. "Here's to Davis, his big-wig mates, and the rally and concert."

The rest of the dinner passes in a blur of excitement, conversation, and good food. The two grans gobble up everything that's put in front of them, so does Fang, Dad, Ajala and Jonno. The rest of us eat most of it, but by the end we're picking at bits and pieces. We all roll out of there at about one am. I had a good chat with Fang about the TV special, he reckons he's already got word out on the street about what's going down.

When I tell him how many we can put up for the night, a total of four hundred, he laughs, telling me, "That's fan-fuckin-tastic mate." He immediately says that we'll probably have to turn people away, which is better than what I've been worrying about the last couple of days. I've been worried that no one would rock up and it would be a flop. He reassures me that he'll get the people there no worries, so I tell him that it's happening at the Monahan Hotel at three pm Saturday. Jeezus, it's only four days away!

I insist that he call me on Friday to touch base, I want to be certain that he's got the numbers and himself sorted. Handing him some cash we shake hands, and he takes off into the night while the rest of us get back into the Hummer to take us home. All of the fans have gone home, so it's a quiet exit from Taxie, which is cool.

$$$$$$$$$

"You're fuckin' shittin' me!" exclaims Bruce, who then starts laughing manically.

This reaction's almost as good as the one I got when I told him I was gonna become a celeb. I invited him to dinner at Taxie last night, but he insisted he didn't want to come. He's been moping around lately, the poor bugger, I know how he feels. He'd already crashed by the time I got home last night, so I've only just filled him in on the concert and rally plans. Needless to say he's blown away.

It's Thursday, and it's a beautiful day, so I suggest that we take the Porsche for a spin, chew the fat, and maybe have lunch somewhere. I've got nothing else on today, everything I needed to do is already sorted. Charlie's happy with how everything's progressing for Saturday, he was so relieved when I told him I'd caught up with Fang. His exact words were "Thank Christ for that!" And I couldn't agree with him more, I was stressing out about the Fang factor too.

I've already touched base with Dad as well, Sexy Juice have contacted him and want me to do some ads for them. Cool. I love their juice range, so I'm happy to give the thumbs up for endorsing the brand. This is the first time I've been asked to do an ad and I'm stoked, I can already picture myself popping up on telly during the ad breaks. Dad's working on getting the best deal he can for me, he reckons he should know the outcome by this arvo. Apparently they're keen to shoot the ad next week, they know all about the respect rally and want to boost their publicity through it. When I quizzed Dad on how they knew about the rally he told me to have a look at today's papers, the rally and concert are splashed across all of them.

"And because of that my son, I'll be able to get you a ripper deal!" he says excitedly. He couldn't hang up fast enough, the scent of the deal egging him on. They'd better watch out, before they know it he'll have squeezed a ridiculous amount of money out of them.

So now that business is sorted it's time to have some fun. Lucky Bruce works from home, it means we get to hang out. I love having him here, the penthouse seemed a bit quiet before he moved in, this is the perfect setup for both of us. With the new security procedures in place, Jonno and Jacobs will have to follow us while I'm driving the Porsche. Jacobs doesn't want to let me out of his sight, and I'm cool with that. They're both hanging out in the games room while Bruce and I decide where we want to go.

Bruce jumps up, grabs his wallet off the coffee table, and declares that he's shouting me lunch. "We should go down the Great Ocean Road, let's go to Lorne for lunch." He looks at his watch, "C'mon, it's only ten, we'll be there by twelve, it'll only take a couple of hours."

I wasn't thinking of driving that far and I say so, but Bruce pushes the button that's guaranteed to make me say yes.

"Maaate, after goin' to the Goldie and learnin' how to drive Black Beauty properly, it's your *duty* to take her for a decent spin. Besides, with all the stuff you've got coming up, when else are ya gonna get the chance? C'mon, it'll be fun."

Jeeze, he must be picking up some persuasion tactics from hanging out with Dad so much lately. Standing up I say, "Enough said, I'm sold. Let's do it!"

I'm glad he talked me into it, the drive down the coast is superb, I'm itching to put the foot down, but stay inside the speed limit.

Black Beauty is *not* a stealth car. People are tooting and waving to us the whole way there. Some chicks in a convertible even give us a flash of their tits! Now that's something that doesn't happen every day. Bruce and I can't believe our luck and have a good old perv, sniggering like school kids. While the chicks are flashing I notice that Jacobs is tailgating us, Jonno's probably ordered him to get as close as possible so he can cop a perve as well. Man, driving the Great Ocean Road in a Porsche is something else. I'm gonna let Bruce drive her back, he's gonna love it.

We pull up at the Cuban restaurant in Lorne that Bruce insisted we go to, and immediately draw a crowd. After some autograph signing and photo taking, the boys escort us inside. I would have been happy with fish and chips on the beach, but Bruce made a big fuss about coming to this place, apparently one of Trace's gal pals raved about it to him a while ago. I'm looking forward to the four of us enjoying lunch together, but Jacobs insists that he and Jonno sit at another table to give us two a bit of space. Jeeze he's a funny one.

The restaurant has a perfect view of the ocean, and I'm glad Bruce brought us here. During lunch we have a man to man about the ex-chicks in our lives. He informs me that Trace has been constantly texting and calling him.

"She was becoming obsessive," he complains. "She was turning up at the penthouse unannounced, lucky you weren't there when she was." At this I snap to attention.

"Don't worry, I didn't bloody let her in!" he sooths. "Porter knows not to give her access. Anyway, yesterday I got a restraining order against her, so she can't come anywhere near me. I've seen a lawyer, I asked Danielle and she put me onto a good divorce one. He's putting it together for me now."

"Shit. No wonder you didn't want to come out last night. Jeeze ya should have told me she was hassling you."

Putting a forkful of food into his mouth he says around it, "Nah mate, you've got enough on your plate. It's all sorted now. No worries."

"Fair enough," I agree.

We decide to have a quick dip in the ocean before we head back to Melbs - much to Jacobs' horror.

"Sir, the logistics. We haven't got enough men for that, we'll need backup," he barks at me, adding, "I strongly advise against it, you saw the crowds here already. It's not a good idea." He's in a real tizz about it. Bugger, I quite fancied a dip and feeling the sand between my toes.

"How about we stop at one of those small beaches along the way?" Jonno suggests. "We can just pull off the road somewhere, that'd be easy, there'd be no one around to hassle ya there."

We all look to Jacobs for his opinion, and after a few seconds to mull it over he agrees. You beauty! I give Jonno a pat on the back, he gives me the thumbs up, puts on his gangsta hat, and we all head off.

$$\$\$\$\$\$\$\$\$\$$

Finding a little beach with somewhere to pull over is easy, the Great Ocean Road's got heaps of them. Bruce and I do a mad scramble to get our gear off, and leaving just our boxer shorts on we run gung-ho into the water at full speed.

"Fuuuuck" we both scream simultaneously. The waters fucking freezing! My dick immediately shrinks to the size of my thumb nail and

I think my balls have disappeared back up inside me. I can't blame the little buggers for trying to stay warm. We should have tested the waters first, but nah, that's not our style.

Jeezus, talk about how to freak yourself out, the day might be sunny and beautiful, but the water's arctic cold. I should have known better, after all it is only the end of September and Spring's just sprung. That's the trouble with living in Melbs, any hint of good weather after a freezing cold winter lulls you into a sense of frivolity, and this is the outcome - freezing your balls off for fun.

But once we've been in for a few minutes it doesn't seem too bad, I think I've gone numb all over to cope with it. We muck around for a while doing normal blokey things, like dunking each other and scaring each other with talk of Jaws, just the usual shit.

Jacobs and Jonno are leaning against their car talking amongst themselves while keeping an eye on us. We got out of Lorne worry free. Once I signed a few more autographs we were out of there and no one's bothered to follow us, which is a big relief.

Bruce starts madly splashing water in my face. Right that's it, it's on for young and old! I splash him back. The splash fest has begun, we're both cracking up trying not to swallow mouthfuls of sea water. We don't see the car pull up at first.

Suddenly we hear Jonno and Jacobs shouting at us, they're waving their arms in the air, trying to get our attention. They both point to the old Commodore that's pulled up next to our cars. A tall blonde chick gets out and waves to us. Fuck me it's Trace! Bruce and I look at each other in shock. Where the hell did she come from? How did she know we were going to be here?

"Do ya want to stay in the water mate? Try and avoid her?" I ask.

His teeth are chattering. "No way, I'll get hypothermia! I'm gonna have to get out."

"Shit," I mutter.

"Fuckin' shit's right, what the hell does she want?" demands Bruce.

Trace teeters down the small embankment and Jacobs and Jonno swoop in, trying to stop her from coming further onto the beach. But she pushes them both out of her way as she tries to saunter towards us, which doesn't work that well because her high heels keep getting stuck in the soft sand, making her stumble. Finally in frustration she yanks them off her feet and throws them away.

"Those bloody shoes cost me four hundred bucks, and look how she treats them. She's got no bloody respect," hisses Bruce.

We're almost out of the water now, it's lapping around our ankles. With the added wind chill factor Bruce and I are absolutely freezing, we're both shivering uncontrollably, wrapping our arms around ourselves to try and get warm. It doesn't seem to be working though.

"I've got a bloody restraining order against you Trace. Don't come any closer to me or you'll be in big trouble," Bruce yells at her.

As if that'd stop her, it doesn't. She just continues on towards us, shouting out, "That's the reason I'm here! How dare you treat me like that!"

She's pretty close to us now, she's standing at the edge of the water. Thankfully Jacobs and Jonno are on the job, each taking one of her arms, holding her in place so she can't get to Bruce. She tries to flick them off, but my boys have got her held nice and tightly now. She's not a happy camper. She's firing a barrage of abuse at Bruce, calling him every name under the sun, as well as repeatedly calling him a loser and a tosser.

Behind her I see someone get out of the driver's door of the Commodore. The car looks kind of familiar, I'm trying to place it. Then the driver hollers out, "Hey Spanxie, you're a fucking wanker!"

Jonno's head whips around, he's recognised the voice, and so have I. I don't bloody believe this, it's Mitch.

"What the fuck are you and Mitch doing together?" I bellow at Trace. She starts laughing maniacally, man she needs some help, she's lost the plot.

"Wouldn't *you* like to know!" she throws back at me, then continues laughing.

"What the hell are you doing with him?" demands Bruce. "Have you been shagging him?" The veins in his neck look like they're about to burst, he is very, very pissed off.

She tries to get free of Jacobs and Jonno again, but she doesn't stand a chance.

Mitch is now nonchalantly leaning against his car - of course it's his bloody car, I recognise it now. He lights up a smoke and yells out, "Tell them all about us sweetie."

Trace looks over at him and scowls a bit, but not much of her face moves due to all the Botox. I've seen that look many times before, she usually reserves it for those she considers dickheads. I used to cop a lot of them. Whatever she and Mitch have been up to, I'd bet that shagging's not on the list.

Turning her gaze back onto me she snarls, "Ha! It's thanks to *me* that Mitch's army have known where to find you all this time."

What the…? I'm trying to compute what she just said, I'm not sure if I've got it right. Bruce takes a step towards her, hands on his hips. "Are you saying that *you* lagged on where Davis was going to be all this time, so that Mitch's shitty protestors could hassle him?"

Giving a defiant head toss she answers, "Yep, and I'll tell you why. I got bloody sick of your Davis updates every night! All I ever heard was Davis this, Davis that, Davis, Davis, Davis. Fuck him and the easy ride he's had." She laughs again like a crazy woman for a minute, then continues, "It was so easy Bruce, you made it just so easy. Always bragging about what Davis did today, what Davis is doing tomorrow. I got so sick of hearing about him, I thought I'd go mental if I heard his fucking name again."

"You have gone mental you silly cow! I can't believe you'd do this to my best mate!" screams Bruce.

She continues ranting, with spittle flying out of her mouth. "I really knew I was doing the right thing when *he*," she points accusingly at me, "stopped me from getting all the VIP contacts at his bloody car auction. I was gonna *milk* that list! It's so unfair!"

Bruce and I look at each other in horror. I think we're both imagining what a disaster it would have been if she hadn't been stopped that night. It was a close call. There's still one thing I don't get though.

"How the hell did you get in contact with Mitch?" I demand.

Trace licks her luber-lips and tosses her hair again. "That was easy, I knew where he worked - we picked you up after work a couple of times when your ute was being repaired, remember? Anyway I met him after work one day, introduced myself, and asked if he wanted the inside goss. The rest, as they say, is history. From then on I just fed him the details of your daily routine, it's as simple as that."

"Fuck me," I breathe. This is like something out of a TV show, not my life. I think I'm still in shock.

"Have you shagged him?" Bruce roars at her.

Eyeing Bruce with distaste she answers, "As if! Although poor Mitch could do with some lovin'. He's had *such* a tough time lately. Poor baby."

I'm up to speed with everything now, man she's a nasty piece of work. I knew she was a bitch, but not on a scale as epic as this. I've got an idea that I know she'll go for. She'll think it's all about her and her fifteen minutes of fame, which it will be, but with a surprise twist.

Taking a deep breath I say, "Trace, I'm really upset about all this, but I didn't know how much *you* were *hurting*." She's looking at me intently. I can see her calculating mind at work, but I've got her Achilles heel here, her soft spot. She won't be able to resist the media spotlight I'll soon be turning onto her. "I think you deserve to tell your story, the world needs to know *your* side of things, and I'd like to make that happen for you. Would you like to go on *Tonight's Current Affairs* and tell Tanya and Australia how you feel?" I coax.

Bruce is looking at me like I've gone mad. Jonno and Jacobs are stony faced, they're not letting anything show. But bingo, I know I've got Trace right where I want her. Her eyes are glittering with excitement and she's pushed her shoulders back so her boobs are jutting out to the max. Hallelujah, there's even a hint of a smile on her face.

"Yes I'd like that Davis," she says solemnly. "Australia *does* need to know my side of the story, when can you get me on?"

Fuck I'm good! I tell her I'll give Big Mal a call right now. My phone's in the Porsche, which is parked next to Mitch's car. I don't want any trouble so I ask the boys, "How are we gonna do this?"

Bruce immediately offers to go and get it, but I have my reservations, there's a good chance he'd punch Mitch, and I don't want that to happen. Mitch'd probably press charges. Jonno looks like he'd like to knock his block off as well, so I dispatch Jacobs to go and get it.

Big Mal can't believe his luck. When I finish running through what Trace's done to me he growls, "Mate let's get her on tonight,

Tanya's gonna eat her for dinner! I can't wait to see it alright!" he cackles with delight, then adds "Has she asked for money?"

"Nup, she'll just be glad to get her mug on the telly."

"Good, she's not getting any - she's a mug alright. She's got no
idea what's gonna hit her. You're a bloody legend Davis. Ten points
for quick thinking." There's a slight pause then he continues, "Maybe
we should get you on the show as well." But he quickly changes his
mind. "Actually no, we'll wait and see what the response is. We might
have to make your segment a bit longer than usual tomorrow morning
though, alright?"

That's fine with me. As soon as I hang up from Big Mal my phone
rings - it's Dad telling me that Sexy Juice have signed me for a one year
contract, and they're going to pay me half a bloody mill to scoff their
products. Cool.

"And," says Dad, "I managed to *squeeze* some more *juice* out of
them!" We both crack up at his corny joke. "You get all the free product you can drink while you're the face of them. How good is that!" he
says excitedly. I think he's more excited about the free juice than the
half a million dollars. Me, I'm rapt about both, this is fantastic. I quickly
fill him in on the Trace story, finishing up with her being on *Tonight's
Current Affairs.* He says to come over for dinner, that way we can all
watch the train wreck together.

As soon as I tell Trace that she needs to get her arse back to
Melbs, that she's going on the show tonight, she demands to be released, which Jonno and Jacobs happily do.

Giving both Bruce and I her best dagger eyes she announces,
"This is the start of *my* celebrity career; *I'm* gonna be a bigger star than
you Davis."

Then she runs back to the Commodore, says something to Mitch,
and they take off. With tyres screeching Mitch gives a final shout of
"Spanxie's a Wanker!" and gives us the finger.

Chapter 19

I'm at Mum and Dad's, and the whole family's here, along with Bruce, Ajala, Jonno and Jacobs. We're all getting ready to watch the big interview between Tracy and Tanya. I've explained to the family what happened at the beach today and everyone's fired up, they're outraged over Trace's behaviour. Dad silences everyone with a clap of his hands and we settle down, we're all looking forward to the oncoming drama.

It's a hoot watching Tanya and Trace on *Tonight's Current Affairs*, it really is top viewing. Tanya's polite, yet lethal. I think she learnt a real lesson from the interview she did with me, because she's nice as pie. She just asks Trace a series of questions that when answered - in Trace's warped way - completely reveal her schizo side to the whole of Australia. Just as I'd suspected she would.

At one point, as we're all glued to the spectacle, Danielle pinches my arm and whispers that I can probably take action against her if I want to. But I immediately tell her that I'm not into it. To be honest I can't be fucked, I just don't see the point, she'd turn it all into a circus about her. She's showing her true colours, everyone can see she's a nasty piece of work, and that's good enough for me. I'd rather just move on.

Holly's the only one not totally disgusted by her behaviour, she wants to know where Trace gets her leopard skin pants from, which earns her a clip over the ear from Grandma Drummond. Man, I haven't received one of those since I was eight and turned her tiny veggie patch into a war zone for my soldiers.

Throughout the interview Trace happily divulges everything she's been up to and why, she holds nothing back. She drones on about how horrible it was having Bruce talk about me all the time, and explains that the reason she did it all is because it's totally unfair that I've become a celeb so easily. She tries to play the poor me role when she reveals to Tanya how I deleted the photos she took of the guest book at my party. Tanya soothingly asks her to explain what happened in detail, so Trace does, digging a nice deep hole for herself.

When Trace finishes her explanation Tanya asks her, "So what you're saying is that you'd happily steal confidential information, and use that information to start your own celebrity career, is that right?"

Trace blinks rapidly a few times, then spits out, "Yeah, what's wrong with that? But I can still be just as famous as Davis, even without his stupid list!"

Then she keeps repeating over and over how I'm really a loser, not a celeb, and launches into her manic new laugh. It's clear to anyone watching that Trace is a vindictive, unstable, lying, gold digging, backstabbing bitch. When Tanya asks her about Bruce and how he feels about all of this, Trace snaps, "I couldn't give a shit what he thinks, he's a loser just like Davis. Those two deserve each other."

Then Tanya asks her about Mitch, and Trace gushes, "He's *so* hard done by. He's had such a hard life."

So Tanya asks Trace if she'll stay in touch with him, adding "Is there any point in continuing your relationship, now that you can't supply him with the information he so desperately wants?"

To this Trace replies that she and Mitch will always be friends. "After all, we've both been through *so* much together. I'll always be there for him if he needs me."

Tanya looks intently at Trace and asks, "And the fact that Mitch has tried to hurt Davis. Both physically with his army of protestors, death threats and the fireworks fiasco, as well as mentally with his horrendous Facebook campaign of bullying. That doesn't worry you at all?"

"Nup, why should it worry me? The only thing I've got to worry about is who's gonna interview me next? I'm a star now aren't I? I'm a celebrity just like Davis is!" she replies, licking her luber-lips and pushing her tits out to get her point across.

The look on Tanya's face says it all, it's a mixture of horror and utter disbelief. She finishes the interview off by saying rather sarcastically, "Thanks for your time tonight Tracy, I think we'll let the Australian people decide if you're a celebrity shall we?" And that's it, beautifully wrapped up by Tanya I thought.

Big Mal rings me a couple of hours later to say that they've scored the biggest ratings ever, they've blitzed all the competition. It even causes a social media meltdown, my Facebook page is flooded with so many hits at once from outraged fans that it crashes, causing a wave of ridiculous rumours about me to sweep through Twitter and other social media sites. They range from, 'I couldn't cope with Trace's exposé, so I've taken down my Facebook page', to 'I've left the country for my own safety', to, and this is my favourite so far - 'I reject fame, I'm going back to work in a factory'. I got a good giggle out of that one, as if I'd ever do that!

$$$$$$$$$$

I had bloody nightmares about Trace coming to get me with her taloned hands last night, it was freaky shit. And this morning she's all anyone can talk about, she's all over the radio, newspapers, Facebook and Twitter. Today the Australian public have declared very loudly what their verdict is, and the answer is a definite no, 'Trace isn't a celeb, she's a pleb!' - that's the headline on the front of *News of the Day*, and it seems that everyone agrees. Even at five am this morning, while Jacobs is driving me and Dad into the studio to do my segment, every radio station we tune into is banging on about what a cheek Trace has got, that she's rotten to the core. We avidly listen as talkback callers rip her to shreds, some of them saying that she should be charged for leaking information to Mitch. Dad agrees with them, he's all for pressing charges, but I tell him like I told Danielle last night to forget it - it's not going to happen.

Now I'm in the makeup room and it's chock-a-block full of people. It's bedlam, everyone wants to have a chat with me about Trace's interview. Ricki and Bria are fawning over me, trying to keep me still, while they elbow people out of the way to try and get enough room to work.

Charlie pushes his way in while clapping his hands, yelling that I've got five minutes. The noise level goes up a notch as everyone excitedly talks amongst themselves. For once Dad's hanging out in the makeup room instead of scoffing coffee and muffins in the green room. It would have been better if he'd done his usual thing instead of turning this place into party central, he's responsible for pulling in anyone who looks even vaguely familiar and asking them what they think about Trace. He then commences to act like the master of ceremonies and tell all and sundry about the family's outrage over her behaviour. Everyone seems captivated by his ranting - everyone except me. He doesn't piss me off often, but now would have to be one of those rare times. I wish he'd just shut up about it all because this constant bitching about Trace is driving me mental.

I'm relieved when it's time for me to get out of there. Bria gives me a wink, telling me to have fun, and Ricki gives me a quick neck rub while purring at me, "Go get 'em tiger! You show that Tracy bitch who the *real* celebrity is!"

On set I quickly get myself settled behind my desk as Kirk and Leeza build up my intro, they've been talking about what happened last night, showing clips of 'Tracygate.'

"Tell us again why you're calling it Tracygate Kirk?" Leeza queries.

Looking directly into the camera Kirk urges for a close up. When the camera zooms in he says, "Because this is a *huge* scandal Leeze, Tracy has not only sold out her friend, but her hubby as well. She's a liar and a thief. I can't believe she thinks she's celebrity worthy. What a joke, she's a joke." He shakes his head, a stern look upon his face. "This is just so wrong on so many levels. I'm sticking with calling it Tracygate from now on."

Leeza flips it over to me, and I'm away, giving my opinion on what's happened and how I just want to let it go and move on. Due to taking lots of live callers' questions, it turns into a half hour segment instead of my usual five minutes. But I still get to play some of the video clips the fans have uploaded onto my site, and they're awesome. One's of a teenage kid helping a wheelchair bound guy reach items high on a supermarket shelf. It's fantastic, it really gives you the warm and fuzzies. Another is of me introducing the crowd to Fang outside Taxie the other night, it's a ripper, and leads me perfectly into a plug for my *Respect the Homeless* TV special.

I notice out of the corner of my eye that Big Mal's just walked onto the set, he's chatting with Dad behind the cameramen. Charlie signals for me to wrap it up, so I finish off with my usual, "Don't forget to respect yourself and respect other people," and we cut to an ad break

"Tracygate - I bloody love it Kirk, alright." Big Mal booms. Kirk grins and does his head bobbing thing, he looks as pleased as punch.

While I was doing my segment I've had a cracker of an idea, and I want to run it by Big Mal right away, I reckon I'm onto another winner. He asks me and Dad to have a pow-wow in his office if we've got time, so I promise I'll be there ASAP, I've gotta get this makeup shit off first.

I love Big Mal's office at the studio, it's like stepping back into another time. He's got it decked out like an old English library, with dark oak panelling, a fireplace, and ornate bookcases. There's a couple of green leather chesterfield lounges, as well as his huge ornate wooden desk. His personal assistant Helen shows me in, where I find Dad and Big Mal sprawled on the chesterfields, a glass of tomato juice in their hands. Moving over to where they're sitting, I decide that I may as well do my pitch to Big Mal now, seize the moment so to speak.

I remain standing, and they both throw smart-arse comments at each other. Dad says, "Watch out, looks like he means business!"

To which Big Mal responds "I can smell success. C'mon Davis, spill the beans alright."

"Yeah what have ya cooked up this time?" demands Dad.

Giving them a cheeky grin I ask them to put their glasses down and get comfy. They both look at each other quizzically, but they do as I ask.

"Close your eyes for a moment gentlemen, and come on a journey with me for a minute or two." They wriggle around, get comfy and close their eyes.

"I want you to imagine its Saturday night, it's six thirty and you've just tuned into 'Show Your Respect' - the show where we play all of your respect videos, a show where the best respect video wins big prizes. It's just like Funniest Home Videos - only respectified! It's a feel good show that gets the public to show their respect and get rewarded for it. I don't know about you two, but I reckon this has the potential to create some real change out there. Whaddaya reckon?"

Both sets of eyes snap open. "Christ on a bike, how do you dig up all these ideas? You're a bloody goldmine Davis alright," Big Mal yells.

Dad's got a tear in his eye. He stands up, comes over and gives me a hug, then launches himself into a huge jump where he punches the air while simultaneously shouting, "My son's a goddamn genius!!"

I just laugh at them both and say, "I take it ya both think it's a good idea then?"

"Hell yeah," shouts Dad.

Big Mal comes over and claps me on the back. "Mate, you're amazing. The viewers'll love it! I love it! A show with a heart. It's exactly what we need alright."

Dad squeezes my shoulder and chips in, "I reckon you're onto something big here son, I reckon this is the perfect platform for your respect message. It's gonna have a huge impact. I love it too!" Then he gets a shifty look. "Of course as Davis's manager, I'll have to give this some serious thought - about what sort of deal we should go for here."

Big Mal roars with laughter. "You bloody Spanxes. Don't break my balls over this ok? Look it's gonna be big. It's gonna go global - if you want it to. The yanks and poms'll love it. Here's a tip though, ya need to own the rights to the show so ya can sell it overseas alright." He gives us both a huge grin and licks his bottom lip thoughtfully. "Now it just so happens I know an expert, he does this kind of stuff all the time and I'm sure he'd be happy to work with you boys on this one. If ya need some help that is." He gives me and Dad a big wink, "I'd be happy to help ya out alright."

We all high-five each other then Big Mal says, "I can't see why I wouldn't pay you say, half a mill *per episode*." He eyeballs Dad "Would that be in the ballpark figure you might consider Mr Spanx?"

"Fuck yeah!" I shout.

Dad's grinning from ear to ear, but crinkles his forehead and replies nonchalantly, "Yeah, that might come close, but we'll need to discuss it though."

Big Mal manoeuvres himself between us and claps us both on the back. "Think about it boys and get back to me. Everything's spot on for your homeless special Davis, Charlie's got it all sorted. We'll blitz Monday night's ratings with it. Now, I've got a meeting in Brisbane, I've gotta get to the airport alright." He holds out his hand and we all shake on 'Going global'.

$$$$$$$$$$

Sweet baby Jesus, I love my life!

It's Friday arvo and Fang, Charlie and I are getting a guided tour of The Monahan Hotel's kitchen. We've already been shown around the restaurant, dining room, and old ballroom, which has been converted to another dining room for the occasion. Mark, the owner of the hotel, is excited to be doing the TV special. He took over the hotel a year ago and has turned it from being a two star dump into the four star beauty we see today. It's an old building with heaps of character, he told us it was nearly falling down when he bought it. He's worked his guts out, and has taken a big chance on turning it around, making it work. Apparently it's his first foray into the hotel business, he was a postie before taking this on, but he's determined to do what it takes to make it work. He's my kind of guy.

He's really pulled out all the stops for us. Yes he's happy to have some of the homeless help out preparing breakfast, but unfortunately they won't be allowed into the kitchen to do any cooking due to health and safety regulations. So Mark's organised to have a special fruit and cereal station set up in the old ballroom which is adjacent to the dining room. He suggests that this can be manned by a rotating crew of homeless volunteers, which will work perfectly. The buffet in the restaurant will be operating as normal, but because we need to feed four hundred people quickly, for both dinner and breakfast, the huge, empty space of the old ballroom has been turned into an extra dining area. Kenny's Hire has generously donated the use of tables, chairs and crockery, which is awesome. I insisted that I pay for the stuff, but they wouldn't hear of it, they wanted to chip in and do their bit to help out.

Sexy Juice rang Dad yesterday asking if they could donate all the juice for the event, and to make arrangements for the filming of the first ad on Tuesday. Sweet! I'm blown away with the response my *Respect the Homeless* special has been getting. Some local restaurants have also offered the services of their kitchens and chefs to help out with dinner, much to Mark's relief. Apparently that was the only thing really stressing him out, his kitchen just couldn't cater to that many people at once, so he's more than happy to have some help in that department. Everything's coming together beautifully. I've got the Streetsmart

Swags stashed in a van so they're good to go. I'm going to hand them out personally as the homeless leave the hotel on Sunday morning. I can't wait to see their faces when I give them something that will ensure they have a goodnight's sleep wherever they go.

The way we've arranged who gets to stay at the hotel works like this. Fang's been on the streets long enough to pretty much know who's genuinely homeless, and who has been for the longest time - they're the ones I really want to give a break to. It'd be great to cater for everyone that's homeless, regardless whether it's been one night on the streets or a month, but unfortunately that just isn't possible. I have to draw the line somewhere, so I wanted Fang to target chronically homeless people, the ones society's given up on. The ones that have really given up on themselves. Dad and I made up some tickets on the computer, we printed them off, cut them up, and I gave them to Fang to hand out to whoever he decided fit the bill. I gave them to him last night, and as soon as we caught up this arvo he told me all the tickets have been handed out. He decided to recruit some helpers, and together they made a list of names as they handed the tickets out. So now, not only do I know the hotel will definitely be full, I also have the count of men, women and children. There's a few families on the list, which totally spun me out. You don't picture whole families as being homeless, but apparently they're out there. Mark gave the list to his reception crew and they're now busily working out room allocations.

Ricki called me last night to ask if he and Bria can help too, they want to set up somewhere to give free haircuts and makeup to the homeless. He said they've got heaps of friends, other hairdressers and makeup artists ready to donate their time, willing to help the homeless look and feel better about themselves. I think it's a brilliant idea, although I doubt we could get all of them done, it would take too long. Charlie and I talked about it and he's all for it. The idea is to get everyone checked into their rooms, let them have a shower and get clean, change into their new respect tracksuits, and then those that want a haircut or makeup done can head down to the underground car park, where Ricki and Bria will have everything set up to do as many makeovers as possible before dinner. I'm so bloody excited about it all, I couldn't sleep last night, everything was running through my head at a million miles an hour.

Mark guides us back into the reception area. The tour's over, we've checked everything out, and it all gets the big thumbs up. He suggests that we'll probably need some extra lighting in the car park for the makeover area, he'll get onto Kenny's to see if they can help out.

Rubbing my hands together I say, "Fan-bloody-tastic! Now you'll make sure all the minibars are emptied yeah? And that there's razors and shaving cream in all the rooms? I'll deliver all the respect tracksuits and hats tomorrow morning, I'm having some kiddie one's made up, they should be ready later on this arvo."

Mark says that's cool, and yes the minibars will all be emptied, no probs, and shaving gear will be supplied, along with shampoo, soap, toothbrushes and toothpaste. Grinning at Charlie, Fang and Mark, I say, "I just want to thank you guys for helping me do this, it really means a lot to me. We are gonna smash it tomorrow! It's gonna be awesome!"

$$$$$$$$$

It's only one thirty on Saturday arvo, we don't officially start filming or checking anyone into the hotel until three, but there's already a long snaking queue of smiling, happy homeless people outside the hotel, as well as a huge crowd of gawking bystanders. I joked to one of the homeless guys earlier when I poked my head out that they were all a bit early, but that it was great to see everyone. The guy cackled at me and said, "Well, we don't got nowhere else we're meant to be eh!" Then he looked shyly at me, held his hands in a prayer position and added, "Bless ya for this Mr Spanx, you've got a heart of gold, ya don't know how much this means to us all, ya really don't."

I gave his ragged shoulder a squeeze and told him I was just glad to be in a position where I could help out. As I headed back inside, the queue let out a loud "Three cheers for Davis," which was pretty cool.

Charlie grabs me and gets busy attaching a Mini-Pro camera to my cap. They're the same cameras all the extreme sports dudes use, they're small and give great quality footage. Charlie wants my whole team and all of Fang's volunteers to wear them, to capture all sides of the action. He doesn't want to miss a thing, and says he'll edit it all together later. Bruce and Ajala are already wearing their newly modified head gear.

I did a double take when Fang introduced me to his four helpers. Three of them I recognised from Colley Lane, the night he tried to mug me and Grandma Spanx. Boy their attitude towards him has changed, he's now the main man. It's great to see them all show him the respect he deserves. It's the other guy that makes me do a double take, I'm sure I recognise him as well, but I'm having trouble placing him.

Suddenly it comes to me, "Hey it's Brad right? I met you outside Taxie that time, you stood up for me and I sent you a t-shirt. How ya goin' man? Good ta see ya." He gives me a huge grin, it's obvious he's stoked that I've remembered him.

His eyes glitter with excitement. "I'm bloody awesome, what you're doin' is unreal! Mate I've known Fang for years. When he told me what he nearly did to you and your gran I almost decked him." We all chuckle and he continues, "But when he told me what was goin' on, and that he wanted to enlist *me* to help, I couldn't believe me luck. Thanks for the t-shirt, it was real nice of ya to give me one."

I'm curious as to how he'd have an address which I could send it to if he was homeless, so I ask him. Laughing at my question, he informs me that the address he gave was for a shelter he sometimes stays in, it was the only place he could think of for me to send it, and luckily they'd held onto it for him.

Now that we're all kitted out with our cameras, it's time for us to quickly help the hotel staff put the respect trackies, caps, and long sleeved tops into the rooms. I decided at the last minute to add the long sleeved tops, figuring that they'll need them. We're running from room to room, placing the clothes on the ends of beds, I feel like Father Christmas. We've only got two more floors to do when Bruce asks me, "What about their feet? They probably won't have any decent shoes."

"Shit," I pant, "hadn't thought of that." We look at each other. Fang and his crew are doing the floor below, so I can't ask him what he reckons. The trouble is that shoes are trickier to fit people than clothes are. "How can we get shoes to fit everybody?" I ask aloud. We both look at each other and are stumped. Why didn't I think of this earlier? I'm pissed off with myself, I should have been onto this ages ago. We decide to keep going with what we're doing, time's ticking and we gotta get these rooms finished.

Just as we're finishing the last room I have a great idea. I call Dad and tell him the situation, that we're shoeless, we need shoes, and we need 'em quick. My idea is to get hold of The Coast Clothing Company. They have mobile shops set up in buses that do the rounds of the beaches in summer, making a killing selling all their surf gear on the spot. They do shoes as well. I'm hoping that we can get them on board and get their buses here stocked full of shoes, so that I can file the homeless through and get a perfectly fitting pair of shoes for each of them. It's a great idea, but can it be done? It's a big ask, but Dad assures me that he's onto it, he'll call them right now. I tell him that I want to talk to Billy myself if he can get hold of him. "Done," says Dad, "talk to you soon."

I've never been into surfing, but Billy Coastley, the creator of The Coast Clothing Company, is an ex pro surfer. He's an Aussie legend who's won heaps of stuff over the years, including several world titles. When he retired from professional surfing a few years ago he set up The Coast. I've always thought it was a brilliant business idea, selling surfie chicks and dudes exactly what they want, where they want it, seems ideal.

Bruce overheard what I said to Dad, he reckons it's a magnificent plan - if I can pull it off. We both snigger when he says "pull it off", God we are so juvenile! Lucky that Ajala went and helped Fang's crew, she doesn't have to put up with our crap.

"Allegedly pulling it off is made me a celeb!" I joke, while doing a wanking motion with my hand. This sends us both into hysterics, we so crack ourselves up! My phone interrupts us, it's Dad.

"Jeeze that was quick. What's the story?" I ask.

"Good news. Billy's in. He should be calling you in a sec, I'd better go. Catch ya later."

Billy calls as soon as Dad hangs up. I can't believe I'm talking to the legend himself, and I say so.

"By the sounds of things you're the legend. Now when do you want the buses there? I'm having them stocked as we speak, I'll be ready to rock and roll in half an hour. It'll take us a while to get up to Melbourne though, our warehouse is in Geelong"

Does he mean that he's coming, that he'll be here personally? I ask him. "Shit yeah" Billy laughs, "I'm not missing out on all the fun. What you're doing's brilliant, bro'. I'm picking up the tab on the shoes too, this is my way of contributing ok? I've heard you find it hard to accept gifts, so let me make this quite clear. You are *not* paying me for the shoes, I want to do this. Ok?"

"If you're sure," I start to say, but he cut's me off.

"Yeah I'm bloody sure, now what time do you want us?"

I look at my watch, it's two fifteen, it'd be perfect if he could get here before dinner. "How about five thirty? That way we could have everyone dressed for dinner. What do you think? Will that work for you?"

"Yep, no worries. I reckon it'll take about an hour to get the four hundred fitted and through the buses."

"Fuck, man that's awesome," I shout.

"You tell the cops we'll need six bus parking bays outside the hotel, I'll look after the rest. Can't wait ta meet ya Davis." And he's gone.

Bruce and I do a chest slam. I fill him in on the details and we go and find Charlie, who's in the car park overseeing the makeover stations. When I tell him the latest development he punches the air. "That's incredible," he says, "bloody hell Davis, this is turning out to be the biggest thing I've ever covered, it just keeps growing." He eyes me suspiciously, "Are you sure there's nothing else I need to know about? You've got nothing else up your sleeve have you?" Shaking my head I say that as far as I know this is it.

Kirk and Leeza stroll into the car park and greet us. Apparently the crowd outside has grown bigger, so the cops have closed the street off for safety reasons. "Well that'll make it easier for the buses," Charlie says. "I'd better go and run it by them. Kirk, Leeza, I need to run some details through with you, meet me in the ballroom in ten." And off he bustles.

I introduce Ajala and Bruce to Kirk and Leeza, who are both very sympathetic to Bruce about 'Tracygate'. They tell him how shocked they were by it all, and that he must be happy to have gotten away from her. I wish they hadn't brought it up, Bruce is looking pissed off and uncomfortable, so I jump in and say the subject is off limits. They quickly get the message and wander over to where Ricki and Bria are holding court to a large number of their helper friends.

The set up they've got going looks great. For the hairdressers there's about fifty salon chairs set up with mirrors in front of them, they've hung long gold curtains behind the mirrors, creating a feeling of glamour. There's even some potted palms dotted around, it's very swish. The makeup section is along the opposite wall, they've opted for shimmering silver curtains, with the same amount of mirrors and chairs set up. The lighting is perfect, and there's even a sound system blaring.

Kirk and Leeza head up to the ballroom, so I go over and give Ricki and Bria a hug, telling them they've created some magic. They introduce me to all of the hairdressers and makeup artists, I can't believe there's a hundred of them here, what a turn out! Switching my hat cam on, I stand up on one of the chairs and get some footage of everyone, panning over the car park as I do so. Then I thank everyone for making such a fantastic effort of donating their time and skills. Jumping down from the chair, I ask them all to line up so I can give everyone a high-five. There's lots of squealing, laughing and bum pinching – I don't think I'll be able to sit down for a week! I tell everyone to go into the ballroom and grab a drink before things go berserk.

At the last minute Mark the hotel owner has printed out a timetable to hand to people as they check in. He gives me a copy for my approval and I scan through it. It reads 'Free shoes will be available from the buses at the front of the hotel between 5.30 and 6.30pm. Haircuts and makeup will be available until 6.30 in the underground car park, provided people shower and wash their hair first. Dinner will be served at 7pm sharp in the ballroom, dining room and restaurant, followed by entertainment in the ballroom at 9pm. Breakfast will be served from 7am tomorrow morning in the ballroom, dining room and restaurant. Any volunteers wanting to help serve breakfast are to report to reception to put their name down.'

Doing a double take I immediately ask him, "What entertainment? I don't know about any entertainment." I wish I'd bloody thought of it though, it's a ripper idea. He just winks at me and says that it's a surprise.

So I have no idea what's going on, but Charlie does, the sneaky bugger. When I ask him if he knows anything about it he assures me that everything's under control. Then he aims his finger at me like a gun and adds smugly, "Who's the one with something up their sleeve now?" Making a clicking noise with his tongue while pulling his thumb trigger, he saunters off, laughing to himself.

$$\$\$\$\$\$\$\$\$\$$

It's show time! Three o'clock on the dot. Giving Jonno and Jacobs a nod, they open the doors to the hotel and take up their positions beside me in the foyer. The homeless begin to file through, making their way to reception. I make sure to greet everyone individually as they come in. The excitement in the air is palpable, the hum of eager voices is music to my ears. The reception staff are doing a stellar job of checking everyone in, the queue is moving along nice and quickly. Shrieks and hollers erupt when people are handed their room key and timetable. Heaps of people rush over to me, saying thanks for the shoes and haircut. I'm trying to keep a straight face, wait till they find out the rest of it! Fang and his crew are at the hotel doors, checking tickets and ushering people through. Everyone's giving him and his boys high-fives as they enter, but a lot of them are shy when it comes to saying hello to me, so I just say "G'day, great to see you."

It only takes forty five minutes and all the room keys are handed out, everyone's checked in. I make sure that Fang and his crew get theirs too. For some reason they weren't expecting to stay, they thought they were just here to help, so I'm happy to tell Fang that he's got the snazziest room in the house, he deserves it, and that the other boys are well looked after too. They all look at me in disbelief, then start shouting and dancing around with excitement for a minute, before sprinting off to their rooms.

I'm astounded that everything's run so smoothly. Mark says it's because we didn't need to take any payment or personal details. "Wish it was that quick all the time," he sighs. "Right, now what's next? Fancy a drink?" he asks me.

"You bet, I need one after greeting everybody, I'm dry as."

We head into the restaurant where I run into Charlie, Ajala and Bruce - they're all propped up at the bar in the corner. Charlie informs us that once we've refreshed ourselves it's time for us to split up, switch our hat cams on, and go room knocking to get some footage of how people are settling in. He wants some reactions to the free respect outfits I've provided for everybody. Kirk and Leeza have been interviewing people outside the hotel during check-in. They've got a proper camera crew with them, and Charlie now wants them to set up in the car park makeover area, ready to do some before and after shots of the homeless.

Turns out we don't even have to leave the restaurant to find out if the respect outfits are a winner. As we're sitting there finalising our plan of action, people start to pour into the room. They're either crying or jumping around with joy. Jacobs and Jonno immediately stand up and race towards the doors, stemming the incoming flow. I'm being hugged, patted, and blessed by the throng that have gained entry. I'm overwhelmed, yet delighted. *This* is what I'm talking about! *This* is the reason I wanted to do this - to make a difference to these people's lives - and it looks like I've succeeded. Sweet! Thanking them all and guiding them back to the door, I tell them I'll see them later, and that I'm rapt that they're so happy.

The makeover station is a mega success. Ricki's team blitzes it and manages to do four hundred haircuts! Everyone gets one, which is bloody amazing, and Bria's makeup crew get through two hundred and twenty people. Unbelievable!

True to his word, Billy easily gets all four hundred people fitted with their new shoes on The Coast Clothing Company buses in time for dinner. He tells me afterwards that his hand's ready to fall off, he had to give so many autographs. He's a top bloke alright, we hang out for a bit, but it's not long enough and people are constantly interrupting us wanting autographs. We'll definitely catch up sometime soon for a proper chinwag. I ask him if he wants to stay for dinner, but he says he has to get back to Geelong, there's a big surf carnival coming up on the Goldie that he's got to get ready for. "Lucky for you it's on, otherwise I wouldn't have had all the buses good to go, we're leaving for it tomorrow. Ya timed it perfectly, catch ya soon bud." And off he goes, job done.

$$$$$$$$$

Dinner runs just as smoothly as check-in did, and it's delicious. I'm sitting at a table in the ballroom with Bruce, Ajala, Charlie, Fang and his team. After dessert Fang gives a speech, saying that this is the best thing he's ever experienced in his life. He finishes off by saying, "Thanks Davis, for showing me that I *do* count, that I *am* important. I'd forgotten that I was worth anything, and you've shown me that even though I may be homeless, I still deserve to show myself and others some respect." As soon as he finishes the room erupts with ear splitting cheering and clapping. I just sit there with a huge grin on my face.

For the first part of the entertainment, I'm directed onto the stage by Fang, who then leads all the homeless people in a salutation to me. They all sing raucously 'For he's a jolly good fellow,' followed by the respect chant - which is spine tingling. Having four hundred people passionately shout 'Respect' at the top of their lungs a dozen times, while punching the air, needs to be experienced to be believed. It makes the hairs on the back of my neck stand up, and brings tears to my eyes.

When they've finish I give a speech, thanking them all for being a part of this, of helping me achieve my dream of making a difference. I tell them that I hope from now on people will look at the homeless differently, and treat them with more respect. I tell them that if they want to share their story on how they became homeless, there's some cameras set up in the hotel foyer. If they can tell their story in five minutes or less, and are happy to have it air on the telly, then go for it.

I also say I need to put a crew together to help hand out drinks and stuff at the respect concert next Saturday. If anyone wants to make some cash and be part of the crew, put their name down at reception and make themselves known to Fang, who's the team leader for the event. The crowd cheers and there's a few cat calls of "Count me in."

Fang's eyes nearly popped out of his head when I said that he was team leader. I actually surprised both of us with that, I plucked the idea out of thin air, it came to me in a flash there and then. It's a bloody good idea though. I finish off by saying how grateful I am to Fang for trying to mug me, because he made all this happen - which brings down the house. Looking out at everyone, I take in the sea of respect caps. It's a total spin out seeing four hundred people decked out in my respect gear. It freakin' rocks! Everyone's having fun, cutting loose and enjoying themselves. I can see that my mission to respect the homeless is a total success. To a deafening chant of 'Davis, Davis, Davis,' I leave the stage and the DJ takes over.

We all dance and party for a couple of hours, then Bruce, Ajala, Jonno, Jacobs and I make an exit. I'm sure my hand's gonna be bruised tomorrow from so much high-fiving, but I don't care. Man I'm knackered. This has been so much fun, it's exceeded what I imagined, and I'd had a pretty big vision for all of this. I'm sure the DJ will keep everyone bopping for a few more hours. Kirk and Leeza are still on the job covering all the action as we leave, Charlie doesn't want to miss a thing, he'll keep them filming until the last person heads for bed. I feel great knowing that everyone's fed, warm, dry and are going to get a good, safe night's sleep.

Back at the penthouse Bruce and I stay up till the wee small hours, talking and finalising the line-up for the respect concert. Frankie emailed the performers list through on Friday, and I've been umming and aahing over it for the past couple of days. I'm having trouble deciding who to include. I don't want to cut anyone off the list, but I know I have to. Frankie left me a phone message yesterday saying that he needs to know NOW so that he can put everything in motion.

So I've decided to bring Bruce in on the decision making process because I'm really torn between who to go for. We can choose a maximum of twelve acts. There's twenty five on the list, and they're all big names. So after dicking around for ages without any results, I figure that what we're doing isn't working, we need a new approach. This in itself causes a major head fuck - how can we do it differently? Then inspiration strikes. The old pull the bands out of a hat trick! Beautiful.

We have our core list of must have's already sorted, so that's what we do, pull the remaining number of bands out of a hat, and I gotta say it's an awesome line up. I email the list to Frankie at three in the morning, as well as my pick for the stage design - so now he can now go ahead and get it all sorted. Cool.

$$$$$$$$$$

No sleeping in today even though it's a Sunday and I've hardly had any sleep. I'm being driven to the Monahan Hotel by Jacobs, I want to be there for breakfast to see what went down after I left last night. The cops let us through the barricade and Jacobs pulls up outside the hotel. For seven in the morning there's a lot of people about. A huge mob of my fans are on the road, a lot of them are holding homemade signs with 'I love Davis' and 'Respect' on them. I'm sure I spot Mitch loitering on the other side of the road with Scott and a small band of their anti-Davis supporters. None of them have got placards or signs though, they seem be lying low, like they're trying not to be noticed. Giving Jonno a poke in the ribs, I point to where they're standing and ask him if I'm right.

"Yep it's him alright. Little fucker! What's he doin' here?"

"Right," snaps Jacobs, "if he's here it's a code red, ok Jonno?"

Jonno grudgingly takes his off hat, throws it onto the backseat next to me and says, "Right you are boss, code red it is. C'mon, let's get you inside sir. No point hanging around here." It still cracks me up hearing Jonno call me sir, I've repeatedly told him he doesn't have to call me that, but he insists on doing so.

I'm escorted inside, then Jacobs disappears, he wants to brief the cops about Mitch's presence. Jonno and I make a beeline for the restaurant, it's time to check out the action. And action there is, it's a flurry of activity. Giving everyone a wave I call out good morning, and all conversation halts as all eyes swivel in my direction. Then suddenly everyone says at once, like you used to do at school, "Good morning Mr Spanx." This immediately cracks me up. I ask how everyone's feeling and a resounding "Awesome!" is shouted back at me. Giving them all a wave I move into the dining room, where the same scene is repeated, then onto the ballroom where it happens again. Fang must

334

have worded them all up about what to say. Very impressive, the guy's got great people skills.

As soon as the greetings are finished in the ballroom, I walk over to the cereal station, grab a bowl, and line up. There's a lot of shocked looks in my direction. People are even more spun out when, after being served by a lovely homeless lady who gushes that this is better than any Christmas she's ever had, I grab a bottle of Sexy Juice and head over to a table where four people are already sitting. I ask if Jonno and I can join them for breakfast. Astonished looks are exchanged between them, but they quickly assure me that they'd be honoured for us to sit and eat with them.

What follows is one of the most interesting and heartbreaking conversations of my entire life. I ask each of them in turn what caused them to become homeless, and how long they've been on the streets for. The answers range from a guy who was born on the streets, to a woman who became a prostitute when her husband divorced her and left her with nothing, to a teenager kicked out of home for stealing, to a guy being sacked and not being able to pay his rent anymore - selling everything just to survive and being left with nothing - and having to learn how to survive on the streets.

The stories are as different as the people, and the time frames differ as well. The shortest being two years, going up to eighteen years of living on the streets. All these people have ended up on the streets through a series of shitty incidents, one rolling into the other, causing them to become homeless. To say it's an eye-opener is an understatement. It makes me feel incredibly lucky to have had the upbringing and security my family's given me. Jonno doesn't say much during breakfast, but when we get up to leave the table he shakes all of their hands, and says that if he can ever help any of them to just let him know. Then he hands each of them a business card.

It's time for the homeless to checkout, and Kirk and Leeza have positioned themselves outside the front doors of the hotel again, they've got it all covered. I've got my hat cam rolling and am about to hand out the first Streetsmart Swag.

The first in line is a little girl. She must be only about ten years old. Giving her a hug I hand her the swag. She looks at it and then at me, and asks if it's really for her. Nodding, I tell her to sleep tight from now on. She grins, grabs the swag and slowly moves off. Looks like the Streetsmart Swag is a hit, I knew it was going to be a winner.

I'm about half way through the giveaway, it's taking heaps longer than I thought because everyone wants a quick chat and a hug, which is fine by me. It seems everyone did help the housekeepers make up their rooms this morning, everyone was happy to take the opportunity to help out, to give a little something back. I'm having a quick sip of water to ease my dry throat, when all hell breaks loose over the road.

What looks like a giant pink dick is bobbing along, high above the heads of the crowd on the other side of the road. Suddenly two giant hands on sticks motion up and down the shaft of it, in a definite wanking motion. Then over a loud speaker comes Mitch's voice shouting, "Davis is a wanker, a capitalist wanker!" which he repeats a few times.

The rest of the street is deathly quiet, the spectacle of a giant wanking dick has rendered everyone speechless - but only for a couple of minutes. Then someone shouts out, "Who's that dick? Who's not showing any respect?"

With that a sea of respect clad homeless dudes and Team Davis fans descend upon the giant dick and hands. Jonno and Jacobs are standing next to me, poised in readiness to protect me.

"Fuck. Mitch doesn't stand a chance against this lot," I breathe.

"Serves him bloody right. The dickhead!" Jonno agrees, and we both crack up. The cops haven't got a chance of getting to him before the mob does. I notice that Kirk and Leeza are both frantically narrating what's happening, while the cameraman pans over the unfolding chaos. Oh man, Big Mal is gonna love this! His will be the only news team to get on the spot coverage, he's gonna go ape shit over it!

Suddenly the giant dick and hands disappear, and Mitch appears, held aloft by the crowd. Two other people pop up behind him, all of them are being held up by the crowd's many hands, they're crowd surfing too. I don't bloody believe it, its Trace and Scott. Everyone's booing and hissing at them. They're being carried along slowly but surely to the cops that are waiting further up the street. The giant dick and hands reappear as well, bobbing along after them. God it looks hilarious! Jonno and I are nearly wetting ourselves watching it, even Jacobs is laughing his head off.

Someone's grabbed Mitch's megaphone from him, and a male voice starts the chant "What do we want? Respect. When do we want it? Now." Everyone joins in, it's almost deafening. When Mitch, Scott and Trace all finally reach the cops, who I noticed were pissing themselves laughing like us a minute ago, but have now got their game faces on, Mitch wriggles, trying to get free. Then he kicks out at the coppers, landing a foot in one of their faces. The crowd gives a cheer as the cops put handcuffs on all three of them. Mitch puts up a mighty fight, but in the end he gets shoved into the back of the divvy van with the other two, and the guy with the megaphone starts up the old Aussie classic, "You're goin' home in the back of a divvy van," then does the accompanying clap to it. Sure enough the crowd responds and copies him, so that's what they drive away to - a very fitting farewell song I must say.

Once they're gone, a cop commandeers the megaphone and congratulates the crowd on doing a great job, for showing respect and keeping the peace. For this the cops receive a big cheer from the crowd, followed by a deafening respect chant. Order is easily restored, queuing for the Streetsmart Swags forms up again, and away I go, continuing the giveaway. What a bloody classic, I'm sure this'll go down as one of the weirdest arrests in history!

Chapter 20

It's Monday morning and Bruce and I have been glued to the telly since six thirty. Channel Six has been running clips of yesterday's 'Dickbarcle' almost non-stop. Yep, that's what Kirk's calling it on *Good Morning Today*, he seems to pepper every damn sentence with it. First it was 'Tracygate', now it's 'Dickbarcle', where does he get this shit from? The trouble is that it sticks, people follow what he says, so I have no doubt that from now on this is what it'll be commonly known as. I wasn't sure at first, but it's growing on me. Bruce bloody loves it, he reckons it's a classic.

Dad calls me at nine, starting the conversation with, "I know you're not going to like this but…"

The bumper issue of G'day magazine, with feature articles on me, Bruce, and the two grans, hits the news-stands today - and I'm under orders from the two grans, via Dad, to buy as many copies as I can get my hands on and hightail it over to Sunny Days Retirement Village. Those two troublemakers have already gone ahead and organised for me to come and host a celebrity morning tea, unveiling the magazine, then giving away my signed copies to all the oldies.

This isn't what I wanted to be doing today, but what the heck. I've roped Bruce into coming along as well, after all he *is* interview worthy. I joke that he'll be able to find himself a rich new wife at Sunny Days, and he rewards me with a death stare, but cracks up laughing after a few seconds. The thought of those crinkled old grannies in the sack is just gross and wrong … why do I even think this crap?

In the car on the way over I touch base with Ajala, and she informs me that someone's uploaded a clip of 'Dickbarcle' onto YouTube. So far it's had nearly two million hits, not bad for only twenty four hours! I haven't checked out how many hits my mariachi or launch vids have had for ages, so I ask Ajala if she can have a quick look.

"No need Mr Davis, I know them off by heart. Forty eight million and fifty six million. By the way this new one's going, it will surpass both of those," she rattles off to me.

Wow, that's a shitload of people clicking. We run through some other stuff. Apparently Mitch has still been posting crap about me on

Facebook, but I don't give a shit. Can't wait to find out what he, Scott and Trace get for pulling their stunt yesterday. I update Ajala on what I'm doing this morning. She giggles, says to have fun, and hangs up.

Well this certainly is a first, I'm being mobbed by a bunch of senior citizens who all seem to have forgotten their manners, because they're being very bloody pushy and rude about it. Jacobs and Jonno are trying to form a barrier around me and Bruce, but it's not working very well. None of us expected this to happen, it's all Grandma Spanx's fault.

Jonno and Jacobs are puffing with exertion, I know Jonno's trying to keep his cool because one of the grandpas has pinched his hat and has plonked it on his own head. Not a smart move, he's lucky that Jonno can't get to him at the moment, but he'd better watch out later. Man this crowd's heaps worse than my normal fans, it's starting to piss me off, but I'd feel kind of bad yelling at them. Then a granny, I'm sure it's Grandma Spanx's nemesis Maisie Smith, reaches over someone's head and pinches me roughly on the cheek. Ouch, that bloody hurt! Stuff feeling bad, this has got to stop right now.

"Right!" I yell. "That's it I've had enough, if you lot don't settle down and give me and Bruce some space, we're out of here. *Without* giving you any autographs for your grandkids!"

Bingo! A loud gasp erupts from them all, and the swarm immediately breaks up, moving back to give us some space.

"Thank fuck for that," mutters Bruce.

The two grans have positioned themselves behind a table at the other end of the common room, which is where I was trying to get to before the oldies mobbed us. The two grans have got their posse of close friends huddled around them, and I can tell they're loving all the attention, they're lapping it up. Jonno grabs his hat back off the old codger who pinched it and wags a warning finger at him, telling him not to pinch it again.

When we finally get over to the table I give both of the grans a big hug and a kiss, making a mental note to keep the table as a barrier between me and the gathering for the rest of the do. Once tea and cakes are served I give a brief talk on how being a celebrity has changed my life, and why I want to bring back the respect. I give the two grans a nice plug, saying that I couldn't have done it without their support and love, then I unveil the magazine with a flourish. It reminds me of being a kid and doing show and tell. The two grans then give a bit of a speech each, telling everyone how wonderful I am and how great it is to get their own spread in such a popular magazine. I notice Maisie Smith's got a sour expression on her face during their speeches. Ah, suck it up lemon lips, my grans rock!

But old lemon lips is first in line for an autographed copy of *G'day*. Everyone else lines up behind her, and shuffles past the table to get their copy. At one point there's a bit of pushing and shoving in the queue, but I tell them to cut it out, there's enough for everyone - which luckily there is.

Just as I get back into the car and take a few deep breaths to settle myself, Big Mal rings. He's over the moon at how well everything went for the special, and he's stoked about 'Dickbarcle.' He can't stop raving on about how this is going to be the most memorable TV special ever.

"Well until the concert on Sat'day night eh!" he roars with laughter, spluttering that I've got the Midas touch. He wants us to do lunch, but when I explain where I am and what I've just been through, and that I need a bit of time out, he agrees wholeheartedly. He bellows "We'll do lunch on Wednesday instead, I'll let ya know where alright," and hangs up.

$$$$$$$$$$

I figure I deserve a bit of rest and relaxation after this morning's Sunny Days shenanigans, and the TV special – Dickbarcle - cockup on the weekend. In the car on the way home I ask Jacobs if we can stop at Woolies and do some shopping as a spa, a beer, and a barbie lunch are called for. Jacobs doesn't really want me going into the supermarket after the surprise mobbing by the oldies earlier, so I'm happy to make his life easier and let one of them run in to get supplies. Jonno put's his hand up for the job, and comes back with a trolley piled high with stuff.

He's got the lot covered, from grog to snacks, to salads and meat, he's even got a pavlova for dessert - you beauty! When we unpack everything back at Paradise Towers I pat him on the back, declaring that from now on he can be my personal grocery shopper. He pisses himself laughing, saying that his wife Rita's banned him from doing it at home because he always buys so much crap.

"It's not crap," I tell him earnestly, "it's man food." We all have a good laugh over this but it's so bloody true, chicks and blokes just can't see eye to eye on this one. Who wants to eat bloody sticks of carrot and celery dipped in yoghurty shit? Chicks, that's who! Give us blokes a man sized bag of chips or nuts any day!

Taking a swig of beer, I move my feet into a better position in front of one of the spa jets, aah that's better. "Nice of you to *not* show up at Sunny Days this morning," I scoff at Dad over the phone.

He chuckles and retorts, "C'mon mate, I don't have ta hold your hand all the time now do I?"

"Nah, course ya don't, only when it suits you eh?"

"Whaddaya mean by that?" he demands.

"Nuthin. Now what's this about Chef It Up? Are ya sure they want me on the show? I can't bloody cook!"

"Doesn't matter, they want you as a special guest next season, which is being filmed next month. Could be a laugh, whaddaya reckon? They're offering big bucks."

"Yeah why not, I might learn a thing or two."

Dad lets out a big sigh and I hear him mutter, "Well that's a bloody relief, phew." Pouncing on his comment, I ask him what he means.

"Well I might have taken the liberty of booking it without running it by you first," he sheepishly admits.

"Dad" I whine.

"Don't you Dad me," he cuts me off, "you said yes didn't you? I knew ya would, so there's no probs."

"Just don't do it again. You know you're meant to run everything by me, and you've been doing a top job at it. That's all I'm saying, yeah?"

Dad mutters that, yes he'll run everything by me in the future. I can tell he's rolling his eyes at me as he says it. Bruce comes out onto the terrace holding a pen, notepad and a six-pack. "Gotta go Dad, talk later eh. Yeah thanks for getting me on Chef It Up" and we hang up.

Bruce is having trouble trying to write while sitting in the spa, surprise surprise. I've been laughing at him for the past few minutes as he tries to juggle his beer, pen and pad. It's a big ask, and he finally admits defeat and throws the pen and pad onto the terrace in a huff. He won't tell me what he's up to. When I asked earlier he'd held up his hand to silence me, saying that he was on a stealth mission. Stealth mission my arse, if I keep bugging him I reckon he'll crack within five minutes.

I'm right. As soon as the pen and pad hit the ground he takes a chug of beer and says, "You need an anthem, a respect song you can play at the concert on Saturday. I was gonna try and write you one. But fuck that shit!"

"That's a ripper idea! Maaaate, you rock." Clinking our beer bottles together we toast his brilliant idea.

We spend the next hour or so trying to think of some lyrics, but everything we come up with sounds crap. After a while Bruce asks wistfully while gazing up at the sky, "But if you could have any band in the world do your song for you, who would it be?"

That's a no-brainer, we look at each other and shout simultaneously, "Flight of the Conchords!" Now I'm excited, I'm imagining that I'm up on stage with them, helping them sing the most awesome respect song in the history of respect songs. Maybe I should have another beer. Yeah why not! Cracking one open I pass it to Bruce, who skulls the one he's already holding. I grab myself another and take a long swig. Man I feel good, this is exactly what I needed. We talk about the Conchords and how awesome it'd be to have them at the concert.

"They're not Aussies though, all the other bands are Aussie," I complain.

"Well they're Kiwis, that's almost Aussie," says Bruce. "We've already claimed Crowded House and Tim Finn as our own, as well as Russell Crowe, Dragon and Richard Wilkins - so why not the Conchords?"

"Yeah your right! They're as good as Aussie," I agree.

"But how the hell would you be able to get in contact with them, to set it all up?" Bruce muses. "And we've only got four days to write a song in, that's a big ask alright."

Bruce saying 'alright' has triggered a thought of Big Mal, which triggers a thought of Frankie Mellor. If anyone can make this happen

Frankie can, and I just happen to have his private phone number. I'm so excited that I shove my beer into Bruce's hand, leap out of the spa and dash inside for my phone. By the time I'm strolling back out to the spa I'm talking to Frankie and running our idea by him. He likes it, he wants to help, and it just so happens that he organised the Australia Day bash at the MCG last January - which the Conchords came and played at. Spewing I missed it, funnily enough I didn't have any spare cash for a ticket! Frankie tells me to ring them myself, and proceeds to reel off their private number. Groping for Bruce's pen and pad I ask Frankie to repeat the number for me again, this time jotting it down. He tells me to keep him posted as to how I go. "If they don't want to do it I'm sure we can talk someone else into it. Maybe Kylie'll give it a shot. See ya mate."

"Fuuuccckkk Yeahhhhh!" I scream as soon as Frankie hangs up, I dance around with the notepad held tightly against my chest.

Bruce is now standing up in the spa, a beer in each hand and a confused look on his face. "What?" he keeps demanding, so I bounce over and show him what I've written on the pad.

His eyes pop, he drops one of the beers into the spa and grabs the pad. "You're shittin' me!" he screams, "Is this the Conchords' private number?" I nod at him. "Fuck Davis, how? Who gave you this?"

"Frankie Mellor!" I shout. "I freakin' love being a celeb! One phone call and it's sorted."

Bruce collapses back down into the water, a goofy look is plastered across his face. "Are ya gonna ring them?" he breathes.

"Hell yeah, I'm doin' it right now, before I think about it too much and freak myself out." I'm pressing the numbers into my phone as I speak, gotta do it right now before... "It's ringing!" I yell at Bruce.

"Hello," answers a deep Kiwi voice. Oh my God, it's Jemaine. Quick I tell myself, say something.

"Aaah, hi Jemaine, this is Davis Spanx. You probably don't know me, but Frankie Mellor gave me your number. I'm a big fan and I need your help."

"*The* Davis Spanx of Dickbarcle fame, amongst other things?" purrs Jemaine.

"Ah, yep, that's me, Dickbarcle, Tracygate, getting fired for being an alleged wanker. Yep that's my claim to fame."

Jemaine's voice warms. "Anybody that's an alleged wanker is a friend of mine, especially if Frankie Mellor's given them my number. What would a fine *upstanding* citizen like you need my help for?"

So I tell him all about the rally and concert, and how I really need a respect song, an anthem. "I realise that it's probably asking too much, but if I was to have one then I'd want you guys to do it for me. It'd be the best respect song ever if you guys came on board. Then, in a perfect world you could perform it at the end of the concert."

There's silence when I finish rattling all this off. Bugger. I knew I was asking too much.

"Give me five minutes, I need to discuss this with Brett - call me back and I'll give you an answer." Jemaine hangs up and I bounce around the terrace in excitement.

It seems like the longest five minutes ever, Bruce has got his fingers and toes crossed for me when I make the call. It's spooky, but he can actually cross his toes, he lifted both feet clear of the water to show me - what a bloody legend.

When I call Jemaine back the phone seems to ring and ring. Pick up, I keep praying. Finally he does. Jemaine answers with "Lucky for you, it *is* a perfect world Davis. We're in, although we do have a couple of stipulations. Brett insists that we play your respect song on the back of a truck a la AC/DC, during your rally through the streets. And I insist that you sing it with us. Think you can manage that?"

"Really?" I squeak.

"Really," he purrs. "We won't be able to get over to Melbourne until Friday. Do you have Skype and a webcam? We can work on the song now if you want, have a little jam session."

"Fuck yeah! That'd be bloody awesome!"

We swap details and agree to see each other online in fifteen minutes. Bruce goes mental when I tell him. I give Frankie a quick call back and fill him in. He loves the idea of playing my respect song on the back of a truck through the rally. "Rock the respect!" he says.

"Hey," I shout, "that's a great name for the song! Thanks Frankie, catch ya later."

$$\$\$\$\$\$\$\$\$\$$

345

When you're working with musical geniuses it's easy to write a song. The Skype session with Jemaine and Brett is magic, we've got the main gist of it down within an hour. Everyone's been bouncing ideas around and it's all just flowing, coming together beautifully. It turns out that they've both been following me from the very beginning. "Who hasn't heard of you and your *rise* to celebrity?" Brett stated at one point. It's great, because they know exactly what's gone on and what I want to achieve, I think it really helped make our song writing easier.

Bruce and I have been kicking each other under the table, neither of us can believe we're doing this. Reality really hits home when Jemaine asks me to sing the chorus. When I do, I can see that they're trying not to laugh at me. Man, singing is not something I'm good at. Sure I can belt something out, but it probably won't be in tune. They pick up on this rather quickly, and ask me to say the chorus instead of sing it. Even after saying it they still look unconvinced, and tell me that they'll work on things and we should catch up on Skype for another session on Wednesday, they'll have got it together by then. Brett says they might email me a sound file of it if they finish earlier, to see what I think. Cool.

As soon as we finish on Skype I ring Eric, Paul, Dad and Doug to share the news of my upcoming Rock the Respect song. It's unanimous, everyone agrees that it's exactly what I need. When I tell them about having a Skype jam session with Flight of the Conchords, and that we're going to perform on the back of a truck just like AC/DC, there's gasps of shock from most of them, and outright blatant jealousy from Doug, who loves the band as much as I do. Dad reminds me to get some beauty sleep, I've got the Sexy Juice ad to do tomorrow. Everyone I spoke to wanted me to come over and watch the homeless TV special air tonight, I was even invited to a few big parties, but I can't be shagged, I need a night off.

Bruce and I fire up the barbie and enjoy a good feed, Jeeze song writing makes you bloody hungry. As we're scoffing our dinner watching *Tonight's Current Affairs*, a news flash comes on showing Mitch giving the camera the finger. He's been charged with indecent public behaviour, being a public nuisance, slander, assaulting a police officer and resisting arrest. The footage shows him exiting a divvy van and being escorted by police into the courthouse. They set bail at ten thousand dollars, which he refused to pay, so he's now in remand until his trial. He's also been advised to take down his slanderous Facebook page, which is unreal - if he does it. Apparently Trace and Scott only got done for indecent public behaviour, and were able to walk away with a hefty fine.

"Serves Mitch bloody right," says Bruce around a mouthful of steak. And I've gotta agree with him, it's about time the law caught up with him. The other two were lucky to get off so lightly.

Bruce swallows his mouthful and says, "Bet she wants me to pay her bloody fine, well she can piss off!" And he angrily shoves another forkful of steak into his mouth.

The news break's over, it cuts back to Tanya who's wrapping up the show by giving a plug to the *Respect the Homeless* TV Special which is coming up next. Then the camera zooms right in on her and she says, "Don't miss tomorrow night's show, we have an exclusive interview with Mr Roland Brooks, also known as Beaker, Davis Spanx's exboss. You don't want to miss it."

What the…? Guess I'll have to tune in tomorrow night to find out what he's got to say.

$$$$$$$$$$

It's Tuesday mid-morning, and I'm shooting the Sexy Juice ad at Luna Park. They asked me if I wanted to invite anyone down to be an extra in it, so I gave the usual suspects a call. Within the hour Mum, Dad, Holly and her daughter Kaci, the two grans, Ajala, Bruce, Eric, Paul, Doug, Janelle and the twins all rocked up. I'm surprised that Kaci and the twins are here, it being a school day and all, but Janelle and Holly explained that it's for their own sanity - they'd never hear the end of it otherwise. Danielle's spewing she couldn't make it, but she's got a big court case on today. Fang wasn't answering his phone so I left a message, I'm not sure if he'll get it in time though.

Luckily I don't have many lines to learn for the ad which is sweet, I just have to say, "I respect my body, and I respect my country. That's why I drink Sexy Juice. Get it into ya!" Ok it's totally corny, yet true. It *is* why I drink Sexy Juice. It's got no shit in it, it's all organic and it's made here in Australia. What more could you ask for? They want me to do a voiceover about the made in Australia and organics thing, which is easy - I just have to read the lines from a script, I don't have to memorise them, it's great.

I get to go on the Big Dipper and all the other rides, while they take heaps of footage of me and everyone else having a good time and drinking the juice. It's a blast, doesn't feel like work at all, and I nail my lines on the fourth take. I must be getting used to this celeb stuff because I blitzed it. Within three hours they've got everything they need and we can all go home. Sexy Juice reckon they'll have the ad on telly by Thursday. I can't wait to see it.

We've all worked up a thirst for something stronger, so the entire Spanx posse decide to wander up to The Espy for a few cold ones. A crowd follows us, but it's fine, there's no dramas. I'm getting used to having my photo taken with the fans and writing autographs, I've got it all down pat now.

Fang never showed up today, he missed out on all the fun. I'm hoping that he's just forgotten to check his phone, I really need to talk to him about the list of helpers for the upcoming concert.

When we get home I check my emails. You beauty, there's one from Jemaine. It's got two music files ready to download. Calling Bruce over to the computer we listen to them together. The first one is just an instrumental, no lyrics. The second one's the complete song. It's perfect, it freakin' rocks! I knew those guys would make the best re-spect song ever, its catchy, quirky, and gets my message across effectively. I love it. We both bop along to it, playing it over and over, trying to memorise the words. I sing the chorus out really loud and Bruce nods his head in approval. Somehow the guys have made my inability to hold a tune work brilliantly.

"It's like you're *meant* to sing like that," gushes Bruce. "Anyone can sing that song – but you *rock* the respect Davis!" We give each other a chest slam for good measure.

I give Jemaine a call, saying the song's perfect, no need to change a thing. When I boast that Bruce said I sounded good, he hoots with laughter and orders me to sing it right there, so I crank up the volume on my laptop and let it rip. When I pick up the phone again, all I can hear is clapping and cheering coming from the other end. He says I should record my voice singing along and email the file to him. I explain that I don't have a clue how to do that, but quickly ask Bruce if he knows, and he gives me the thumbs up, sweet. Jemaine insists that we get the song out as quickly as possible so that my fans have got a chance to get to know it before the concert. I like his thinking. He reckons we can all get in the studio together on Friday to put it down properly, but for now let's just get it out there. Far out, I'm gonna record a proper single with the Conchords on Friday, this is unbelievable! Jemaine asks if I've thought of what to charge people to download it.

"How about a dollar?" I suggest. "And would it be ok if the money raised goes to my charity? Would that be cool with you guys?"

"Sure, no probs. Yeah a dollar sounds good, everyone can afford a dollar eh," Jemaine replies. I announce that I've already booked him and Brett into the presidential suite of the swankiest hotel in the city for a couple of nights, and ask what their fee for doing the song and gig is going to be.

There's silence on the other end for a sec, then he says, "We watched your TV special last night, and you know what? Brett and I have decided that we'll waive any fees. Man, this concerts gonna be awesome. I took the liberty of ringing Frankie for the lowdown, and he said the truck's a goer, which is the icing on the cake. We've always wanted to do that. I've gotta say I'm blown away with the line-up you've got going on there. So no fee for you bro'. Sound good?"

Jeeze, I would have paid them whatever they asked for, but I'm getting better at accepting all the good things that come my way. So I shout ecstatically, "Fuck yeah, you guys are the best. I'll learn the words, get Bruce to help me record it, and email it to ya ASAP. See ya Friday for our recording session." I give him Dad's number as a backup. Then Bruce and I get busy making my recording. Just as well he's a computer nut. It must be the day for getting things right because I nail the lyrics in a flash. By dinner time it's done and dusted, email sent, game over.

I look at Bruce, "I think we deserve to par-tay! Shall I give Bambi a ring and see what's happening on the scene tonight?"

His face lights up. "Hell yeah!"

$$$$$$$$$$

Having my wing-man *and* my wing-girl out with me is a blast. We've already been to an art opening, which was different, very hoity-toity, but jam packed with A-listers. Now we're at some model's birthday bash in Brighton. My eyes have been popping out of my head at the bevy of gorgeous, scantily clad goddesses that are frolicking and shimmying on the dance floor. It's a feast for the eyes. Bambi tells us both to get a grip when we spot the pool area, which is decked out with columns and stuff and resembles a roman bath. Bruce whispers that he knows what he'd like to get a grip of. Bambi must have heard him because she smacks him on the shoulder and tells him to behave.

"But why should I? I'm a free man now," he turns to me and says excitedly "And so are you! Jeezus Davis we're free agents, we can do whatever we bloody want." He's right, wow.

"So Mr Free Agent, who would you do what to, given half a chance?"

He points to a drop dead gorgeous chick that's just getting out of the pool. It's like we're watching a slow motion scene from a movie. Water's dripping off her perfectly toned, white bikini clad body. She pauses for a second, shaking her long auburn mane of hair, causing droplets to fly everywhere. Then her tight arse starts undulating as she climbs up the rest of the ladder. When she reaches the top she stretches luxuriously, turns around to accept the drink someone hands her, and takes a seductive sip.

"Her," Bruce breathes, "I want to kiss her."

"Go on then. Do it. You're hot property mate, you can do what ya want," I tell him.

To my utter astonishment Bruce shoves his drink at me and makes a beeline for her. Bambi and I look at each other, then watch Bruce strut over to her.

"Fuck me, he's gonna do it!"

"Yep, that's a man on a mission alright," Bambi agrees. "That's hot. I didn't know Bruce had it in him."

We both stand transfixed as Bruce boldly walks up to the goddess, confidently takes the drink out of her hand, gives it to a passing waiter, then holds her face between both of his hands and gives her a deep lusty pash. It's a true movie star kiss. Confident, passionate, hot. When he's finished he says something to her, then swaggers back to us. His hard on is blatantly obvious, but he doesn't seem to care, he's grinning from ear to ear. The chick just stares after him as he returns to my side, a look of lust and bewilderment on her face. I can't believe what I've just seen. Bruce has transformed himself from Mr Pussy-Whipped to Captain Courageous. That took a lot of guts. I'm so impressed I'm speechless. The only thing I can do right now is give him a man hug. Bambi wants to know what he said to her.

Smiling at her he says, "Thanks. That's all I needed to say. For the first time in years I feel like a proper bloody man. That was awesome!"

"You freakin' rock!" I shout, giving him a high-five and telling him how he's gone from Mr Pussy-Whipped to Captain Courageous.

He pisses himself laughing but jokes, "That's my call sign from now on ok?"

"Roger that Captain Courageous. Over and out." I chuckle.

Taking his drink back, he has a sip, eyeballs me and says, "Now it's your turn."

"How old are you two? You're unbelievable," Bambi scoffs.

She's about to say something else, but I shove my drink at Bruce. Putting one hand behind Bambi's head and the other around her so it's in the small of her back, I dip her backwards while giving her a very long, deep, thorough kissing. I eventually bring us both back up to a standing position, and we stand there panting, looking deep into each other's eyes. I've got the biggest hard on ever, it's throbbing angrily in my pants. Fuck that was awesome! All I say to her is "I've wanted to do that since we first met. Drink anyone?" and snap my fingers to get a waiter's attention.

Bruce hollers "Way to go!" Holding our drinks out at arm's length, he chest slams me before handing my glass back to me.

Turning back to Bambi I take her hand, give it a kiss, and look deeply into her eyes again, saying "That was magnificent. Thank you."

It's the first time I've ever seen her beautiful feathers ruffled, she's clearly not sure how to take all this. I can think of exactly where *I'd* like to take it, preferably somewhere private, but I'm sure I've freaked her out enough for the moment. I ask her if she's ok. Nodding her head she assures me that she is, but I can see the question in her eyes. Did I really mean it? Giving her tiny hand a squeeze I whisper in her ear "Honey, you'll always be my wing-girl, but I'd like to make it more than that. It's up to you."

Squeezing my hand back she gives me a saucy wink and says, "Thought you'd never ask. Now I must go and mingle for a bit."

I watch her sashay off to a group of nearby chicks who engulf her. I'm sure they all saw what just went down, now they probably want to pick her brains about it. Bruce flicks me on the arm.

"Maaaaate. Apart from the pash, which you rocked, have you two just become an item?"

"Something like that, yeah. Fuck, I can't believe I just did that! And she wants me as much as I want her. She said yes to taking it further."

Nudging me in the ribs Bruce affirms, "You two'd be great together man. She's awesome. Remember the first time we met her?"

"Hard-on city," we say together, and crack up laughing at the memory.

Bruce is looking at me like a proud father, he's got a big smirk on his face. "Cheers to that then. You deserve a good woman. And a good shag."

Clinking my glass against his I reply, "Amen to that brother."

We mingle. Everyone wants to have a chat, and soon Bruce goes his own way, the chicks are crazy for him and he's enjoying all the attention. Excusing myself from the group I've been chatting to, I head over to the roman style pool cabana, which is amazing and huge. There's lounges everywhere, groovy music is playing, and the buzz of conversation fills the air. I spot an empty seat and grab it. I need to rest for a minute.

No sooner have I plonked myself down than a set of long legged, dark haired identical twins pounce on me. One perches herself on the arm of the lounge and the other squeezes in next to me. Their miniskirts ride up, showing acres of luscious bronzed skin. Both of them start playing with my hair, and introduce themselves as Tatyana and Serafina. They talk in unison, saying the same thing at the same time, which is really bizarre.

"We are Russian models. We win top model. Yes?" they drawl together. I just nod at them with a smile firmly plastered onto my face.

Serafina leans down from the arm rest and says, "You are very sexy man. We like sexy men."

Then they both say together, "I bet you have big pant sausage."

I'd just taken a sip of my drink as they said this, and their comment about my big pant sausage causes me to spray my drink all over a guy standing in front of me. He looks at me in disgust and quickly moves away. I can't help myself, I start laughing hysterically. And that's how Bambi finds me, with drink dribbling down my chin, flanked by identical Russian twins, laughing uncontrollably. She coolly takes in the scene.

"Need some help sweetie?" she coos. I nod and she literally shoos the twins away, throwing a "Sorry he's taken girls," in for good measure.

When I can finally speak I tell her what happened and she cracks up. Arching a manicured eyebrow, she asks if I'm ready to go home and show *her* my pant sausage, which cracks us up again, but I quickly jump up. I don't have to be asked twice! Bruce is happy to keep partying so Bambi and I make a speedy exit, the vibe between us is electrifying.

On the drive home Jacobs keeps glancing at us in the rear view mirror, I'm sure I saw him give me a quick wink at one point. Bambi and I aren't acting all lovey-dovey, we're trying to keep our hands to ourselves and I thought we were holding it together pretty well. But our horniness for each other must have registered on Jacobs' radar, I'm sure he's onto us.

The situation becomes blatantly clear when he pulls up outside Bambi's house, ready to drop her home. We're trying not to giggle as I ask her exaggeratedly "Would you care for a nightcap at my place?" She can't help herself, the giggles take over, and through them she agrees that that would be lovely. During all this Jacobs has been staring at me in the mirror.

When I say, "On to Paradise Towers thanks Jacobs," he smirks and I see his eyes crinkle with humour in the mirror.

But all he says is, "Very good sir," and moves the car off into the traffic.

Jonno's a different matter entirely. His head whips around and looks from one of us to the other, assessing the situation. Then a grin spreads across his face and he says, "Nudge nudge, wink wink, say no more!" I can see his shoulders heaving with silent laughter as he sits facing the front again.

$$$$$$$$$

As soon as we get into the lift at Paradise Towers it's game on, we're all over each other, kissing, licking, and groping. Stumbling from the lift we bounce off the walls of the foyer, conjoined at the lips before becoming conjoined at the hips. I know damn well that Porter and his crew can see me and Bambi on the security monitors going for it in the lift and foyer, but I'm beyond caring.

When we get into the penthouse lounge I push her up against the wall. She stops me for a sec, rummages around in her handbag and thrusts a condom into my hand, before tossing her bag onto the floor. Then the mad kissing starts again. Suddenly her legs are encircling my waist, and a quick fumbling to get my dick free and move her G-string aside ensues. Lucky she's wearing a mini skirt and lucky she's got thighs of steel, because she has to pretty much support herself while I do the freeing of our bits and get the condom on. All this time our lips and tongues are devouring each other. The moment she lowers herself onto my shaft is mind blowing. I want to come there and then, but luckily I hang on for at least twenty strokes. I know this because I'm madly counting them, trying to distract myself from blowing. But I lose count at twenty one and have the most intense, electrifying, out of his world orgasm that makes me roar with pleasure. After I blow, I have to put her down, man that's a hard position to hold. They make it look easy in the movies but it's not, especially when you've been drained of all your strength. I can hardly stand up, let alone walk!

But I make it into the bathroom where we undress each other. Fuck she's beautiful, her body is amazing. The sight of her naked is giving my dick twinges, and once we start washing each other in the shower I can't help but get hard again. We kiss each other all over as we're supposedly drying each other off. I'm lingering on her amazing boobs, licking the water off each nipple with relish, then moving down her glorious body to her landing strip. Pushing her legs apart I administer some much needed tonguing to her clitty. Fuck I can't get enough, and neither can she, her groans of pleasure say it all. Then it's payback time, but the naughty minx bypasses any semblance of seductiveness and goes straight for my now ramrod hard cock, and who am I to complain? Sweet Jeezus she knows how to work a cock with her tongue. At one point she even draws my balls into her mouth, much to my shock and delight. Then she works her way back up my body, licking and kissing it all the way. I pull her into the bedroom, almost dragging her in my eagerness to continue our explorations.

The second time we take it much slower, savouring the opportunity to discover what turns each other on, learning which buttons to press for maximum pleasure, and the third time is a combination of frantic lust coupled with lazy intimate interludes. To say I'm shagged after all this is an understatement, but oh what a way to exhaust one's self. It's pure bliss.

$$$$$$$$$

The next morning I feel kind of weird, Bambi stayed the night and we have a good chat while we are still in bed. It's bizarre how you can be so intimate with someone the night before and then feel so awkward the next day. Bambi's awesome, but I'm not ready for a relationship just yet. I still think about Claire all the time and, even though it's over between us, this morning I feel guilty for what I did last night. Bambi must have known what I was thinking because she snuggles up and says that she's glad about what happened last night but she doesn't want to have a relationship.

"Really?" I ask in surprise.

Stroking my chest she says, "Sweetie, you're on the rebound, you're not ready for anything serious. And I'm not looking for that at the moment either. How about we just be fuck buddies?"

A grin spreads across my face, is she for real? "So you'd be my wing-girl-fuck-buddy huh? You'd be happy with that?"

"Yep. Suits me fine. I want some more of that good lovin' you're so masterful at. But with no strings attached ok?"

Laughing, I pull her on top of me and tell her that that's just perfect. It's everyman's fantasy to have a hot chick for fun times with no strings attached, and this is just what I need right now. We celebrate our new agreement with a quick hot shag.

Bruce is lounging on the terrace when we finally appear. I lent Bambi some respect trackie daks and t-shirt to wear, they're swimming on her but she looks so cute. Giving a hoy I wander out on to the terrace, and am blown away when two heads pop up from the adjoining loungers on either side of Bruce. Fuck me, it's the Russian twins! Bruce looks like the cat that got the cream, and I'm betting that he certainly got plenty of *that* last night. I give everyone a good morning, even though it's nearly lunch time. The twins chorus their greeting, and Bruce just gives me a nod and a wink, then introduces me to them. Bambi pipes up that I had the pleasure of meeting them last night.

The twins smile greedily and say together, "We think Bruce has bigger pant sausage than you."

Bruce, Bambi and I piss ourselves laughing. Bambi wags a finger at them and says, "That's something you two will never find out."

Then she marches inside, announcing that she's making coffee and does anyone want any. I go in to help, grab her around the waist and ask her what she meant by that comment.

"I thought there were no strings attached? That I was still a free agent."

Kissing the tip of my nose she replies, "You are Sweetie. But I *know* you'd have better taste than those two skanks. You've got more class in your little finger than those two have got between them. Bruce better watch out, or they'll gobble him up and spit him out, they've got quite a reputation you know."

Chapter 21

Thank God Big Mal's organised to have lunch in the city. I've decided to jog there from Paradise Towers, much to Jacob's disgust. He insists on running behind me to keep an eye on things, make sure I'm ok. We're both kitted out in respect trackie daks, caps and t-shirts, and we blend in with the public pretty well. It's so much easier going incognito these days because masses of people are wearing my respect merchandise, which is so cool.

I figure it's time to get a bit fitter, I'm gonna need all the staying power I can muster for my new improved sex life. It's just as well I've given up the smokes, I'm having enough trouble breathing while jogging as it is. Technically it should only take me ten minutes to get to the restaurant, but I have to stop a couple of times to catch my breath. I'm an absolute disgrace compared to Jacobs, who's whistling the Rocky theme while he runs. I'm sure he's doing it to show off, he hasn't even worked up a sweat, the fit bastard.

Taking off for the last stretch I have a flash back to last night's love fest, man she's incredible. Parting from Bambi this morning was such sweet sorrow. Fuck, I'm turning into a poetry spouting, namby-pamby dickhead. But if that's what having four shags in eight hours reduces a man to then I'll happily reel off Shakespeare or any other poet all day long!

I make it to the restaurant just in time, I know Big Mal's got something big to show me. He left a message on my phone early this morning reminding me about lunch, saying he's got a surprise that I'm gonna love. Dad and Ajala left messages too, but I'll have to get back to them later, after lunch.

The restaurant is on the banks of the Yarra River, and of course Big Mal's got the best seat in the house. Frankie's sitting at the table with him, they're both in deep conversation but stand up to shake my hand as soon as I arrive. There's a bottle of champagne in an ice bucket next to the table, and when I sit down a waiter rushes over and pours us all a glass.

"What are we celebrating?" I ask raising my glass.

Frankie and Big Mal look at each other, then Frankie says "Here's cheers to your new number one hit Davis. Rock The Respect is a chart buster; it's already hit number one."

"It's a bloody sensation alright," adds Big Mal.

I don't understand, and stammer, "But how can it be released already? How can it be number one, when I haven't even heard it yet?"

Big Mal rolls his eyes at me and says, "Have you had your head in the sand or something? This is huge. How come ya haven't heard about it, what's your media chick Ajala doing?"

I tell them that I haven't spoken to her today, I've been busy. Another flashback of last night hits me. Yeah I've had my head in a much nicer place than in the sand!

I must have blushed because Big Mal pounces. "I saw that photo of you and that photographer girlie having a pash at that party last night. Keep you up all hours did she?" He and Frankie both give a knowing chuckle.

"Shit did someone take a photo and post it?" I ask in shock. "Man can't ya keep anything private these days?" I'm horrified that this has leaked. Claire's sure to see or hear about this. Shit.

Big Mal takes a delicate sip of his champagne and says, "Get used to it Davis. It's plastered all over *News of the Day*. Front page. Anyway she looks like a good sort. Now let's talk business alright."

I ask again how the song has managed to get out there so quickly. Frankie licks his lips and replies, "We fast tracked it. Jemaine sent me your vocals plus what he and Brett had put together. I simply gave it to the best record producers I know to mix, then I uploaded it to your site and pulled some strings to get it onto iTunes. Easy. Once you boys go in the studio on Friday to lay it down properly, we'll just send out a free copy to anyone who's already bought this first version. They'll love it - it's all sorted, no worries."

Shaking my head in amazement I ask, "And it's already gone to number one? Are you shittin' me?"

"Yep, and nup," they say together, then shut up, letting it sink in for me.

Big Mal waves his hand in the air, then points to a certain waiter. Seconds later music fills the restaurant. The unmistakeable music of…holy shit, that's my song! I sit wide eyed throughout it, I can't help singing along to it, and I notice Frankie and Big Mal are bopping along and singing a few of the lyrics too. It sounds different, yet similar to what I've heard. It's a total spin out hearing my voice with the Conchords, it freakin' rocks.

When it finishes all I can say is, "Fuck me, that's awesome!"

"Ha!" shouts Frankie, thumping the table with his hand. "I win, I win. Hand it over mate." He's now got his hand out motioning Big Mal to give him something. Resignedly Big Mal takes out his wallet and hands over a hundred dollar note.

"What did you two jokers bet on this time?" I ask, shaking my head at them. Man those two are unbelievable, they'd bet on anything.

Frankie laughs and says, "*I* bet that your first two words were gonna be fuck me. Buggerlugs over there bet that your first two words would be fuck *yeah*. So I win! You little beauty!"

We talk about the homeless special for a while. It blitzed the ratings, and has set a new benchmark in feel good TV. Big Mal is stoked and so am I. He asks if Dad and I have thought any more about Show Your Respect, the show I want based on respect clips that would be similar to Funniest Home Videos. He wants to lock it in, and the sooner the better, but I palm him off onto Dad, saying that I've left negotiations up to him - I just want to get it out there. I mention to them that I'm going on Chef It Up and both of them hoot with laughter, telling me good luck with that one, neither of them can boil an egg. When I tell them that my specialties are tacos, curried sausages or anything BBQ'd, they piss themselves laughing, saying that at least I'll be entertaining viewing.

Big Mal wants to know if I saw Tanya's interview with Beaker last night. I'd totally forgotten about it. So he whips out his smartphone and brings it up for me to have a look at. Turns out that Beaker's fired Mitch! And he's thinking of firing Scott too, but hasn't done so yet.

He pompously tells Tanya that he had no choice given Mitch's behaviour. "That phallic display in the streets was the end," he says. "I can't very well let him get away with that sort of behaviour when I sacked Davis for a similar kind of situation. Those boys need to learn to keep certain things a man does private, not go gallivanting around town making a nuisance of themselves." He rambles on about how all this has had a huge impact on his business, how he's finding it hard to get staff, that's why Scott hasn't been sacked yet … blah blah blah.

I switch it off and hand it back to Big Mal, then we talk about the upcoming rally and concert. Frankie confirms that all the acts I picked are booked in and are rearing to go. He's already got his crew working on the stage set. Because it's a free concert he's happy that only minimal security fences are needed to protect the stage while everything's being set up, they'll be dismantled for the actual gig. Big Mal wants the concert to remain free, but still give the punters the chance to donate to my charity if they want to, so he's getting Frankie to set up lots of donation booths. He wants them dotted all around the park. Frankie's also got my merchandising stalls good to go as well, and all the proceeds from any sales at the concert will also go to my charity.

The first three rows of seats at the music bowl will be taken up with my family, friends, and VIPs. I suggest that we auction off the rest of the seating area to raise more money for the charity. Big Mal and Frankie look at each other, then nod together.

"I'll get it plastered all over Channel Six for the next few days. That should do it. They'll be sold out, no probs alright," says Big Mal.

Sweet. I love how these two work, when they want something done, bam it's done, no mucking around, no dithering. They always make quick decisions which they take immediate action on. It's so cool.

Rubbing his hands together Frankie happily divulges that he's got the truck for the Conchords and me to play on all good to go. He's having it draped in respect banners, it'll be pimped to the max. Big Mal has been onto the council and has sorted out the route we'll take, starting at the mall in Swanston St, heading out along St Kilda Rd to the Sidney Myer Music Bowl. I wanted to start at the Treasury Building at the top of Collins St, but unfortunately we couldn't get clearance for it. Everything's set to kick off at four o'clock on Saturday and I can't bloody wait.

$$\$\$\$\$\$\$\$\$\$$

For the past two days I've been fluctuating between terror and a heightened state of excitement. I'm so nervous and excited about tomorrow's rally and concert it's totally doing my head in. Bria even comments on my skin this morning, saying that I look very pale as she's making me up for my morning segment. Ricki wants to know all the goss about me and Bambi, but I tell him a gentleman never reveals their lady's secrets. To which he cattily replies that he'll just have to read about us in the trash tabloids then.

Thank God it's Friday and I've only got one more sleep to go, don't think I could handle living in suspense like this for any longer. We taped most of today's respect segment yesterday. I took to the streets to get the lowdown on what people thought of the *Respect the Homeless* special, and ask if they were coming to the rally and concert on Saturday. It was heaps of fun, I'm really relaxed doing that sort of thing now. I know Jonno and Jacobs hate it though, because as soon as word gets out about where I am and that I'm interviewing people, the crowds build up quickly. From the response I got on the streets yesterday everyone loved the homeless special, and my 'Respect The Streets' rally is gonna be huge.

Fang finally got in touch with me yesterday, which is cutting it a bit fine, but I'm just happy to hear from him. I thought he might have gotten cold feet but he said that he's been in contact with some of his family who he hasn't seen in fifteen years. When they saw him on the homeless TV special they somehow got in contact with him. So he's spent the past few days with them, catching up on lost time, which is so cool. I'm really happy for him, it's a great outcome.

Yesterday Jacobs assured me that together with Frankie's security crew we can employ some homeless to not only hand out drinks at the rally, but to assist with the security side of things as well. I suggested that they also help us man the donation booths and merchandising stalls. I asked Frankie and he gave it the green light, but he wants some professionals on hand to make sure everything runs smoothly. He's worried about too many five fingered discounts happening, so he wants his usual crew there to make sure everything stays legit. Makes me happy, the more we can employ the better as far as I'm concerned.

Charlie sticks his head in the makeup room door to tell me I've got five minutes. Ricki gives a squeal and quickly presses the remote for the TV monitor, then leans over to switch on some music. Rock The Respect blares out of his iPod dock while the Sexy Juice ad plays on the TV.

"It's a Spanxfest!" he screeches and starts dancing around the makeup room.

Bria joins in and hauls me up off the chair, so we're all bopping around like dickheads, having a good old time. I love it. Now's the perfect time, so I present them with front row tickets for the concert, which causes them to both shower me in kisses and hugs. Jonno and Jacobs put their heads around the door to see what all the fuss is about, and as soon as Ricki finishes smothering me, he spots Jacobs and holds out his arms for a hug, puckering up his lips for a kiss. The look of distaste on Jacob's face is priceless, he looks like he's eaten a sour lemon. Ricki gets the message. I know he's still got a big crush on Jacobs because he's always asking me stuff about him. Poor Ricki, he doesn't stand a chance. When my song finishes I give him and Bria a high-five and head out onto the set. It's time to spread some respect!

I'm surprised to see there's a live studio audience here today, that's really strange. And sitting behind my desk is Tanya Gilmore. That's even weirder. Alarm bells are ringing in my head, what the hell's going on here today? Tanya waves me over, patting the chair that's next to hers, and I take a seat. Kirk and Leeza are crapping on about something so I whisper to Tanya, "What's going on?" She gives me the old twist of the fingers against her lips mime, signalling that her lips are sealed. I notice there's a seat placed in front of my desk, in an interview position. What the hell's she up to? My mind is racing, maybe Beaker is coming on.

Kirk and Leeza do my intro and then we're on. Tanya immediately takes control of things and tells the viewers that they're in for a real surprise this morning. Then she asks me if I'd like to show what I got up to out on the streets this week, so I do a quick intro and they roll my taped segment. As soon as they cut to it I nudge Tanya with my elbow and ask her what's going on again. She gives me a cheeky grin and tells me to wait and see. Once the taped bit is done she gives a brief rundown of my successes. She shows the Sexy Juice ad and has my song playing in the background throughout it all. She tells everyone how I now have a number one hit, and that my success is all thanks to an allegation made at my old workplace.

Looking at me she says, "Some very nasty things have been said about you over the last month haven't they Davis, a lot of untruths have been thrown in your direction, wouldn't you agree?"

"Ah that's right Tanya, they have." Where the hell is this going? I'm trying to catch Charlie's eye, but he's deliberately ignoring me for some reason.

"There was one particular untruth that set this whole respect revolution in motion wasn't there? And you got fired for it didn't you?" she continues.

I affirm that yes, we all know the reason I got fired, and from that misunderstanding I started my mission to become a celebrity and to bring back the respect. I narrow my eyes at her, I know she's up to something, I just can't figure out what it is yet. I don't have to wait long to find out though.

"Well today we've got someone here that can once and for all clear your name from any wrongdoing. Would you like to see who that is?"

"Hell yeah," I say.

The studio audience gives a shout of agreement. All eyes are on me.

Someone starts to walk out onto the set. I can't see them clearly at first, they're hidden in the shadows. But I can tell it's a bloke. As he moves forward his face comes into the light. Oh my God, it's Scott!

My head swivels from him to Tanya and back again. Scott walks up to the desk and holds out his hand for me to shake. Standing up I take it and say, "Well this *is* a surprise! What are *you* doing here?"

Tanya asks Scott to take a seat, then tells me that it was very nice of me to shake his hand, seeing as Scott was one of the ringleaders of Mitch's army. She asks if I feel any animosity or anger towards Scott for what he's done to me. I don't, I just feel sorry for him. It looks like he's always been a follower, and I bet Mitch isn't the first person to take advantage of him.

Looking at Scott I say, "Nah, there's no hard feelings on my side. Mitch probably threatened you into it or something eh? There were heaps of opportunities for you to really hurt me if you wanted to. I spotted you heaps of times with Mitch's mob, but you never really did anything. You always kept in the background like ya didn't want to be there. Except for that first time outside Paradise Towers, and then at Dickbarcle." I give a little chuckle as I picture him carrying one of the big hands that was stroking the giant dick. I shake my head at the memory. God that was funny.

Tanya asks Scott to tell me what he told her earlier. Scott runs a hand through his hair, I can see his face start to break out in a sweat, he looks really nervous. Taking a deep breath he sits up straight and starts to talk.

"Davis, I know for a fact that you're not a wanker, that ya never did anything like that at work that day." He pauses and looks out at the audience. "I know this because *I* was in the other cubicle having a dump while you were in there."

The audience gasps and so do I, but he continues on. "I was there. I heard you open the mag, turn a couple of pages, which only took a couple of minutes, and then ya left. You never even pulled ya pants down, I would've heard. And there's no way ya could have brought yaself off that quick. No bloody way. And ya didn't flush or nuthin."

The audience laughs at his colourful language. I can see Charlie going nuts, this is all going out live and he won't have had a chance to censor anything.

I'm stunned and shocked by Scott's confession. I can't believe he's known all of this, yet hasn't spoken up and told the truth. But not only that, I'm stupefied as to why he'd continue helping Mitch for so long, knowing everything they did was based on a lie.

"Why? Why haven't you said this before?" I ask in amazement.

He looks down at the floor and seems to shrink into himself. He doesn't say anything for a few seconds, which seems like hours. Then he finally admits, "I told Mitch when it all happened that it was just a misunderstanding, that you hadn't done anything, that ya weren't a wanker. And he threatened me. He said that if I told anyone the truth he'd torch me car." He looks up at me imploringly. "You've seen what he's like, he's capable of anything. I was scared. He said that we could make some big bucks off ya, and I should just leave everything to him."

Scott runs his hand through his hair again, takes quick a sip of water and confesses, "Then everything just got out of hand and I *couldn't* say nuthin, it was too late. Mitch unleashed all that shit, he seemed unstoppable, and I felt trapped." Wringing his hands together, he says, "But then ya started doin' all this nice stuff to help people and I felt like shit, I couldn't live with me secret any longer. I'm really sorry Davis I really am. I'm a stupid dickhead. I shoulda said something earlier, I shoulda known better. Sorry mate."

Far out, this is unbelievable. I take a few second to process it all, then standing up I walk around the desk and face him. He's still sitting down, so I ask him to stand up and I give him a man hug. He immediately bursts into tears, so we just stand there for a minute.

Then I take a step back and hold him at arm's length, saying, "Mate we all do stupid things, the important thing is that you've spoken up now. That took a lot of guts, you should be proud of yourself."

He sniffs and wipes his eyes with the palms of his hands, then wipes his nose on his shirt sleeve. The audience cheer and clap.

I give him a minute to get himself together then say, "You're not gonna let anyone else talk you into doing anything stupid ever again, are you?"

Giving me a weak smile he answers, "No bloody way, I've learnt me lesson, that's for sure."

Clapping him on the back I say, "Well that's good then. Now what *I* want to know is how you guys made that giant dick, it was a ripper." Giving me a cheeky grin I give my chin a thoughtful rub and add, "You know, you could make a bit of money from selling that story to say…*G'day* magazine. Whaddaya reckon?"

$$\$\$\$\$\$\$\$\$\$$$

Hooley dooly what a day! Scott sure took me by surprise this morning, but it hasn't put a dampener on things. I'm super excited about getting to spend the arvo in the recording studio with the Conchords. The mixing booth we're in is chock a block full of people. Doug, Dad, Eric, Paul and Bruce *had* to come along and watch the magic happen. And magic there is, we laid down the official version of Rock the Respect in less than two hours, Jeezus we bloody rocked it alright! This is a dream come true - Hugh Jackman might be my man-idol , but Brett and Jemaine are my rock gods. They're so cool!

After the recording sesh we all head down to the music bowl to check out what Frankie's done. It looks incredible, the crew are still putting the finishing touches to the stage and doing the sound checks, but they give us clearance to go wherever we want. We all head backstage to check it out, which is totally cool, no one else is there but it's still fun having a look. Then we all go up on stage and dick around for a bit. I'm trying to picture how the music bowl will look tomorrow when it's full of thousands of people, but it's hard to imagine. Man, I can't wait to experience it! Rock the Respect is dominating the charts, it seems all the radio stations are saturating the airwaves with it, it's freakin' awesome. Everyone's gonna be able to sing along to it at the rally and concert tomorrow.

$$$$$$$$$$

Thank God it's Saturday at last. Scott's bombshell revelation yesterday has turned into a complete media frenzy, he'll be able to make some money alright. Dad got sick of being bombarded by the press, so he decided to give an emergency press conference at Paradise Towers this morning. He reckons it's important to reassure my fans that I'm ok. Apparently the public are worried about me being devastated by Scott's confession. Giving a press conference is the last thing I feel like doing, but my fans are important to me, without them I wouldn't be a where I am. So I announce to the gathered media that the way I see it is like this. I'm a big believer in things happening for a reason. If Scott hadn't kept his mouth shut then maybe I wouldn't have been fired and I wouldn't have started my crusade to bring the respect back. Maybe Beaker still would have fired me, who knows. I'm just glad that things have happened the way they have. I finish up by *thanking* Scott, and I tell everyone that I'm fine with his revelation, I feel that things have panned out perfectly for me. After I answer some questions from the press Dad butts in and announces that we have to finish up – today's a big day, we've got a rally and concert to go to.

Oh. My. God. This is un-bloody-believable! The noise from the crowd is deafening, I can hardly hear myself think. I still dunno what the Myer Music Bowl's gonna look like when it's choc-a-block with thousands of people, but I now know how it feels to be surrounded by thousands of people in Swanston St. It's bloody incredible.

The moment has finally arrived and I still can't believe I'm doing this. I'm standing here with the band, up on the back of the truck ready to rock and roll. Literally! The rally's just started, just moved off. The crowd is unbelievable, there's talk of over forty thousand people showing up. It's so big the cops had to block off more of Swanston Street to accommodate everyone. The atmosphere is charged with excitement, everyone's on a high.

A fleet of my mobile billboards head up the front of the rally, closely followed by Bruce, Eric, Ajala, Fang and Paul. They're all holding aloft a massive 'Respect the Streets' banner. Fang's got a megaphone and he's giving the chant "What do we want? Respect. When do we want it? Now!" There are lots of other people with megaphones dotted throughout the procession as well.

The two grans and the rest of my family are sitting in open topped sports cars near the front of the march, waving to the crowd, like in a Grand Final Parade! All except Dad and Doug. Unsurprisingly, they managed to talk their way into coming on the truck with me and the band. I didn't stand a chance when they both unleashed their verbal assault on the merits of them accompanying me. Jonno and Jacobs are stationed on the truck as well, they really look the part. They've got their wraparound sunnies on, Jonno's got his hat on, and they're both standing with their arms crossed, legs apart with their backs to the truck cab, surveying the scene. We've got a bevy of other security dudes walking all around the truck as well, protecting us from the masses. Our truck's quite a way back from the front of the rally, so everyone can sing along if they want. I'll probably lose my voice before we even get to the Myer Music Bowl.

We're now moving at walking pace, Big Mal's got cameras set up at various points along the route ready to capture every glorious moment. The concert doesn't start till seven, he's gonna broadcast it live, but he wants to film everything for the TV special that's airing tomorrow night. "It's a double whammy alright," he'd roared with delight when we had lunch on Wednesday.

We're getting ready to sing Rock the Respect for the first time, I'm so nervous. Suddenly the boys start playing, and while counting myself in I grab the microphone stand, then let it rip. Oh my fucking God, I'm singing the greatest respect song in the history of respect songs, with my favourite band, on the back of a truck surrounded by forty odd thousand people. I fucking love my life!

As soon as I start singing all my nervousness and concept of space and time disappears. I *am* a rock god, living the dream every warm blooded male has dreamt of living. Walking, or rolling as the case may be, in the wake of the Aussie legends AC/DC.

I have no idea how many times we play Rock the Respect, but I know it's a lot. We make sure to have a short breather between sets, and during these intervals the crowd launches straight into chants of 'Respect, Respect, Respect' or 'Davis, Davis, Davis'. It's freakin' awesome! Then we all do the 'What do we want? Respect' thingy, which leads into another round of Rock the Respect. It's shit hot! Time must have sped up or something, because it seems like a blink of the eye and we're at the Sidney Myer Music Bowl.

Our truck heads to the backstage area while the crowds disperse at the front, making themselves at home on the lawn. True to his word, Big Mal plastered Channel Six with ads about the seated ticket auction. They all sold out in six hours flat. Dunno how he managed it but it ran like an eBay auction with a six hour time limit. The charity's made a heap out of it, sweet! I'll be able to fund some more amazing respect projects in the future.

I spot some of the homeless helpers doing a stellar job directing the incoming flow of people, and helping out at the donation booths and merchandising stalls. All the booths and stalls have got huge queues snaking out from them, which is unreal. The music bowl looks amazing, respect banners are draped everywhere. There's a few ginormous TV screens at the stage area and further back on the mounded grassy area, which in a normal concert is where the ticket booths and fences are set up. Having the giant screens positioned on the mounds is pure genius, because it allows the whole park to be utilised, allowing tens of thousands more people to enjoy the show.

The open topped sports cars that are carrying the family have already arrived when we get to the backstage area. Looks like everyone's gone inside, no doubt to peruse the buffet I've got set up in there. Frankie's idea is to give the crowd an hour to settle in before some guest speakers take to the stage. Not sure who he's got up his sleeve, he wouldn't tell me. He wants me to be the MC for most of the event, just not this first bit, although he still wants me to welcome the crowd which is kind of weird, but he's the guru. If Frankie says that's the way to do it, by jingo that's the way we'll do it.

When we jump down off the truck Jemaine, Brett and I do a funny bouncy thing, and before I know it Dad and Doug have joined in. We're all pumped up with adrenaline and excitement, bouncing around high-fiving each other. Jonno and Jacobs look cool, calm and collected, as if chaperoning rock gods happens all the time.

We find the family in the green room, where the line-up of talent is unbelievable, and so is the buffet from what I can see. The two grans have cornered Big Mal near the smoked salmon, no doubt trying to talk him into taking on their grannies behaving badly show as they stuff their faces. They're always pestering me to ask him about their show, so I told them a few days ago that Big Mal would be here tonight, so they could ask him themselves.

Ah yes, my family certainly aren't shy. I notice Holly stroking the arm of a well-known guitarist and shake my head. He doesn't stand a chance, she'll chew him up and spit him out in no time. Mum's showing off her lucky ABBA handbag to anyone who'll listen to her, recounting how being here reminds her of when Dad and her first met. I'm pretty sure the whole of Australia now knows the story about Doug being conceived here, but she's determined to remind everyone again. Doug's dragged Dad as far away from Mum as possible, they've latched themselves onto Kylie's entourage, although she's not here herself yet. I bet they're trying to get some inside goss on her, like whether she sleeps in her hotpants, or maybe even in the nude?

Spotting Bambi talking to Barnsey, I stroll over and give her bum a pinch. Squeaking in surprise, she turns her baby blues on me and they immediately light up. She's looking as hot as ever, Jeezus I've hit the jackpot with our fuck-buddy setup. Barnsey introduces us to some other guys, which leads me into doing a full circuit of the room, chatting with and thanking all of the stars for coming and performing tonight. They all seem as stoked as me to be doing this gig, which really blows me away. Just as I'm about to hit the buffet Charlie comes over and tells me that it's show time, I need to get up on stage and get everything started.

$$$$$$$$$$

Holy shit, that's one hell of a crowd. As I walk onto the stage a deafening roar erupts from the audience. I ask them if they had fun at the rally, and an ear splitting cheer rewards me. I then ask them if they're ready to have some more fun, that we've got an amazing line up here for them tonight, are they ready for it? A louder cheer erupts from the crowd.

Then Dad walks out and stands next to me. This, I wasn't expecting, and the crowd clap and cheer. He says into the microphone, "Bit of a bigger crowd than at your launch eh son." I nod my head in agreement and he says to the crowd, "Get comfy everybody, we're about to re-live all of Davis's magic moments. Would you guys like that?"

They scream their approval, and with that the stage lights dim and the giant screens take over, showing a montage of everything that's happened to me over the last month. God, I can't believe it's only been a month.

It starts with the mariachi band, which makes me feel sad about Claire and me, then some clips of the launch video - and the two grans pashing, to my billboards and the nude photo of me getting out of the spa, and some shots Bambi took of my ute auction party. Heaps of fan respect vids are shown, even the one taken that day outside the café, where the very first respect chant was born. Some clips of my respect segment are shown too. It's amazing watching it all, the homeless special is there, and Mitch and Beaker bullying me that day on *Tonight's Current Affairs*. The Sexy Juice ad gets a plug, then it cut's to some shots that have just been taken of me singing my heart out on the back of the truck, panning over the massive crowd all marching in the streets doing the respect chant. And it finishes with Scott confessing that he'd known all along that I'd been wrongly accused.

As that fades away Dad stands up and says, "I always knew Davis wasn't a wanker," and the crowd roars their agreement. When they settle down a bit he adds, "There's not many people I know of, that can get a crowd as big as you lot to turn up, who can make a difference in so many people's lives so quickly, who's got a heart as big as this." He throws his arms wide apart and the crowd cheer him on. He gives my shoulder a squeeze and says, "I'm so proud of you Davis, I think we all are."

Again the crowd goes ballistic and immediately launch into a respect chant. Dad quietens them down and says, while looking me in the eye, "You've had a lot a lot of surprises over the last month son, but I reckon this one'll top it off nicely." Looking out over the crowd he tells them, "When Davis first started on this journey, he told me that his aim was to become a celebrity so he could make a difference, and bring back the respect. His *other* aim was to stand on the red carpet next to his man-idol Mr Hugh Jackman." Holding his left arm out Dad says, "Ladies and gentlemen, Davis, I give you the wonderful Mr Hugh Jackman."

The crowd goes wild, and I nearly fall over from shock, I've got to hang onto Dad's arm for support, is he for real? The stage lights dim again, and all the big screens light up, showing Hugh's smiling face.

"Sorry I can't be there with you tonight Davis," he says, "but I'm in LA getting ready for the premiere of my new movie. And guess who's going to be here on the red carpet with me? That's right, you are! Get ready mate, 'cos you're coming to LA – tomorrow!" He chuckles then says, "Show him the tickets David."

Dad whips out an airline ticket and waves it in my face.

Hugh continues with, "I love what you're doing at home in Oz and I can't wait to meet you here in LA. Have a great night Davis, see you tomorrow!" then he shouts "RESPECT!" gives a cheeky wink and the screens go dark.

I stand there like a stunned mullet for a second, then it all sinks in, and I start screaming like a lunatic. Lifting Dad up off his feet I spin him around a few times, then drop him unceremoniously and start running around the stage punching the air. I'm crying too, I've lost the plot completely, but who gives a shit! The crowd's loving it, and of course the cameramen have caught every second of my madness.

Finally I calm down, and Big Mal comes onto the stage with Frankie. They give a speech about what respect means to them and how it's so refreshing to have someone like me come along and shake things up a bit, get people talking about the important things in life. Then it's show time.

This is by far the best night of my life! Every band gives a talk on what respect means to them and how it's great to see it being brought back, then they kick off their set. Unfortunately everyone's been limited to four songs, due to noise pollution we have to wrap things up by ten thirty. Bloody Victoria is such a nanny state!

The crowd's loving it, I'm loving it, it's the best concert ever. Once Kylie finishes her last song I take to the stage and give a speech about how amazing my journey has been over the past month, and how I'm blown away that everyone's so open to bringing back the respect.

"Our streets *could* be safer," I say passionately, "we *could* look out for each other more and bring back the respect. All it takes is for each of us to *decide* that we'll do our bit, and make it happen. That's what *I'm* planning on doing, how about you? Are you gonna help me bring back the respect, yes or yes?"

The response is unlike any other, everyone goes all out in declaring their "Yes." It's mind-blowing, ear splitting confirmation that people are ready for my message. Wow.

Once they quieten down I continue on, telling them that I feel blessed to be in a position where I can get the word out and hopefully make a difference. I tell the audience how great they all are, and how I want to thank everybody for their support in taking the time out to come along today. I give Fang a special thank you, and thank all the volunteers for helping, saying I couldn't have pulled this off without everyone's incredible assistance. Then I ask Big Mal and Frankie to join me on stage and I give them an extra special thanks. I ask the crowd to help me give them a thank you chant and lead them in it. It's awesome, I can tell Big Mal and Frankie are blown away by it. After that I give Frankie's crew a special thank you for making the music bowl look so awesome, then I thank all the performers for coming on board at such short notice and making this a night to remember. I again lead the crowd in a deafening thank you chant, which is fan-bloody-tastic.

Then all of the performers, Big Mal, Frankie, my family and mates, Bambi, Jonno, Jacobs, Ajala, Ricki and Bria, all crowd onto the stage together holding hands, and we all sing Rock the Respect. Fuck we rock it alright. The crowd have got their fake candles lit up, it's a sea of smiling, illuminated faces all singing along, all eager to bring back the respect. At the end of the song the audience and everyone on stage launch into a massive respect chant. The power and energy of this chant is electrifying. Together we are one unified, passionate force, declaring change, declaring respect. For me this is a life changing moment, I feel totally unstoppable.

Gazing out at the crowd I now know what it looks and feels like to stand in front of thousands of people - it's spine-tingling magic, pure magic. I also know how incredible it feels to be able to make a difference in other people's lives. I'm grinning from ear to ear, delirious at the realisation that tomorrow I get to meet my man-idol - in LA - on the red carpet! Basking in this incredible moment, I drink everything in, trying to savour it all. I'm amazed and so grateful that I created all this. I'm living proof that one person *can* make a difference in the world. All you have to do is believe in yourself and follow your dreams. I bloody rock!

Watch out America, here I come.

A Final Word from LJ

I hope you had as much fun reading about Davis as I did writing about him – he's such a cheeky charmer isn't he?

If you enjoyed being part of his crazy world and want to spread the respect then give Davis a review at www.amazon.com – and tell your friends to grab a copy - that would be bloody awesome!!!

I'm busily working on the next instalment of Davis' antics, so stay connected with my Facebook page - L J Grandi - or my blog www.writeongrandi.com where I'll be sharing some inside goss, updates and sneak peeks.

I really appreciate you taking the time to read this kick arse novel – thank you so much. As Davis would say, don't forget to respect yourself and respect other people!

xxx L J Grandi

PS: Imagine if this book really kicked off a respect revolution – how cool would that be!

PPS: A great big thank you to my editing and design team at Pink Diamond Publishing – you guys rock!

www.ingramcontent.com/pod-product-compliance
Lightning Source LLC
Chambersburg PA
CBHW022205030726
47494CB00019B/360